THE TRAITOR OF
SHERWOOD FOREST

Amy S. Kaufman has a PhD in medieval literature and has written about the Middle Ages for both academic and popular publications, including *The Washington Post*. She currently resides in Vancouver, Canada. *The Traitor of Sherwood Forest* is her debut novel.

--‹‹‹•›››--

Praise for *The Traitor of Sherwood Forest*

"A dazzling tapestry of history and legend, this is Sherwood Forest as you've never seen it: through a woman's eyes. Kaufman delivers a medieval England so real, so full of light and shadows and nuanced characters, you can't help but wonder if this is what really happened."

—Mary McMyne, author of *The Book of Gothel* and *A Rose by Any Other Name*

"Peasant girl Jane Crowe enters the dappled glades of Sherwood Forest seeking safety and freedom. Instead she stumbles upon a darkly woven web of danger, deceit, and violence with none other than Robin Hood at its center. Kaufman paints fresh shadows upon an ancient tale, entwining new characters with old history for a satisfying and compelling read."

—Liz Michalski, author of *Darling Girl*

The
Traitor of
Sherwood
Forest

Amy S. Kaufman

PENGUIN BOOKS

PENGUIN BOOKS
An imprint of Penguin Random House LLC
1745 Broadway, New York, NY 10019
penguinrandomhouse.com

Set in Baskerville Regular
Designed by Alexis Farabaugh

LIBRARY OF CONGRESS CATALOGING-IN-PUBLICATION DATA

Names: Kaufman, Amy S., 1974– author.
Title: The traitor of Sherwood Forest / Amy S. Kaufman.
Description: [New York] : Penguin Books, 2025.
Identifiers: LCCN 2024039985 (print) | LCCN 2024039986 (ebook) |
ISBN 9780143138129 (paperback) | ISBN 9780593512241 (epub)
Subjects: LCSH: Robin Hood (Legendary character)—Fiction. |
LCGFT: Historical fiction. | Novels. | Adaptations.
Classification: LCC PS3611.A8238 T73 2025 (print) |
LCC PS3611.A8238 (ebook)
LC record available at https://lccn.loc.gov/2024039985
LC ebook record available at https://lccn.loc.gov/2024039986

Printed in the United States of America
1st Printing

The authorized representative in the EU for product safety and compliance
is Penguin Random House Ireland, Morrison Chambers, 32 Nassau Street,
Dublin D02 YH68, Ireland, https://eu-contact.penguin.ie.

For Mike,
who believed before I could

The
Traitor of
Sherwood
Forest

PART I

A Gret Wager

Chapter One

You've seen him before." Bran led Jane through the forest with a blindfold tied around her eyes, his hand a gentle guide on her arm. "You just don't know it. Fox-colored hair, narrow eyes that change color. He blends in, at the market, at worship. That's how he stays hidden."

Jane smelled woodsmoke close, from an old fire. Ale as well, stale on the wind, and some kind of herb. And Bran, whose horsey, straw smell from the stables clung to him like a wet shirt. "Don't you ever worry what will happen if you're caught with him?"

His chuckle echoed a foot above her head. "Oh, I ain't seen with him. No one is."

Bran was the tallest man she'd ever been courted by, and the biggest too. Like a great, sweet ox. Hard to imagine him pulling off capers and robbing nobles. But he was quick with a joke and a smile, and people bent to him, so perhaps he wasn't lying. Still, Jane wouldn't really believe him until she saw Robin Hood with her own eyes.

"Do other women ever come out here?" she asked him.

Bran laughed. "Not the kind you'd want to know, Janie."

She stumbled over a fallen branch and grunted. Her boots were a little too big. They were her brother Adam's, and although he was two years younger than she, he had already grown past them. She couldn't wear them to town, but they were sturdy for fishing, or working the garden, or running off on stupid rides to the forest with Bran.

Bran rested his hand on the small of her back. "Steady, girl," he said as though she were one of his horses. "Quiet as we come up. Don't want to spook them."

Finally, they stopped, and Bran let out a low whistle. The forest became very still. Jane couldn't even hear him breathing anymore.

Then a whistle came back, twice as long, and Bran took her arm again. That was the sign, she guessed. She wondered if she could repeat it.

Why would you want to do that, Jane? What are you even doing here? she asked herself, though it sounded like her mother's voice in her head. But her mother was the last person Jane would listen to now. It was Sibyl's fault she was out here, after all. Sibyl was abandoning their house, wooed by her latest lover's promises. Jane was certain her mother would be betrayed again, but she never could sway Sibyl's mind once a man was in it. Nor could Jane keep the house on her own, not with her brothers leaving too. She had nowhere to go.

But Bran had promised that Robin Hood would find her a place. That he would give Jane a way out of the grinding, dull ache of hunger, of thin winter pottage and twice-mended stockings and early frosts that could turn the whole of harvest season bitter. Who would say no to that?

"Oy, Bran!" Jane jumped as a shout came from high over her head, higher than Bran, even. "Whatcha got there?"

"This is my girl, Jane!"

Jane stiffened. The voice sounded like it was coming from high up in the trees. Was that Robin? Did he live up there, like a feral animal? She felt herself shaking, and couldn't stop, even though she knew Bran would tease her for it later.

"Relax, Janie," he whispered. "Wyll is just the lookout."

She tried to calm herself, but the blindfold suddenly felt like it was cutting off her breathing, and she gripped one hand with the other to keep her fingers from scrabbling up her face to tear it off.

"You can take that off 'er now," the voice from up high said, like a benevolent angel.

"He won't get mad, then?"

"Not for her."

Her hands trembling, Jane reached up and brushed against Bran's fingers as he took the blindfold off. The forest light was dim, filtered through the towering trees, but it still stung her eyes. She rubbed them fiercely, not caring about the mud or stains on her hands, then blinked up at the voice.

Wyll, skinny as a pike fish, stood atop a hunting stand in a great oak. A bow leaned against his leg, arrows scattered at his feet. "Well, good day, Jane!" He grinned down at her. "Welcome to our little kingdom."

Jane smiled shyly. She wasn't used to men paying any mind to her, and it made her toes tingle.

"Hey, enough flirting! Jane's here to meet Robin."

"Oh, is that right? Well, good luck, Jane. And good luck, Bran. He tell you how handsome our Lord of the Greenwood is? You might lose your heart out there, or worse." Wyll's grin grew wider, stretching out to large ears that framed his face like wings.

Jane didn't know how to respond, so she reached for Bran's hand instead, twining their fingers together.

"That's right, Janie, you show him." Bran laughed. He always knew what to say.

He led her along quietly, but not so quietly that it would seem like sneaking. When they got closer to the smell of stale smoke, Jane heard voices—one in particular, melodic and insistent.

"Oy, he's goin' on again," Bran muttered. "Wait 'til he's done. He don't like interruptions."

"Who, Robin?" Jane looked up at him, pushing her hair out of her eyes.

But Wyll had climbed down from his post to join them, so Bran shook his head and swallowed whatever he had meant to say.

"And what's King Edward done to win your loyalty? Turn against his own father? Ride off to the Holy Land only to be scared home by a single dagger? God's bones, it took the man two years to claim his crown! Do you think he cares for you? Do you think he cares for England? We can't even feed our own. Why should your coin go to swords and blood in other realms?"

Robin came into view right as he was gesturing grandly, his eyes bright with fire, sitting with one leg up on a log as though it were a woodland throne. He had fox-colored hair, just as Bran had said, and his eyes flashed as green as new growth in the forest. Jane watched as Wyll went to his side as if drawn by his words, a cup of ale in his hand.

"'Tis the French," someone shouted. "Get them off the throne and we'll go back to the old ways!"

"'Tis not the French, Mooch. French, Welsh, Scottish, or Castilian, like the fool-headed queen. 'Tis all the rich. They'll steal the coin from your purse as sure as we will, but make up pretty lies about the cause. And where does your coin go? Not to fill John's cookpot"—he nodded at the hulking, gold-bearded man who shadowed him—"nor to feed your sisters, nor to fatten your sheep. It goes to castles far from here, and pretty baubles, and it pays the men who fight their foolish wars."

It was hard not to be stirred by Robin's speech, and a fiery current ran through the men, even as their ale turned flat and stale. Jane knew what angry men deep in their drink could do, especially to women. She had learned that lesson in her own home—first from her father, and then her eldest brother, Peter, after their father left and he thought to become man of the house. Jane fought the urge to shrink behind the shelter of Bran's body, or to run right back into the woods.

Bran must have sensed her fear, for he cleared his throat a little too loudly.

Robin's eyes faded to hazelwood, his mouth twitched, and he glanced at Bran, then down at Jane. "Ah. I see we have a guest."

Jane watched the men's shoulders drop, their faces lighten, as they turned to look at her.

"We taking the toll, master?" asked the one called Mooch, his face shadowed with sparse black hair.

"Women don't pay the toll," Bran answered. "As you'd know if you ever had one." The men laughed, and Jane felt the tension fly up into the wind, whirled up with the leaves. Bran could just do that.

"Brave girl, to ride all the way out here." Robin's stare was a challenge.

"This is Jane," Bran said. "The one I told you about."

"All right, Jane." Robin stood, balancing on his log playfully, but his face wasn't playful. "Your toll is a question. Do you pray to the Virgin?"

"She ain't no virgin, riding with Bran." Wyll snorted.

Quick as a snake bite, quicker even than a strike of lightning, Robin bloodied Wyll's face with the back of his hand.

Jane's spine went straight as a wooden pole. She hadn't even seen him move.

She couldn't bring herself to look at Wyll, but she heard him moan as another man laughed and slapped him on the back. Her face burned. Bran stayed at her side, tense but silent.

Robin's face didn't change. Not at all. He went back to balancing on his log, like it had all been a dream. "The question stands, Jane."

"I do pray to Her, m'lord," she stammered. "Every day, and . . . and more on holy days."

"What do you pray for?"

"M'lord?"

"What do you ask of our Holy Mother?"

Jane hesitated. She had dreamed the night before of running through the woods, a wolf on her heels, its jaws dripping, and a boar rushing toward her ahead. Just when she thought she would be trampled, sunlight flashed between the trees. She couldn't see a clear path there, but the ray of sunlight glittered as it fell upon the wet leaves, urging her to hide in the brush among all the snarls and tangles and let the boar and the wolf pass her by.

Sibyl loved dreams and their meanings, and Jane knew what she would say: the wolf was hunger, the boar was a man who would keep her, and Jane was afraid of being grown. So Jane had not told her about this dream. Instead, she decided that the Virgin had sent the sunlight to guide her, as She did for the bold knights who fought in Her name, or the frightened children who prayed to Her in the dark. The hidden path through the brush would be her escape.

That path had led her into Robin's wood.

But Jane knew that wasn't the answer Robin was looking for.

"I . . . well, I pray for my brothers, I suppose, and . . ." Jane thought back to his words, his speech. "I pray we'll all be fed and clothed and shod, by the Lady's grace. For things to be well, and to stay well, and for no one to suffer." There was truth in what she said, but her real prayer had been selfish, and the false words felt like mealworms in her mouth.

Robin looked at her for a long moment. "Follow me, Jane," he finally said. "I have need of a girl like you."

-‹‹‹◆›››-

Robin led them to a small copse of trees. Their branches formed a canopy, and someone had draped it with a tarp of oiled cloth. Robin ducked beneath the tarp, and Jane followed him at Bran's nod.

The little pocket in the forest was a shrine. A portrait of the Virgin stood on a tree stump. It must have been taken from one of the churches—one of the nice ones. Gilt framed Mary's face, Her eyes sapphire, Her skin bronze like an old coin. Scattered around the stump that served as Her altar were endless small treasures: seashells crusted with salt; a gem-studded drinking horn filched from a lord; arrowheads, one tinged dark brown at the tip; brooches that sparkled even in the dim forest shade.

Robin sat right down in the dirt and trampled grass, and she and Bran sat before him. "Bran tells me you'd like to work at the King's Houses."

"I hoped we could get her the job in the kitchens," Bran said before she could answer. "I thought she could listen for us, keep an ear out."

Robin's thin nostrils flared, his stare piercing Jane. "Bran won't always be here to answer for you. So answer me yourself. You're marrying age. Why serve ladies and lords and sleep in a lonely bed, passing us secrets in the dark, when you ought to marry a decent man who will spare you this kind of work?"

A laugh escaped Jane's lips. "Begging your pardon, m'lord, but there will always be work, husband or none. More so once I wed."

Something flickered across Robin's eyes, but it was surprise, not anger. "Why not take holy vows, then?"

"The church wouldn't have me, but to sweep their floors."

"No." Robin smiled, back on surer ground, and drew closer to her. She could smell his woodsy scent, the campfire in his hair, the musk of his sweat, and something sweet on his breath. "They only take wealthy girls, don't they, to steal the dowries from their families?"

Jane nodded as though she agreed, but, inside, she was thinking of her brother Adam, who had apprenticed with a priest. It had cost them so much to provide for him while he slept on the floor of the small, drafty church to learn his mass. Jane had sewn his clothes with her own hands and sold all her summer conserves to buy his post. Even then, if it hadn't been for Adam's kind demeanor, his aid to Father Gilbert, and the deep friendship they had formed, her melancholy brother would be laboring on a farm instead of listening to the Lord's call.

"Do you think it's odd, Jane, that we are told Christ's love can only be bought with coin? That God is to be found in gilded halls, spoken to in strange tongues that will never pass your lips or mine? That the Virgin will never glance at us unless we empty our purses for the greedy men who tend to Her candles?"

The sun shone through the trees in a dim autumn ray, bathing Robin in warm light. "They try to hide Her in their churches," he said, "but I believe the Virgin's grace is right here, in this wood, and in every mist from the sea's waves, and every star above us in the dark, and in the call of birds and the rustle of stoats beneath our gardens."

"I think so too!" Jane said breathlessly, and she saw from the flush of his cheeks and the glittering light in his eyes that she had pleased him. Jane had always felt at home in the woods, at peace among the trees. It was the only place she felt like she could breathe. Perhaps Robin was right, and that was because the forest was where God's grace found her. "I believe we may pray anywhere, m'lord, and the Holy Mother will listen."

Robin grasped her hand, his palm firm and strong, calluses woven into his skin, and a small shock traveled up Jane's arm with his touch. He pulled her to her knees and knelt beside her, turning them both to face the Virgin's portrait. Mary beamed above Her little palace of stolen shells and gold, as though She had indeed sent the dream to Jane, guiding her right here, to Her shrine between the trees.

"The rich are liars, Jane. They lie about what is right, and what is holy, all so they can stand on your back to lift themselves higher. They would have you serve yourself to them like a fatted goose upon their table, devour you, and call in more of your kind to clean up the bones."

Heat pricked Jane's skin, then guttered quickly, like a fire on a wet night. Robin was right, she was sure, but she had never even spoken to a rich person herself. The wealthy circled the earth in their own sphere, high above her garden and the tiny house where the walls always seemed to be closing in. But it would be different now, at the King's Houses. Jane would be thrust into their world, lost within it. Robin meant to flame her anger, but, instead, a deep sadness rose inside her, and his hand pressed harder, so hard that the bones in her fingers began to ache.

"What is it, Jane?" Robin had seen the shadow cross her face. Bran's eyes were wide with warning, and he shook his head as subtly as he could.

Jane thought quickly. "It's just . . . I'm sure you're right, m'lord, but what is to be done about it?"

Robin leaned closer, perilously close. "You mean, what can *you* do about it?"

Jane nodded, her breath caught in her chest.

"What havoc can a single mouse wreak in a farmer's field? Very little. But an *army* of mice, slipping through the night, can drive the farmer from his home. And that one mouse"—he pressed her hand harder still—"can fatten himself and his family, and sleep in his warm den as soundly as you please." Robin smiled. "I didn't notice you when you arrived, not at first. That could be very useful."

Jane tried to imagine herself among an army of rodents, but all it did was make her skin crawl and her mind race with questions. What about the cats, and the sickles, and the poisoned leaves farmers used to clear their fields of pests? Had Robin ever actually worked on a farm? She fought an urge to look at Bran the way she did when a person said something foolish, to see his eyebrows quirk and force a laugh out of her. But Bran still seemed deadly serious, and she knew she must say something to show she was not making a joke of Robin's words.

"So, I'm to be a mouse, then?"

Robin laughed—a great, surprised chuckle—and finally dropped her hand. "No mind for metaphor, this one? No matter, so long as her heart is with us." He said it to Bran, though his gaze was on Jane, and it was warm and fond. "We'll have a trial, of course, to see if she's worth what you say."

"Of course," Bran said, and Jane could feel his eyes steady on her, willing her to say the right thing. He had warned her about being tested, but he had also told her she would pass whatever trial came with ease, so long as she kept her ears open and her mouth closed. Jane took a steadying breath. What was there to worry about? She would only need to listen, after all. They wouldn't force her to steal, or fight, or break any laws. Bran had promised. And what were a few whispers in the dark?

"I'm with you, m'lord," Jane said, "whatever trial comes."

"Then pray with me, Jane," Robin said. "Pray the Virgin shows you light and grace and truth."

Jane felt the warmth of her dream then, as gentle as springtime sun. All would be well. Robin would guide her, show her the path away from the hungry beasts of womanhood and time. She'd had a true dream after all.

Before she bent her head to pray, Jane could have sworn she saw the little portrait of the Virgin Mary smile.

Chapter Two

Bran wasn't the first man Jane had bedded—Wyll was right about that. But he was the first to bring a little spark of sunlight into the gray days of Jane's life, the first one to show her that there was something more to herself than washing, cooking, and scraping weeds out of the garden, or worrying about her brothers' futures or her mother's many heartbreaks.

Before Bran, Jane hadn't felt drawn to anything. Things happened to her all the time, and they always would. That was how life worked, and you made the best of it if you could. If she hungered for anything, it was for peace and silence. She loved to walk through the woods, to revel in the quiet and stillness, no one needing anything from her. Her brothers often accused her of being a daydreamer, of being lost in her own thoughts, but Jane wasn't really dreaming of anything. She was watching. Watching the leaves fall, and the squirrels fill their cheeks, and the little spring birds sing to each other about the sun.

Jane's penchant for long, lonely walks in the woods was how she'd met Bran. She had seen him riding past the village once or twice, stopping to show a new horse to the children. That spring day, he had taken a shy mare out running and come across Jane. He'd offered her a ride home on his horse. He was tall and broad, with hair the color of sweet winter chestnuts and warm brown eyes that shone with a buried joke. Jane had refused, of course. She was no fool. But Bran had come to find her the next day, and the next. Then one day, when the rain burst out of the sky earlier than it should have, and her boots and clothes were all over mud and filth, she'd let him take her home. He'd taxed her for the ride— the promise of a kiss the next day, when the weather would be fine. "We'll see," she'd said, but she had kissed him, and he'd begun to come around every day to see her, just like the sun rising and setting.

Jane supposed she was being courted. But it wasn't a proper courtship. Bran wouldn't talk about the future. That's what she liked about him—he came and lit things up like a firefly, then went away and left her to herself. He didn't seem to need anything from her. Not like everyone else in her life, who would bleed her dry like a pack of leeches if they could.

One night they were drunk on blackberry mead, sitting by a stream on one of those blissful, breezy days warm enough for bare feet but cool enough for the flies not to bite. She wished everything in her world could slow down like it did with Bran—that life could be sipped this way, like spiced wine, instead of rushed. Leaning in close, his eyes unfocused from drink, Bran tried to tell her she was beautiful. "You have hair like river sand," he had said. "And eyes like . . . like river sand," and they had laughed. Jane knew he was being kind. She had seen her reflection in the glass: lips that chapped in hot or cold weather, narrow but round eyes, dull hair that turned gold in the summertime, freckles across pale skin. But she kissed his cheek for the compliment, clumsy as it was.

"You know I'm not the marrying kind," he warned her, attempting to be stern with a frown that wouldn't stay on his face.

Jane, who could hold her drink far better than he could despite his size, burst out laughing. "As if I'd marry an outlaw!" Then she said, after some thought, "Maybe I'm not the marrying kind either." After all, what good did it do? Her da was gone, and when he had been in their home, he'd been like a smothering force, a hot wind, with his moods and his rage. The air was cooler without him. There was space in the house, room to breathe. Except when Sibyl's lovers made themselves at home, as Hugh, the newest one, seemed to be doing more and more. As if he didn't have a wife and children of his own.

—«‹«•›»›—

Hugh didn't have the dark fire of Jane's father, but it was clear why her mother had chosen him. He was tall and lean, deceptively placid, with a voice like weathered stone. A habitual, easy shrug of the shoulders that made it seem as if he would never play games when, of course, he always was. Small eyes and a narrow chin. Clean-shaven. Shoulders slumped to make himself shorter, more innocuous, less of a threat.

What was not entirely clear was why Hugh had chosen her mother. His own wife was meek and kind, without the raw, wild laughter that Sibyl Crowe fell into when she drank. Jane's mother had been a beauty in her youth with a fire to match her father's, but, now, lines gathered at the corners of her eyes. Her hair had silvered early, thick, winding streaks in her long, dark braid. "You children drained the color out of me with my milk," she'd say with a smile, as though it were a joke, but Jane couldn't help but wonder.

At first, her mother seemed bent on winning Hugh, as though there were a contest between her and his wife, Phillipa. She would study Phillipa with fascination, cataloging her faults, as though finding just the right flaw would be the rot that spoiled the apple. "Did you see the fine cloth she wore today, green as moss?" Sibyl would complain. "Who can afford such a thing in a lean winter?" When she'd had enough to drink, she would whisper, "Some women just don't know what a man *needs*." It was no secret what Hugh "needed"—their little home was not large or quiet.

But over the summer, Hugh's wife had grown sick, and Sibyl had stopped speaking of her. This unsettled Jane even more. Now, everyone behaved as though Phillipa did not exist at all. And Hugh was always around.

He was sitting at the table with her mother when Jane came home with her heart still pounding from meeting Robin. His nose and cheeks had grown bright with wine, and her mother, her hair mussed like a pup's fur, stroked his face as though they were alone in the room.

But they weren't. Little Ralf ran up to Jane and thrust a stick against her belly when she came inside, a threadbare, hole-infested blanket draped across his shoulders like a cloak.

"Stop, villain!" he squealed. "I am Robin Hood and I shall take all your gold and hide it in the forest!"

Jane jumped, cold shock making her knees buckle. How could her brother know where she had been? But her mother and Hugh snickered. "Leave off, now, Ralf," Sibyl scolded. "You're too old to play make-believe."

Ralf frowned and shook his stick at his mother. "You'll see," he growled. "You'll all see!" And then, laughing maniacally, he dashed out the door past Jane and into the yard, where he poked at the poor, groveling chickens.

"Well," her mother asked, "how did they like you up at King's Houses?"

Jane smiled to help her swallow the truth of where she'd been. "I think it'll work out."

"Ah, thank God!" Jane's mother heaved a sigh of relief, and Hugh squeezed her closer.

"See, dove," he chided her mother. "I told you." Jane cringed at the ill-fitting nickname. Sibyl was no dove. A hawk perhaps, or a true crow, even though the name had come to her by marriage. But no dove.

Jane busied herself tidying the hearth, sweeping the ash and stoking the dwindling fire. "Were you worried, then?"

"Janie," her mother wheedled, "you know I'm always worried about you." Jane knew no such thing, and she frowned at the hearth. She had turned nineteen in the summer, late in June when the fruit swelled, but Sibyl had never once uttered a word about her leaving before Hugh came along.

"I told you she'd make a life for herself, dove," Hugh said. "'Twas nothing to worry about."

Jane felt pulled in two. Hugh was trying to defend her, but she still didn't like it when he turned against her mother. "It's not forever. They only need help making things ready for the new king, and the feast days."

"But if you work hard," Hugh blared, though he was a landowner himself and rarely had to soil his palms with work, "you'll impress them, and they'll ask you to stay."

"Well then, you'd best impress them, Janie," her mother said, "if you can't get that boy to marry you."

"Mother!" The word burst out of Jane even though she knew she was being provoked. It was ridiculous for Sibyl to push marriage on her when all she did was interfere with marriages.

"Be kind, dove. The girl has a right to celebrate. Get us some more wine."

Jane tried to smile at him, but it strained her heart. She didn't know why Hugh wanted to be in her good graces, but he always tried. They all tried. How could she warm to them when it was only a matter of time before they left her mother staring out the window again, her heart broken in two, her eyes ragged with loss.

"'Tis easy for you." Sibyl wiped the rim of the wine cup she had been sharing with Hugh and passed it to Jane. "Your eldest daughter is married off. Mine has the heart of a nun!"

"Jane'll work hard and then she'll settle down," Hugh assured her. "You'll see. She's a good girl. Not like her mother." Then he winked and squeezed her mother's flat arse, which made her giggle like a girl. "When do you start work, then?" Hugh asked as though they were a normal family, and this was a normal conversation around a normal table.

"Just before All Hallows."

"That's plenty soon enough," her mother said.

"Soon enough for you to leave?" Jane tried to keep the hurt out of her voice, but it was plain, and she flushed, ashamed of her reaction. A gust of wind whipped in through the open door, and ashes flew from the fire where she had just swept, a little cloud of them dancing through the room.

"Janie." Sibyl's voice softened, laced with false concern. "You know Phillipa is very ill. It's only a matter of time until . . ."

Bile rose in Jane's throat. "Until she's dead. I know." Jane's voice was winter frost, and her mother was startled into silence, for once.

"It's a tragedy, to be sure." Hugh drank again and wiped his mouth, not looking the least bit tragic. "But I've sworn to care for your mother, and I intend to make an honest woman of her."

"As much as anyone can," Sibyl cackled, but Jane could still see the wound her too-blunt words had carved on her mother's face, and her eyes when she looked at Jane again were as still and dangerous as a frozen lake.

"It's the house, Janie." Hugh gestured to the roof, where rot crept in the corners and one of the beams sported a long, thin crack. "You've done the best you could, without a man around. But the house has reached its time."

Jane bristled at the use of her nickname. That was meant for family and for Bran. "My brothers are around." Though that wasn't exactly true—Adam had gone to the priesthood, and Ralf was hardly a man; he'd apprentice soon, probably with Peter, who had moved to Newark-on-Trent and married a merchant's daughter. "They'll help fix it."

"Don't be silly, Jane," Sibyl said. "There's no need to cling to old things. We move along with the turning seasons, as we must."

Jane's jaw throbbed with all the words she wanted to shout. Of course Sibyl would think that. She had never met a bond she didn't want to break, no matter how much she suffered when her lovers abandoned her afterward. Sibyl's men were like marigolds in the garden, blooming bright but gone when the cold came.

But perhaps all men were like that, Jane thought to herself. Perhaps it was best to feed and water what you knew would remain instead, what would sate you in the lean times and not just show up to turn its face to the sun.

Chapter Three

J ane walked to Mansfield market on a beautiful October morning, clear and crisp, the dawn still gray with streaks of peach and blue, her basket of conserves heavy on her hip. The sun grew bright as a ripe quince, and it was almost possible to forget that every step she took brought her closer to leaving home, to putting her trust in someone who was more legend than man instead of into the work she did with her own hands.

Jane had taken over selling her mother's conserves once she was old enough to walk to Mansfield on her own. When summer faded, she would pluck ripening berries and boil them with honeycomb, following Sibyl's recipes. But she learned, and she tested, drying flowers when their petals drooped, mixing wardens with violets and custard apples with rose, and now she sold more conserves than her mother ever had.

"Have you got the pear one? 'Tis such a treat in winter." Margery, the butcher's wife, had cheeks as full as a chipmunk's, red with the flush of her waning years.

"Of course!" Jane was especially proud of that one. She'd

mixed in all the rowan berries she could rescue from the birds with honey and half-turned hypocras for a bright and festive flavor.

"Shall I trade you for soaps again?" Cleverer than her husband by far, Margery had turned his castoff, coarse fats into a trade of her own, her baskets full of soaps. The hides she sold to the tanner, to feed and house her family far above their station.

Jane shook her head. "I'll take pennies if you can spare them."

"Oh." Margery's kind brow furrowed. "Is there trouble at home?"

There was, but not the kind of trouble that Jane would ever share. "I'm taking a new job at King's Houses," she said. "I won't be home much longer."

"King's Houses! My word! What a blessing!" Then her mouth fell open. "Don't tell me this is the last I'll see of your conserves."

"I'm afraid it is, for a time."

"I'll take three," Margery whispered conspiratorially.

"You're too kind!" Jane laughed. "But you mustn't. I'll empty your purse!"

"Give them over, no more arguing. We'll save these 'til you come to market again."

Things were much the same at her other friends' stalls, and Jane began to feel lighter and lighter, as if she might float away, and not just because of her emptying basket. The more she told her story and heard the way everyone talked about King's Houses, the clearer her future became in her own mind. It *would* be grand, wouldn't it? She would wait on knights and nobles and cook with spices from faraway lands. And she would never go hungry.

So long as she passed Robin's test.

Jane tried again to push the trial out of her mind, as she had each time the shadow of it rose up and threatened to cloud out the sun. There was no sense worrying about a thing until she knew the shape of it.

"Grand, Jane!" Old Jankyn said as he took the last of her plum conserves. "I suppose we won't see you 'round the market now, will we? Too refined for the likes of us?"

"Hardly! I'll spend my days in the kitchens, same as you." Jane turned down his salt fish, even though it was a fish day and Sibyl could have used it, and asked for coin instead.

Waiting for him to sort through his purse, Jane heard a whisper in her ear like a hot wind. "If only they knew what you're really getting up to at King's Houses."

Bran's voice, filling her up like a cup of cider, making her toes tingle.

"Hello, you." She turned to him with a smile. The morning sun lit his cheeks, and he looked so strong, young, and solid in that marketplace full of aging merchants that she wanted to wrap herself up in his warmth, as if he were a great, sturdy tree and she could shelter from the wind beneath him.

But Bran looked more serious than usual. "Robin needs you," he said. "East entrance. It's time, Janie. Be a good girl and show him what you're worth."

Jane felt cold and hot all at once. Here it was: Robin's trial, right in the middle of her Friday. Right in the middle of the market, where everyone could see. Her mouth was suddenly dry as summer dust.

"I'll sell the rest of these." Bran tugged at her basket.

Jane took a step back, pulling her basket with her, hoping her worry didn't show on her face. "They won't give you a good price," she argued, feeling foolish even as she said it.

"Everyone gives me a good price!" Bran smiled, teeth white and strong, but did not let go of the basket.

"There's but a few left. It'll only take . . ."

"You need to go *now*, Janie." Bran grew stern, like he did when he was leading horses, and Jane felt as if the earth were dropping out from under her, as if she might fall into a pit and never see her way out. "When Robin calls, it's always now."

"Is this boy bothering you?" Jankyn asked, handing Jane her coin.

She stumbled over her words. "No . . . I—"

"Just lending an arm," Bran said, all smooth humor and musk. "Pretty girl like Jane shouldn't have to twist herself sideways carrying these, should she?"

"You watch out for that one. He's a rogue if he's anything." The fishmonger waggled his finger and flashed a grin with his few remaining teeth.

"Kind thanks," Jane muttered, and then felt like an ass. She knew they were both having a joke, but she couldn't think of anything clever to say. She felt, as she often did, like people's words were racing around her, somewhere over the top of her head where she couldn't grasp them.

Bran looked apologetic as they walked away, and his voice was gruff, but he sounded as if he were struggling to keep it so. "Robin is not a patient man. Best to learn that early."

Jane still felt roughened by the whole exchange and by the loss of her basket. Her voice cracked horribly as she said, crossly as an old grandmother, "Those are the last of the strawberry, and that's the blacksmith's favorite, though he likes to say it's for his wife and not for him, so make sure to . . ."

"Jane." Bran put a firm hand on her shoulder, his gaze warm

and soft as a wool blanket. "Robin's plots can get a bit odd, but you'll have fun, I promise."

She nodded but could not quite smile back, nor could she put her finger on what was bothering her. All Jane knew was that she had felt like a soaring hawk for a moment, and then been yanked down as if by a master's tether.

But she was being ridiculous, wasn't she? After all, Bran and Robin were the ones placing her at King's Houses. And where would she be without them?

"East, you said?"

"Yes, and I'll walk you if . . ."

"No need." She tried a bright smile like Bran's own, but she imagined it looked false on her, for her heart did not feel bright at all. "I know the way."

The Sext bells rang as Jane hurried east, only to stumble over her own feet when she saw Robin. He wore an enormous hat squashed down over his pretty hair, and his slim figure swam in a baggy gray tunic. He was ill-dressed, ridiculously so, and dragging a massive cart full of pots.

Jane was unsure what to do. Was she supposed to approach him, or pretend not to know him? She wished Bran had given her some kind of instruction.

Finally, Robin's eyes found hers, even though she stood still as a statue. "Fair maiden," he called in a voice much older than his own. "Would you help me lead my pots to market?"

His words sent a charge up Jane's frozen legs, and she started forward again. "Of course, m'lord!"

"I'm no lord, my dear, by the grace of the Virgin," Robin said too loudly. "Just a humble potter here to sell his wares."

Jane stifled a nervous laugh as he bowed. She placed her hand on the cart, though she was not sure where to lead him. Potters usually stayed near the entrance, for their carts were heavy, awkward to maneuver through the square.

Jane was close to Robin now, close enough to smell his earthy scent and the lingering smoke of a campfire. He'd used wood ash in his hair to gray it, stooping a little and slowing his speech to age himself, but he still cut too fine a face to go completely unnoticed— he couldn't hide his twinkling eyes, his straight nose, that smile. Sweat marred the armpits of his tunic, but the stains hung well below his own arms, and a rope fastened the too-large garment about his waist. He had a nasty bruise on his hand, all red and purple at the edges. His neck too bore a red streak and a fine scratch.

"Are you well, m'lord?" Jane asked softly.

"Sharp eye," Robin murmured under his breath. Then he bellowed, "Well as can be, fair maiden! Ruffians accosted me in the forest, but I got the better of them. An easy task for a stout craftsman with a strong heart."

Jane's stomach sank as she looked over the cart. It did look familiar, now that she thought of it. And the usual potter had not arrived. If Robin was here, wearing bruises and another man's clothes . . .

She swallowed and sent a small prayer to Mary that the true potter was safe and unharmed. Surely Robin wouldn't hurt an honest man just to pull a prank.

Robin interrupted her worries with another ostentatious shout.

"Now, fair maiden, where is the market center? I want to be in the best place to sell these wonderful pots!"

Jane's mouth creased, her face hot. Did he have to bleat like a stuck sheep and turn so many heads? "This way," she said, leading him past the other merchants, who stared with open mouths at the strange potter pulling his cart through the market, the copper inside clanking like a smith's hammer as the cart bounced over stones and pebbles.

"Here we are." She helped him ease the cart into a space between a fishmonger she never spoke to, for he sold fish from the sea that was too fine for the Crowes, and her friend Thomas, who sold carrots, cabbages, and onions. The air was unpleasant between the dried fish and the cabbages, and Jane tried to keep from wrinkling her nose as she greeted them both.

Robin bid Jane to help him lift the tarp off of his cart. Grabbing a pot from the top and swinging it wide, he bellowed, "Pots! Pots! Pots for sale! The more you buy, the more you get!"

A few women stared, whispering to each other. "Is he daft?" Thomas asked Jane. "What's that even mean? Of course the more you buy, the more you get!"

One woman stopped to peek into Robin's cart, then turned down her nose and walked away. She didn't even look at Robin. They all knew the real potter here, just as she did. There would be no reason to stop for a stranger's wares if the pots you trusted might be waiting at the entrance. No reason to look at Robin twice at all.

Robin frowned at Jane as the villagers hurried by him without a second glance, but there was a smile in his eyes. "Bran said you sell here all the time. That you're good at reading people—at finding out what they want. So tell me, Jane: how would you earn a buyer's trust, if you were me?"

Jane flushed at the compliment, and it made her bolder than she would have been before. "You should take off your cap," she said.

"What?"

"Your cap. I just mean . . . if you want the ladies to buy your pots, you might show them . . ." Jane stumbled. How could she say this without seeming immodest? "You might let them see your face, is all."

"My face, is it?" Robin's smile was sharp as a blade, and dangerously intimate. Her heart jumped. "Will this face sell pots, little Jane?"

It surely would, but Jane would admit no such thing. Not under the heat of that gaze. Not with everyone at market staring at her like she'd lost her wits for following this strange potter around. "For trust, m'lord," she said. "People here don't trust hidden faces."

"Clever girl." Robin, mercifully, turned his eyes back to the market crowd. He removed his cap, ran a hand through his ashy hair, then leapt atop the cart with the grace of a cat. "Pots!" he cried loudly. "Have a gift, the more you buy—a special gift, from me!" He winked at a young woman who had turned to stare, causing her to flush red as cherries.

Sure enough, women began to circle Robin's cart, murmuring among themselves, some of them laughing.

"Must be new to potting," one woman said.

"Won't be at it for long." Another snorted.

"What's the gift?" a third woman called out, her basket already burdened with grain, her face creased in a disdainful frown so deep it looked etched into her bones.

"A bold one, aren't you!" Robin dropped his voice low and sultry. The woman giggled then, a sound as strange as a frog croaking out birdsong. "Buy a pot and find out."

Blushing furiously, the woman shook her head and disappeared back into the crowd.

"I'll buy one," a skinny woman said, her hair like hay straw, her eyes sharp. "How much for brass?"

"Two pennies!" Robin announced, and Jane's eyes widened. The pot was worth five pennies at least, and he could have gotten twice that out of a noblewoman. The crowd warmed to him now.

The woman pressed the coins into Robin's hand, leaning closer. "And my gift?"

Robin looked at Jane, all traces of that intimate smile wiped away, as though they truly were strangers to each other, just as they were pretending to be. It stung, irrationally, and left Jane cold in the pit of her belly. "Be a help and give me that pipkin, would you, girl?"

Trying not to bristle at her transition from "fair maiden" to "girl," Jane dug a small pot out of the cart and handed it over. Robin bestowed it upon the woman with a grand bow, as though he were handing her a precious jewel. "Your gift, good wife." He squinted. "You are some lucky man's wife, aren't you? Fate could not be so kind to me today."

Bold as she was, the woman flushed and sputtered before a friend in the crowd called out, "She's married to a big one, potter. Watch yourself!"

Robin clucked his tongue. "Alas." And then his eyes moved to another woman in the crowd, as though the first had melted away the moment he shifted his gaze.

"Come now!" he called out. "Who gets the next gift? I'd hate to have to haul these heavy pots back home!" Jane studied his face, the strong hands that yanked his collar up over the scratch on his neck each time it slipped, but his eyes were everywhere else, not on her. Was this all she was meant to do? Would he release her from his game once the cart was empty, or had he forgotten her completely?

The fishmonger sidled up to Jane as a crowd of women swarmed the potter's cart. "You should tell your master, girl: he'll never be prosperous giving away his wares as though they aren't worth a penny."

"He's not my master," Jane snapped, harsher than she meant to be. "I'm just helping for . . . for charity." But the fishmonger was right, and perhaps this was part of her test as well.

She tugged on Robin's sleeve. "You'll be out of pots soon," she whispered, "and have nothing for it. Perhaps . . ." She chose her words carefully. "Perhaps, if you were quieter, there wouldn't be such a crowd."

Robin watched her, that smile still playing in his eyes. "And what if I want us to be noticed?"

Jane was struck silent. *Whose notice could he want?* she wondered. Being noticed was the last thing she had expected for her trial, the very last thing she would have wanted, something that could shame her in front of everyone she knew. But she was in it now, she was. There was nothing left to do but play Robin's game.

Robin's wares continued to dwindle as Jane waited and watched. As the sun slipped behind a cloud, a fine woman strode past their stall, tall and clad in green silk and a fur mantle, her chestnut hair clutched in a net woven with beads. She looked like the sort of woman who ought to have a retinue behind her, but she was trailed by only two old servants, their arms full of trinkets and sweets. People scattered as she passed, some bowing their heads deferentially.

"Who is that?" Jane asked Thomas.

"The new shire reeve's wife," he said, his breath like a stale onion.

"There's a new reeve for Nottingham shire? What's he doing all the way up here?"

"Hunting outlaws, I expect." He spat in the dirt. "'Bout time too, I'd say, if that potter got robbed on his way to market."

Hunting outlaws. She froze as Robin's eyes latched on to the woman in the fine clothes. Jane shoved toward him through the greedy shoppers, leaning closer to his ear than she was comfortable with. "Not that one," she said. "You'll be found out. Her husband is . . ."

Robin didn't turn his head, but he said softly, "The shire reeve of Nottingham, of course."

Jane felt as if all the dust and dirt from the market had flown up into her throat. Was this who he had been waiting for? But that meant—

And Jane understood now; his game had only begun.

"Ah!" Robin cried out, looking directly where he shouldn't. "Now here's a woman worthy of my gifts. Why"—he gave Jane a sly smile—"God's bones, I think that's Lady de Stircheley, is it not, gracing the market on this fine October day, and so far from Nottingham town!"

Lady de Stircheley raised one sharp eyebrow to assess Robin. She had a square jaw and strong neck. If the reeve was anything like his wife, he would have a formidable stare indeed. "Do we know each other?"

"Who wouldn't know of you, my lady?" Robin said. "Mansfield rarely gets such guests as yourself and your good husband, protector of the land."

"What can I do for you, potter?" the lady asked, her eyes wary.

"A gift." He bowed magnanimously. "A welcome to our humble town. Every new household needs pots, even those as rich in stature as your own."

The reeve's wife glanced between her servants. "And what will your gift cost me?"

"Why"—Robin looked up at her from under his lashes—"not a single penny! I have five pots left, and all of them are yours, for nothing but my lady's grace and favor."

The crowd gasped.

"You're having me on," the lady said, but she strode over to the cart to inspect the remaining wares. "How much, in earnest?"

"Do you doubt my word, disparage my honor?" Robin asked. "Is the oath of a mere potter worth less than a shire reeve's under the eyes of God?"

Robin met Jane's eyes, and gave her a small nod, barely noticeable.

Summoning all her courage, Jane stepped forward, hoping Lady de Stircheley wouldn't notice that her spine was frozen, that her walk was more like a lurch. "He's honest, m'lady," said Jane, her eyes on the woman's jeweled slippers, which were too tight for her large feet. "I've seen him give his pots away for pennies all this day."

"And why would he do such a foolish thing, when clearly he needs those pennies?"

Jane followed Lady de Stircheley's stare to Robin's ill-fitting tunic, which had slipped, again, to show the angry scratch on his neck. The reeve's wife seemed a proud person. She would not want charity. And suddenly Jane understood what Lady de Stircheley needed to hear.

"Our potter was nearly robbed today, m'lady," Jane said. "But he escaped. Perhaps he feels grateful for Mary's grace. Especially since your husband has come to drive the thieves away." There was a warning in what she said too. She hoped Robin heard it.

Robin beamed at her, and despite her fear, that smile warmed Jane like the sun. "'Tis true, just as she says. Our Lady has given me two gifts this day: my freedom, and our new shire reeve. Surely I must give my own gifts in return."

"You're very generous indeed, potter, for a man so recently imperiled." Lady de Stircheley studied Robin closely now, lingering on his fine features, his sparkling eyes. "It speaks to a stout heart." Then she looked back at her overburdened servants and sighed. "But I'm afraid I'll have to come back later to collect your gifts."

"Why, we can carry them!" Robin cried, and Jane's heart dropped into her stomach. "That is, if you're willing, my dear girl. You've been ever so kind to me today. Could I press upon you for a single favor more? There's a penny in it for you, by my word."

Jane struggled. Was this part of her test? Afraid and painfully conscious of all the eyes on her, she nodded.

The reeve's wife was rosy-cheeked and in excellent humor now. "Grammercy, good sir," she said. "If you will not take my pennies today, I'll make it worth your while. When you come back to market, I'll send my staff to buy pots from you and you alone!"

Robin bowed low. "My lady, I swear myself to your service, now and forever more, if only you might smile at me again, for one smile from you is as a spring flower in winter's dark."

The reeve's wife laughed. "A spring flower, is it? And this from a potter who has tasted his autumn years?"

"Autumn fires burn the hottest," Robin said, a grin slithering across his face. Jane's ears burned as the reeve's wife grinned back. Were all married folks so inconstant, wives and husbands? And who was Jane to be embarrassed by it—some kind of fine lady or nun? Her head down, Jane stacked pots high enough in her arms to hide the look on her face as she trailed after the flirting couple.

They followed an uphill path from the market to the town's old longhouse. It had been neglected after King Henry's death while his son Edward took the long journey back from Crusade to claim his throne, but the place had been polished up for the new shire reeve: the stone freshly scrubbed, the roof patched, a field of herbs and a large garden thriving beside it.

"What a fine home, Lady de Stircheley," Robin said. "Your husband must keep you well indeed."

"There's no need to be so formal," Lady de Stircheley said as she led them all, Robin and the servants with their baskets and Jane with her arms full of pots, back to her house like a pack of ducklings. "You may call me Betrice."

The path was muddy, grooved deep by cart wheels, and strewn with horse droppings. Jane craned her neck to look past her full arms, trying not to step in the filth; it would hardly do to enter the shire reeve's home trailing horse dung.

"I've never known a potter to have a servant," Betrice said, not asking what she really wanted to ask. "You must do very well for yourself."

Jane looked desperately over at Robin. Betrice would likely be invited to dine at the King's Houses, and if she recognized Jane as a potter's servant, that could be the end of her position there before it even began.

"This girl?" Robin asked, all innocence. "She's not my servant."

Betrice looked at Jane crossly and not a little sheepishly. "Ah, my mistake. So she's your . . ." She let the words trail off, but her eyes remained fixed on Jane, one pointed brow raised.

"I . . ." Jane stammered.

"She's a fellow merchant," Robin said, and Jane could have thrown her arms around him in gratitude, had her arms not been overfull with pots. "She was kind enough to help me once her goods were sold."

"Ah." Betrice seemed relieved. "Then I'm afraid I've been horribly rude. I'm Betrice de Stircheley, and you are . . ."

"Jane, m'um. Jane Crowe," Jane muttered, grateful that she didn't have to bow with the pots in her arms.

"And what do you sell? Perhaps I'll buy from you next time."

"I sold conserves," Jane said, "but I'm taking up work at King's Houses soon, in the kitchens. I won't be at the market."

"So you *are* a servant." Betrice sounded pleased, and her sharply angled nose pointed straight up as the order of things was restored.

Jane had gotten so many congratulations at the market that Betrice de Stircheley's dismissal of her new role tasted like a draught of fish stock. She glanced at Robin, whose knowing eyes met hers, and thought about what he'd said to her in the woods that day—that rich folk would devour her like the fattened geese on their table, and call in more of her kind to clean up the bones. It seemed he was right, wasn't he?

"To be selected for King's Houses"—Robin took the tone of a proud parent—"is quite an honor. Jane made the staff for her excellent skill with cookery. Perhaps you should have snatched her up for your kitchen first, my lady."

"Oh, but we have a proper cook," Betrice said, and then her fair skin turned pink, as though she'd suddenly realized her insult. Jane controlled her expression as best she could even as her cheeks began to burn. She gathered her courage for whatever trick Robin had planned, for surely the reeve and his wife deserved it.

"A *proper* cook," Robin said, his voice teasing. "A lowly potter like myself can only dream of the delicacies hidden beneath your roof, my lady. Or do you think them too rich for my tongue?"

Betrice's laugh was deep, hearty with lust. "But, where are my manners? You could try these delicacies this very day! We're to have a modest feast at Nones. You simply must dine with us."

"With us?" Robin asked. "With you and the shire reeve?"

"Just so," Betrice said. "And you can tell my husband all about your thieves."

"I couldn't possibly impose on your good husband's hospitality," Robin started, but Jane could tell from the lift in his voice that his words were false, that he had been counting on this very thing from the moment he dragged that cart into the market, and her stomach clenched again.

"But I insist!" Betrice said. "You swore yourself to my service, did you not?"

"God's mercy," Robin said. "I shall do your bidding, then, fair lady. But I insist that Jane join us, for she was kind enough to carry all your pots. She is the real hero of this story."

Jane took a deep breath. Playing a trick on the reeve's wife in the safety of the market was all well and good, but what if the reeve caught on to the game in his own house, and she and Robin were trapped inside? "I don't know," she stammered. "I . . ."

"I insist." Robin bowed to her, as if his invitation were a favor rather than a trial.

Jane could see the discomfort, the struggle, on Betrice's face. To have two merchants at her table would be one thing, but to invite a servant to her table was something else entirely.

"Yes, really, you must," Betrice finally said, her stiff tone implying that, indeed, she must not.

"'Tis settled, Jane. Carrying pots is hungry work—believe me, I know. And you'll need a proper send-off to King's Houses."

"Indeed." Betrice's smile bared all her teeth.

Chapter Four

Walter de Stircheley was not what Jane expected. She had been certain Betrice's husband would be as tall and pampered as his wife, pillowed in silk and soft shoes. Instead, Walter was smaller than Betrice, but not small. He was thick, skin sun-browned and sagging where the muscle had lain fallow for too long, like a forgotten field. His gaze, brown between a wild sand-and-salt brush of eyebrows, was intense, hard, as though he knew something about you that you might not even know yourself. His nose was round and pockmarked, his jaw firm, the veins in his neck pulsed when he spoke, and his hands were not the soft, smooth hands of an untested lord. This was a man, Jane thought, that you could not hide from, and she worried for Robin, and worried for his plans, whatever they were.

Robin assessed him with a hungry look, like a cat staring at its prey, and Jane decided she never wanted to be on the other side of that stare.

The reeve was surrounded by fighting men, mercenaries, not a one of them with the hope of becoming a lord himself. They were hard men, sooty beards and lost teeth and scars, and even though there were only three of them, along with the reeve it was enough to set Jane's teeth on edge. A bald man with a neck as thick as a bull's let his eyes crawl over Jane, and she fought the urge to shift closer to Robin. She stood her ground instead, staring only at the reeve as he spoke. Strange that she hadn't felt quite so threatened in Robin's forest, surrounded by outlaws.

"I see my wife has picked up more strays." Walter chuckled as though he had made a clever joke.

"Walter!" Betrice's voice was suddenly octaves higher, a tall woman squeaking like a mouse. He pulled her close and kissed her full on the mouth, but it was a hard kiss, an attempt to display some kind of power rather than show affection. "Be kind," she said, surreptitiously wiping her mouth when his head turned. "The potter was almost robbed today!"

Walter's eyes fastened on Robin, taking in the bruise blooming on his hand, the scratch at his throat. "Is that so? How did you stop the thieves?"

"A stout heart," Robin said, thumping his chest with a sly glance at Betrice, "and a stouter stick."

The reeve laughed, missing the joke. "Fortune smiles on you, potter"—he gripped Robin's hand—"for I'm here to find those thieves, and drag them off in chains. Your name, good man?"

Betrice flushed, mortified. "Oh, I'm afraid I didn't ask!"

"Robert," Robin said immediately and smoothly, as though it were the name he had been born to. "Robert Wentbridge. Named for the place I grew up by."

Betrice looked confusedly at Jane. "And Jane is . . ."

"I sell conserves," Jane said more sternly than she meant to, "at Mansfield market. Very pleased to meet you, m'lord."

"Indeed." Walter's eyes assessed her, cold and hard, and then

shifted back to Robin, as if satisfied that Jane was no one important, not a threat. Her shoulders eased considerably when his attention moved past her. "Well, bring them in, then. Our potter
here deserves a drink, and you can tell me how much of my coin
you threw away at market."

"Oh, Walter," Betrice muttered, but she sniffed as if she were
irritated rather than contrite. Their manners were so different—
his so low, and hers so high—that Jane suspected the reeve's wife
must be the one with the moneyed family. She had seen the reeve's
arrogance and bluster in her older brother, Peter, after he married
Cecely de Thornton, a merchant's daughter. Walter de Stircheley
had won Betrice in some way, though Jane was not sure how, and
he used her coin to fill his table.

And the shire reeve's table was full—full and covered in fine
white cloth. The table overflowed with food, wine, ale, and steaming, gold-crusted loaves. Sun beamed in through the tall windows,
seeming to shine on different dishes as though they were being
shown off by heaven itself: pies glittering with yolk, a whole pig
roasted with apples, bowls of leeks and onions in the purest white
sauce, and a dish of colored salts at the table's head. The scents
alone nearly brought Jane to her knees, the savory aroma of
roasted game covered with a wild and spicy burst she couldn't
place. She hadn't seen a table so heavy with meat in all her life.

"Serve yourselves," Walter grunted as he reached for the fine,
light wastel bread that had been set before him, pulling it into
flaky layers. "We don't put on airs here." It would be hard for them
to do so, Jane considered, since the two servants who brought the
finger bowl around to clean their hands were the same two who
had followed Betrice to market.

"Don't tell the priests how full our table is on fish day," Betrice

A GRET WAGER *41*

whispered intimately to Robin as she filled her trencher with an impossible amount of food.

"I wouldn't dream of it," Robin said. "We are all of us brimming with sin, so what's the harm in a sin that injures no one and brings only pleasure?"

Jane found herself blushing almost perpetually, seated as she was between Betrice and Robin, who charmed the reeve's wife with a smile so playful that Jane was sure Walter would reach over and stab Robin with his eating knife. The rough men sat at a smaller table, farther from the giant hearth and swallowed in shadow.

Jane took a slice of pie that had rich, crumbled venison pouring from its glossy crust, a small roll, two slices of pork with apples, and just enough of the leek and onion dish to be polite, though she loathed onions. She watched Betrice carefully—she had no idea how fine people made their table, and she did not intend to embarrass herself in front of Robin. After Betrice picked up her meat pie in one hand, Jane took up her own and almost swooned at the first bite, her senses filling with smoke, wood, and sweetness, almost like the incense from a church's censer, but warming instead of cloying. "This is wonderful," she said. "What flavors the pie?"

"It's canelle," Betrice said. "Can't get that from Mansfield market. We had to bring our own stock."

"It's lovely." Jane sighed in wonder. "I've never tasted such a thing."

"Have you never been to Nottingham? Never been to the spice market there?"

Jane shook her head, but before an explanation could leave her lips, Betrice laughed, her cheeks high with color, her eyes on Robin.

"Imagine a cook who doesn't know spices. And at King's Houses, of all things!"

Robin's eyes tightened, though his smile remained. "I find the simplest things are often the most beautiful—unadorned, with no foreign wiles to mask their nature."

Jane stared furiously at her trencher. "Of course," Betrice murmured, but she was not so easily daunted. "We're headed back there in a fortnight, by God's grace, and this time I'll bring back sugar. The Saracens have the stuff, and our men brought it from Crusade. It's delightful—so much lighter and more delicate than honey!"

"That stuff addles the mind," Walter grunted. "As do all the fruits of the Moors."

Betrice flushed. "Men are so contrary." She wiped her lips on her sleeve before she took a sip of wine, and so Jane did the same, then caught Robin watching her, eyes twinkling with humor. She stared back, frowning, the wine emboldening her. What had he expected, bringing a peasant girl to such a rich table?

"Did you go on Crusade, my lord?" Robin asked, turning his attention to the reeve. "I'd no idea we were dining in the presence of a knight."

Walter frowned as though he had tasted something bitter. "Me? No. Not so lucky as to be born to a gilded scabbard. I *earned* my reeveship."

"How did you earn it?" Robin's teeth glittered. "I love a good tale of battle."

"I hunted the cowards who tried to overthrow King Henry in the Barons' War—that traitor de Montfort and the other filthy dogs who fled when their rebellion failed. But I didn't catch them

A GRET WAGER 43

all. I hear a band of them camp in your Greenwood, like animals. Like as not, they're the ones who robbed you, potter."

Jane stared at Robin. Was he a baron, then, playing peasant among the trees? The thought irked her.

Betrice clapped her hands, her face glowing. "Oh, is it true, Jane? You have a pack of rebel barons hiding in your forest? How exciting!"

"The men who robbed me were common thieves, not soldiers." Robin laughed to make light of it, though there was no laughter in his eyes. "Else I couldn't have fought them off with my stick."

The reeve snorted. "These men were swords for hire in the war—men who would sink to anything, and did."

Robin fixed his eyes on the reeve like a hawk on a rabbit, all the lightness fleeing his voice. "The barons only had to pay a toll and grovel to keep their lands. The fighting men saw no such mercy. Your barons betrayed them just to save their own skin. Why hunt for those who bloodied their swords for coin or cause, like any man would?"

And then, Jane saw clearly who Robin was. Why he was hiding. He would have been young when the barons tried to overthrow King Henry—barely more than a boy—but a peasant need only be old enough to hold a sword when war came calling. The barons had sent him to attack his own king, and then abandoned him when they'd lost.

The reeve chuckled and patted his stomach. "Simon de Montfort didn't keep his skin. They chopped him up like a Christmas pig and spread him six ways across England."

"*Walter!*" Betrice turned purple, her white tablecloth clutched in her hands. She looked as though she might storm off in a rage. The rich food twisted in Jane's stomach, her heart beating faster with the memories of all the storms she had weathered at home—and so, Jane did what she had always done when people wanted to make war at the table. She distracted them.

"What did the rebels want?" Jane asked, the words clunking loudly in the volatile silence. "The barons, I mean." She laughed nervously when she felt the weight of everyone's stare. "I was but a child then. The war didn't touch us out here."

"No." Betrice sniffed, her skin cooling. "I suppose it didn't." She took another drink of wine and cleared her throat. "They had principles, some of those men. People were hungry, and King Henry had his ear bent too far toward foreigners. He had spread his wealth thin and wide, with none of it going back to England, and the barons wanted . . ."

"To take power for themselves," the reeve interrupted her. "'Tis what all men want when they go to war, no matter how lofty their claims."

"Is that so?" Robin's eyes lit with fire. "Then what drives you to chase the men who lurk in our woods, who have no power at all, and never did? The Barons' War is ten years past. You must have the drive of a bull, my lord, to hunt the rebels still."

"Our new King Edward has tasked me with it," Walter said proudly. It had been a bright morning, but as the clouds came, the reeve's house grew darker, and the fire lit the room in strange ways. Red sand and silver danced across Walter's battered jaw when he smiled.

"Didn't Edward himself fight against his own father at first, on the barons' side?" Robin frowned. "I remember when men would follow Edward into any battle, he fought so well, before he turned his eyes to treasure and the Holy Land."

"They were fools, as he was a fool, and a young one at that. Edward grew up. Those cowards ran from their mistakes instead."

Jane's heart dropped as the men locked horns once again. She had taken a second serving of pie, trying to savor the taste, but now it was turning hard and slick in her belly. If Robin and his men had rebelled against the king, and Walter was here to hunt them, then what was Robin doing dangling himself like a prize boar right beneath the reeve's nose?

And what about the rest of them? What about Bran? He was far too young to have fought in the Barons' War, on either side. Did he know who he was working for?

She found Robin studying her face again, his green eyes exposing her to scrutiny like moonlight on a rat. He must have known that his old war would come up tonight; he had dredged the past up himself. But why? Did he want to see how she would react? Was the real test whether or not Jane could keep his secrets?

Then a shout went up from the other table, and Robin looked away and Jane could breathe again. She turned to see ale sloshing onto the table's sticky surface, the floor beneath the fighting men's feet littered with crusts. Jane could not help but stare at the bounty on the floor. They would set the dogs upon it, she knew, even though the alms bowl had nothing but a stale loaf of brown bread in it. Bran had told her stories about how nobles were callous and wasteful at their feasts, but it made Jane heartsick to see it when her task at home had been to save and make use of anything she could.

"What's on, lads?" de Stircheley called. Something in him that was tight as a whip when he spoke to Robin and his wife loosened when he addressed his men, like a flower easing open in the spring.

"The boys have made a wager," a tall, older mercenary said. "A shooting contest!"

"Aye!" a man called, his beard slick with grease. Had Jane not bothered to wipe her mouth like that, she'd have been tossed out on her ear. But she supposed table rules were different for fighting men. "Ox here"—he pointed to the bald man with the roving eyes—"says he can outshoot me. I says he can't. So we'd like to have it on and see."

Ox, squat like a toad, cleared his throat. "If you'll allow it."

"What's the wager?" Robin asked, and Jane saw annoyance flash across the reeve's face. He was meant to hold court here, in his dark little hall, and Robin had beaten him to the question.

"Ten shillings."

Robin whistled. "A fair wage your shire reeve must pay, for you to bet that kind of coin. I've half a mind to give up selling pots and try your game myself!"

"Ten?" The reeve snorted. "That's beggar's coin. I'll give twenty shillings to the man who wins the shooting, and I'll give it from my own purse!"

"Hurrah!" The three men pounded the table, and Jane winced again at the spilling drink, reminding herself that she wouldn't have to be the one to clean it up this time.

"Robert, my good man"—the reeve slapped Robin hard on the back, forcing a small cough out of him—"if you want to see how men of war spend their days, come out to the yard. We're about to have a little game of bows and arrows."

"I should very much like to see that." Robin cocked his brow. "And will you shoot in the contest yourself, good Shire Reeve?"

"Ha!" Walter's laugh was loose, good-natured. He had won, after all, putting up the coin as he had, and proved himself a lord, at least in the eyes of his shadowed table. "Let the lads show off. They've earned it."

"Well then, I expect to be impressed." Robin's mouth twitched, and Jane found she could not look at him for fear she would burst into laughter.

"And Jane shall lend me an extra pair of hands in here," Betrice cried merrily, looping her long arm through Jane's own.

"Oh, no," Robin said. "Jane deserves a cup of ale and a show after all her labors. Surely you wouldn't deprive her. What sort of hospitality would that be?" He did not look at Jane, but she felt his warmth emanating in her direction, and she was immensely grateful. No one had ever tried to ease her burdens in such a way.

"Oh." Betrice looked hurt and shamed again, but brightened quickly with false light. "Then we shall both join you! Perhaps you'll let the ladies judge the game, as they did in Arthur's court!"

"This is no pleasure hunt. A shooting contest is a man's game," the reeve said curtly. "*I* shall be the judge."

Robin's verdant eyes glittered. "Long gone are the days of Diana the huntress, little Jane, and of chivalry and manners and romance. 'Tis a man's world now, the magic gone cold as stone. Let the shire reeve choose his man. I, however, am no man of arms." He dropped to one knee, his tunic billowing around him like a great gray pool. "This humble potter shall ask the ladies for their judgment and take them at their honorable word."

Walter scowled. "Do what thou wilt, potter. The men grow thirsty, as do I, so let's get on with it."

Betrice rose to follow her husband to the courtyard, and Robin came up beside Jane to whisper in her ear, his scent all ale and woodsmoke. "You soothed them at the table, Jane, but I wanted them angry."

Jane nearly jumped out of her skin. "I'm sorry, m'lord."

"No matter. I've learned much from them." He leaned closer, his breath hot on her neck, sending a small shiver through her. "What do you think of our shire reeve? A man's man, is he?"

"Yes," Jane said, but then she frowned. "Well, maybe. But not to be one of them. He likes to be above them."

"Tell me more. What have I missed? You've a gift for knowing people's tempers. I've seen it now myself."

Jane flushed hot. She wanted to tell him it was no special gift. She had learned it because guessing wrong could earn you shouting or a hard smack in the face at home. "I can't really say, m'lord. I've only just met him."

"Make a game of it, then. What do you guess?"

"Well, he's proud," Jane said slowly. "And covetous of coin, though he doesn't want to seem so."

"Why not?"

Jane hesitated.

"Go on," Robin urged, fire in his eyes. "It costs you nothing if you're wrong."

She chewed on her lip as he stared at her, then finally blurted out, "I think the money's not his."

"Is that so?" Robin's eyes widened.

Jane nodded toward Betrice, whose back was straight and stiff in the crowd of brutal men who stalked the courtyard, readying their bows. Her skirts swirled, kept from dragging on the muddy ground by the grip of her own fist. "She's higher born than he is. He won her, somehow. Perhaps some gift for his service."

"Now that"—he tapped the tip of his nose—"is worth a gift of your own. Watch, and I shall win it for you."

"Wait!" Jane grabbed his wrist. "Are you the one he's hunting?"

Robin grinned. "Well, if I am, he isn't hunting hard enough."

"He's a dangerous man," she said urgently, fear flooding her. After all, what good would passing Robin's test do if he wound up hanging from the gallows? "I wouldn't cross him."

"No," Robin said, "*you* wouldn't." And he strode out to the courtyard, his potter's disguise swishing around him, blowing dust.

Chapter Five

The courtyard wrapped around the house, sheltered by a stone wall. The land had been stripped in the back so that only a single oak remained, shedding its yellowing leaves across the hard-packed dirt.

"I'll send a servant for stools," Betrice said.

"Oh, that's not necessary." Jane prepared to settle onto the earth and rest her aching back against the longhouse wall.

"Don't be silly," Betrice replied. "You'll muss your clothes!" She pointedly did not look at Jane's stockings, which already had a layer of dirt and market mud climbing up them.

The old serving woman tried to slide a stool beneath Jane, who leapt up and grabbed it from her. "I can arrange it," she said, horrified. "Thank you ever so much!"

The woman merely nodded, eyes fixed upon the ground, and arranged another stool for Betrice, who was twice the woman's size and half her age. Betrice noticed the look on Jane's face, even though she tried to hide it. "They've been with my family a long time," she said with a coy smile. "Can't let them go. They wouldn't know what to do with themselves, no roof over their heads, no work for idle hands."

Jane nodded as though she understood, but stayed silent, not trusting her tongue. Her back screamed as she tried to find comfort on the stool.

The game was dull to watch at first. Drunk and sloppy, the reeve's men shot wide of the mark, some even sending arrows flying into the stone wall. They punched each other in the arm and swore foully, spitting in the dirt like beggars. Jane had grown up in a house full of boys, but poor as they had been, they had not been nearly so rude. Perhaps the poorer you were, and the less you had, the more you valued how you seemed to others.

But Robin wasn't bored. He was transfixed. He watched every shot, every stance, listened keenly to every insult hurled, every word spoken. And he watched the reeve too, at ease among his men, slapping shoulders and trading japes.

Finally, when Foulke, the skinniest and quietest of the reeve's men, dropped his arrow before he could even shoot it, Robin cleared his throat. Jane reached for his sleeve when she saw what was happening, but it was already too late.

"What game is this, Shire Reeve? I've half a mind to think you've overfed and besotted your men just to keep your coin!"

Ox staggered forward, his eyes unfocused, his lips a snarl. "And you think you can do better, potter?"

"Had I a bow, by the Rood, I'd show you in one shot! Any man may hit a hare in the wood better than these louts, even a man who sells pots!"

Ox turned hot as a blacksmith's bellows. He growled and stormed over to Robin, who sat unperturbed even as the man's rancid breath hit his face. "Get on your feet, old man, and back up those japes with your fists!"

"Old man?" Robin smiled, but it was cold. "Reeve, is this how your yeomen speak to guests?"

Ox churned up phlegm in his throat and spat at Robin's feet. "You're all talk, potter. A real man backs up his words."

Robin stood then, right in front of Ox, sending him off-balance and stumbling backward. "I would shoot, by God, but I have left my hunting bow behind. Had I expected to encounter animals"— he raised his eyebrows at Ox—"I would have kept it at my side."

"Oh, I'll loan you a bow," said the reeve with a hungry look. "If you're brave enough to shoot."

"I'll shoot." Robin kept his eyes on the large man before him.

"Then go on, potter. But if you lose, you'll pay back what my lady gave you for your pots."

Jane and Betrice exchanged a glance. The pots had been free, after all. Betrice winked and whispered, "Let's not tell him. Your potter is sure to lose, and it will be a great game when we reveal that he owes nothing."

"And if he wins?" Jane murmured.

Betrice guffawed and elbowed her in the ribs, none too gently. "And swine will fly this day too, I suppose?"

"What's the joke, ladies?" A slow, easy grin spread across Robin's face. "Reeve, you haven't laid a trap for me, have you? You wouldn't give me a bad bow just to win back your wife's coin?"

The reeve snorted. "As if I'd notice pennies lost to the likes of you. If there's a trap here, potter, you've laid it yourself. I'm a man of honor, and should you choose to make an ass of yourself in front of fighting men and ladies, I won't be to blame for your embarrassment. In fact, you may choose the best of my own bows. Fetch them," he ordered his men, "and set them up."

Jane glanced nervously at Robin. When he shot—and surely he would shoot well—would the game be up? Would they see that he was no old man, no mere potter, in spite of his grayed hair and billowing clothes? And what would happen to Jane when he was caught?

The men came back with three weapons: a massive bow the height of a tall man, and two shorter bows for hunting, one with a serpent carved into its grip.

Robin chose the tallest one, and Walter's men snickered, nudging each other and smirking.

"You're sure that's the one you want?" the reeve asked with half a smile. "It takes a strong arm to pull that bow back, much less string it."

But Robin strung the bow smoothly, expertly, the loose potter's robes hiding the tautness of his muscles, the strength of his lean grip, and everyone's laughter died away.

"I think this one will do," Robin said calmly. "Twenty shillings, you say, to hit the mark?"

The reeve nodded, stiff.

Robin took an arrow from the quiver and, without any fanfare, he shot. The arrow landed with a thunk in the wooden target, an inch from the mark, the base of it vibrating in the silence. Betrice cheered, her shoulder glancing off Jane's as though they were friends sharing a joke.

"Luck!" Foulke shouted.

"You didn't hit the mark," the reeve said, his thin mouth a frown.

"He came the closest!" Betrice called, her skin flush and merry with drink.

"The shire reeve is right." Robin bowed, a sly smile lurking on his face before his body dipped down. "I missed it by a finger's breadth. Shall we shoot again to settle the matter?"

"Aye!" The men leapt up, eager to redeem themselves. They had treated it as a mere game thus far, but now it was a challenge.

"But . . ." Robin spun the reeve's bow as though it were a child's toy. "Let's raise the wager. Forty shillings for the mark."

"Forty?" Walter stammered, his face draining of color.

Jane gaped. Should he win, Robin would be hauling away a whole chest full of pennies in his potter's wagon.

"The coin will not be missed, you said, so why not spend a little more?" Robin's face was pleasant, but the glare between the men was hard. "As you say, it is nothing to a man of means such as yourself."

Robin looked at Jane out of the corner of his eye as the reeve's face twisted with suppressed rage. Jane realized she had been right all along. The coin was not his. The reeve was caught now, like a stupid, proud beast that thought it was too clever to be hunted. He could not say no.

And Jane finally saw Robin's trick, from the ridiculous potter's costume to his strange spectacle at the market. It was all for this moment: to humiliate the reeve, to strip him of his coin, and to mark him—another corrupt nobleman pinned by Robin Hood's arrows. She felt a tangle of excitement and fear. Robin had hit his mark, exactly as he'd planned. And he could not have done it without Jane. Part of her wanted to run—but a larger part of her wanted to see what would happen next, for there was more to Robin's plan, wasn't there, with the Barons' War and the new king? Jane would not forget. She would have to watch and tread carefully.

"Oh, come, Walter," Betrice urged. "It's nothing to us!"

"Fine," the reeve grumbled, his voice almost too quiet to hear. "But it's coming out of your spending purse."

The men lined up, trying to steady themselves for the sake of coin, and shot. Foulke came the closest to Robin's last shot by a hair, and he hooted, his friends offering a sloppy toast, pointing mockingly at Robin.

Robin smiled softly, as if to himself, and took his turn.

One swift, easy shot, like a starling shooting from the sky, and a sharp crack as the arrow slammed into the center of the target. Jane's mouth fell open.

Robin had cleft the peg in three, his arrow humming at the center of the shattered mark.

Silence swallowed the courtyard until Betrice, finding her voice, hooted and leapt out of her seat, toppling the little stool beneath her.

"By His nails!" she cried. "He's done it!" She grabbed Jane's arm and yanked her to her feet. "He's done it!"

The men cursed and swore, and Jane clapped, though her arms shook violently. "You have the devil's own luck, potter," she said.

Robin bent on one knee in a deep bow. "God is with me by our Holy Mother's grace, young Jane. Follow the path She shows you and you will never fail." Then he lifted his head, the dimming sunlight showing the ash in his hair and a glimmer of the foxcoat red beneath, like a lover's secret. "And will the queens crown their champion this day, as they did in days of old?"

Betrice giggled like a girl. She curtsied, lifting her skirts a little too high, then took the fillet off her own head and laid it upon Robin's drunkenly, so that it sat askew and shrouded his face. Her own lovely hair fell out of its netted binding. "Good Sir Robert Wentbridge," she declared, "I dub you . . . the Knight of the Pots!" Then she burst out laughing, and Jane forced a laugh out of herself as though she were drowning and it was her last breath of air. She looked at the reeve surreptitiously, at the shadows darkening his face. Betrice was taking things too far. Walter was moments away from violence.

Jane lifted the ridiculous fillet off of Robin's head and brushed the ash off of it, restoring it to Betrice with a gentle hand. "You'll spoil your hair, good lady. Let me fix it for you."

The reeve's wife ducked her head obediently, but she had eyes only for Robin.

Seeing Betrice's wild locks covered and arranged again seemed to settle the reeve, a restoration of order in the chaos. He rose slowly from an uncomfortable crouch, as though his legs were stuck in mud, and clapped loudly, so that the whole party quieted for the sound. "So you might be a man after all, worthy of bearing arms. Were you a fighting man, once, and kept it secret?"

Jane felt danger slice through her belly, and she strained to keep a smile on her face, her cheeks aching with the effort.

Robin abandoned Betrice's regard and rose gracefully to face the reeve. "A fighting man? I'm afraid not. But I am a fair shot with a bow. A master archer trained me, even gave me his bow once. I had to leave it in my cart when we delivered your wife's pots, else I would have had it for your game."

Walter's eyes brightened, sunlight on coal. "Who is this friend?"

"Why, Robin Hood, my lord. Do you know him?"

Jane's whole chest seized. She thought the courtyard couldn't get any quieter, but she was wrong. It had the hush of the grave now.

"Is that a joke?" the reeve spat.

Robin's smile tilted. "And why would I mock a man who means to pay me forty shillings? I know some say Robin is a myth, but I've shot a hundred rounds with him under his trysting tree. He beats me every time. If only I'd had as lucky a shot with him as I had here!"

"And this . . . tree," the reeve said, eyes blackening like a hunting cat's, "can you bring me to his hiding place?"

"Robin doesn't hide, good Shire Reeve. He makes his home in the pines west of Rufford Abbey. Everyone knows it."

Jane swallowed her fear. She didn't know exactly where Robin's hideout was, but she knew he had given the reeve the wrong location. When Bran had set out for their hideout, before he covered her eyes, she had noticed that they were riding north.

"I'll give you another ten shillings in the morning," the reeve said, his teeth sharp, "if you'll bring me there."

"My lord, you've been generous indeed, but I could not impose again upon your treasury, grand though it is. Besides, you'll need a full purse if you mean to see the Lord of the Greenwood. He takes a toll"—he smiled sheepishly—"though not from men of low means such as potters."

Walter snorted. "Lord of the Greenwood indeed. Let him try."

"Perhaps you'll find your thieves too, good potter," Betrice added.

"Aye. I expect to find them in the very same place!" The reeve chortled, and his men laughed right along with him.

"Tomorrow will be good hunting!" Foulke said.

"Oh, but your men must follow at a distance." Robin lowered his voice with warning. "You should look as though you ride alone. Fill your purse, bring only your bow, and ride with me, or the Lord of the Greenwood will not appear."

"I thought you said he wasn't hiding." The reeve smirked.

"He's a cautious man is all, and one who respects tradition."

"Sure, sure. Now, let us put you up for the night, potter." Walter forced a false smile onto his face and patted Robin on the back. "With a shooting arm like that, I'd best not let you out of my sight."

"Yes, do stay the night, potter," Betrice cried. "What fun!" But then she remembered Jane, like a forgotten pet. "Oh, but I'm afraid we don't have space for a young lady."

"You're very kind," Jane said, "but I'd best be getting home before the sun sets. My beau will be waiting for me at the market."

"Your beau!" Jane didn't think it was possible for Betrice to brighten any more, but she was practically glowing now. "How wonderful!" She caught herself. "Young love, I mean. Isn't it wonderful, Walter?"

"Wasted on the young," Walter grumbled.

"Cheer up, good man!" Robin said. "How about another round of drinks in honor of our judges?"

It was more than another round of drinks. It was another, and another, and another, until the sun was dangerously low. Jane wondered how long she was meant to stay. Surely she had passed Robin's test by now. She looked around for him, or for Betrice, to make her apologies and leave, but she realized with a sinking feeling that they had both disappeared. She had been left alone with the men.

Jane excused herself—she had been as moderate as she could,

but her bladder forced her to seek out the cesspit, which she found, to her relief, to be enclosed within a privy. On her way back, Jane heard Betrice's laughter out by the garden. She followed the sound, rounding the corner, and nearly stumbled into Robin and Betrice, who were pressed together in the dark, her neck in his mouth, her head tilted back in ecstasy, his arm all the way up her skirts.

Jane's breath caught in her chest. Her heartbeat quickened as she felt a flash of longing, and then, just as quickly, rage. She felt as she did when she had watched her brothers finish all the stew in the winters, when things were scarce. Jane hungered, hungered in a sharp, sudden way that made her want to claw Robin out of Betrice's arms, as though Jane were a starving wolf and Robin, a hen.

Robin pulled back, just a little, and began to turn his head. Shaking off her tangled feelings with a start, Jane ran. She burst back into the feast hall, trying to keep the distress off her face, and heard Betrice rushing in behind her.

"I really must get back, my lord," Jane said to Walter, trying to steady her voice. "Thank you for your hospitality. It was . . . far more than I imagined."

Walter's laugh came from deep in the center of his gut. "I expect so. It's not every day a servant girl feasts in a shire reeve's hall! Let's get you back safely." He gestured to Foulke. "Walk her back to market, will you?"

Foulke rose with a lascivious look in his eyes, strands of his dust-brown hair, thin at the top, clinging to his sweaty head.

"You're very kind," Jane stammered, "but that's not necessary, I . . ."

"I insist," Foulke said. "It isn't safe out there." His yellowed grin spread across his face, showing black gaps where a few teeth had been knocked out in a fight, or worse.

"I . . ."

Robin came up behind her then, heavy with ale and Betrice's perfume, and laid a hand on her back. She bristled at his touch. Here she had thought his aims were noble, but he was base as an animal, wasn't he? "Jane, I nearly forgot, my mind was so muddled with fine food and drink. Your young man told me he'd wait for you at the bottom of the hill, right here. A good lad," he said directly to Foulke. "Keeps the horses for King's Houses. Strong as a lion, isn't he, Jane?"

"He is," Jane breathed out, gratitude and rage at Robin competing for her heart. He was going to get himself killed, no mistake, but at least he had offered her a way out of the mess he was making.

"Jane." Robin's voice forced her to turn around and face him, although she did not want to. He pressed something into her hand. "Your share of the winnings, fair maiden. For your help with the cart and the loss of your day. You're kind to entertain an old man and his games." His eyes searched hers, as if testing her once again, seeing if she would share his dalliance with the reeve's wife. As if it was part of the trick, and all Jane had to do was hold her tongue.

The purse was so fat in Jane's hand that her eyes widened. "My lo . . ." She cleared her throat. "Good sir, I couldn't possibly."

"Get yourself a nice new tunic for your work at King's Houses. Better to impress your masters *and* your beau."

"Ah, a potter who plays at being a lord." The reeve smirked.

"And a bowman," Robin said brightly.

The smirk folded. "And a bowman. Of course. As if I could forget."

—⟨⟨⟨◆⟩⟩⟩—

Bran was waiting right where Robin said he would be, along with his horse. "Well?" he asked, his broad face beaming. "How was it?"

Jane collapsed into his arms, letting out a huge sigh.

"God's bones, you reek of ale!"

"I'm just glad it's over," she said. Then she pushed back and stared up at him. "It *is* over, isn't it?"

"Eh, not quite." Bran was still smiling, but with that guilty look in his eyes he had whenever he was late or had forgotten to meet her. "Someone needs to warn everyone that the reeve is coming. Robin wants it to be you."

"How did you know about Robin's plans with the reeve? They've only just agreed to it!"

Bran grinned. "Robin has eyes and ears everywhere, among the servants and runners, people no one cares about or sees. They got word to us."

Jane thought of Betrice's elderly servants, hauling stools and market wares and food until their backs had bent into curves. Were they the ones whispering for Robin? Was that to be her life, her future, just another invisible set of eyes for the heroes of the wood, who drew their bows for glory and drank their winnings away in the shelter of the trees? "So I'm meant to be one of them?"

"It's not like that, Janie." Bran kissed the top of her head. "You're special—special to *me*, at least."

But not to Robin, she thought, no matter how important he had made her feel. Shame washed over her at the way her heart sank. What kind of a fool was she?

"Why should they need warning? He's sending the reeve the other way entirely, into the pines near Rufford."

"And that's where they'll be waiting," Bran said, his eyes grave, "to spring the trap. That's where you're going too. Come now, let's get you home. You'll need an early start tomorrow."

"What's Robin going to do to him?"

"Just show him what's what, and where not to stick his nose." He patted his horse, who neighed softly. "With any luck, he'll be headed back to Nottingham before All Hallows."

"He's headed back anyway." Jane took his hand to climb onto the horse. "So what's the point of shaming him further?"

"Have you taken a liking to the new shire reeve, Janie? Not even started at King's Houses and you're already too good for us?"

"Hardly." Jane snorted. "But I can't go out there, Bran! The reeve knows my face. He knows I'm to work at King's Houses. If he tells anyone . . ."

"Robin has a plan for you, Jane. Trust him."

"Bran, I . . ."

"He's relying on you, Jane. You mustn't let him down." A shadow crossed his face, dark enough that she worried for what would happen if she *did* let Robin down.

"Are you afraid of him?" Jane asked softly, for she had seen gentleness in Robin, but also hardness. He had been so kind to her, but there had been blood in his eyes when he looked at the reeve.

"Don't be silly." Bran's voice was full of false cheer. "Robin's arrows only fly for thieves and traitors. And, besides, you want to know how all this turns out, don't you?"

Jane wasn't sure she did. Not anymore, not now that the excitement and the drink had faded and she was left with nothing but her fear. She would have said so, but Bran had kicked the horse to a gallop, its feet pounding on the dirt, and her words would have been lost to the wind.

Chapter Six

The sun was barely up when Jane set out the next morning, the sky pale gray, thick with shredding clouds. She hurtled through the forest, tunic clinging to her body beneath her stifling cloak. It was misting, not raining, which was better, but her boots were caked with mud.

She cursed Bran under her breath. He could have given her a horse. She could have bought a horse of her own with the money Robin had won her, but Bran had warned her to move silently and said she could not be followed. Still, she had been hurrying through the woods for nearly an hour and still hadn't reached the trysting tree—if she didn't find it soon, she would be too late to warn Robin's men, and she'd fail her test. And then what would become of her?

Jane walked faster, glancing behind herself frantically, as if she were being chased. Her mind spun, her face as hot and clammy as if it were July, not October. She shrugged her cloak off her shoulders, letting it fly out behind her to snag on tree branches and bushes and God knew what else. She had barely slept the night before, spinning the events at the reeve's house over and over in her mind, her body shifting, her dreams—when she had them—a sweaty turmoil. Thanks to the restless night, her mind was a fog, her mouth crusty, her thoughts slow. None of this had been what Bran had promised her. She had thought all her work for Robin would be at King's Houses, cozy and warm in its kitchens, listening for whispers, not stealing out of her house in the dark with nothing in her stomach but nerves and bile, traipsing through the woods before dawn, ruining her boots, her legs aching, her back stiff, alone and vulnerable and tired—where any manner of predator, man or beast, could easily overcome her.

Was she just a fool then, like Betrice, or Sibyl, a grown woman making herself silly over a man? *Nonsense*, Jane thought sullenly. Betrice might have gone soft in the loins over Robin, as Sibyl had for Hugh, but even they wouldn't have let themselves be run this ragged.

It was just then, when Jane's head was spinning on a wild course, and she was about to give up, and it was light enough to see her hands and the twigs and mud stuck fast to her stockings, that she finally saw the trysting tree.

A massive oak held court in the forest's center, thick and strong among the birch trees' snow-white bones. Seashells danced on ropes throughout the oak's branches, tangled white and gray and pink among the crisping leaves. The shells sang like tiny church bells when the wind swept through.

But Jane didn't have time to marvel at its beauty. The sky was paler now, and the shire reeve would be coming. She whistled once, short and sharp, then twice more, just as Bran had instructed.

"Who goes there?" Wyll's voice, high and reedy as a bird's, came from somewhere above her.

"It's Jane!" she said, and felt like she was shouting, her heart pounding red and raw within her breast. Her name caught in her throat, and she coughed to clear it. "Robin sent me."

"Did he manage it?" Little John lumbered out of the trees like a giant of legend, axe clinging to his hip. "Did he trap the bloody shire reeve?"

"He did," Jane said, mouth like sand. "They're on their way here." She collapsed against the tree, panting, taking the misty air into her burning lungs.

"Take a breath and a drink, girl. They didn't give you a horse?" Another man, dark and clearly foreign, with curling silver hair, a wooly beard, and a lilting tone to his words, handed her a skin of ale. Jane took it gratefully and shook her head.

"Robin can be a right ass when his head's in a scheme," John said.

"Stuff it, John," said Wyll. "This here's Little John, Jane. You met him last time. And this one . . ."

"Call me Tuk," the older man said, with a sharp look at Wyll.

"Tuk's short for his real name." Wyll grinned. "Though he won't tell us that, nor where he's from."

"There's a whole sea between myself and that name," Tuk said. "And I mean to keep it there. Drink up," he added. "There's more where that came from. We thought we'd have a longer wait." The ale was almost on the edge of turning, but it warmed Jane's throat and cleared the morning's fog from her mind. She drained half the skin before she handed it back.

"Right," John grumbled like a sleepy bear. "I lost good coin on that. Never thought the new reeve would be fool enough to be tricked so."

"Shouldn'ta bet against Robin," Wyll chirped. "Men see what

they want to see, that's what the master always says. Listen to him, Jane, and you'll learn all you need to know."

John rolled his eyes. "Boy thinks Robin is an angel come down from the skies, he does."

"What's Robin going to do to the reeve?" Jane asked, for she had not liked Bran's response the day before, nor the way his eyes had wandered into the graying sky when he answered.

"Show him whose woods these are." Wyll puffed out his chest. "Make sure he never comes back."

But Jane had met Walter. She knew he wouldn't be deterred by a challenge. He was a bull who would charge once he got something in his sights. Besides, these were the king's woods, and the shire reeve was the king's man. If Robin bested the reeve, wouldn't King Edward just send another man after him?

She said none of this out loud but couldn't stop herself from making a face.

Wyll caught her look, and his eyes narrowed, his cheeks sharp with color. "You *are* with us, aren't you, girl? Bran said you could be trusted." He grabbed Jane's wrist, his grip damp and sweaty as a child's. She jerked her arm away instinctively, as she would if one of her brothers had reached for her in anger or in sport.

"I *can* be trusted," she started, but before she could finish, John stepped between them, shielding her with his bulk.

"She don't need to think the master walks on water to work with us."

"What if she's a spy, meant to send us to the gallows?"

"Raise a hand to the girl again and you'll wish you'd seen the gallows." The words were hot, but John's voice was suddenly a cool, low growl, as if he was used to making threats. Wyll paled then, shrinking like a flower in the frost.

He shot Jane a sour look. "He's doing this for your kind, you know. You could show a little more respect."

"My kind?"

"You know what I mean." But Wyll was embarrassed, and Jane saw him for a coward, his anger and suspicion as fleeting as an ornery cat's. She had known what he meant, and she'd wanted to shame him for it. People like Betrice or Wyll never let her forget who and what she was—and how she was beholden to them.

Little John was having none of Wyll this morning. "So Robin and the reeve cast piss on each other while we hold the bowl," he grumbled. "Big help."

Jane could see their tempers brewing, and she knew it was a fight she had no place in. "I should go now," she said, "before the reeve comes."

"But the trick isn't done yet." Tuk gave her a sly grin and thrust a bundle at her. "Here, you can't ambush the shire reeve looking like that. He'll know you."

Jane found herself shrinking, stepping backward a little, as though the bundle were on fire. "I was only supposed to warn you. I'm not supposed to . . . I couldn't . . ."

"'Course you can!" John encouraged her. "What's the fun in a trick if you can't see the man's face when he's caught?"

Jane shook her head. "But Robin already took his shillings. They played a shooting game, and he won."

John handed her back the ale, nearly empty. "There's more coin to be had," he said. "There's *always* more."

His face was full of welcome, and a tiny, warm thrill went through Jane's spine like a current of flame, searing away her fear and exhaustion. John treated her like she was already one of them—not just a mouse under the nobles' feet but a brave outlaw, a hero. And what would that mean for her?

It would mean she was someone of consequence, someone who could press the world with her finger and force it to tip.

Jane drained the ale and opened the bundle from Tuk, her heart knocking against her breastbone. It was a cloak and a strip of long, dark cloth. The cloak was a marvel, fur-lined and thick and oiled for the damp. It was rich enough to have belonged to a lord—and it buried her from her shoulders to the tips of her boots. Jane wondered who they'd stolen it from.

She held up the strip of cloth. "What am I to do with this?"

John grinned, then wrapped his own black cloth around the bottom of his face. Jane copied him. Then he reached over, pulled the cloak's hood over her hair, and stood back to admire his hand-iwork.

"There," he announced. "Now she's a *proper* bandit."

Tuk thrust a rusted sword into her hand.

"I don't know how to fight," Jane pleaded, her voice muffled behind her makeshift mask.

"Don't need to." Wyll spat on the dewy ground, then tied on his own mask. "Just point that at the reeve when I point my bow."

The sword wasn't heavy, but its meaning was, and Jane's wrist shook as she lifted it.

"She can barely hold it!" The force of Wyll's laughter nearly blew his mask down.

No sooner had Jane hoisted her sword higher, just to spite him, than they heard the potter's cart rattling through the woods from the west. Two riders sat atop it, and it was hitched to a horse—the reeve's, Jane suspected—ambling over broken branches on the dirt path. Wyll pulled Jane behind a cluster of trees, pressing a finger to his lips, as John and Tuk strode out to greet the cart, their weapons flashing in the pale light.

"Come, now. Behind them," Wyll whispered, and he moved through the trees toward the back of the cart, Jane scrambling to follow.

Robin and Walter hopped down to face John and Tuk, the reeve with a keen hunter's eye and a small, satisfied smile on his face.

"So, which one of you . . ." Walter's bold voice wavered as he heard Jane and Wyll come up behind him. His shoulders went rigid. The silence grew sharp, as if charged by a lightning strike.

And like the man of war he was, the shire reeve went for his sword.

"I'll hold that for you," Robin said neatly, and before anyone could blink, the reeve's sword was in the "potter's" hand.

Walter's mouth fell open. "Shit," he said, and reached for the horn hitched to his waist. At that, Wyll aimed his bow at the reeve. Jane pointed her sword as well, struggling to steady her shaking shoulders, the morning's stale drink crawling back up her throat.

"Now, now, king's man. Don't go telling." Little John barreled up, sword out, and wrenched the horn from the reeve's hand. "This will fetch a pretty price."

Robin shrugged. "He can blow as loud and hard as he likes—no one will come when he calls. Remember that drink we shared this morning, Shire Reeve? Your men sleep like stones. They'll be lucky to make it out of bed before nightfall."

Even weaponless and surrounded, Walter kept his edge. He surveyed his captors, examining their masked faces, and stopped to stare hard at Jane, his lips pressed together. She didn't see the fear she should have seen in his eyes. He hadn't lost his color. He did not cower. He was a hard man, harder even than she had realized the day before.

"Is it the small one?" he demanded. "The one in the rich cloak, hiding behind a hood? Show your face, man!"

Jane nearly stumbled under the heat of his gaze, the fury in his voice. *The cloak*, she thought. *A rich man's cloak, one that should belong to a lord.* Had they known what the reeve would think when he saw her? Had they tried to make her look like Robin Hood, to act as bait?

Walter didn't take his eyes off Jane. "Come now, man to man. If you're here to rob me, don't do it behind a mask. Here." He cast his coin purse on the ground, right at Jane's boots. "You can try to hide yourself from me, but I see you for what you are: you're the very coward and traitor King Edward said you were. A man without honor."

Jane kept her sword up, her arm as rigid as bone. Sweat poured down her back. The reeve's weapon was gone. His horn was gone. But if he fell upon her with his fists, and Robin's men weren't fast enough . . .

Then Robin spoke, his voice breaking the spell that kept Jane's knees locked together as if they were the only things holding her up. "The honor," he said, "is all mine, Shire Reeve, now that I have seen exactly who *you* are, and who your lovely wife is, and how you keep your home."

And at that, the reeve finally paled, the color draining from him like a star blinking out in the night.

Walter turned slowly, as if he were waking from a dream, and saw Robin, his foolish hat discarded, his fox-colored hair clean of ash and grime, the thin morning light weaving it with gold.

Jane let her breath out in a gust, her mask puffing from the burst of air.

"Coward! Give me back my blade and horn! If you're a real man, fight like one!" Walter demanded.

Robin took the horn from John and studied it. It was yellowing and curved, like a giant's tooth, but banded with shining gold. "Be sensible." Robin hitched the horn to his own hip. "How could I kill you and leave that hot-blooded wife of yours alone? She's a lustful woman, Walter. I wouldn't leave her to follow her own whims if I were you. Not for a moment's time."

"Why, you . . ." The reeve burst forward, face flush with fire, but John caught his arms behind his back. John's laugh, which had so warmed Jane when he shared it with her, suddenly sounded cruel.

"Let me go!" Walter spat. "My men know I'm here! They'll win me justice even if they do it for my corpse. They know exactly where you rest your head, traitor!"

And they know me, Jane thought. *And so does the reeve.* Shock made her rigid once again. What would this mean for her work at King's Houses? Had Robin ruined his promise to her with this foolish game?

What a thing to worry about now, when she had almost felt the reeve's fists against her skin. Robin must have a plan. He *must*. He was a legend for a reason.

"Is this how you repay my kindness? After I invited you to my home"—Robin smirked, gesturing to the forest— "just as your generous wife invited me to yours?"

Walter scowled. "You've played your trick. Why don't you free me and see if you can best me then!"

"I'm not here for blood, Shire Reeve. The day is too fine to spill it all over the floor of my palace. Surely you've heard, since you've been hunting me, that I don't take such a heavy price from travelers. I merely take a toll."

"You have my silver. What more do you want?"

"Let's see . . . I also have your horn, your weapons, and this fine horse you've loaned me. You know"—Robin cocked his head—"I think that's enough for one morning. Go home to your wife, Walter. Treat her kindly. Then leave. Take her back to Nottingham, where she can have the spices and the sugar she longs for. We have our own justice here in the Greenwood, Shire Reeve. The king's laws aren't welcome."

Jane felt dull, numb, as the exhaustion she'd been battling all morning washed over her, like a weight pulling at the back of her neck, so heavy she could have dropped into the grass and slipped into dreams. Was that all there was to Robin's elaborate scheme? The reeve was *already* leaving for Nottingham. Did Robin put her through all this just so he could mark his territory like a dog?

"And how do you expect me to *get* home? You've stolen my horse." Walter sounded bitter now that he was beaten, but cold as a deadly winter.

"Aren't you a man's man, as you said? A soldier and a hunter?" Robin taunted him. "Surely you followed the terrain when we rode out here. Surely you marked it on the map in your mind. It's a lovely day, and your boots are very fine indeed."

The moment stretched out in silence, the reeve burning with pent-up heat like a smothered flame. Robin beamed, uncaring, as if he were the sun and the reeve's mad fire were nothing to him. Jane had to look away. Her eyes found a rotted birch log, black fungus grasping its base like a corpse's fingers.

"You may have won today," Walter said after a long stretch, his voice redolent with threat, "but this isn't over."

"You had best hope it is," Robin said courteously, his own voice light and measured. "For all that's left to take from you are things that cannot be replaced."

Robin's words hung in the air like a thundercloud. Finally, just when Jane thought she had forgotten how to breathe, Walter backed slowly into the woods. He kept his eyes locked to Robin's until the trees came between them. Then, just as Jane lost sight of him, she heard his footsteps quicken as though he had broken into a run.

Robin's sunny, smiling mask slipped into something grim and hard. "Follow him at a distance," he told Tuk. "Make sure he doesn't come back." Tuk nodded, wordless, and disappeared after the reeve.

Robin joined Wyll and John as they clustered around the tree, and he pulled a jug of wine from the reeve's cart. "We've earned the good stuff, I think."

Jane, still masked, still clutching her sword, swallowed, feeling the dryness of her own throat as the men laughed and passed the wine between them. Their cheers, their jostling, all sounded dim and far away. She had been so tired, and she had thought she would never stop sweating, but now she was wide awake and cold from the toes up, as though she had plunged her foot into a boot full of snow.

"Girl!" John called to her, not unkindly. "I think you can rest your sword now. He's not coming back."

At that, the men's laughter broke through the fog in Jane's mind. She lowered the sword and tried to laugh with them, but her laugh was a soft, muffled thing that made no noise at all.

John cleared his throat with a deep cough. "So that's our new shire reeve, is it?"

Robin wiped his mouth, handing him the jug. "So it is, though a mite poorer than he was before I met him." He smiled, but there was no fire behind it at all, no warmth.

Wyll's laugh was like the bark of a puppy that did not yet know its place. "A hot-blooded one, wasn't he, calling you a traitor! That's a strange and grand term for a thief in the woods!"

Robin's green eyes flashed at Jane, ever so briefly, as if daring her to mention what Walter had revealed about the Barons' War. Jane realized his men didn't know his past, that he had been a part of the rebellion—at least, Wyll didn't—and Robin was testing her again.

Once he was sure of Jane's silence, Robin shifted his attention back to Wyll. "A man given to high temper has a mind clouded with stories. In the tales he tells himself, he's a knight whose knee bends to the king, making traitors of all who oppose him."

"Y'see, Jane," Wyll said enthusiastically, "I told you you'd learn from the Lord of the Greenwood! Wise words."

Jane tried again to laugh, but the sound disappeared behind the cloth around her face. John laughed at her instead, bold and hearty. "Look at that one! Scared stiff as a rabbit! Come now, girl, you've earned another drink!"

Jane *was* scared, but she didn't want them to know it. Her mind swirled. Perhaps the reeve would depart for Nottingham, just as he and Betrice had planned, but today's shame would only inflame him. It wouldn't keep him away forever. And when he did come back, wouldn't he search for the girl who had come with the potter? Would the reeve believe her innocent, if he came to King's Houses and pressed her for her role in today's scheme, in the loss of his silver? Who would protect her then?

Jane glanced at Robin to see that he was studying her, his face inscrutable. She was not safe yet, no matter how warm Little John had been. Bran was not here to whisk her away if Wyll, or anyone else, questioned her heart. She would have to show her fealty. Revel with Robin's men, as if she saw the sense in what he'd done to the reeve. Play her part.

Somehow, Jane forced her limbs to move. She pulled the cloth down under her chin and walked to John's side, handing him back the sword. "I'll trade you," she said, and her voice rasped unexpectedly, causing all three men to chuckle.

"A girl after my own heart!" John said. "You can keep your wisdom, Lord of the Greenwood." He placed a hand on Jane's shoulder, lighter than he would have if she had been one of the men, almost delicately, and she found herself warming to the big bear of an outlaw even more. "Jane and I will keep your drink."

Robin smiled, finally, his sly grin lighting up his face, a little flash of relief in his eyes. "Jane can keep everything she earns. She's one of us now, after all."

One of us. She had finally proven her worth, finally passed his trial. That was a balm for Jane's worries, stronger than any drink, if a fleeting one. As one of Robin's mice at King's Houses, she would have more trials to come. And unlike the men of the Greenwood, she would have to face her trials alone.

Chapter Seven

Jane had a few more days before her duties at King's Houses would begin, and waiting around at home, in the house Sibyl and Hugh meant to abandon, felt like waiting for the sun in winter, grim and tiresome and choking. She could hardly breathe there, not when she had to hold her tongue to keep from saying what she really thought about them. There was only one person who felt like home to Jane now, one person who really knew her, and that was her brother Adam.

He tended to a little church hidden among the trees near the neighboring village, and Jane set out for it that day. She could have sent word through her mother about her new post at King's Houses, but she wanted to tell Adam herself, wanted to see the pride shining in his eyes that she had made a new place for herself, just as he had. So Bran loaned her an aging rouncey named Moll for the ride, since Tuk and Little John teased him so fiercely for forcing her to run through the woods on her own two feet. Bran had also tried to ease her fears: he was sure Robin had a plan to protect her should Walter or his men come looking for her.

But while his kisses still stirred her, his promises did little to soothe her nerves, and she was sure he knew it.

Jane found her brother Adam shuffling across the church's floor, dragging a broom around, his tread heavy but his eyes as light as if he were in a proper town church with music and stained glass that turned the sun into colors.

"Jane!" He leaned the broom against a bare wall and hurried over to embrace her. "How wonderful to see you!"

Jane smiled broadly, setting down the bundle she had brought, and gave him a long, warm hug. She had missed Adam so much—his melancholy, studious air, his reassuring presence in their home, and the sharp jokes that seemed to come from nowhere, piercing a tense room when you least expected it. The house had felt cold and spare without him.

"A drink?" Adam asked. "I've the last of an autumn cider."

"I can't finish your cider! It will be winter soon, and you'll sup on bread and water rather than ask for more."

"I won't . . ."

"I know you," Jane scolded him, crossing her arms.

"I won't taste it at all if I miss my chance to share it with you." He pointed to her bundle. "Can I put that away for you?"

"Actually . . ." Jane smiled sheepishly, her heart thrumming with excitement. "It's for you."

"For me?" Adam unraveled the man's cloak Jane had worn to trick the reeve, its fur hood cleaned of grime and soil, its torn patches mended by her own hands in the candlelight. "But Jane! This is very fine. Where did it come from?"

"I bought it at market," she lied, "when I sold off the rest of the conserves."

"You sold them all? But you need . . ."

"I have work now, Adam. At King's Houses. Pour the cider and I'll tell you about it."

The table in the back room of the church was tiny, one of its too-short legs propped up by a whittled triangle of wood. There were two small chairs, but only one had scored its drag marks into the floor. Tears stung the corners of Jane's eyes to think how lonely Adam must be. Her brother liked his solitude, but now that old Father Gilbert had passed on, Adam supped alone every night within these dark stone walls.

"Do you miss home?" Jane burst out once they had finished talking about her new post and the cider had warmed her belly.

"Will *you* miss it, when you finally leave?" Adam asked gently.

"It will be different for me. I'll hardly have a moment to myself, living among the servants. It's just . . ." Jane looked around and shivered. "It's so quiet here."

Her brother let out a satisfied sigh and leaned back, straining the little chair. "Quiet and peaceful. I can read by candlelight if I wish, sleep through a dark and dreamless night, and break my fast listening to the birds. Our home was a tempest, Jane. Always raging, and you never knew when the storm would knock you down. You'll see once you're away." He cocked his head. "Although perhaps not. Perhaps the servants you live among will have their own storms."

"Does anyone ever visit you?"

"Besides you?" He grinned. "Who else do I need?"

"Adam." She flushed. "You jest, but everyone needs people."

"I see people every Sunday, and at mass, and when they need comfort or aid, or they're grieving or scared. I see plenty of people."

"But they all *need* things from you," Jane insisted. "They're not your friends!" Even as she said it, she thought of the long day she had spent trailing after Robin, carrying out his plans, and the morning after in the woods, a target for the reeve's misdirected rage. Was she any different?

"Friendship is a strange thing," Adam said. "You can start out helping someone, and you never know when they'll help you in return. Like this cider we're sharing"—he gestured, looking much older than his eighteen years—"it was a gift from a friend. A man I helped when his wife passed. I listened to him for months, I heard his heart, and then one day, we were talking about fishing and the weather and our hopes for the new king instead of his life troubles, as if we were true friends indeed."

"You don't fish," Jane murmured into her cider.

"What about you? Have you made new friends? I hear there's a boy hanging around."

"It's just Bran." Jane waved her hand, embarrassed.

"And where is 'Just Bran' from?"

"He works the stables at King's Houses."

"Is he the reason you got to work there?"

Jane's face grew hot. "He gave me the chance, is all. But I earned it myself." She had earned it because of what she had done for Robin, but Adam couldn't know about that.

They talked for a while about easier things—Jane's future, Ralf's ever-growing feet. They laughed about Hugh together, joking about his airs but skirting around their fears. And Adam shared more stories of the people he had healed, or guided, or merely sat quietly beside while they grieved.

"I have something more for you," Jane finally said. She handed Adam the little purse she'd brought with her.

"Jane, you didn't have to . . ."

"I had extra." Jane felt nervous with the lie, her back hot in her woolen tunic, which was damp with sweat.

Adam opened the coin purse. He looked at her in astonishment, his eyes glittering with what might have been tears. She had given him half her earnings from Robin. And why not? He needed it to buy his bread, and she wasn't going to give a single farthing to her mother, not when she had Hugh to care for her.

"Perhaps this won't be the last of your cider after all," she said to break the tension.

But Adam's voice was cold. "Jane, where did you get this?"

"I told you, I . . ."

"Did this Bran give it to you for . . . for favors?"

Jane nearly spit her cider out. "*Bran?* Bran doesn't have that kind of money!"

"Then who?" Adam was hardening. He drew back from her, as though she were poisonous. "Who is he? What kind of vile things is he making you do for all this coin?"

"Adam! I didn't get it for *that*!"

But his gaze didn't soften one bit. "And the cloak? Is it a castoff from your lover?"

Jane felt the heat and warmth flee her belly and travel up to her face, her cheeks flaming. "You think I . . ." She shot to her feet. "*Adam*, how could you think that of me?"

"Jane," he said sternly, as if she were a child who needed scolding. "I don't want you to turn out like Mother. I don't want you to think that what she does is right. You know she . . ."

"I *know*. I'm *nothing* like her." Now Jane was the one who had grown cold. She was the one who spat out her words as though they were rotted meat.

"You might think it's different, but men who lead women into sin are the same. They have the same wants, the same devilish desires. They'll ruin you—and you're so young, Jane. You have your whole life ahead of you. You haven't even made a family yet!"

"*You* were supposed to be my family!" Jane fought back the tears that rushed into her eyes, the swelling hot salt in the back corners of her mouth. "How could you think this of me?"

Adam stood too, his lumbering form shaking his chair. "What am I supposed to think? Am I supposed to believe you made this much coin through honest labor?" Had it been her brother Peter, he would have shouted. Adam never shouted at her, not once. He was gentle even now, even angry, and somehow that made his scorn feel worse.

"If I were a man"—Jane trembled violently—"you wouldn't question the money at all! You would be grateful for the gift. You wouldn't throw it back in my face!"

"If you were a man, I *would* question it. I would think you'd stolen it, or worse. This is a huge amount of money, Jane!"

"Well, perhaps I'm a thief, then, not a whore!"

Adam's face twisted at the crass word. "You're no thief, Jane. I know that if I know anything."

"But you think me a whore? That's a kinder story?"

"This is a house of God. Mind your tongue."

She snorted. "Mind *my* tongue? After the way you spoke to me?"

Adam sounded tired. "Then where did you get the money? Perhaps you can explain it and we can both calm down."

"It's an early payment," she said stiffly, "from King's Houses. They wanted me to get some proper clothes."

There was silence between them then, and in that silence hung the cloak—fine, ostentatiously fine, and definitely a cloak for a man.

"Then you should keep it," Adam said softly, "and get some proper clothes." He did not believe her—Jane could see that on his face. She scrambled for a story that would make sense but saw with sadness that Adam had made up his mind. For all he knew of her, for as close as they were, Sibyl's shadow was too great and too dark for Adam to see Jane in truth. Had it always been that way between them, him sitting on his lofty perch, waiting for her to fall because of the nature of her sex? Had Adam never really seen her at all, when she thought he had always known her heart?

Suddenly, Jane felt more alone in the world than she ever had.

"You don't want the coin? Fine," she snapped. "Give it to the poor, if you're afraid of its taint."

"Jane . . ." Adam's voice sounded so far away, buried in his throat.

She snatched up the rest of her things. "And it's a good cloak. Someone can make use of it. Maybe your friend with the cider."

If Adam called after her again as Jane stormed out of the church, she couldn't hear him, not with her blood pounding in her ears. No matter how hard she worked, no matter how she provided for them, her family would never approve of her. It had always been that way. So why bother helping them at all?

When Jane was fifteen, her oldest brother, Peter, had come all the way from Newark-on-Trent to show off his new wife, Cecely. She was a delicate, pale-haired thing, fragile as a precious cup. Though Sibyl's lover—it was Elias Frye back then, not Hugh—had made himself scarce upon Peter's arrival, his presence permeated everything: a pair of boots by the fire, a spare cloak by the door, and Sibyl, smug and satisfied, speaking of his generosity and kindness with every tale she told. Jane could see the rage growing in Peter, ready to burst out, and it didn't take long. He was so much like their father in that way. So when Sibyl told yet another story of how shrewd Elias was, how wise and how bold, Peter slammed his hand on the table, sending his new wife skittering back in her chair.

"Enough, Mother!" Peter bellowed. "All of Clipstone knows of your shame! I've no need to hear more of it!"

"My shame?" Sibyl drew her shoulders back, as though she had been prepared for this battle and had kept her tongue sharpened for this very purpose. "And are you ashamed of the ale you drink, of the meat you had for supper? For they would not be here without my shame."

"There must be another way!" Peter leaned forward. "Think of Jane, of her reputation. What kind of example are you setting for her?"

Sibyl raised an arched eyebrow. "Jane is not bedding him."

Peter shook his head, glaring into his ale. "I'm sorry, Cecely. I had no idea I was bringing you home to meet a common whore."

"Peter!" Jane shouted, suddenly on her feet, but at the same time her mother had risen, reaching across the table to smack her son's face and sending his ale flying across the room, spattering the wall.

"This is my house," Sibyl said with a voice of steel, "and you will not talk to me that way in my house. You are not here to feed the children. You are not here to see them in clothes and shoes. You will hold your tongue, or you will leave this place right now. And you will not darken my doorstep again."

Then she grabbed her cloak and thrust open the front door, a gust of chill wind threatening the fire.

"Where are you going?" Peter demanded, his hand smacking the spilled ale.

"Out to earn more bread," she snapped. "Remember what I said. I'll expect to see you gone if it displeases you."

When she left, everyone stared at the spilled drink until Cecely got up, shaking, and asked Jane where a rag could be found.

"Sit." Jane patted Cecely's delicate hand. "I'll get it. You're our guest."

Peter sighed and sat back in his chair, running a hand through his hair and tousling it like a bed of black leaves. "I'm sorry, Jane," he said, but he didn't move to help her as she wiped up the mess. Cecely sat uneasily, watching Jane as though she were trying to memorize her movements.

"You should be sorry, you ass," Jane grumbled. What did he think would happen when he said such things?

"Is the shouting over?" Adam stumbled out of the little bedroom, his worn stockings snagging on the dirt floor, his nightcap askew.

"Have we woken you?" Jane asked. "Is Ralf asleep?"

"*You* haven't woken me," Adam said with a pointed look at his older brother. "And Ralf is only pretending to sleep."

Peter folded his arms across his chest. "You're the man of the house, Adam. How can you let this go on?"

Adam rolled his eyes. "This *man* is just trying to recite his prayers. I begin my training in a fortnight, as you would know if you'd had anything to do with us before showing up out of nowhere and deciding everything we did was wrong." Adam's tone was light, but his face was dark and heavy with old resentment.

"Aren't you worried about Jane at all?" Peter demanded, and Cecely reached over and squeezed his hand, wordless, as if exchanging some silent secret. He let out a long breath, then soft-ened his voice. "Jane, Cecely and I have been talking. We"—he glanced at his wife, and she nodded encouragingly—"we'd like you to come live with us."

"Live with you." Jane's mouth fell open and she froze, rag dripping ale on her feet. "That's absurd, Peter! Who would care for Adam and Ralf?"

"Mother should care for them!"

"There are many things that should be," Jane said, "but they are not. You should be more respectful when you're here, Peter, and mind your tongue."

"And what is there to respect?" His sneer made his face ugly, pointed like a rat's.

Jane snorted in reply and went to the door to put the rag out. Perhaps it would rain overnight, and she wouldn't have to waste the fresh water she'd hauled in earlier that day to wash it off.

"Be reasonable, Jane," Peter said. "Adam will be gone one day, and Ralf will be grown, and you must think of your own pros-pects. The gossip about Mother hasn't reached Newark, praise God. You can start over there, find a husband."

"A husband! I'm but fifteen!"

"That's old enough, Jane." Peter pressed his wife's tiny hand, and Jane flushed as she realized she did not know how old Cec-ely was.

"You didn't marry until you were two and twenty!"

"It's different for me. I'm not a burden on the family."

A burden. Jane felt a quiet fury building inside her, like a storm of ice in her chest.

Adam had been sitting by the fire, staring at it as if it were a door that could free him from this uncomfortable argument, but now he lifted his head. "Jane is the reason we're all still here. If anything, I'm the burden, deep in my studies instead of working with my hands."

"You're no burden," Jane said quickly, her heart thawing a little. But she was still angry. How could Peter not see everything she had done for her brothers, for their mother?

Was this all her family thought of women? Suddenly, Jane found herself thinking of her mother with pride, as if to spite all her brothers. She had been by Sibyl's side at dawn, feeding the geese and chickens, cooking at the hearth, and weaving cloth by candlelight. Jane and Sibyl were the ones who kept the roof clean and the walls patched. They were the ones who made the bread and cakes and pies, who fed Adam and Ralf and fetched water from the well and eggs from the hens and churned the butter and plucked roots from the ground for soup. How could her brothers refuse to see it?

"It's not the same," Peter argued. "You have your studies with the priest now. You have a path forward. But who will care for Jane?"

"I will." Adam's face dimpled with a coy smile. "She'll be one of those old ladies doddering around the church, staring daggers at the miller's wife when she passes the alms bowl without putting in a coin."

Is that what Adam wanted for me? Jane wondered now as she rode home, the chill autumn wind sharpening her anger into points. *To be his burden instead of someone else's?*

Jane wanted to live a life where no one could tell her who or what she ought to be, which path she ought to take. This was why she had been led to Bran, and to Robin and his men. Like the forest in her dream, the men of the Greenwood had opened their secrets to her, showed her a way to follow her wits and her heart. They could be her brothers now. For one thing was clear after today: there was no place in her old life, or her old family, for Jane and her dreams.

PART II

A Gentyll Knyght

Chapter Eight

Jane had only seen the King's Houses from a distance, so she hadn't known what to expect inside. Something like the shire reeve's house, perhaps, but bigger. Instead, she found a small village within a massive circle of fences and trees. She spent most of her days in the main kitchen, but there were multiple kitchens, and multiple feast halls, and whole separate chambers for the king and queen and any guests who came to visit. There were chapels for prayer, and more horses than Jane could count. She'd foolishly thought Bran would be the only man in the stables, but he worked with several others, though most of them were merely boys. She wondered, in passing, what had kept him with the horses at his age. Was it loyalty to Robin Hood? Or simply a desire not to be tied down?

Kitchen work was hot, despite the open air, and sometimes difficult. During the first few days at King's Houses, Jane had sliced, pared, plucked, and scrubbed until she thought she would drop— all under the stern eyes of Master Eudo, the manor's head cook, a portly man with a bald pate and a drooping white mustache. He looked like a jovial grandfather, but guessing at his nature from his pink face and friendly form was a mistake you would only make once.

Most of the time, though, Jane felt her position was a great luxury, especially compared to the work she used to do at home, with one cauldron and one pan and no oven except the one used by the whole village. So much of the dull work she'd had to do just to prepare a meal at home was handled by someone else now. King's Houses had a buttery, a dairy, huge gardens, and even a deer park and a pond full of fish! Meat came to Jane clean of skin and bone, butter already churned, cream skimmed from milk, and flour milled. She ate fresh bread every single day—even though servants had pea bread rather than the fine-milled bread saved for guests—and she had butter for it too, and ale and ripe cheeses. Her belly was starting to swell pleasantly, and Bran said her cheeks were looking full as roses. He even asked once, nervously, if she might be with child, but she wasn't, and that was another blessing.

But the people of King's Houses were confusing, a knotted tapestry. King Edward had visited only once since Jane had arrived, and she hadn't even caught a glimpse of his royal robes. He'd brought his own kitchen staff, so Jane, the other scullions, and a grumbling Master Eudo had been trundled off to the queen's kitchen to do preparatory work for the "real" cooks: kneading dough, slicing endless piles of apples and pears, and plucking juniper berries from their prickly branches.

The rest of the time, Lord Alan de Beauchamp, the king's distant relation, was acting lord of King's Houses—and he and his wife behaved as if they were royalty themselves, entertaining a whirlwind of guests and friends. Jane's head spun trying to keep track of who was coming and going each week, let alone their various tempers and demands, especially because none of them stepped a single foot into Jane's world—not the ovens where she worked or the dusty old room in the maids' chamber where she slept with twelve other girls. It was as if the servants were all mice indeed, scurrying around in the darkness, trying not to get underfoot as the important people trod around over their heads.

And then there was Robin, whose tasks Jane had to carry out in secret. Sometimes it was as simple as reporting how many and which nobles were attending an afternoon's feast. Other times, Robin wanted gossip: who was cross with whom, who was sharing a bed when they shouldn't be. Growing up, Jane's ability to read people had always been about survival—but here, it helped with her reports to Robin, for she could see plain as day what people wanted, even when they didn't know it themselves, and they would grow to like her for it and tell her secret things—their grudges and their wishes and their fears. She would whisper to Bran that Lord Alan had trysts with the dairy maid when his wife was away, and that his eldest son was cruel to the servants, and that the cellarer was stealing wine, or so Master Eudo suspected. Robin never did anything with her whispers, so far as Jane could tell, but they did seem to please him—at least, Bran *said* Robin was pleased. Jane never heard directly from the Lord of the Greenwood. It was always Bran who moved between them, turning Jane's time with him from a blissful distraction into something heavier, more serious. It made them awkward with each other, as if Robin was always with them, watching, and judging—a ghost haunting their trysts, no matter how private their moments. And it made Jane feel as if every moment at King's Houses, even the ones that were supposed to be for herself alone, she had to be on her guard, always listening, and always worrying about being caught.

Sometimes Jane would escape to the long, narrow room she shared with the other girls and breathe in the darkness, dust, and quiet. She had thought she loved being around people, but she had taken for granted the silence of her afternoons, her walks in the woods where no one chattered at her but the birds, and no one was there to order her around. At King's Houses, she had days where she thought her head would fly right off her neck because she could not get one spare moment, one spare thought, to herself.

Jane would have been very overwhelmed indeed had it not been for her new friend Emelyn. Bright, confident in a way that Jane had never been, and cheery as a chirping bird, Emelyn seemed as if she were born to the strange, sprawling grounds of the king's estate, its rules and its quirks.

"New girl, aren't you?" Emelyn had said on that first day in their dim, windowless room.

"I'm Jane," said Jane in greeting.

"Right, Jane! The girl from Clipstone!"

"Near Clipstone," Jane had muttered, unwilling to admit that she and her family had lived at the outskirts of the village, far enough away that no one could see what her mother got up to with the straying husbands of Mansfield. And before that, far enough away that no one could hear her father shout when the drink got into him.

"Well, don't worry, Jane from near Clipstone. It gets better." Emelyn linked her arm with Jane's. "Eudo can be snarly as a mean old cat, and watch yourself around Master Ancel, the steward, for he's always got his eyes on us for stealing, but I'll tell you what's what and things will be sweet as a summer cherry in no time. You'll see!"

Emmie was a wonder, her braids neat and brown, lips pushed forward like a little duck's. Men kept their eyes on her; they seemed to like her long waist and spoon-shaped hips. Or perhaps it was Emmie's cheer that drew them. No matter what went wrong, she would make you feel you could get 'round it.

Jane and Emmie would often sneak off together after serving the lords and ladies their evening sop—eels and crusts, pasties with bits of venison, or cheese and herb tarts, with which they took dizzying amounts of wine, red and clear as glass and finer than anything Jane had ever tasted. Emmie would steal them a tipple, and the two of them would wrap themselves in cloaks and creep out to the frost-covered gardens, whispering gossip, their breath hot and sweet in the icy, starlit air. Emmie was always a comfort to Jane, for she didn't mince words or tell people what they wanted to hear. She said her piece no matter what she felt, and, still, everyone loved her. Such a thing would never have worked for Jane. She didn't have Emmie's confidence, or her merry spirit.

After Candlemas, when the snow began to clear and turn to rain, Jane got word that her youngest brother, Ralf, had gone to apprentice with Peter, and that Hugh's wife was getting sicker and her mother's house would be empty soon. She grew melancholy. She still felt out of place in her new life, but her old life had slipped away as soon as she turned her back, as if her will had been the only thing making any kind of family out of the Crowes. Emmie found Jane crying softly in her bed that night, and she sat down and wrapped her in a tight hug, letting Jane sob into her shoulder to stifle the noise so the other girls wouldn't hear it.

The next day, Jane explained herself, saying she was sorry for crying to Emmie like a babe in her arms. The other girl gaped at her. "Have you never had a bosom friend, Jane?"

"I've been surrounded by boys," Jane admitted. "Three brothers and . . ." She shrank back from the sudden urge to reveal everything to Emmie, her whole secret life, and destroy her work for Robin Hood. "Boys from the village, you know."

"No wonder you're so shy! Well, we're to be here for each other, from now until we're married off to dukes and princes, so be ready for a cup full of my tears the next time my cakes burn in the fire and Eudo makes me do them again from scratch." But there never were any tears, not for Emmie, light and spirited as a colt, and when Jane's worries came because she had to sneak away with news for Robin, she couldn't share the truth of things with Emmie; there would always be secrets between them.

Her new friend had noticed Bran's attentions right away, though, and that was something Jane *could* talk about. "That one," Emmie had said, "is the apple of many a girl's eye, and you've got him hooked like a fish on a rod! Well done." She beamed, her thin cheeks streaked with color, and then she said a thing or two about Bran's broad shoulders and his fine form and firm and manly chest, and other things that must be firm and manly, until she drove Jane into an embarrassed squeak.

Once Jane had settled in, she started paying more attention to Emmie's gossip. When Emmie told her how much Master Eudo disliked the gardener for being stingy with his herbs, Jane made sure to complain about him under her breath, just loud enough for Eudo to hear, which earned her a crusty, conspiratorial smile. And when Emmie said that Eudo had fired the last kitchen girl without a word of warning because she didn't knead the pasty dough fine enough, Jane made sure to put her back into it and was rewarded with an admiring, if startled, "My, they grow them strong out in Clipstone, they do."

⋘◆⋙

One morning when they were simmering the last of the pigs' bones for brawn—it all had to be used up before Lent came, when there would be nothing but fish for the table—Eudo stomped past Jane with a stormy face and shoved a bundle of herbs into a chambermaid's arms. "It's for *her*," he growled. "And if she wants anything else, remind her that my kitchen is for food, not witchery."

Eudo had complained about people before, but Jane had never seen such a mixture of resentment and fear on his face. "Have we another guest?" she asked cautiously.

"The prioress is here," Eudo grumbled, his tongue worrying the back tooth that always pained him. "Came in the dark, no warning to any of us. Her and that knight who follows her around all moon-eyed. Always hovering around the kitchens, she is, and she can get her long nose right out."

"A prioress? Why would a holy lady be at King's Houses?"

The cook snorted. "Holy lady, my arse. As if we don't know what she really gets up to."

Jane couldn't get another word out of Eudo, who would only mutter, "The devil's always listening," so she went to Emmie, whose nut-brown eyes shone with mirth. "Oh, don't be asking Master Eudo about *Ibota of Kirklees*." Emmie drew out the woman's name in hushed tones, as if it were a blasphemous oath.

"But who is she?" Jane asked. "Why is she so awful?"

"You'll find out for yourself," Emmie said, "when you see her creeping shadow in the kitchens, picking through the herbs, lurking in the hallways like a graveyard spirit."

"Is she a midwife, then?"

"Hardly!" Emmie waggled her fingers. "She's a sorceress, she is! They say she trained with the Moors in secret, while our own men were fighting them, and that she reads in tongues and can curse you in every language and even with the devil's sigil. They also say"—Emmie leaned close, whispering—"that she poisoned the man who would have been her husband so she wouldn't have to wed him, then bewitched her knight to be her lover instead."

"You're having me on." Jane laughed. She didn't believe in silly things like witches and spells. There were real enough dangers in the world—no need to go spinning fantasies about false ones. "Besides, the king wouldn't stand for a murderess running the priory."

"She's his cousin, and you *know* how royal blood will cling to its own." Emmie picked up a bowl of eggs and started whisking them fiercely. "Move, now—we can't keep them waiting on their omelets."

Despite Emmie's warning that Ibota of Kirklees was always hovering around the kitchen, Jane didn't see the prioress until days later, when she was carrying caudles up from the kitchens to the main house and almost spilled them all over the prioress's fine, blood-colored gown.

"Oh!" Jane stumbled backward. "I'm so sorry, m'um! Please, forgive my clumsiness."

"No need to grovel." The woman waved her gloved hand dismissively, and Jane nearly swallowed her own tongue, her face flushing with fire as she realized who it was. She rarely had a chance to talk to anyone Robin might be interested in, but here was the prioress, right before her, her lips pressed together in the telltale expression of a frustrated noblewoman who didn't know where to direct her orders.

"May I fetch something for you, m'um?" Jane blinked innocently.

"Are you new here?" The woman's quick assessment, her sharp, attentive glance, gave Jane a start. She wasn't used to being noticed.

"Yes, m'um, I'm Jane, Jane of . . ."

"The kitchens, clearly." She nodded at the caudles, her words slicing through Jane's like the blade of a razor. "Can you bring me a bunch each of laurel and mustard, when you've the time?"

"Yes, m'um. Where shall I bring them?"

"Tell the girls it's for Mother Ibota," the woman said with a heavy sigh. "They'll know where to find me." She was tall, almost as tall as a man, lean on top but with healthy hips and thighs. Jane had expected her to be an old crone, but Ibota was Sibyl's age, if better fed and with much finer clothes, and with a neat, gray-black widow's peak emerging from beneath her wimple. Her nose was indeed long, and bent on its bridge, but her eyes were blue as an icy lake, set deep in her pale face like a bird's eyes, clear and watchful.

"Yes, m'um."

Jane bent her head. She was wondering how to break the news to Eudo, when Ibota said knowingly, "And never mind what Eudo has to say about it. Tell him I insisted. You may say that I was very menacing."

Ibota did not sound menacing at all. She sounded exhausted, and Jane couldn't help the smile that bloomed on her lips as she scurried away.

Master Eudo did grouse at Jane, but he pointed to the right herbs and told her the way to Ibota's room. "You be careful now, girl. Those sorceress types can suck you in, keep you from knowing what's what, with a few devilish words." He sniffed. "Nice girl like you, I'd hate to see you go astray."

"Why, Master Eudo, if I didn't know any better, I'd say you'd taken a shine to me."

Eudo scowled and swatted at her with his cloth. "Well, you do know better, so get going." Jane hid a grin, scampering away. Anyway, she did know better. She knew about Eudo's trysts with Master Ancel, their long nights together under the dim light of candles, when they thought no one was watching. Emmie said it was a sin, but Jane wasn't so sure. She saw their love for each other plain enough, and it seemed so pure and simple—not fraught with struggle like her mother's affairs, no teasing or testing or gamesmanship like whatever she was doing with Bran.

That was one secret of King's Houses she would not pass on to Robin Hood. Perhaps the Lord of the Greenwood wouldn't have used it against Eudo—but perhaps he would have—and Jane felt protective of the old cook now that she had won him over.

The prioress had her own room at the far end of the guest chambers. Jane shuffled past the guards, their padded shirts stained with sweat. When they were in their cups or felt the budding lust of springtime on warmer days, she could feel their eyes following her, focused and deadly as one of Robin's arrows, but today, thankfully, they ignored her—just another servant girl with her head bent. Tapestries hung heavily on the stone walls, full of mythical creatures cavorting with deer and birds, and Jane immediately felt her shoes too shoddy and her footsteps too loud in the darkening hallway. She had to gather all her courage to rap on the prioress's door.

"What?"

"I have your herbs, m'um." Silence met her announcement, so she tried again. "Your mustard and your . . ."

"Yes." Jane heard a chair slide across the floor, an irritated sigh. "Well, come in."

The prioress's room was massive. Her bed was covered with books, books that should have been chained up in a monastery or hoarded away in a king's library. The books were a fortune on their own—and that was not counting the clothes, furs, and silks draped across nearly every surface.

The knight Eudo had mentioned was there too, tall and lean and weathered as an old tree. Ibota waved her hand to dismiss him. "It's all right, Roger. You can go."

He nodded and stalked out, closing the door behind him.

Ibota looked sheepish when she followed Jane's astonished eyes around the mess. "Ah, yes. You can see my maidservant left me before my travels. Pregnant, if you can believe it. Don't ask me how she got pregnant in a nunnery," she added. "It happens more often than you might think."

"I've brought your herbs, m'um," Jane said again, unsure what else to say. Sometimes nobles just liked to hear themselves talk, especially about their servants.

"Set them over there." Ibota gestured to a long sideboard, and Jane obeyed. Leaves and dried flowers covered the table, alongside tiny casks and bottles in colored glass. There seemed little room for what Jane had brought, so she moved some of the bottles together, trying not to get them out of order, although it looked as though, like everything else in the room, the prioress had given them no order whatsoever.

When Jane turned around again, Ibota was studying her with those ice-colored eyes. "Do you need anything else, m'um?"

"You don't fear my potions?"

"*Should* I fear them?" Jane met Ibota's stare, surprising even herself. "It's only plants and flowers." Something about the way the prioress looked at her drew boldness out of her, as if she wanted Jane to feel that they were equals. That was dangerous, Jane knew well enough. A high-born lady might treat you as a friend, like Betrice had, then forget you as though it meant nothing to her at all, or even snap at you for stepping out of line when the game was over.

"You see, had the last girl not been too dull-witted to confuse proper alchemy with witchcraft, she'd be here with me instead of raising the shepherd's brat. Do you know your plants and flowers, Jane?"

"Yes, m'um." Jane felt strangely flattered that she remembered her name. Ibota had seemed busy and distracted, but the knife-sharp stare told Jane that was just a game, perhaps one she played to avoid being beholden to anyone. Jane had known widows aplenty, ones who seemed sure of themselves, unafraid to take up space, like their souls filled them from their shoulders to their hips, like they could broaden now without a man around to shrink them. Everyone pitied them and made up stories, but they seemed calm and settled and peaceful, like sturdy trees rather than petals blown this way and that by the breath of their lovers and husbands.

Perhaps it was the same with Ibota, who lived like a widow without ever having suffered an actual marriage.

"So you know why I've asked for laurel and mustard?"

Jane hesitated. "Have you a headache?"

"Very good." Ibota pressed a finger to her lips in thought, and Jane noticed her fingertips were stained deep green, as though she had been digging in the garden, and were chapped and rough as a peasant's. Perhaps that was why the prioress wore gloves outside her chambers: the people of King's Houses would have judged her harshly for such large, indelicate hands. Jane couldn't help but wonder what Ibota did to cover them when the weather was warm. Would she smother her hands in gloves just to keep up appearances? "You wouldn't be interested in a job as a lady's maid, would you?"

Jane laughed at the absurdity of it. "Oh, no, m'um. I'm just a scullion. You can't have me plaiting your hair and drawing your baths and so forth. You'll need a maiden for that, one born to fine clothes and furs, who knows how to care for them."

"Yes." Ibota rolled her eyes. "So they tell me."

They stared at each other a moment, awkwardly, and Jane grew hot despite the draft coming in from the window. Her mind was reeling. Could she really have become a lady's maid? A proper one? Dressed nearly as well as her mistress, her fingers flying through fine thread in the cool, herb-scented breeze of Ibota's chambers, instead of grating turnips in Eudo's kitchen?

And what would Robin say, or Bran, if she rode off to a priory full of soft-living nuns instead of doing their spying for them, after they had both worked to get her a position at King's Houses? It would be poor payment for their favors indeed if she abandoned them to spend her days in plants and herbs and lonely silence. It didn't even bear thinking about, so Jane pushed it out of her head and offered Ibota a small curtsy.

"If there's nothing else, m'um," she said, her chest crushing under the weight of the prioress's keen stare.

"Not now, there isn't. But for tomorrow, and for after, we'll see, won't we?" And at that, Ibota pulled back, draping on hurried indifference like a fine cloak. "Best get back to work. Eudo can be a bear when he's feeling neglected."

Jane hurried past the knight who stood guard at the prioress's door and went back to the kitchen, ready to mull over the strange exchange in her mind—Ibota's offer, her interest in Jane's knowledge of herbs. Was she a witch after all? Had Jane been naive to dismiss Emmie's and Eudo's superstitions? The prioress didn't seem threatening. But then again, she didn't really seem like a prioress, or much like a noble at all. She had the frank, sharp tongue of a brewster but the clothing and airs Jane would expect from a king's cousin.

She didn't have long to consider Ibota's character, much less her very strange offer, because Bran was waiting when she got back, his big form leaning against the rock wall between the stables and the kitchens.

"Hello, you," he said, his voice like warm butter.

But Eudo was already annoyed that Jane had run off with his precious herbs. She didn't have time to linger. "Let's be quick," she said as he pulled her close for whispering.

Bran's brow creased with concern. "Why? What's wrong?"

"A prioress has come, all the way from Kirklees. Running everyone ragged, she is. Including me." Jane regretted the words as soon as they had come out of her mouth. It wasn't the way things had gone with Ibota at all, but it was the tale everyone told, so it came to her with ease.

"A prioress, eh? Those holy women are always so full of airs."

"She's the furthest thing from holy," Jane began, but then Eudo's sweating face appeared around the corner.

"Get in here, girl! No one pays you to gossip!"

Jane flushed. Everyone knew Bran was her beau, and it was perfectly natural for her to whisper to him, but it made her nervous all the same, even if Eudo hadn't any way of knowing where those whispers were really going.

"Mind if I steal Jane away?" Bran asked Eudo in a tone that said *Man to man, you understand, be a friend*, and Jane felt a spark of irritation. Eudo was already cross, and she would have to work doubly hard to turn his heart toward her again. But she needn't have worried. She could already see the *yes* forming on Eudo's face in the warmth of Bran's camaraderie. "It'll only be a moment."

"Fine," Eudo grumbled with false gruffness. "But she'll have to work extra during cleanup."

"Of course." Bran took her arm and grinned, and Jane's agitation grew, for after all it wouldn't be him, would it, working extra?

"You watch that boy," Eudo called over his shoulder. "He's trouble."

"So everyone keeps telling me." Jane managed a smile and followed Bran to an empty corner in the stables, where the long wooden beams sent shadows across his face.

"I'm trouble, but you like it." Bran pulled her close, crushing her against his broad, soft chest, his scent filling her. She reached up to kiss him, to see if she could wash out her annoyance with lust. It *almost* worked, when he kissed her long and slow, lifting her onto the tips of her toes with his strong arms.

"So," he said with feigned casualness, setting Jane down but keeping his arms around her, keeping her tight against him, "tell me more about that unholy prioress. Did you find out why she's here?"

"She's the king's cousin, apparently, so she can be anywhere she pleases," Jane mumbled into his chest.

Bran whistled low. "King's cousin, is she? He'll want to hear of that."

Jane pushed away from Bran, playfully, although she meant it. "That's right. You're not here for me, are you? What does Robin want this time?"

"I'm *always* here for you, Janie." Bran reached for her, but she swatted him away.

"Come now, let's have it. You heard Master Eudo. I have to get back to work."

Bran recited Robin's message to her. "You'll see a high-born man brought low in a fortnight's time," he said. "Notice where he points his finger, and tell us whether his cause is just."

"Robin wants *me* to judge a man's cause? But that's mad! How can I . . ."

"Says you're a good judge of character. Though you can't be too good a judge, spending time with a rogue like me." He pressed toward her, and she pushed him back again, frowning.

"It's another trial, then. I thought I'd passed his trials."

"That's Robin. The big man never stops testing his arrows. Wants to see if you're sharp enough. But don't worry, Janie. Things will become clearer than they look now, I promise."

"So you *know* what Robin's message means, then? And you're meant not to tell me?"

"I don't know much," Bran admitted, "but I know Robin always has our backs, if we're loyal, if we keep our eyes open for him."

Jane thought of Ibota, who had noticed her sharpness straight-away and wanted to reward her for it, without the need for end-less tests. Had Jane been too hasty turning her down, closing a door that she never thought could have opened for her? "Some of his arrows have turnips to peel," she grumbled, "while he's busy testing."

"What's really vexing you, Janie?"

Jane feigned embarrassment, trying not to let her frustration show through the mask. She didn't want Bran to think she needed worrying about. And she didn't want Robin to think that either. "I'm just tired. It's Lent soon and Eudo is complaining about pre-paring all the fish, and there's the cleaning to do, and—well, it's nothing that would interest you."

"You always interest me." Bran kissed her sweetly on the cheek. "Come and find me later, then. When you have more time."

"Come and find *me*." Jane teased him, to make him think that she felt light in her heart, that she was strong enough not to need his reassuring. "And we'll see."

Chapter Nine

Wake up, sleeping kitten!" Emmie shook her. "The abbot has arrived. Everything will be all frowns and dourness until he's gone."

"I thought we had another two days." Jane rubbed the crust from her eyes and immediately regretted it when they began to tear and sting. She had been slicing onions well into the candle-light, for the abbot was said to love the vile things—with eels and in pasties, raw and cooked and even charred, especially now that it was fish days when he couldn't get meat or butter. Jane had gone to bed exhausted, her fingers and hair stinking, the odor of onions coming out in her sweat. So far as she could tell, the Abbot of Saint Mary's had ridden all the way from York for the sole purpose of eating King's Houses out of all their onions, and she'd be glad if he did, for she never wanted to see another onion again.

The manor was short-staffed to serve all the monks who traveled with him, so Jane and Emmie would have to clean themselves up to bring out food and wine while averting their eyes so the monks wouldn't have to trouble themselves about women.

And in all the chaos, and throughout all her labors, Jane was still waiting for the man she was supposed to judge. He should have come within a fortnight, and it had been that and two days, by Jane's count. She had been listening to every passing conversation, trying to catch every breath of gossip, her neck sore from straining. "A high-born man brought low," Bran had said. That would be something people talked about. And Bran had implied that she would see it with her own eyes. Surely the abbot was not the petitioner he spoke of, but she suspected they were connected, in the same way she expected rain on days when the sky filled with fat, gray clouds.

Jane sighed, her whole body aching. All she really wanted to do this morning was close her eyes again, but Emmie was merciless, dragging Jane out from beneath her stinking blanket. "Come now. Today it's caps for us and wimples for the ladies, and stare directly at your feet and try not to spill on anyone."

"What's that?" Milla laughed. "Is the abbot afraid we'll be tempted by his onion-breathing majesty?" Milla had been at King's Houses for ages and ran the buttery all by herself. Nothing ever rattled her and she seemed able to make a joke out of everything. She was cold to Jane when they were alone, but she and Jane got on through Emmie, as everyone did. Emmie was like the spoke in a grand wheel that kept King's Houses moving.

"Or him by us, lovesome as we are, so attired." Emmie straightened the frilled cap on her own small head, and it tilted all the way down over her arched eyebrows. She looked like a child wearing her mother's clothes, it was so ill-fitting, and Jane burst out laughing when Emmie batted her eyes, causing it to slide down to the tip of her nose. She scowled when Jane put her own cap on, tucking her mussed hair beneath. "At least you have a proper head," Emmie lamented. "Oh, alas and woe, for the abbot shall turn his lecherous eye to you."

"Like our prioress has?" Milla asked.

"I can't believe the abbot is so particular about his service," Jane complained, swiftly changing the subject.

"Only about women," Emmie said.

"And what would *he* know of women?" Jane asked.

"More than any woman would like, I'll tell you that," Milla said.

"I can't wait to see how *Ibota* takes his visit." Emmie rubbed her hands together with glee, drawing out the prioress's name and lowering her voice like she always did.

Master Eudo seemed to share Emmie's delight at the prospect of Ibota's misery, for he was downright cheerful when they hauled themselves into the kitchens. "Perhaps he'll finally put that woman in her place," he chortled, and his full, jolly cheeks went pink with pleasure at the thought.

What place is that? Jane wondered, but she didn't ask because she needed to stay in Eudo's good graces. She found herself bristling at the idea that a woman as grand as Ibota might be smothered like an overboiling pot.

But Jane had more important things to worry about than the prioress, for throughout the hurried preparations of the abbot's first meal, which he would be taking with Mother Ibota and a whole herd of monks from Saint Mary's Abbey, she had to watch out for whatever surprise Robin had planned.

The Great Hall was up a flight of stairs, and it would have bloomed with light had the day not been rainy and dreary. One side opened to a balcony overlooking the deer park, and the other was lined with stained glass in a rainbow of colors. A small table at the far end of the room bustled with monks, while the abbot sat at the head of the main table with Lord Alan and Lady Felice de Beauchamp, who had dressed as if they were greeting King Edward himself. Ibota sat beside Felice in a fine gown and wimple, gloves covering her hands.

The dinner conversation began slow and stilted, and Jane dashed back and forth from the sideboards, eyes lowered, serving up everything Eudo could muster while still following Lent restrictions: fresh fish cooked in milked almonds, salt fish with mustard and onion, peas and onions in almond cream, and hot loaves of bread to fill everyone's suffering stomachs.

But the conversation soon grew heated, either because of the thinness of the Lenten table or the wine required to wash down all that onion and fish. By the time Jane was bringing out pies made with the sweet conserves she had potted herself, the abbot and prioress might as well have been flinging fire at each other.

Ibota was leaning forward, her face bent in irritation, and the abbot, who was much older than Jane had expected, his hair white around his tonsure, was scowling back at her, his face dripping jowls and condescension. Unlike his monks, who sat like shadows in their habits, the abbot of Saint Mary's wore robes of gold and white silk, and a massive jeweled cross that bounced against his chest as he bellowed.

"It's *Provence*, Prioress. Provence may listen to one woman's whims, but this is England. And Edward is not his mother."

"But it bodes poorly, Father Simon. You must know that. We can't allow such barbarous ignorance here. My people are frightened, and . . ."

"*Your* people?" the abbot sneered. "And why do you call the Jews *your* people, when you claim to be running a good Christian priory?"

"The nuns at Kirklees serve the whole community. We have relations in the town—we assist them, and they assist us, with our trade and our crops and with merchants. They're our partners, and they deserve protection like anyone else under our care. We Cistercians are not content to hole up in our stone walls with our books." She sniffed, leaning back. "Unlike *some* orders, we work in the world."

Alan de Beauchamp looked as though he had caught a foul wind, his round nose crinkling. "Well," he said diplomatically, "you're all doing God's work, you are, Cistercians and Dominicans alike."

"And we're ever so grateful," his wife, Felice, added smoothly, though she didn't sound grateful in the least.

The warring parties ignored their hosts. "You should take care who your associates are, Mother Ibota," the abbot said, drink turning his purple veins bright against his pale flesh. "Your kinship with the king won't always protect you."

"Oh, you'd like that, wouldn't you," the prioress snapped. "Shall I warn my cousin there's a traitor seated at Saint Mary's, one who plots for his demise?"

"That's not what I meant!" Father Simon stammered. "You . . ." And then Jane could hear no more, for a great shout came from the bottom of the stairwell, drowning out the abbot's words.

"I don't care *who* he says he is," Master Ancel yelled from the stairs. "Get him the hell off our grounds!" He rushed into the room, pale-faced and sweating, and offered an abrupt bow. "My apologies. We have a . . . visitor outside, but he'll be removed peacefully."

"But he has a sword!" said Milo, a young spit-boy who was a bit slow in his wits. "And he's calling for Father Simon!"

Emmie stared at Jane with exaggeratedly wide eyes beneath her too-large cap. Jane blinked back, feeling a slow chill. This must be the man Robin had told her to watch for; he was the first person to arrive at King's Houses who didn't belong. But how was Jane meant to take the measure of anyone with the eyes of the entire feast hall on her, everyone waiting for her to serve the next course?

Master Ancel shoved Milo back down the stairs. "Get your fool arse out of here and stop interrupting dinner!"

"But he said he's a knight! And that he—mmph!" Milo's words were smothered by Ancel's swift hand, but it was too late. Everyone was thrilled to have a distraction from all the bickering.

Lord Alan laid down his cloth, trying to cover his curiosity with concern. "I suspect we should go and see who it is. Ancel, you've called the guards?"

Master Ancel dropped his grip on Milo long enough for the boy to squirm away, and he sighed heavily. "I have, my lord. I assure you, you need not disturb your meal."

"Oh, never mind that," Lady Felice said. "I've already eaten enough fish to last the rest of my days."

The nobles rose and walked out onto the balcony, shoving Jane and Emmie and the other servers aside as though they were nothing more than furniture. Jane strained to see past them, as if she could transport her spirit out onto the balcony through force of will, while her body remained obediently in the room.

Master Ancel shook his head, then snapped at the serving girls, "Well, go follow them! They'll need you sooner or later."

Relief warring with worry in her heart, Jane hurried onto the crowded balcony where the nobles and other servants clustered like a pack of eager ducklings. She peered down through the rain, which fell jagged and streaked with ice in little, clear-colored knives. A man knelt in the courtyard, his clothes far too thin for the cold. A great brown puddle formed a soggy stage around him, and rain streamed down his haggard face, which twisted as if he were in pain.

"Father Simon," the kneeling man wailed. "My life is in your hands! I only ask that you hear me out before you send me to my fate!"

Lord Alan's mouth twisted in disgust. "Begone, wretch, or I'll have you dragged out. We don't take in beggars here at King's Houses. Try your luck at the church in town."

"I am no beggar," the man declared, his voice muted by the driving rain. "I'm a knight! Ask Father Simon! Oh, I see him slithering around behind you, like the serpent in man's garden. Go on! Ask that coward my name."

"What's the meaning of this?" Lady Felice pressed close to her husband. "Father Simon, do you know this man?"

"Oh, he knows me. Ask the holy abbot whose lands he means to steal. Ask him of the debt he drank from me with his devil's tongue, and how he'll take all I have in three days' time and leave me destitute!"

The prioress lifted a kerchief to her mouth, but even Jane could see that she was smiling, her eyes sparkling with this sudden discovery. "Oh, do tell us his name, Father Simon. I would be delighted to learn more about *your* associations."

The abbot scowled, but he knew he had been caught. "That," he said with a cough and a small, almost imperceptible stammer, "is Sir Richard of the Lea. I presume he's here to confess that he has sworn a false oath and cannot repay his debt to me."

"Is that true, Sir Richard?" the host demanded, his tone gentling with the possibility of being outranked. "Are you here to break your oath? Are you new to knighthood, or did you squander your wealth away on sin?"

"I am a noble knight, and true, by God that made me!" Sir Richard shouted through the rain. "My ancestors have been knights for a hundred winters!"

"Was he the type to raid his neighbors?" a chambermaid whispered beside Jane. "Had a knight like that around when I was a girl; village all turned on him, and his house burned up in a fire after he took one sheep too many."

"Good men don't fall, that's all I know," Milla declared. "Must've stumbled down some wrong path, this one."

Lord Alan was beginning to enjoy the show. He had one arm around his wife, sheltering her from the cold and damp, and his wine cup in his other hand. It sloshed slightly, drops of rain turning it cloudy. "Have you no friends to aid you, sir knight?" he called. "Surely your family must have made some allies serving all those hundred winters."

Sir Richard stared up at all of them, rain pouring into his eyes and nose, down his throat. "They're strangers to me now." He spat out water. "When I was rich, they boasted of my friendship. But now, my only friend is God, who died on the Rood to save me."

"Oh, spare me your false faith, Sir Richard," the abbot finally blurted, shoving his way out from behind his host and spilling wine in his haste to defend himself. "You killed and coveted like the rest of them, until you caught poverty like a bout of leprosy and it turned your lips to God's ears."

"If you *are* noble and true, Sir Richard," Lord Alan said with a chastising glance at the abbot, "then you understand the meaning of a man's oath. Why do you expect Father Simon to offer you relief when you cannot keep a simple vow?"

Sir Richard's face hardened. "Oh, I expect nothing. The wheel of Fortune turns, and a good man is brought low, and a bad man is risen up. Only God may amend what Fortune spins astray. Know my words, Abbot, and know that as high as you have risen, God will have the balance in the end."

"You speak as if you were forced into your debt," Lord Alan said. "But if you're a man and a knight, as you say you are, you ought to know the price of a thing, and whether it's beyond your means."

"The folly is my own," the knight replied. "And the serpent played on that folly, and on my kindness, and on my love for my son and heir."

Father Simon puffed up like a rooster, his face red with indignation. "Tell the truth, Sir Richard. If you choose to kneel like a beggar in the muck, don't soil yourself further with your lies. Your son was a murderer! I loaned you money for his bail despite my better judgment, never dreaming you wouldn't repay me. You've had a year to pay your debt, and what do I have to show for it? Must I have warned a man of such noble blood as yourself what would happen if you broke your oath and failed to pay your bond?"

The knight staggered to his feet. "You should have *warned* me that it was all for nothing. You should have warned me that no matter how much gold I paid, no matter how I filled the earl's coffers and pled my case, I would be forced to bury my son, my heir, when he was twenty winters old!"

"He's the one, then?" Master Ancel murmured beside Jane. It seemed even the steward's curiosity had gotten the better of him, for he too had come out onto the balcony to watch the scene. "The one whose boy slew the Earl of Lancaster's son on the jousting field?"

"Do you know him?" Jane asked.

"Aye, a good man, if a proud one. But no fool. He should have known Lancaster wouldn't let the boy keep his head after such an insult."

"Nobles are the last ones to realize the harshness of their rule until they're bleeding from the stab wounds in their own backs," Milla said bitterly, but looked away at Ancel's warning glare.

Jane studied Sir Richard closely. At first, she had found it difficult to see a proud man in all his despair, until the fire awoke within him at the sight of the abbot's face. But pride was in him now, and it burned strong beneath his anguish. The knight's voice rose to echo in the courtyard, rain streaking his thinning hair steel-colored, slashing his pockmarked cheeks. "You should have told me that no price could spare my son the axe, even though his only crime was being better with his lance!" His voice peaked and pitched, escalating to a shout. "I sold everything to save him—my land, my bond, my honor—and only then, with nothing left to my name, did I come to you for grace. But there was no saving him, was there, Abbot? And you knew it all along!"

"Did you know, Father Simon?" Ibota asked. "Did you know there was no saving Sir Richard's boy?"

"Get him out of here!" The abbot gesticulated wildly at the guards, who were as awed by the scene as the nobles and servants were. "For God's sake, men, can't you see he's lost his mind? Or will you wait until he sticks his knife through my liver to find your courage?" He rounded on his host, frothing. "Lord de Beauchamp, is this how you would see the king's guest treated, accused of crimes by wild beggars in the courtyard?"

The guards began approaching Sir Richard cautiously, torn between the abbot's orders and the knight's accusations. But Sir Richard held his hands up in surrender, backing away.

"There's no need, good men. Do not follow this snake into hell for his false words. Trust me, I know well the price of hearing them. I merely came here to say my piece. You might have won on this earth, Father Simon. You might take my goods, and all my lands, when my debt is due. But I will board a ship over the salt sea and pledge myself to Christ on the mount of Calvary, where He too was betrayed."

The abbot rolled his eyes. "Oh, for the love of . . ."

"You can keep these earthly treasures, but we will see, Abbot, which of us sings at God's side, and which of us turns on the spit in hell."

"How much did you loan him, Father Simon?" Ibota asked.

"Why?" the abbot scoffed. "Do *you* intend to pay his debt?"

"I'm just curious," she said mildly. "But if it's a small sum, I don't intend to shame you for your lack of generosity. Perhaps it's not worth mentioning."

"A small sum?" Spittle flew from the abbot's lips. "It's four hundred bloody pounds!"

"Well"—Ibota smiled with satisfaction—"God must be pleased with your devotion indeed, to grant you such a sum to lend. And now you have Sir Richard's lands in recompense. Land in the high lea, if I'm not mistaken. Famous for its sheep." She blinked at him, feigning innocence, but it looked like a ridiculous mask on her penetrating, focused face. "Quite a lucrative acquisition."

"Indeed!" Lord Alan, missing the point entirely, cuffed the abbot on the shoulder. "We should celebrate!" The abbot looked as though he might slap his host's face in response. "I'll send for the finest wine, and a king's table full of venison. Er . . . fish," he said as the prioress's eyes widened, for it was Lent, after all. "The finest of fish from our own pond."

Lord Alan nodded to Master Ancel, who snapped his fingers, sending Jane and the others scurrying back to the Great Hall. The sight of Sir Richard's face, raw and haggard in the streaming rain, the loss that hollowed a path through him like a worm burrowing through soil, made Jane ache deep in her chest. She could not imagine how she would feel if she'd had a child ripped away from her, if she'd had to bury a boy when she should have seen him knighted.

But then again, the Earl of Lancaster had lost his son as well. Was he not entitled to his grief, and his justice?

Jane swore under her breath. How was she meant to judge such men, whose lives played out in grand songs, the whole world chanting along with their victories and losses, while her own life was barely a whistle? She tried to imagine her father mourning her death, or Adam's or Peter's or Ralf's. Sibyl had lost a child between Peter's birth and hers, and Peter said that was when their father turned to drinking, but Jane didn't believe it. Not of him. Sir Richard's heart had been torn open by his son's death. Her father barely *had* a heart, so far as she could tell.

And didn't that settle things? Any man who put the love of his son, and of God, over earthly gains had to be in the right. The judgment she must make was not between Sir Richard and the earl, who both grieved their losses. It was between Sir Richard and the abbot. Sir Richard's cause was just, Jane decided—she was sure of it, just as she was sure that the abbot was a cruel man. Not even *Ibota* liked the abbot.

As Jane was scrubbing pots an hour later, Emmie brushed by her with her lips pursed and her brown eyes bright. "Witch wants you," she crooned. "Says to bring her mint for her stomach and a lemon, she does."

Jane groaned. "Must it be me?" Her arms were deep in dishwater up to the elbows, and the sun had nearly set, and she still had to speak to Bran. If she left now, she'd have to finish washing up by candlelight again. And what if Bran showed up wanting her answer for Robin and she couldn't be found?

"Come now, I've got these," Emmie said. "But only if you promise to tell me what she says about the abbot."

Jane snorted. "As if she talks to me about such things." She grabbed the mint and lemon. She knew what drink the prioress would make for herself—she had seen it often enough—so she crushed the herbs and sliced the lemon, poured in clean water from the pot over the fire, put a cloth over the top, and trudged through the rain to the prioress's chamber.

Ibota's wimple was off and she was seated at her dressing table before a looking glass, her callused, knotted hands working her steel-and-cinder hair into a long braid. The prioress looked younger without her headwear, though there was a heavy crease between her brows, beneath her sharp widow's peak. "Jane," she said wearily. "You've come. You may place the ingredients on the . . ." Her eyes dropped down to the cup in Jane's hands. "Oh!" Color flooded her cheeks. "Well, look at that. You've gone and made it for me."

"I thought you might be tired." Jane lifted the cloth and handed her the cup. The room filled with the scent of lemon and mint and the sweet drops of honey she had added when Eudo's back was turned. "It was . . . well, it was quite a day."

"A gift for understatement, I see." The prioress took the cup and gave it an exploratory sniff. "Mmm, and a gift for blending herbs as well." She sipped, her eyes closing in relief. "Lovely, and just the right amount of . . . oh, have you spoiled me with honey?" She smiled like a child receiving a present. "And it's not even springtime."

"'Twill help you sleep," Jane said. She wondered if Ibota could tell her anything about Sir Richard, such as *why* his son could not be saved, so she could be more certain of her verdict. Jane gathered her courage and asked boldly, "Did you know him, m'um? The knight, I mean?"

"I knew *of* him." Steam drifted in front of her face, blurring its harsh lines. "Who hasn't heard of the knight whose son slew Lancaster's boy?"

"It sounds like an awful incident."

"Oh, it was. But it was the last apple in a rotten barrel. Lancaster and Sir Richard were ever at odds, back to the Barons' War." Ibota drank deeply, then sighed, contented. "It was only a matter of time before he lost his fortune, one way or another."

Jane's shoulders tensed with the mention of the Barons' War—Robin's war. She hoped Ibota didn't notice. "Was Sir Richard one of the rebels?"

Ibota's eyes sharpened. "Why so curious, Jane? What have the barons to do with you? Are you a princess in disguise, like in the old stories, come to shame us all for our dealings with the poor?" She smiled kindly, though her words stung. She knew Jane was no such thing.

"There are outlaws, I hear, in our woods," Jane said rashly. "They fought for the barons against the king, or so I'm told. The new shire reeve is hunting them." She regretted her words immediately, for they came from resentment at the way the prioress had belittled her. She had wanted to feel bigger because of what she knew, but it was a foolish way to salve her own hurt feelings.

Ibota leaned forward. "Outlaws, you say? Who fought against the king? Do you know where they're hiding?"

Jane cursed her own tongue. "It's just gossip. I was foolish to mention it. If there's nothing else, m'um?"

Luckily, the prioress's watchful gaze had turned, her mind chewing something over. "No." Ibota shook her head. "That will be all," and Jane rushed out, leaving the soothing scent of mint and the prioress's warm fire for the chill of the stone hallway.

Jane felt her talk with Ibota had gone badly amiss, although she wasn't quite sure why. The prioress could have nothing to do with Robin Hood, whether he fought for the barons or not. Robin would have been a young man on the battlefield, and Ibota a young noblewoman locked away in her nunnery, probably well on the other side of England, safely away from the war. And Jane had learned more with her boldness, hadn't she? The blood between Richard and Lancaster had already been sour, and perhaps the abbot was playing out the earl's vengeance in the guise of a loan he never expected to have repaid. Curse it all, she had forgotten to ask Ibota about Father Simon.

When she returned to the kitchens, Bran was waiting for her.

"I know the answer," Jane told him eagerly. "The knight's name is Sir Richard, and his cause is just. They killed his son, and now they mean to steal his land, to ruin him. It's the abbot who's done it—made him a loan to save his son when he knew the boy would die despite the bail."

"The abbot, eh?" Bran was clearly impressed. "No surprise

there, is it? The church is always trapping good men to bring them low. I'll send word to Robin. He'll want to help."

"I don't know where Sir Richard went." Jane worried her lip. "The guards ran him off."

"Never mind that. We know exactly where he's gone, and where he's been."

Of course you do, Jane thought sourly, *but you didn't think to share it.*

"Be here just before dawn in three days' time," Bran said. "I'll have another task for you."

"*You'll* have another task?" Jane asked, annoyed. "Giving orders now, as if you're Robin himself?"

"Janie . . ." Bran pulled her close again, all musk and kindness. "Don't be like that."

"Don't." She pushed him away. "I smell of onions."

"Silly Janie." He kissed the top of her head anyway, and Jane felt herself melting toward him, despite her frustration. "You smell of sex and sweetness, and summer afternoons."

Suddenly, Jane thought of what Ibota had said about the barons and the war. If it was tied together, Robin would want to know it. "Bran, there's one more thing."

"What is it?"

"Tell Robin . . . tell him Sir Richard was on the wrong side of an old war."

Bran pulled back, his face puzzled. "What's that now?"

Jane shook her head. She wasn't about to explain it if Bran didn't already know. Not when he was plenty happy to keep secrets from her. "Robin will know what I mean."

"Oh, will he? You and the master have your own secret whispers, do you?" Bran's tone was teasing, but his eyebrows lowered.

"Maybe," she said, happy to see him caught off guard. "Or maybe *I'm* testing *you*." And then she smiled, to show it was a joke, and that she was still soft for him. "Go on. Let me get back to work."

Bran bowed low, as though she were a queen and not a servant girl. "As you wish, my lady." And Jane felt light in her heart then, as though she'd been freed from a heavy weight. Bran was pleased, and Robin would be pleased, and she was working for a good cause: to help a man who'd had his child and his fortune stolen. She, like Robin, would be the hand of justice in an unjust world. The poor knight brought low wouldn't have to wait for his heavenly reward to see his wrongs righted: she and Robin could correct them, right here on earth. Even if no one knew what she did in the shadows.

Chapter Ten

It wasn't Bran who came to Jane in three days' time. It was Robin himself, lurking outside like a slender wolf, his face hidden by a hood. Jane jumped when she saw his lithe figure leaning against Bran's spot on the wall between the kitchens and the stables, a spark of flame in the gray light of morning.

"Why, it's you!" Jane cried out. She flushed despite the cold air, felt heat prickle across her back, and she struggled to keep from pulling her hair out from beneath her foolish cap so she could look less like the faceless drudge the abbot seemed to want them all to be. Something about the way Robin watched her made her feel stumbling and stirred, more aware of herself than she should be.

"Are you certain?" Robin pulled his hood back, and his green eyes twinkled as if he were a forest spirit come to brighten the dull, mundane stables of King's Houses. "You might still be asleep and dreaming."

"Well, I hope I wouldn't dream myself into this cap," Jane quipped, and that earned her a surprised laugh. Her jokes always did—as though people forgot every time that she could be clever. "Isn't it dangerous for you to be here?"

"What is life without risk?" he asked with a slim, sharp smile. "Besides, I've a brave thing to ask of you, and I cannot ask you to be brave if I play the coward myself."

"What do you need of me?" Jane asked shyly. Robin stared at her a moment, holding that coy smile on his face, until she realized he wanted her to come closer. So she did, looking around to see if anyone was watching.

Robin used his foot to push himself off the wall, so that they were closer still. "Just open up a door." His breath was sweet with apple and fennel.

"Open a door? That sounds a small thing, not a brave thing."

"Small actions matter, Jane." He brushed his hand against hers, sending a shiver through her whole body. "Even if they seem invisible, even if you *feel* invisible, you can change everything just by opening a door."

Jane cleared her throat, deeply nervous, though she tried to remain calm and still, and she did not move her hand away from his. Under his gaze, with that barest of touches, Jane felt suddenly as if she mattered. "All right, then. Which door shall I open?"

His mouth was close now, so close she could feel the wind from his breath moving the little hairs on her neck. "Do you remember Sir Richard?"

Jane nodded, trying to still her leaping stomach. "Has he . . . is he well?"

"He's better than when you last saw him, thanks to your own honorable judgment. He'll return to King's Houses today, right by the scullery door. I need you to be here when the sun begins to fade. I need you to let him in."

Jane's eyes widened. People came and went from that door at all hours, and the servants were nosier even than the guards. It would be hard, if not impossible, to smuggle a man into the Great Hall, but especially Sir Richard, since everyone was still talking about his spectacle in the courtyard. But she could not say no to Robin, *certainly* not to his face, and she and he both knew it. "Yes," she said. "Yes, of course."

"Good!" Robin drew away then, satisfied with her word, and Jane felt as though a flaming hearth at her feet had suddenly guttered. "There will be a show today, you wait and see, Jane. I hope you enjoy it as much as you enjoyed our last caper." He winked. And then he pulled his hood up and slipped away into the dawn, as quickly as he had arrived, taking with him the sweetness of his scent and the cloudy spell his presence always seemed to cast on her.

The morning felt colder once Robin was gone, and Jane returned to the kitchens preoccupied. She stumbled to see Ibota waiting for her, watching her; it was early enough that Jane had been expecting the place to be empty.

"Was that your beau?" the prioress asked, as casually as if she were a maidservant and they were friends enough to gossip.

"Him? Oh, no!" Jane could feel the color draining from her own face, and she turned her head toward a sack of flour, away from the prioress's sharp eyes. "He's, um . . . a friend of Bran's, Bran my beau, that is . . . I mean . . ."

The prioress laughed loudly. "Oh, never you mind, Jane." She waved her gloved hand as if swatting at a moth. "I shan't tell your first beau about your second."

"It's not . . . I don't . . ." But then Jane stopped, for she realized that Ibota thought she was embarrassed over some normal, lustful thing, and that letting the falsehood seem like truth would alleviate her suspicions about anything else. "Well, I suppose," Jane muttered with a guilty smile. She wiped a dusty hand across her brow. "We'll see what it comes to. You never can tell with boys, now, can you?"

"What makes you think I would know?" Ibota smiled cryptically. "But you know your herbs, Jane, and how to keep yourself from trouble?"

"Parsley and pennyroyal," Jane recited, though she flushed to talk about something so private, so earthly, with a fine, holy woman like the prioress.

Ibota shook her head. "So much better than my maidservant. Are you *sure* you can't be tempted to join me at Kirklees? The abbey is such a light for women. Where else can you learn to read and write and have peace all around you, without being expected to answer a man's call or shepherd a herd of children?"

Jane flushed, for she already knew her letters. Adam had taught her. But something told her the prioress might be disappointed to hear it. "M'um, I'm honored, I am, but I've told you . . ."

Ibota's eyes narrowed. "Is it these boys keeping you here? Ah, I should have seen it. The chaste life is not for all women, although there is room for . . . well," she said when she saw the alarm on Jane's face, "never mind that now. I'm here for chamomile to soothe my nerves. Today's feast is bound to be long and dreadful, and I'll need to hold my tongue more than I'm accustomed, what with that dullard of a reeve *and* the abbot croaking at each other like toads."

"The shire reeve?" Jane's heart froze, all the blood rushing out of her fingertips. "Is he to come today?" Suddenly, the promise she had made to Robin felt far more dangerous. He had made it sound such a simple thing, but he must have known the reeve was coming. He *always* knew.

"Does that trouble you?" Ibota frowned, those watchful eyes searching.

"Only for the extra seats and servings," Jane lied, shoving the bundle of dried flowers into the prioress's hands too quickly, smearing them with yellow dust. "Will this do?"

"Thank you, Jane," Ibota said, but she had drawn back again, distant and dismissive, and Jane knew that her hasty answer had not satisfied her. Before Jane could try to explain herself again, Eudo stalked in with his face tense. Emmie trailed after him, breathing hard beneath her giant cap.

"Good. You're here," Eudo barked at Jane. "Where's the dough you were supposed to make me?" He grunted at the prioress and her chamomile.

"If there's nothing else, m'um . . ."

Ibota took her leave, and from that moment on, Jane was absolutely buried in work, covered in flour and the skin and dust of almonds, even before the sun truly cleared the morning fog. Emmie stayed close beside her, whispering dirty jokes about the prioress and the abbot, making Jane's face burn, until they had finally finished the last of the candied violets, Eudo's pride—for violets had come early to the garden and they would be a sweet surprise after a meal so heavy with fish and flour. As often as she could, Jane checked the sun. It was a long way from fading, and as the hours crawled by, the great knot in her stomach only seemed to grow.

At one point, Master Ancel appeared outside the kitchen and cleared his throat to get their attention, not daring to tread on the muddy floor, not before they brought the dogs in to take up the scraps. "There's a whole tun of wine missing from the cellar," he announced with a sour look on his face. "Any of you know about that?"

"That dullard boy was the last to the cellar," Eudo grumbled.

Jane knew he meant Milo, whom Eudo never had a kind word for, despite him always nipping at the cook's heels trying to please him. "He'd lose his own head if it wasn't attached to him."

Ancel's lip curled as though he had walked into a field of pig shit. "I'll find him. Clean up, girls. We'll need you to serve." His face was stern, lean with Lenten fasting. Ancel took his Lent rules seriously, which meant the whole staff had to take them seriously, although Jane knew that other households bent those rules in the privacy of their own kitchens. Here, the buttery was barren, Milla repurposed to serve the table and clean the nooks and crannies they'd all neglected in more festive seasons. But, Jane supposed, if you were constantly hosting prioresses and abbots and monks, your cooks could hardly get away with dropping an egg in the sauce for thickening. They would know, and your whole staff would be in the chapel doing penance instead of toiling away on the next batch of almond cream. Foul stuff, grainy and thick; Jane missed fresh milk terribly.

"I reek of wet eel," Emmie groaned as they trudged to their chambers to wash up.

"Eels and onions," Jane agreed, grateful for the silly conversation, which kept her teeth from grinding together with worry.

"Oh, the onions! Don't remind me! I thought we were done with all those onions the day that poor knight arrived and turned the abbot's visit sideways. Although . . ." Emmie lowered her voice in case anyone was listening. "I hear he's had the chance to better himself since then, he has. Father Simon should watch his coffers."

"What d'you mean?" Jane plunged her hands into the basin and watched with dismay as it turned cloudy with flour. She'd been too distracted to brush them off first.

Emmie clucked her tongue at Jane's mess but stuck her hands in the basin anyway. "I heard Robin Hood helped him. Gave him the four hundred pounds *and* a set of fine clothes, even a pair of shining spurs."

"Robin Hood?" Jane tried to control her shaking voice, the way her heart threatened to tunnel through her chest. "Honestly, Emmie, where do you hear such nonsense?"

"A boy or two, here or there," Emmie sang, loosening the lacing on her kirtle and wiping her throat clean with a cloth.

"Well, that's absurd," Jane scoffed. But her voice sounded higher than it should have. Had it been anyone but Emmie, whose mind danced everywhere like a rabbit's, Jane was sure she would be caught in her lie.

Emmie turned to her, the curves of her little breasts peeking out between her laces. "Think the abbot will like this with my cap?"

Jane sputtered out a laugh. "Merciful God, Emmie, put those things away or you'll get us both whipped."

Emmie stuck her hands back in the cloudy water. "You don't think the stories about Robin Hood are true?"

"People will tell their tales, but anyone claiming to know him is playing you for a fool. You shouldn't be so gullible." The words felt cruel as soon as they came out of Jane's mouth, but it was too late. She couldn't quell the ball of anger that had bloomed in her chest like the sun. Robin Hood was supposed to be *her* secret— and Jane had only found out Robin was helping Sir Richard this morning. She hadn't even been told the details—not about the four hundred pounds, and certainly not about the spurs. Though, she thought to herself smugly, she never would have spilled those secrets as carelessly as Emmie had.

Emmie's face fell. "Well, there's no need to be a shrew about it.

I s'pose you're right, though, for if Robin Hood were a true story, we'd all be clad in silks and shining gold and the abbot would be serving *us* a grand feast of onions instead of the other way 'round."

They made their way up to the Great Hall, Jane gnawing on her worries, her eyes still on the sun whenever she could catch a glimpse of it. The sideboards absolutely overflowed with food. Jane knew how it had all gotten there—she had peeled and kneaded and scrubbed and pounded for days, wearing calluses into her hands—but all that food still seemed like a miracle. Perhaps she would never be used to the way nobles feasted, not after she had spent so many years making meals out of scraps.

Master Ancel had made the mistake of seating Ibota beside the abbot, who headed the table, with Walter and Betrice across from her. Had anyone asked Jane, she would have said to put the prioress anywhere but next to Father Simon, but there was nothing to be done about it now. Lady Felice sat on Ibota's other side, and a few of the monks from the abbey were sequestered at their own table, quietly grumbling among themselves as if they would prefer to be reading in their stony monastery, or working their gardens, or whatever it was monks did with their time.

"Lady de Stircheley, when did you and the reeve return from Nottingham?" Lady Felice, slim and delicate, her chin pointed like a wood fairy's, made Betrice look like some sort of giant Dane woman beside her. The reeve's wife wore her wimple for the abbot, her forehead pale and drawn without her lustrous crown of chestnut hair.

"We've just been back a week's time," Betrice chirped. "And we . . . oh, my goodness, Jane!" she cried out as Jane set a huge dish of eels in herbolace before her. Betrice looked down at the dish and shuddered, then tried to cover her disgust with a weak smile.

"Hello, m'um." Jane blushed fervently beneath her cap.

"You two know each other?" Lady Felice's hazel eyes sparked at the promise of gossip.

Betrice looked up at Jane helplessly, obviously embarrassed, so Jane said, "We know each other from market, m'um. I sold conserves."

Relieved to know her choice of dinner companions would not be revealed in such company, Betrice asked softly, "And how is your potter?"

Jane froze, trying with all her might not to look at Walter. So he hadn't told her. "Gone," Jane said with forced brightness, though she could feel the reeve's gaze upon her. "Haven't seen him since that day at market."

"How strange," Betrice murmured.

Jane noticed Master Ancel staring daggers at her. "Sorry, m'um. I really should get back to serving."

"How kind she is to the help." Lady Felice exchanged a long look with her husband, her voice dripping poison with the false compliment, as Jane continued setting trenchers among the monks at the smaller table.

"Indeed," Lord Alan said to Walter. "Your wife has a generous heart."

"Generous to a fault," Walter grumbled. His eyes that had been so fixed on Jane at the mention of Robin Hood's false identity had drifted now, down to the table, his stern face purpling with anger.

"Jane is very bright, and very capable," the prioress announced loudly, as though she were giving a sermon. "To my mind, she's wasted as a pair of kitchen hands." Jane's chest swelled with pride in spite of her distress, and she tried to keep her eyes down as she served so that no one could see her cheeks flush.

"Yes, well"—Betrice's high voice floated over to them—"we can't any of us help our circumstances."

"I think many can rise above their circumstances, can they not?" Lord Alan goaded them with a sly smile at Lady Felice.

"Indeed," his wife quipped. "We'll all be rubbing elbows with peasants in no time. Betrice, you *must* try the herbolace."

"Yes, do!" Lord Alan said, his chest straining against his silk tunic. "We have our own pond here at King's Houses, and the eels are fresh as you please!"

"You mean King Edward's pond, of course." The abbot wiped almond cream from his mouth. "You are only its stewards."

Lady Felice rolled her eyes at his insult. "Are you feeling un-well, my dear Betrice? Or"—she leaned forward—"do you have exciting news?"

Betrice, who had gone pale, shook her head. "It's just the eels, my lady. I . . ."

"The woman has no stomach for it," Walter growled, and he nodded at Emmie to add a heaping serving of eel onto his own trencher, as if to make up for his wife's squeamishness.

"There's just so much of it at Lent," Betrice said weakly.

"Never turn aside what the Lord provides, my dear," the abbot chastised her.

"Now, Father Simon," Lady Felice retorted, "not everyone has the appetite for fish that you do. Nor your appetite for wine." She muttered the last words under her breath.

Her husband heard her, though, and raised his cup. "Fish must swim, as they say!" he declared. "A toast to changing circumstances: the good abbot's, and our good reeve's!"

Walter's knife clattered onto the table, and he gripped his cup with a fist, avoiding Betrice's uneasy glance. "I'm sure I don't know what you're implying."

"All I mean," Lord Alan said, "is that these days, a strong man of solid heart can prove himself and rise." His eyes twinkled with delight. "You yourself had quite the rise after you helped King Henry punish the rebel barons."

This seemed to appease Walter, and he puffed up like a morning rooster. "Well," he said, his voice unnaturally low and gruff, "*I'm* a man who gets things done, not a man who sits on his arse in silks. Our new king has entrusted me with more important work than counting crops and collecting coins."

"Edward values diligence and honor over blood," Lord Alan said, poking at the reeve's sore feelings. "I'm sure he sees your worth."

"Perhaps high birth is no guarantee of honor," the abbot muttered, "if Sir Richard is any proof."

"Who is this Sir Richard?" Betrice asked, her voice pitched high and false, like it had been when Walter's temper threatened her own table.

"Why, he's the reason for our feast!" Lord Alan declared with a broad grin. "Father Simon will be a very wealthy man at sundown."

"Wealthy?" the abbot scoffed. "When I've lost four hundred pounds to a knight with no honor and no means?"

"But think what you stand to gain, Father. Sir Richard's wool is worth far more than his honor—or yours, for that matter," the prioress interjected loudly. She wanted the whole room to hear her, and she knew just how to do it, Jane thought. "The way I see it"—Ibota sipped delicately, once she was sure she had everyone's attention—"your four hundred pounds will be repaid by summer's end, and you'll earn triple that in a year's time."

The abbot's face struggled between pride and rage before Ibota added, "And it's all for the good of Saint Mary's, of course, and for your service to Our Lord. Think of how many hungry children you'll be able to feed with the proceeds."

Ibota's back was to Jane, so Jane could not see her face, but she watched Walter assess the prioress as though he had just realized that there was another predator stalking the hen yard.

"Of course," Lord Alan said, "a man might take a little for himself. This was a private loan, wasn't it, Father Simon? You wouldn't have used the church's funds to help a friend."

"Nor to bankrupt him, surely." The host's wife giggled into her drink.

"Are you sure it's not a bit early to be celebrating?" the prioress asked, her tone all courtesy, but her words like blades. "The day is not yet done. And Sir Richard does have until the sun sets to repay you." Jane's spine turned to ice. Did Ibota know something? Had she been listening to Jane and Robin as well as watching?

"Faugh, you heard that fool in the courtyard," Father Simon snapped, his face hot with drink and frustration. "All of England heard him. Sir Richard is far beyond the sea by now, spending the last of his sorry days kneeling at Christ's feet."

The prioress patted her mouth with a clean cloth. "You must be very certain that your claim is just, to ruin a man's livelihood for silver."

"You are always in my beard, woman!" the abbot cried. "The man's an oath-breaker and a debtor! There's a good chance he's dead or hanged by now. I paid dearly for my trust in him and I can't be the only one he's wronged."

"And if he dares to show his face today, the shire reeve is here to arrest him for you," Lady Felice said dryly. "How fortunate."

"Jane," a soft voice said, and Jane startled, torn away from the nobility's war of words by an older woman, one who did the washing and who was so bent and withered that Emmie always joked she had been there since before Adam fell out of Eden. "It's time," the laundress said.

Jane blanched. She didn't even know the other woman's name. But, obviously, the old woman knew Robin, and she knew Robin's plans, and he had used her precisely because she would be invisible among the other servants. *He's got a whole field of mice sneaking around King's Houses,* Jane thought, and the realization was so bitter that she almost forgot to be afraid. Would she wind up like this bent and whispering crone, her hands raw with lye and her bones thin with a servant's wages? Would her whole life be spent in these halls, Robin's woman on the inside, with nothing to claim for herself but a head full of secrets?

-◀◀◀◆▶▶▶-

Jane made an excuse to Master Ancel about needing the privy, then raced downstairs. Clouds masked the sun; she hadn't noticed how late it had gotten. She thrust open the scullery door, and there stood Sir Richard, hunching over beneath the eaves. Emmie's gossip had been right. His clothes were fine, silk and gold thread and rich saffron and blue, perfectly fitted to him despite his thin frame and long limbs. His face was still pale and drawn, haggard as a beggar's, his eyes pink around the edges, but he had been shaved, and he smelled of the wood and spice that lingered on all the men of Robin's camp.

"Sir Richard?" She greeted him. "Follow me." She led him to the servants' stairs, which would take them to the main hall.

"Wait," the knight whispered, his voice gentle and melodious, nothing like the shouting, wild man he had seemed in the courtyard three days ago. "My dear, I would know your name."

She bristled, both because no one had told him—had they just said "Wait for *the girl*," as if she could be anyone?—and because there wasn't much time before someone came along and found them, and then Jane would be out on her ear if she was lucky, and hauled off in irons if she wasn't. "It's Jane," she said, more curtly than she should have. He was a knight, after all.

To her horror, Sir Richard took her hand in his own and dropped to one knee. His palms were rough as raw wool, and the top of his head shone bald beneath a spray of thin, salt-gray hair. His eyes met hers, watery and weak. "Jane," he said, "I am honored to meet you. God has sent you here to right a wrong. I shall never forget what you've done for me."

"I . . ." Jane's annoyance fled her, and tears stung her eyes. "The honor's mine, sir." No one had ever spoken to her in such a way, nor taken her hand so, not without looking for a tumble, and she felt as light and lovely as a maiden, her hand smooth and delicate in his own.

"Thank you, Jane," Sir Richard said gallantly. "And if there's anything I can do for you when our work here is done, you need only ask, and you shall have it."

Jane's heart swelled. "Now, now," she said gently, "you can leave off your kneeling. Your hard days are behind you."

Sir Richard eased himself upright again, the ache of the movement revealing itself in a wince. "My grief will always be with me," he said. "The grief of loss and betrayal. But there is also kindness in this world, and I thank you and yours for showing it to me, and for reminding me that God watches out for His servants, and He will always rule in favor of the just."

Will He? Jane wondered. It struck her then how well Sir Richard had been lifted up from his disgrace, while she and all the other servants helping Robin had never known such fine clothes, such a full purse, and must still bow their heads and bend their knees for Robin's cause. The thought vexed her, but it felt selfish, and foolish, especially now, when she had to hurry the old knight along or risk her neck. "Will you be safe alone?" she asked as they reached the end of the corridor, for she could not take him any further, or they would both be caught.

"I know the way," he said. "And your men have already taken audience with the abbot, as a distraction."

"They have?" Jane flinched, imagining Robin facing down the reeve again. Even if he disguised himself, he would never fool Walter de Stircheley twice.

But it was not Robin standing guard in the Great Hall, clad in Sir Richard's coat of arms. Instead, it was Tuk, and Little John besides, his gold beard blackened with soot, weapons at their hips and heavy sacks at their feet, as though they were prepared for a siege. John looked up at Jane as she scurried along the edge of the room to join the other servants, and he unabashedly winked. Terror filled her up like an ice-cold bath. What a fool he was! Had de Stircheley seen?

But no one would have, Jane quickly realized, for no one was paying any attention to her. Everyone was shouting.

"What does he want?" the abbot demanded. "We're done hearing him plead his case. His debt is due at sundown. There will be no extensions!"

"Our lord will speak for himself," Tuk said mildly. "You need only await his entrance."

"Well"—Lord Alan frowned at Tuk—"if he can afford Saracen soldiers, perhaps he has his debt with him after all."

Emmie caught Jane's eye across the hall, her own stare wide and mocking from beneath her cap as if to say, *Didn't I tell you?* Jane would never hear the end of being wrong about this, she knew. And she would have to pretend she had no part in it, which chafed her even more.

"If he *dares* to enter here," the abbot yelled, "I want him taken straight to prison. He's a debtor and an oath-breaker!"

"Do you mean to tell me my job?" the reeve snapped, and Jane could see from the color on his face that something had raised his temper all to edges. Betrice's head was low, her face white as a lily, and Lady Felice was looking on her with hard, cruel eyes. Perhaps she had been tormenting her further.

Suddenly, the doors flew open and Sir Richard strode in, looking twice the man and half the age as he had when Jane had smuggled him in through the scullery door. With a grand, sweeping movement, he knelt between his fake retainers, fur cloak blooming around him like a great rose.

"Greetings, good gentlemen, fair ladies all." Sir Richard's voice was strong and steady. "By your grace, Abbot, I have come on the day we have agreed upon, true to my honor and my debt."

"And have you brought my silver?"

"Not one silver coin"—the knight smiled—"by God that made me."

A slow smirk spread across Father Simon's face. "Then drink to me, Lady Prioress. The debtor has brought himself to us, no need for a chase. And you are wrong yet again."

Ibota said nothing. She merely watched, face shrouded in her wimple.

"What are you doing here," Lord Alan asked, "if you haven't come to pay your debt? Surely you know we'll have you hauled off to jail. The shire reeve can see to it himself."

"I am here," Sir Richard said with a glint in his eye, "to test the abbot's mercy, to pray for a few more days to gather his coin."

"You already broke one oath," Lord Alan said. "Your lands are forfeit. By God," he quipped, "he really is the fool they say he is. Prison would be a blessing for this one."

"Will you have mercy on me, Shire Reeve?" Sir Richard turned to Walter. "You know what it is to ride Fortune's wheel. Those who sit high can be brought low again with a single spin. A new shire reeve will need new friends, and I shall be yours, should you take my side this day."

The reeve was unmoved. "Fortune didn't make you break your oath. A man does what he will with the gifts God has given him. Should they slip through his fingers, he has no one to blame but himself."

Jane thought of Walter's own losses in the woods and stared furiously at the stained glass behind his head.

"And you, Father Simon," Sir Richard asked, smiling incongruously, making everyone uncomfortable, "has God shone enough light to illuminate the error of your ways? Out of courtesy, and the friendship we once had, at least swear to me that you will protect my lands and return them once I have repaid my debt." He bowed his head. "I'll even offer myself as your servant until I earn back your four hundred pounds."

"What a deal," Lord Alan muttered. "A madman for a servant. Who could pass that up?"

"By God that died on a tree!" Father Simon rose, slamming his fist on the table, his face purple as beetroot. "Get your own bloody land! The lea is mine!"

Sir Richard looked unsurprised—only satisfied. "Good lords and ladies, you believed you shared your table with a man of God, and yet he hurls blasphemies like a churl, and his heart is just as closed. You heard me offer him a chance to show Christ's mercy, but he bargains like a devil instead. Know this, Abbot: I will have my lands again, and sooner than you think, and your own honor will be the price."

"Get out, false knight!" Father Simon bellowed. "Get out before I have you dragged out of here in chains!" The guards started forward, shaken out of their shock, and John and Tuk put their hands on their swords. Jane's heart leapt into her throat. They wouldn't dare, would they? Not here. She and the other servants would be cut down if they couldn't get out of the way. It would be a slaughter.

"You lie, Abbot, with your twisted tongue, before God and all these men and gentle women. I have never been false. Not for a single day." The knight drew himself taller. "You haven't a drop of courtesy, despite your golden cross and your robes, to suffer a knight to beg for so long before you. Step back," Sir Richard ordered John and Tuk, and they obeyed his command, as if they were his men indeed. "There will be no violence. Not on my orders."

"What good are your damned guards, Lord Alan, if they're just going to stand there?" Father Simon shouted frantically. He smacked the table in front of Walter. "And you, Reeve! What good are you?"

Walter glowered back, his dark stare a challenge.

"You can call your guards, and you can test my strength," Sir Richard said, "but I have stood before fiercer foes than you, Abbot."

Lord Alan paled. "If there is to be war over the knight's lands, it won't be here at my table. Perhaps you two can come to terms, Father Simon. As you said, the lands are worth far more than the four hundred pounds you loaned."

Father Simon looked between Ibota and Lord Alan, his eyes bulging, so unsure where to place his rage that he could only sputter, "*I* didn't say that!"

"So," Sir Richard said, "you admit before all these gentle folk that my lands are worth more than my debt, that you have taken far more from me than you ever gave. You're no man of God. You're a usurer, a sinner, and nothing less. And I accuse you, here before the shire reeve and all this company."

"But . . . but that's ridiculous!" Father Simon slammed his fist down on the table again. "You can't just stand here and accuse me . . ."

"It does sound a bit like usury to me," Ibota mused. The abbot lost all of his color when she turned to Walter and asked, "What do you think, Shire Reeve?"

Walter's eyes sparked with delight. "You're the expert on sin, Prioress. If you think it's usury, I think I ought to take you at your word."

"Perhaps," the abbot stammered, "perhaps we might come to terms. How much would you . . ."

"There will be no terms," Sir Richard declared. "You could give me a thousand pounds, and, still, I would not surrender my lands. You have already taken my heir from me. Did you really think I would let you toss my family into landlessness and infamy for any amount of silver?"

Sir Richard nodded at Tuk, who handed him one of the two large sacks he and John had brought with them. And then the knight strode up to the table, upended the bag, and shook it out all over everyone's dinner.

Gold coins fell like warm rain: on the abbot's lap, on his plate, filling up the wine cup, until a mound of gold buried the abbot's portion of the feast. Betrice gasped.

"Here is your coin, Abbot," Sir Richard said. "Four hundred pounds. The same amount you loaned to me. I wanted to see if you were truly God's servant, to give you a chance. But now, I swear to you, I shall see you ruined. Defrocked, cast out, and driven to begging like a mendicant friar, if God will listen to your serpent's hiss at all."

"Well, look at this!" Lord Alan held up a coin, examining it with amusement. "King Henry's golden pennies! I haven't seen their like since the war." He turned to Walter. "Reeve, it seems we've been served the abbey's four hundred pounds instead of a sweet course. We're lucky to have you here to judge Sir Richard's bond. Are his lands his own again?"

Walter savored the moment. He drank long of his wine, then squinted at the coins on the table, and at the other sack at John's feet. "As you're all so fond of pointing out, I'm no high-born knight. But I know the weight of coin well enough. Seems to me there's plenty here to call the debt repaid."

The abbot, struck silent, turned as white as fresh-fallen snow.

Sir Richard bowed deeply. "And so, good lords and ladies, I shall take my leave. If you ever find yourself in Verysdale, you may stop by my door for a good meal and a warm hearth. Some of us"—he glared at the abbot—"have not forgotten courtesy."

The feast was over after that, Eudo's candied violets forgotten.

Before she retired to her chambers, the prioress sidled up to Jane. "It seems you have many friends among the nobles."

Jane tried to keep the tangled flush of pleasure and fear from reaching the expression on her face. "I try to serve well, m'um."

"Strange that Sir Richard made it into the Great Hall on his own, through the guards. How do you suppose that happened?"

Jane faltered. "I can't say, m'um, but there was chaos in the kitchens, to be sure. We were short of hands, and some wine even went missing, and . . ." She realized she was rambling, which would only make her look guiltier. "Well, you can't trouble your-self with such things, m'um. They're far beneath your notice. Someone will get the switch for sure, is all."

Ibota's smile was a false one; she looked like a cat that was about to bite. "I'm sure you're right, Jane. Each of us reaps what we sow, in the end."

"Of course," Jane murmured, but not even the prioress's warn-ing could dampen her mood, or her sense of pride. Robin Hood was right. Small actions like hers did matter. And for once, Jane did not feel invisible. Sir Richard had noticed her. Had really *seen* her.

Wasn't it worth the risk to do the work for Robin, if it meant seeing a villain like the abbot brought low, and right in front of her own eyes? What did it matter if the other servants, who laughed and joked, cheering the abbot's humiliation, didn't know she was involved? *Jane* knew, and Sir Richard knew, and most im-portantly, Robin knew. And for Jane, that was enough.

Chapter Eleven

Father Simon departed in the night, much to everyone's relief. Soon after, Lord Alan and Lady Felice took advantage of the warming weather to travel to the coast. No guests remained at King's Houses besides the prioress, who took meals in her chambers. She claimed she was staying until some trouble with the roof was resolved at Kirklees, though, to Jane's mind, fixing a roof should not have taken such a long time, unless the roof was very large indeed.

It had been nearly a week, but the household staff still gossiped about the abbot's great humiliation. None of them imagined they would be a party to anything so delightfully shocking ever again. Not out here, where people only visited to feign loyalty to an absent king.

Emmie had taunted her about Robin Hood, since she had been proven right, and Jane seemed to be the fool. "I hear he's as gallant as Lancelot, handsome as Gawain, and smells of rose petals and honeycombs," Emmie said in her joking way, tickling Jane in the ribs and forcing a cup of wine on her.

He doesn't, Jane wanted to say. *He smells of firewood, and musk, and the clean, soft fur of a hare in springtime.* But instead, Jane just groaned and muttered that Sir Richard must have found a friend to take the money from, because didn't nobles all help each other in the end, even if they had their petty squabbles?

At least Bran knew what Jane had done. He had given her his soft, secret smile and told her how proud he was of her, and how much he wanted to bed her. And so he did, hot and fast in the stables, and Jane had to admit that the sex was better and more fervent than it had been between them in quite some time. It made her feel giddy, like a lusty girl again.

Sometimes, though, when she closed her eyes, Robin's smooth, sensuous smile slipped into her mind, his long legs as he leaned against the wall. And though Jane tried to drive him out of her thoughts, a little piece of her thrilled at the danger. What was the harm to anyone, if those thoughts only stayed inside her head?

Today, though, her secrets felt more dangerous, for Bran was taking her out to the Greenwood, and she would see Robin again. As she rode behind Bran, hair flying loose in the warm sunshine, her eyes wide open—no blindfold, which meant she was trusted— she couldn't help the shiver of anticipation that rattled her all the way from the nape of her neck to her toes.

The ride out to the woods was invigorating too: the sweetness of woodbine, the pale clouds of lily dust, the fresh smell of fallen logs as they dried off from yesterday's rain—even the quivering worms in wet patches left by the downpour. Until this very day, Jane hadn't realized how much she missed fresh air and the forest, her solitary strolls, even her long walks to market with the heavy basket at her side. There was a whole world out here, big and broad and natural, cycling like the moon and the sun and the seasons, and the worms, snails, and birds didn't care if Lord Alan had enough salt for his afternoon meat, or whether the sideboard that was always just a little bit crooked needed a new wedge carved for its leg. *This* world, huge and limitless, felt meaningful, felt right, as if it were Jane's true home. Her chest expanded with every breath in the woods, her shoulders widening, her neck loosening as her chin turned up to greet the sun. She felt like a summer queen, as though she were riding to her court crowned with hawthorn, the men of the Greenwood ready to kneel at her feet and take vows in her honor.

The first thing Jane noticed when she climbed down from Bran's horse was the smell of roasting venison. Lying beneath it was campfire smoke and the tang of juniper boiled with honey. Jane's mouth watered and her stomach howled with eagerness. Clearly, Lenten fasts weren't followed in the Greenwood.

"There she is!" Little John announced. "Our brave kitchen squire!" Robin's men were all planted in the dirt, stockinged legs sprawled out with the ease of ale and spring warmth: Little John, Tuk, and Wyll, who leaned his thin body against a tree as though he were an errant branch. Another man roasted a deer over an enormous spit. "This here's Mooch," John announced. "He's our cook today. That's why we brought him 'ere, ain't it, Mooch? That and your pa's stout ale."

Mooch bowed low. He was thick-limbed, with a stubborn, greasy lock of dark hair that fell over his eyes and a forehead that was a little too pale, though his cheeks were red with mirth and good humor.

"I remember you," Jane said shyly. "From when Bran first took me to the forest. The food smells wonderful, if a little sinful."

"Mooch is the old man miller's son," Bran explained. "He fetches bread and butter and even cheese for us . . ."

"Though we fetched the deers ourselves, we did," John boasted, patting his stomach.

Jane felt strange, flailing and lost, watching someone else toil over food. "Let me know if I can help," she offered.

"Don't you lift a finger, Janie!" Little John handed her a mazer fit for a king—perhaps a long-dead king—with old, gold-colored dragons fading into the silver. She had to hold it with both hands. "You don't have to cook for no one else today." Pride washed over John's face, sparkling in his eyes.

Robin sat apart from the others, an arm draped lazily over his knee, a cup dangling from his hand. She could feel him watching her. When she finally grew brave enough to look back, his slow smile sent a shiver through her in spite of herself.

He rose, gesturing like a lord welcoming his barons to a feast, which Jane supposed he was, in his own way—the great, wild Lord of the Greenwood and the men who fattened their purses on his orders. "You've earned your feast, Jane. Today, you'll be served as well as any fine lady, just as you deserve."

"Aye, and you'll see why we want to take what the rich have for ourselves." Wyll was the smallest and thinnest of them, but he made it a point to take up the most space, all bent knees and sharp elbows. He made his voice deeper than it really was too. "'Tis our money, after all, and our labor, as they feast upon our backs."

"Come now," Bran said. "No need for grim talk on a fine day." To Bran, everything was light as summer, and should stay that way. Wyll drew a finger across his wet mouth, as if to seal his lips, and they all laughed, for Bran's gentle scolding had set everything at ease.

The ale was stout and rich, and, soon enough, Mooch spread

out a glorious feast before them upon a yard of clean cloth. Jane tried not to agonize over the cloth being smeared by dirt and grass as he filled it with smoked venison and sweetbreads fried in flour, hunks of fresh cheese and fine-milled bread. There wasn't a single fish in sight.

And that wasn't all they had. They opened a tun of fine wine and passed great cups of it around. It tasted of cherries and plums—familiar—and Jane realized, with a shudder of guilt, that this must be the tun that had gone missing the night of Sir Richard's spectacle. Milo had been blamed for its loss, and Master Ancel had boxed his ears and ordered him fed nothing but stale bread until Lent was over. Had Robin smuggled it out himself when he came to see her that morning? Had he known what the consequences would be? She glanced at him over the top of her cup to see if she could read the truth on his face, but he only wore that same soft smile, beckoning, fixed on her, without a trace of guilt.

Once they had eaten their fill and passed the wine around again and again, Jane began to feel pleasantly swollen, like a fat little bird flapping from branch to branch, thick with summer seeds.

"Ah . . ." Little John leaned back, his hand on his enormous belly. "Let's drink a toast to Sir Richard! Patron of the Greenwood, destroyer of abbots, wearer of fine spurs!"

Jane giggled into her wine. "He was quite a sight at the abbot's table! How did you get him so well-clothed in such short time?"

"Now, this is a great tale," Mooch began, his dark eyes sparkling, but John cleared his throat and glared. "Oh, all right, word hog. You tell it."

"I tell it better!" John grinned. "So this knight shows up here with naught but ten pennies in his purse—I know, 'cause I checked."

"And you can bet he took a share for himself." Tuk chuckled.

"As if this one"—John jerked his thumb at Robin—"wouldn't have turned me upside down like a caught fish and shaked out my innards!" Robin's smile broadened. He enjoyed this, Jane realized, being the center of the story but taking no part in telling it. He saw her watching him, and his eyes widened a fraction, his smile deepened, and then they both looked back at John.

"So Master Robin had given him the coin, but then I says, you can't have him show up and repay the abbot in them shredded clothes. He needs to look a proper knight, show the abbot what's what!"

"What, then?" Jane snorted a little, then blushed at the indelicate sound. "You sewed them up yourself?"

"Took the measure with me own bowstring, I did!" John boasted. "The devil's draper, they call me."

"The devil's horseshit." Mooch handed Jane a hunk of bread, sticky and glistening with honey. "He stole those clothes, and don't let him tell you different."

"You'll ruin the tale, you will!" John clapped Mooch on the back of the head, but it was a fond blow.

"Then," Wyll said, eager to add his own voice, "he hires himself and Tuk out as squires!"

"Got to see the innards of the king's grand house, I did."

"Did you get to see that serving girl? The one with the . . ." Wyll made a gesture with his hands like a pair of women's hips, and Jane found her good humor dampening as all the men laughed. Did he mean Emmie? Her face felt hot.

Bran shoved Wyll, but it was gentle, for Bran was always gentle. "Quiet, churl. There's a lady present!"

"Right, a lady. The one you rode out into the woods . . . I mean the one you rode *with*." Wyll grinned at his own joke, but no one else smiled, and the woods grew thick with silence. Everyone looked away, laughter and cheer dying in their throats. Jane, though, turned to look at Robin.

His face was frozen, his stare fixed on Wyll with a dark intensity that made her stomach churn.

"Watch your mouth, Wyll Scathlock," Robin said, "or I'll pin you to that tree by your throat." Then he slammed down his cup and stalked away into the trees.

"Oh, now you've done it," Little John said. "He's gone to brooding." But his voice shook just slightly, and, still, no one laughed.

Wyll looked more nervous than anyone, and he turned to Jane, eyes pleading in his skinny face. "Our Jane can give as good as she gets, though, can't she?"

Everyone's eyes were on Jane, but not in the way she would have liked. She felt like a mother yanking on her sons' ears, or a fragile flower that needed protection, and not a worthy rogue capable of bravery and honor, like John or Tuk or Bran. She drank and stared after Robin, suddenly lost.

"No harm meant, Janie, I swear it," Wyll kept on, and Jane bristled as she always did when someone she disliked used her nickname. "What I mean to say is . . ."

"What he means to say," Bran interrupted, "but he's too much of an ass to say it, is that he's sorry."

And how would Emmie, loved by everyone, have responded to Wyll's ribbing? Emmie would have made a joke instead of sitting there mooning with big, sad eyes like a cow.

"He's sorry, all right," Jane said boldly, then took another huge gulp of wine.

They all burst out laughing, even Wyll, who blushed shyly and smiled at her for the first time. Robin was still gone, sulking, but at least the men would stop treating her like she didn't belong.

"D'ya think he'll come back," Wyll asked eventually, "or should I go and get him?"

"Maybe he went to walk it off," Tuk said. "You know how he hates you loosening that foul tongue."

"No fun, that one," John agreed. "But he tolerates us, though he's not keen on revelry himself."

The image of Robin and Betrice together thrust suddenly into Jane's thoughts, hot and heavy and unbidden, and as quickly as her courage had bloomed, it wilted, for she wasn't Emmie, was she? She couldn't bounce back from a wound as though nothing could shift her bright feelings. She looked down to hide her blush.

"You're ram's shite, Scathlock," Mooch said. "Always pushing. You broke the rules, so what do you expect?"

"You have rules, all of a sudden?" Jane laughed, but her heart wasn't in the joke anymore.

"Aye, of course we merry men of the Greenwood have our rules! Just as King Arthur's knights did, in their time." Little John leapt on a log with surprising grace, as if he were Robin himself, then cleared his throat. "No harm to farmers, yeomen, or good knights who might be friends. And we never harm women—nor say coarse words about them," he added with a pointed glare at Wyll. "But, abbots, reeves, and lawmen who haunt and hound the poor, and all those churchmen who steal from God's cup to fill their coffers . . ." He raised his cup, expectantly.

"We beat, we bind, we rob them blind!" all the men chanted.

"Fuck the church!" Wyll added for good measure.

"Surely it's not the whole of the church that's gone wrong," Jane said, the drink and Wyll fanning her ire. She couldn't help but want to defend her brother Adam, despite what had passed between them. "Some join to do good. Poor priests in the villages, and—"

"That's the lie they tell you, tell all of us, so they can take from you and from me." Wyll's face had turned to fire. "They think they can do whatever they want to whoever they want. They think we won't make them pay."

Jane looked over at Bran, and he shook his head slowly, his eyes wide with warning. He knew her brother was a priest. He just didn't want her to say so. Anger rose in her chest like a foul belch. Is that how it was, then? They could laugh and jape and say all manner of things, insult Jane and her friends, be crass and rude as you please, but *she* could only share a small part of herself—the most pleasing part.

Well, why not? That's how it had been at home, hadn't it, her brothers speaking with wide-open mouths and Jane quiet, tactful, keeping everything close. Why had she expected anything different?

Jane needed a breath. The drink was getting to her. She rose to her feet, her back weak and her legs wobbly from sitting for so long.

"Where are you off to?" Bran asked gently, as if apologizing for quieting her.

"I need to make water," she mumbled.

"Oy, bring back Robin if you find him!" John said. "He's had enough pouting."

"Sure you want her running off after Robin?" Tuk warned with a wink to Bran. "Best watch your girl, stable boy."

Bran laughed it off, but he looked uneasy, and he didn't look Jane's way when she left. *Good*, she thought. *Let him worry, even if he's a fool for doing so. As if someone like Robin would want to warm his bed with someone like me, a lowly serving girl. A mouse.*

Jane went far from the camp to find a private spot. None of the men would follow her, she knew, but Robin hadn't come back and she was worried that he might stumble onto her when she was in the middle of something base and lowly. Of course, the last time she'd gone to make water at a feast with Robin, she'd found him with his hand up Betrice's skirts, and . . .

Her thoughts flooded in with the drink, jumbled, flashes of rage and shame and envy that would not cohere. *It's the wine*, she thought. *Never mix wine and ale—you know better.* It was something her father would do, and look how it would set him off. She pushed her thoughts down, boxed them up in a coffin. There was no chance of finding Robin in another woman's arms tonight. There were, Jane thought smugly, no women in the woods besides her.

On her way back, Jane passed by the little shrine to Mary. The sun was drawing down, close to the edge of the trees. It was springtime, so darkness would take longer to set in, but it would come. And then the celebration would be over. Bran would expect her to stay the night with him above the stables. No one would talk about her being gone all night at King's Houses, and no one would worry, so long as it didn't interfere with work. No one bothered with women like Jane—women who, she'd heard Master Ancel say once, were born to rut and breed and die. Like a yard full of pigs. No wonder Wyll Scathlock thought no one would defend her honor. And no one had, not even Bran, except for—

A shadow moved in the shrine, like a long wolf was stalking it, and Robin slunk out, a mixture of arrogance and guilt on his face. She should have known he would be right here. Here was where he felt safe, felt guided. Here was where he heard answers.

It must be nice, Jane thought, to believe that Mary was looking out for you, that God and His Holy Mother cared what you did from moment to moment. To feel that you weren't beneath Her notice.

Robin smirked at her, but it was stiff. "Have you come to lead me back, then, like a stray sheep?"

Jane hadn't, of course, but she didn't want to tell him why she'd really wandered off. "We've smoothed it out," she said instead. "Wyll and I, that is. It was foolishness. Just a joke gone wrong."

"Yes, you're very good at that." Robin studied her. "Smoothing things out."

Jane shrugged away the observation. "Do you come here to think?"

He nodded, solemn. "Many men refresh their spirits in the church, but I find the Lord's grace out here, in the church He made with His own hands."

"I know just what you mean." Jane clasped her hands and stared at the trees, bright green and budding, filling her heart with hope. "It wasn't until I came out here that I realized how much I'd missed these woods, missed roaming free beneath the sun." Robin smiled, canny, regretful, and she realized he might have mistaken her words. "Not that I'm not grateful for the work, m'lord, but . . ."

"Jane." He drew closer to her, churning the twigs beneath his feet like wind before a storm, that smile still on his face. "You mustn't call me that. We're all equals out here."

His closeness, his heat, brought back her dreams of him, and

Jane felt suddenly like she needed to look anywhere but into his eyes, which were green as the shoots sprouting from the trees, his autumn-colored hair lit by the fading sun. Her gaze danced around until it found Mary's shrine. "Do you hate the church as much as they do?"

"The church isn't God," Robin said, and she felt his presence closer now, the warm glow around him, his words tickling her ear. "There's the nobles and the abbots, growing fat in the castle, and they've shut out God, for all their gold. God doesn't touch their hearts. Not in the way He does out here."

"God can touch any heart, if it's open enough." It was something Adam always said, but she wasn't about to admit that to Robin. Who knew how he would react to finding out she had a brother in the church?

"And how open is your heart, Jane?" Robin's voice was soft and sultry. Was he mocking her, or . . . ? She turned to face him and found him studying her, curious, gentle. "I feel less alone out here with Mary than I do among the men sometimes."

Jane nodded. "I know. I feel the same about the kitchens."

"They're good men, but they don't always understand. They don't always see me. You're different, Jane." His fingers grazed hers. "You can always come out here, you know. If you don't want to feel alone."

"Bran said he'd bring me," Jane demurred, "when I want to come."

His eyes were a challenge. "Bran doesn't have to bring you. You're your own woman, aren't you? Have your own thoughts, your own feelings?"

Jane swallowed, and it turned into a gulp, and she was immediately ashamed. She tried to pretend it was a laugh. "Well, I don't have my own horse," she said, and was relieved to see him smile at the joke.

"You see so much, Jane. You're not a stupid girl. Tell me . . ." And now he was closer to her than was strictly proper, like he had been that day when he had asked her to open Sir Richard's door. She could smell him, almost taste him on the tip of her tongue. "What do you see in Bran?"

"In Bran?" She laughed, startled. "You mean . . . you mean because we . . ."

"Because you're bedding him." His mouth twitched. Her face was on fire. "You're not just bedding him out of boredom, are you? Not a smart girl like you."

What if I am? she thought wildly, recklessly. A part of her, somewhere deep down, considered whether it might be true. Bran wanted her, and he cared for her, and he made her laugh, made her world fill up with light like a night full of stars. But she was too smart to fall in love like a fool, to have expectations, to get trapped by her loins and her heart. A dalliance was a simple thing. A husband could wreck your life.

At least, Jane had thought she was too smart, until Robin, who pulled at her like the wind pulled at torches. Robin was the one who made her feel like a fool. Robin could wreck her life, if she wasn't careful.

Jane stood, flapping her wrists uselessly, as if she didn't know what to do with any of the limbs on her body. "Well," she stammered as Robin moved even closer, and she realized suddenly that he was tall, almost as tall as Bran. He towered over Jane, his shadow hanging over hers like an embrace. "Bran is kind, and steady and warm, and he never lets his temper go . . ."

"So he's safe, then?" Robin asked in a whisper, and as he said it, Jane realized it was true, and that Robin had read her as easily as she could read anyone else. Fear and excitement gripped her at once as he shifted behind her, his mouth near the top of her head, his breath moving her hair like a breeze, his hand dangling beside hers. She couldn't hide things from him. She saw that now. Not like she could from other people. And if he saw this about her, could he also see . . .

"And what do you see in me?" he murmured from behind her left shoulder, his arm brushing her flank, fingers grazing her wrist again, ever so gently, dancing across the skin, almost too light a touch to feel.

But she felt it. Oh, did she feel it, and a wave of heat ran through her.

Jane coughed a little, stumbled, turned the side of her face to him, too shy to look him fully in the eye. He brushed her hair aside and ran his fingers down her cheek. His other hand closed around her wrist, and as he moved his lips to her jawline, Jane thought her heart would seize right then and there, and she'd be found dead, turned to a puddle of water by Robin's breath.

His lips on her ear, soft and warm. "I know you see me, Jane. See me more than anyone ever has. So what do you see in me?"

"I . . ." She was turning to him, her lips about to graze his, because what did it matter now, now that he had come so close, when a shout rang out from the woods and they both jumped.

Robin moved backward, eyes on her, steady as a cat on the hunt.

"Oy, there you are!" Little John bellowed at them. "Thought you'd been eaten by wolves, the both of you!"

"Jane's just come to round me up." Robin was all smoothness, his voice loud and confident with the lie. Jane suddenly wished the ground would swallow her.

"There might just be enough wine left for you, if you hurry," John said, walking a few yards away from them, far enough from the shrine for decency, but not for privacy. "Now, get out of here." He loosened his trousers, and Jane gasped shyly, turning her head. "I've got to piss."

Jane started to leave, only to feel Robin beside her again. "Bran didn't come to find you," he murmured as he brushed by her, hand touching hers with another sparking shock. "And he didn't stand up for you. Remember that." And then Robin was gone, melted back into the woods, and the only thing Jane could think to do was follow him back to the fire.

Chapter Twelve

J ane stood alone at the threshold of the old house. That was
how she had already begun to think of it, she realized—"the
old house." And why not? Hugh's wife, Phillipa, had died
at Easter, and not a week later, Sibyl had sent word to King's
Houses—through a hired messenger, as if money no longer mattered to her—that she had moved into town, and that Jane ought
to come and fetch her things before the woods or bandits or God
knew what else came to claim them. Her brothers wouldn't come,
Jane knew. Ralf had left little behind when he joined Peter in
Newark-on-Trent, and Adam seemed to want nothing from his
old life if it didn't fit perfectly into his new one. To Peter's mind,
and Adam's, and maybe even Ralf's, Jane and Sibyl—who had
fed and clothed them for most of their lives—had only weighed
them down.

The house was on the edge of the forest, so it had never been
bright, but it seemed especially dark now, eerily silent. The hearth
was cold, clogged full of gray ash, the abandoned poker stained
white beside it. A steady drip came from the roof, pattering beside
the desolate hearth like the long, slow melt of snow in early spring.

It was making a mess of the floor, and a few leaves had fallen in too. They must have been bright green before they drifted inside, but now they were brown with rot.

The Crowe family furniture, such as it was, still lingered: the cast-off chairs, the crooked table. The table had seemed so large when Jane was a child, but it looked tiny now. Like furniture for children. Hugh would have better, surely—and likely more than one fire in the house, so that the cold never touched him. Her mother's straw bed was tucked behind the crumbling daub and twig panel her father had built for privacy. Some of Sibyl's things would be there, anything that was too poor for her now, but Jane decided she wasn't even going to look. It wasn't as if her waiflike mother's clothes would fit her. They would all be too short at the ankles, too tight at the waist.

The only thing left was to check her conserves. Surely Sibyl had taken those with her—why waste good food? But Jane climbed to the storage loft with a feeling of foreboding. And sure enough, her pots were abandoned, white mold coating the oldest ones. The strawberry and rose pots she had left to sweeten would be close to going off, if they hadn't already. If they were still good, they could be sold. But what was she supposed to do: bundle them up and carry them back on her horse, praying they wouldn't break? What could Master Eudo possibly do with potted fruit on the verge of spoiling? And the coin her conserves might bring at market was nothing compared to the wages she'd miss if she skipped a kitchen day to sell them.

Jane decided to abandon them, pots and all. The whole morning had been a waste, like a visit to a graveyard hoping to speak to the dead. She felt foolish for coming. Despite Sibyl's cold message, Jane realized some part of her had expected to see her mother sitting at the table just the way she had when John Crowe left, crying that it hadn't worked out with Hugh after all, that he had tossed her over like all the others had, and that she had been a fool. Jane had been prepared to tell her not to worry, that her pay from the kitchens would support them both. That *she* would help keep Sibyl fed and warm and free from having to please a man.

But that wasn't what had happened, was it? Hugh had kept his promise to marry Sibyl, and Jane's mother had forsaken her old life with glee, as if her years with Jane had meant nothing. And Jane knew better than to try to visit her mother in Mansfield. Sibyl wouldn't want any reminders of where she came from, not when she could play the caring new wife comforting a grieving widower. Sibyl would spin her story in a way that made her look like a hero, and she would come to believe that the lie was true simply because it favored her.

Jane felt suddenly restless, as if the old house were crashing down around her and she needed to run anywhere, to anything, in order to be free of it—free from the dust and the mold and her rotting conserves, from the old anger and sorrow that threatened to crush her. She should return Moll to Bran now that she had no use for her, but she didn't want to go back to the kitchens, where she would disappear again, just another mouse scurrying underneath the nobles' feet, as easily forgotten as she had been here at home. And she wasn't dressed for town. She'd ridden out wearing a tunic and stockings and her brother's old boots, and Emmie had mocked her for wearing "boy's clothes," but they were just peasant clothes. Jane had worn them every day of her life, unless she was going to market or to worship. She wondered how Emmie had come up so differently, thinking she was some kind of fine lady when her family fed themselves with their hands in the dirt just as Jane's had.

There was only one place Jane really wanted to go, she admitted to herself. One place she could feel like she mattered to someone. Robin had told her she could come out to the Greenwood whenever she wanted. *Bran doesn't have to bring you*, he had said. *You're your own woman, aren't you? Have your own thoughts, your own feelings?*

Just thinking of seeing Robin, standing with him under the shelter of trees again, hearing the breeze rattle Mary's seashells, made Jane sick with longing, like a great rope in the center of her chest were pulling her out into the woods. It wasn't lust, she told herself. It was the spark that Robin had awakened within her, like a tiny, glowing ember in a hearth full of ashes. For Robin had taught her to hope. To hope that something in her life could be more, that *she* could be more than she had ever been before. It was as if she had spent her whole life in a dimly lit cellar, surrounded by dust and spiderwebs, breathing stale air, until all of a sudden, Robin had told her to look up—and there, shining overhead, almost close enough for her to touch, was the sun.

Before Jane could let her racing heart dissuade her, she leapt onto Moll and urged her north. She thought of all the nights in her long, dark room at King's Houses, where she slept surrounded by the soft snoring of other girls, secretly remembering the heat of Robin's lithe body as he stood behind her, the touch of his hand, his lips brushing her jaw. She flushed and tugged Moll to a stop, her courage faltering at the sight of the trees that marked Robin's camp. Was she lying to herself, just as Sibyl had? Was she telling herself grand stories when her heart was after something base, something treacherous?

But it was too late for Jane to turn back, for there was a stirring in the trees. Whoever the lookout was had already seen her.

"Who goes there?"

Jane's heart lurched. It was Robin himself.

She grasped frantically for an excuse to have come to the Greenwood all alone. Last week, she had sent word through Bran that one of the monks of Saint Mary's Abbey, Brother Godric, was back at King's Houses. He had filled his face with ale and revealed that the abbot was trying to overturn the reeve's judgment and take Sir Richard's lands again. Had anything happened since then that she could pass on? But her mind had frozen stiff, and she could think of nothing as Robin emerged from the trees.

They stared at each other in silence, Jane astride Moll, whose hooves jostled nervously, Robin with his green-lined cloak billowing around him in the wind, rustling with the leaves, as though he were part of the forest. Jane thought from his silence and the wary look on his face that he might be angry with her for coming, and she cursed herself again, flush with humiliation.

But Robin's expression shifted from puzzlement to delight. "Jane! Is everything well?"

Jane scrambled for an explanation. "I . . . yes, m'lord," she stammered, the words coming out far too quickly. "I had a free day, and I was nearby, and I thought . . . I thought I might find Bran here." She could have kicked herself then. What if Bran really *was* here? What if she had been wrong about his plans? What would he say if he found out she had ridden off to see Robin alone?

"Is that what he told you when he loaned you that horse?"

Robin's words hit her like an arrow to the chest. He knew she had spun a story, but what was left for Jane to do besides keep spinning? "I thought he might have got done early, is all, and I was just at my old house, which is close . . ."

Robin grinned at her stumbling and held out a hand, gallantly, to help her down from her horse. "You're always welcome here, Jane. You don't need a reason. It's a sanctuary for you, just as it is for us." She took his hand, so grateful he had saved her from herself that she could have wept. His palm felt hot, but his fingers cold, as if from nerves. Of course, her own hand was as soggy as a wet fish, from the ride and from the overwhelming sense of her own stupidity.

"You've come on a very special day, Jane." Robin steadied her with a hand on the small of her back, sending a charge through her. He held her eyes as he always did—but his smile was slow, almost predatory. "Are you ready for a game today, Jane? Is that why you're here?"

The air went out of her. "What d'you mean?"

His look was knowing and intimate enough to make her ankles weak. Her breath shortened. Did he know the truth of what had driven her here? Did he see her as a harlot, like her mother?

Then his eyes widened, like he was sharing a secret. "You must always be ready for adventure, Jane, now that you're one of us." He drew away then, his hand gone from her body, his eyes turning back to the woods as he tied Moll's reins to a tree, and she felt like she could breathe again. She was being foolish. Of course that wasn't what Robin had meant. What was she thinking? She tried to turn her words to other matters as he studied the trees, searching for something.

"Is it true that Sir Richard hasn't repaid you?" she asked, for Bran had complained of it the last time they were together.

Robin laughed. "'Tis true, though I told him not to trouble

himself. Sir Richard has turned to charity, I fear. He was never meant to be an outlaw. Not like us."

"Won't you miss the coin?"

"I'll get it back my own way." Robin was still peering through the trees. Jane's relief at being out from under his stare was turning into discomfort. "Our good Sir Richard is raising up poor men to be his yeomen, giving them fine swords and clothes and bread and ale. It's a worthy cause, and I'd rather get the coin from someone else. Someone who would spend it ill."

"It sounds like he's raising an army," Jane said, her eyes trying to follow Robin's into the woods.

Robin turned away from whatever quarry he was hunting to examine her. "Perhaps he is, at that. I hadn't thought of it, I'll admit. But should his case go wrong, he'll fight for his home. He won't lose it again, not if there's a chance that blood could save what coin would not." He strode close to her then, shockingly close, and studied her face. "You're a wise one, Jane. Like the crow you're named for, hovering above us, seeing us all run around like rats."

She screwed up her face, trying not to laugh. "I'm a crow, am I? I thought I was a field mouse."

"Perhaps you've risen with the turn of the sun. Or . . ." His eyes burned into her, and she tried to stare at his nose. It was pointed at the tip, like an arrowhead. "Or perhaps I missed the full sight of you, at first. Perhaps you were too much to see all at once, like one of the old gods. Do you know about the ancient goddess of wisdom, Jane?"

She shook her head and finally forced herself to meet his blazing stare. The blacks of his eyes had gone wide, like a stalking cat's, almost swallowing the green.

"Minerva, they called her. Goddess of wisdom and war."

"Goddess of war?" Jane asked softly, conscious of her breath, and of his, and of the way their breaths mingled in the small space between them. "Am I to wield a spear, then, like some kind of Amazon?"

His hand reached for her cheek, but instead of touching it, he brushed a stray hair away from her eyes. It must have flown everywhere from riding, she realized. She fought the urge to smooth it herself.

"Minerva whispered to men, telling them of the world's secrets, of their own strengths and their enemies' weaknesses, which only she could see. She, and the other old gods"—his finger traced a line through the sweat-damp hair behind her ear, making her tremble—"sent birds to inspire their heroes."

"Like robins?" Jane asked, trying to keep things light, trying to keep herself from being devoured by his gaze.

"Like crows." He dropped his hand gently, grazing a knuckle across her jaw. "But there's no time for old tales now. Do you hear that?" He stepped away from Jane, leaving her bereft, as though she stood over a yawning pit. "Horses, in the distance. He's almost here."

Jane gave him a smile that she hoped looked wise, like an ancient goddess. "Who's almost here?"

"Our special guest, of course!" Robin whispered, his eyes teasing.

"Shall I go, then?" She glanced down at her boyish tunic and stockings, her old boots. "I'm hardly dressed for guests."

"Oh, you're nearly perfect. But whether you stay or go is entirely up to you." His eyes challenged her, measured her.

"Well, I guess it depends." Jane tried to keep the nerves from her voice. "What kind of person is coming? Is it someone who shouldn't see me?"

"Well . . ." Robin mocked her voice by making his higher. "I guess it depends." Jane found herself suddenly irritated. He'd been acting like a lover, wooing her, and now he was behaving like one of her brothers. Perhaps he saw the look on her face, for he dropped his voice again. "What kind of person are *you*, Jane? Are you a crow in truth? Or are you just a mouse, waiting to be snatched into the sky and swallowed up?"

The horses' hooves grew louder now. Soon, it would be too late to run.

More noises came from the woods: crashing feet and laughter, and then a baleful moan. Robin tore off his cloak and thrust it into her hands. "Put this on, little crow," he said with a sly grin. "Keep your hood up. And cover your face." He started off in the direction of the noises. "Follow when you're ready."

Her heart racing, Jane tossed her own cloak into her saddlebag and draped Robin's over herself, bathing in his scent: woodsmoke and sweet leaves and sweat. She shivered, and not from the cold. She had a plain scarf with her to keep her head warm when she rode out to her house in the morning chill, and she tied it around her face the way John had done when they ambushed the reeve, tethering the too-large hood into place and covering everything but her eyes. Her heart thudded. It wouldn't be the shire reeve again, would it? Jane didn't think she could face that kind of confrontation again.

When she caught up to Robin, she heard John, angry and shouting. "I told you this was a fool idea! You ought to finish it here and be done with it."

"Where's the fun in that?" Robin was teasing him with the same voice he'd used to provoke Jane.

"I'll shove your fun up your . . ." John turned as Jane wandered up, shuffling her feet loudly to make sure they didn't think she was spying on them. "Oh, piss on the devil! *She's* here?" John's face shifted between anger and disgust, so vehement that Jane nearly staggered backward and fled into the woods. "As if this plan wasn't fool enough!"

"What's wrong? Do you mean to be a miser with our feast, old man?" Robin asked, but he was grinning. "Jane, did I tell you we're having a feast?"

"Stuff your feast, you right arse!" John stomped off, grumbling foul curses.

"Is something wrong?" Jane asked, her voice muffled by the scarf. "Are you sure I shouldn't go back to King's Houses?"

"It's too late for that now." Robin, sounding gleeful, put a finger to his lips to quiet her. "The game's afoot, and it's time for us to play it. If you're brave enough."

"Brave enough for what?"

He leaned in, his eyes glittering, and he thrust something into her hand. "Take this," he said. "Keep it close." And then he was gone, and Jane found herself staring at a long, thin knife, polished silver and engraved with interlocking knots, the hilt circled by strange serpents that looked as if they might swallow the blade. Its handle was worn. It had been held—*he* had held it—time and time again. And now he had put it into her hands. But for what?

Jane stumbled after Robin. She emerged from the cover of the trees to see a group of men—Mooch, Wyll, Tuk, and someone else. Someone with his hands and feet bound, wearing a long cowl. A monk's cowl.

And Jane was glad for the mask, and for the cloak, and for everything that hid her face and muffled her voice, for she gasped aloud when she finally realized who their "guest" was. Right there at her feet, trussed up like a Christmas pig, his eyes wide with fear, was Brother Godric, the very same monk she had served salt herring to at King's Houses the day before.

Chapter Thirteen

The men had gagged Brother Godric with filthy cloth. A rope around his torso bound his arms, crushing his shoulders together. A bruise bloomed over his left eye. His habit was shoved up over knobby ankles, another rope around his calves. His legs, bared to the cold, were scattered with curling black hairs and bloody scrapes. He was so unsteady from his bindings that they'd had to prop him up against a tree to keep him from rolling onto his side.

Jane reeled. She tried to slow her breathing and detach herself. As if it didn't involve her. As if she weren't at fault. But Robin never would have known the monk was visiting if it hadn't been for her. He would never have known about the abbot's plans either. The information she'd been feeding Robin for weeks had led to this moment, to Brother Godric brutalized and humiliated. He was a man of God, and he was here under their rough care, being treated like a common criminal—all because of her.

Jane wondered, as fear pressed her heart against her chest bones, if God would punish her for this. She hadn't thought much about heaven or hell before. She thought if she said her prayers and didn't sin too much, everything would probably be well. She had never done anything important enough to need proper penance. Until now.

Jane squirmed, thankful for the mask and cloak, though the smell of Robin's sweat and musk, so pleasing before, was beginning to stifle her. She whispered a prayer to Mary under her breath, thinking of Her portrait under the forest canopy, surrounded by seashells and treasures. There must be a reason for all this, some kind of plan. Perhaps Jane was being punished for her lustful feelings for Robin. Perhaps none of this would have happened if she hadn't ridden out here like a hare driven mad by springtime.

Jane tried to calm herself. If she panicked—if Robin and his men saw her panic—well, they claimed to be her friends, but they were also men with swords and knives and secrets. She had to prove her stomach and her steel. She was not sure if they were planning to kill the monk, but they had hurt him, and if they were willing to do all this to a man of God, what would any of them care about a servant?

Little John glowered beside Brother Godric, looming like a beastly giant. Mooch was masked like she was, and so was Wyll, but Robin, Tuk, and John went barefaced. It worried Jane. Whatever they were going to do to the monk, they didn't expect his vengeance.

"Free his tongue," Robin said to Tuk, who bent down and removed the cloth from the monk's mouth. "Let's hear what he has to say for himself."

The monk shook his head like a wet dog, gasping and spitting out threads. "I know you from somewhere," he said to Tuk. "Sir Richard's Saracen." He wiped his mouth on his shoulder, brown eyes shot with red, but defiant. "Is this how the knight proves his chivalry? Rounding up holy men to torment?"

Robin knelt in front of him, soft mockery in his voice. "My good monk, you're hardly holy, are you? Not a man as well-fed and wine-sodden as yourself."

Robin's face, his eerily calm smile, seemed to make the monk more cautious, his anger dampening in a draft of icy fear. "Look," he stammered, "you can tell Sir Richard I've nothing to do with the abbot's plans. And I've no power to stop him. In fact, I've . . ."

"Little monk," Robin said, tapping Brother Godric rudely on his nose, as if he were an errant child, "you're giving your secrets away too soon. Don't go spoiling the game."

John groaned audibly.

"Dine with us first, and hear our case, before you judge us simple blades for hire." Robin sprang to his feet, leaving the monk stuttering. "For I am no one's man, and certainly not Sir Richard's. Sir Richard is chivalrous, and noble-hearted, and good. He would never give me leave to do something like *this*."

Robin's back was to the monk, so he couldn't see all the color flee the man's face. But Jane could.

"Something like what?" the monk rasped, all heat gone from his voice. "Who in the hell are you?"

"Hear that blasphemy?" Wyll scoffed. "Holy man, indeed. They're all the same, ain't they, Master? Bunch of liars and users who sin as easily as breathing."

"What do you want from me?" the monk asked. "Is it coin you want? Are you just common bandits?"

Wyll bent down and slapped the man's face, a sharp crack

with his thin hand, and Jane nearly jumped out of her boots. "Watch your tongue, monk!"

"Now, now, Wyll Scathlock," Robin said. "That's no way to treat our guest." John's face reddened, rage flickering across his bent brows, for Robin had given the monk Wyll's name. His full one. John's warning rang in Jane's mind: *You ought to finish it here and be done with it.* A wave of nausea rose in her, and she struggled against it, rocking in her boots to steady herself as if she were standing on a rickety boat. Robin wouldn't really bend to John's plan, would he? They wouldn't murder a man in cold blood, alone out here in the forest? If that was Robin's game, why would he draw it out for so long?

If I were truly an ancient goddess, she thought desperately, *and I could whisper in Robin's ear, I'd tell him to stop all this. I'd tell him to get out of Sherwood and run as fast and as far as he could, until a dozen forests stood between his body and the law.*

The woods were taut with silence, as if even the birds were waiting to see what would happen. Just when Jane considered running away, wondering if she might be shot in the back as she fled, Robin bowed to the monk, sweeping his arms wide. "On my word, monk, I mean what I have said. Won't you join us for a meal, and some wine? If you are a true man and an honest one, we might be able to help each other."

Godric's face stilled. He had seen a door open up, a way out, one that depended on the cleverness of his tongue. His cheeks warmed with sudden hope. "Well"—he let out a false, shaky laugh, as though he wanted them to think he were completely at ease while strapped to a tree like a rebellious hound—"you can hardly expect me to eat and drink with my hands tied."

"Of course not!" Robin nodded at Wyll. "Free him from his

bonds, Wyll. I'll bring him a bowl for washing. Mooch," he said, and Mooch winced at the use of his name, even though it was merely a nickname, "bring the bread, the cheese, the wine."

"This is a bad idea," John grumbled under his breath, but loud enough for everyone to hear. Jane stood wishing she could disappear into the shadows. What would Robin call on her to do? And would he call her Jane, as he was naming all the others? If he did, her job at King's Houses was ruined for certain. Brother Godric couldn't see her face, but he would know her name. He would remember everything about this moment in the woods, all the names and all the faces he could see, and everything he suffered.

"This monk is no threat to us," Robin said. "Isn't that right, good monk? And if I'm wrong, our arrows are surely faster than his feet. Little John," he called, "bring over that basin so our guest can wash."

John growled at the use of his name, and Jane nearly sighed aloud as well. Until suddenly, she realized that when Robin spoke, he wasn't looking at John at all. Wasn't even speaking to him, in fact.

Instead, Robin was looking directly at *her*.

"The bowl, John," he said to Jane again. "And make haste."

Jane stared dumbstruck from under her hood. The real Little John's eyes widened now that he had caught on to Robin's trick, and he looked so indignant that she thought he might burst out and claim his name back.

"Little John." The monk laughed at her as if he and Robin had become fast friends. "He is a wee one, isn't he?"

"Don't let that fool you," Robin warned. "He's quick with a sword in your gullet, even if his mind is a bit on the slow side. *Now*, John!" he snapped.

Shaking herself into action, Jane sprinted over to the wash basin that Mooch had left alongside a spread of fresh cheese, early spring berries, and hard bread. She lifted the basin and carried it over to the monk, setting it before his feet, trying to bend as a man would rather than a woman, crooked and awkward rather than graceful, letting her sleeves fall over her hands to hide them, praying that the monk couldn't see how much she was shaking, how the water sloshed about in the basin as though it were an angry sea.

"Thank you, my good man," the monk said. Jane backed away as quickly as she could, worried he'd notice something if she got too close, something that would give her away.

When he finished washing the blood and dirt off his hands, Brother Godric poured the water over his head, letting it run through the mud and blood as if he were a barn animal. Jane handed him a clean cloth from the pile beside the food. The monk wiped his face clear and grinned at her. "Quiet one too, eh?"

"It's a sad story, it is," Robin said gravely, but he winked at Jane as the monk wiped his face again, then pulled his face grim and serious when Godric could see him. "The law cut out his tongue."

The monk lost all the color he had gained. "My . . . my God, I . . ." He stared rapidly between Robin and Jane, stricken, and Wyll and Tuk had to turn their heads to keep from laughing.

Jane's face burned behind her mask. Tears stung her eyes, suddenly, stupidly, as if it had really happened. She truly had become a fool. What would Bran say if he were here? He'd tease her mercilessly about this. He'd probably say he wished it were true whenever she scolded him, and that thought just angered her more.

But Robin shrugged as if he were speaking of a lost lock of hair. "'Tis a trying life, monk, outside of your abbeys and your castles and your manors. But we in the forest still know how to feast, tongues or no." Jane had been so afraid that she only just now noticed the smell of roasted meat, seeping in through her mask and through the blood she'd drawn worrying her cheek in an effort not to speak, as though she could sever her tongue with her teeth and make Robin's words true.

"This is a fine feast indeed for forest men." The monk tore off a hearty hunk of bread.

"Take what you will of food and wine, monk," said Robin. "Consider it payment for your rough journey here." They ate in silence, at first, Jane pulling her scarf down but keeping her face turned away from Godric. She could barely stomach anything more than a bit of cheese and bread. Mostly, she drank wine, until the sharp edges of the day began to scatter and blur.

Once the monk had a few mouthfuls and a good guzzle of wine, Robin asked, "Where is your abbey, monk, when you're at home?"

"Saint Mary's," the monk began. "Though that doesn't mean I have the abbot's counsel . . ."

Robin blinked as though Godric's words meant nothing, but Jane could see that they meant everything. She had seen the same focused look on Robin's face when he drew his bow and hit the target in the reeve's game.

"So you're devoted to Her, then, our Blessed Mother?"

"Well, of course," the monk said. "A good and honest woman, that Mary, none of that fussing and frippery you see in women today. She knew Her duty."

"Indeed. They say that Mary knows a lie before it even dances on the tongue, and that She'll turn her head from the dishonest when they pray, for their words sting Her ears like a bee's touch."

"That's why women don't pray to Her," Brother Godric quipped, "only girls, too young to jump into men's beds and tell tales about it." He laughed heartily at his own joke, and some of Robin's men chuckled too, though no one looked Jane's way. She drank long at her cup of wine. It was quite a joke indeed, Jane thought, that this monk should talk in such glowing terms about a woman he'd never know in this life, and have so much disdain for the women he saw every day.

The monk had sensed that devotion to Mary was a topic his captor liked. "I am Mary's servant," he added, a little too eagerly, "as we all should be. I serve Her every day. I act and speak on Her behalf, in all things and in all ways."

"As do I, good monk." The mocking tone was back in Robin's voice. "And in what office do you serve Her?"

"Well"—the monk cleared his throat, suddenly embarrassed— "I'm, er . . . the abbey's high cellarer." He looked up, sheepish, as if they all knew that pouring wine for abbots was hardly service to the Virgin.

"Well, you're more than welcome here," Tuk joked, "if you bring the wine next time."

Everyone laughed except for Jane and Little John, the real one, who hadn't said a word since the meal began, as though he'd lost his tongue the same as his imposter. He had been eating little but drinking steadily, staring unkindly at Robin, and at Jane, as though they were serpents slithering around his ankles and he had a mind to strike them down.

Robin's smile rose and fell as quickly as a ripple in a pond. "I wonder what Mary thinks of men who serve Her in such differing ways. What if their services should be at odds, such as a poor man who kneads fine dough with his hands, and a wealthy man who takes the bread for taxes and hoards it within his walls? Whom do you suppose the Virgin would favor?"

The monk smeared another hunk of bread with soft cheese, but Jane could tell the question vexed him, his dark brows meeting as he struggled to understand Robin's challenge through a cloud of drink. She could also see that Robin was in the mood to toy with his prey and had just now drawn his claws. She put her own cup down, wishing suddenly for water.

"You never told me who you are." The monk asked his own question instead of answering. "Or how you serve the Maid yourself." He stuffed the bread into his mouth, a crumb lingering on his lip.

Robin's face didn't change at all, and neither did his form, seated lightly on the ground, an arm draped casually over his bent knee. "Whatever Our Lady commands of Robin Hood, She'll find a friend in him."

The monk sputtered and began coughing hard until Tuk reached over and thumped him on the back.

"You're . . ." he finally managed after a gulp of wine. "You're . . ."

"I am indeed the Lord of the Greenwood," Robin said grandly, as though he sat upon a throne and not on soil and stones. "Welcome to my kingdom."

"I just . . ." The monk's voice turned gritty, food still clogging his throat, and he cleared it, thumping his own chest. "Thought you weren't real, lad," he said finally. "Thought the shire reeve was after a fairy story."

"Well, here I am. Real as the spots that take a sinner. Although . . ." Robin traced a finger through the dirt, idly. "I have been wondering, lately, if I've angered Our Lady. I loaned good Sir Richard the money in Her service, and yet I haven't seen a penny of my pay. Not for months." He tilted his head to the side. "Perhaps you've brought it with you? Since you're so favored in Our Lady's gaze, and since you act and speak on Her behalf?"

Wyll grinned, finally catching on to the game. "He is from Saint Mary's Abbey, ain't he, Master?"

Anger reddened the monk's ears, and not a little bit of wounded pride, for he too had begun to see the trick. "By God's arms, lad, it's not *my* debt," he said defensively. "*I* didn't promise you anything."

"But Sir Richard swore to Mary as his surety," Robin said slowly, as though this were a solution he was just puzzling out. "And *you* are Mary's servant. Her high cellarer, in fact, who serves Her in all things and in all ways. Isn't that what you said?"

"I did." The monk frowned, and looked down, as though an answer to his predicament might be crawling somewhere among the insects and the worms. "I did, good man, but you see . . ."

"And aren't you, as a man who is kept and fed and speaks in the name of Her abbey, Her messenger, sent to act in Her name?"

"Now, look here, lad . . ."

"That's Master Robin, to you, monk," Robin said. "Only my friends have earned the right to be fond with me. And it seems you are not my friend, despite sharing my wine and bread. Are you saying you didn't come as Mary's surety, to pay me back my debt?"

"No," the monk said firmly. "No, I did not. But if you free me, I'm sure I can arrange to send . . ."

"Are you quite sure?" Robin asked. "What do you have in your saddlebags?"

"Oh," the monk said, his eyes shifty with the lie. "A few shillings."

"Well," Robin said cheerfully, "if that's all you were given for your long journey back to the abbey, *I* should be loaning *you* money." He grinned, and everyone had a laugh, except for John and Jane, who knew better. "But if there had been any more, I suppose it would rightfully be mine."

"Well"—the monk was blushing hot, he hid his lies so poorly—"I'm sorry to say my horse will have run off by now. If your men hadn't spooked her . . ."

"Oh, they caught her when they caught you. Didn't they tell you?" Robin tsked, shaking his head, and said to John, "Very unkind of you, Greenleaf, to make a man worry about his horse all through a fine meal such as this one." He pointed with his chin. "That's Reynald Greenleaf there, if he didn't introduce himself. He's rather cross today. He doesn't like errands. Or monks."

John frowned at Jane, but his anger seemed tinged with something else too, a darkening cloud of worry.

"Go on, now, Little John. Check the man's belongings and tell us true. If there's no more than a few shillings, I won't touch a penny of it. Indeed, I'll send our monk home with even more silver to spend."

Me? Jane almost sputtered, but instead she pointed to her chest and raised her eyebrows.

"Yes, you, John. And hurry. I'm sure our guest is eager for his pay."

Jane stood, her legs shaky with drink, and stumbled off to find the monk's horse. The poor thing was frightened, and probably hungry, its eyes wide and watchful. Jane clucked at it gently, soothing, copying the words Bran said when he wanted to make a horse feel safe, even when she wasn't. "Easy now." She stroked the horse's mane. "It's all right." The horse nickered, shook her head. Jane would try to bring her bread from the feast, if she could sneak it, once she had done with this.

Godric's coin purse was nowhere obvious. He was not a stupid man. But men hid things on horses—Bran had told her so. Wealthy men who wanted to travel safely would have their saddles made with little pockets for hiding treasures. She ran her hand beneath the saddle, cooing to the horse as she probed, but found nothing.

The saddlebags, perhaps? They hung on either side of the horse's flank, thick with sheep's wool and tanned hide—thicker than they needed to be, and broad. They would be heavy on the horse, and the monk was heavy too, making the whole journey slower. It was no wonder he couldn't escape John and the rest of Robin's men when they came for him.

Jane felt around the lining of the saddlebags, which bulged as if woven from stones instead of cloth. Something hid within the linen, and she didn't think it was a cluster of prayer beads. There—beneath her hand, a loose stitch, a hanging loop of thread. Jane used Robin's knife to pry open the lining. She slipped her fingers inside and found something hard to the touch. When she pulled it out, she found herself holding a full coin purse. So here was where the monk hid his money.

Jane peeked inside and gasped. Surely this was more than a few shillings' worth. And her knuckles had knocked against something beside it. Could there be two purses hidden in the saddlebags—or more?

Jane pulled the bags off the horse, opening each one and placing the monk's belongings gently on the ground: fresh underclothes, a jug of wine, and an ornate gold chalice that would pay much of Robin's debt on its own. Once she had emptied the bags, Jane went at the thread with Robin's knife some more, curiosity burning her as she loosened the stitches.

Purses upon purses. The monk's saddlebags were lined with coin. She could have taken that coin, and the horse, and ridden off into some other county and lived like a duchess, if she'd had the blood for it. The sight of all that silver in one man's traveling bags put things right in Jane's mind. How could she ever have doubted Robin? Wasn't it clear, right here in front of her, just what kind of treachery he was fighting, and who he was fighting for? The paltry leavings at her old house, the rotting conserves and the moldy floor, the sagging roof and walls, the thin garden she had scraped for winter food: that was the whole of her life. All she had known. And here was a monk she bent her head to, a man whose cup she filled, carrying enough to feed her and her brothers for ten lifetimes in his saddlebags. Hiding it. For himself, and for his own brothers, these men who claimed to give up everything for God.

And Brother Godric had the nerve to call women liars.

Jane was still fuming when she heard her name—or, rather, John's name—shouted from the clearing where the men were finishing their meat, draining the wine. Robin was summoning her back. Godric must be sweating rivers, unless he thought her too fool to find his coin, which he probably did. And why not? Her kind were all fools, weren't they? Bowing and scraping to men of God who hoarded the silver from their levies, riding it all over England hidden on their horses. She had been cross with Wyll for the vile way he talked about the clergy, but everything he'd said was true, wasn't it? Perhaps not about low clergy like her brother, but about the higher ones, the ones who walked on rose petals and sat on thrones of gold. She thought angrily about the way she had worked so hard to make sure Adam could take his vows, and about how hard *he* had worked, bending to the will of greedy men like Godric and Father Simon because everyone believed that God had chosen them to rule.

Jane was surprised at the fire inside herself. But it helped her feel more like Little John, the man she was supposed to be that day. The disguise freed her, in a way. The rage she'd had to stuff down as Jane the servant, who had to show a pleasing face, could burn behind the safety of her mask, and no one would think less of her. Not among Robin and his men.

Jane stormed back to camp and took pleasure in watching the monk's eyes leap to the saddlebag slung over her shoulder, the jug of wine and the gold chalice in her hands. She delighted in making him skittish as a mouse, just as he was when Robin revealed his name. Jane had that power now, the power to make a man lose his courage, and she felt it like a surge of lightning.

She allowed herself a luxurious moment of anticipation, her eyes meeting Robin's, seeing the warmth there, seeing the approval. And then she upended the saddlebag onto the cloth they had laid down for the monk and the others to dine on, just as Sir Richard had done at the abbot's table. The monk's purses broke open in a thunderstorm of coins.

Robin's men watched in reverent silence until the last coin tumbled off the cloth, into the grass. Jane dropped the empty saddlebag and crossed her arms over her chest, looming over the monk as though she were Little John indeed.

Wyll whistled. "That'll be Sir Richard's debt there, Master, sure as Mother Mary sent it Herself."

The monk looked up at Jane in horror. "How did you . . . ?" he started, his voice a hoarse whisper.

"Little John sees what's hidden," Robin said. "He's good at ferreting out men's secrets, aren't you, John? Like a crow watching for his prey."

The real John snorted in disgust. Jane couldn't speak, so she met Robin's eyes again and smiled behind her mask.

Godric struggled to explain around the dryness in his throat. "Look, my good man," he started. "This isn't my coin, you understand? These are taxes, collected from Mansfield. This coin goes to the abbey. To the church. To Mary's own cause! You wouldn't steal from the Holy Mother, would you?"

Robin crouched down in front of the monk, close enough to Jane's leg that she could feel his warmth. "And just what does the abbey use the coin for, good monk?"

"For . . . for charity!" the monk sputtered, but he had a tell, the monk did, and that was in the fiery flush around his throat.

"I want to believe you," Robin said softly, "but you've proven yourself untrue. You lied about your coin. You took my meat and my bread, but you're a sour guest indeed, your tongue heavy with falsehoods. So how can I believe you about such a thing as this, when you've so much cause to be untrue again, caught like a rat in a kitten's paws? How do I know those coins won't go to fattening your waist, filling your cellar with fine wine? Is that how you serve our Holy Queen? Shouldn't you hope to restore Her good name, and Her virtue, rather than see it besmirched by debt?"

"It's not my debt!" the monk shouted, but he knew it was over now. He knew that whatever game he thought he could play to manipulate Robin, he had already lost.

"And now"—Robin rose—"it is not your coin. It belongs to

Mary, as you have said, and Mary is an honest woman, a true one, as you have also said. And so I shall serve as Her knight, and count Her debt repaid, as courtesy demands. Mooch, fill our cups with the good monk's wine," he said. "By the token Mary has sent me today, I'll lend any worthy man my coin upon Her word."

"By Our Lady," the monk snorted, "courtesy, my arse! You could get it yourself from Sir Richard! You could forgive his debt! You can't call yourself courteous when you invite a man to dinner only to rob him. You're nothing but a glorified thief!"

Jane felt rage rise up inside her again. Who was he to call them thieves, when he rode around with all their tithings hidden in his saddlebags, jangling against a golden cup? The stolen tun of wine flashed into her memory, the beating Milo had taken for it, but it tilted her only for a moment. Robin wouldn't have taken it if he had known what would happen, she was sure. He meant it only to spit in Lord Alan's eyes, and the eyes of all the nobles. But Brother Godric *must* have known what would happen to the peasants who paid the coin he stole to gild his hall. He must have known he was starving people to fill his purse.

It seemed Brother Godric's words had angered everyone. John scowled, and Wyll raised his fist, but Robin stayed calm, merely clucking his tongue. "Now, Scathlock, he'd paint us all for churls if you strike him again, so let's not prove him right. Show him, instead, a looking glass to reflect upon his words. For he has stolen this coin from the people of Mansfield, not for Our Lady's good name, but to hoard away in his cellar. We are merely retrieving stolen goods, bringing them back to their proper place."

Jane's heart swelled. Robin had said just what she had been thinking.

"And I suppose you'll give it all back to the people, will you?" Brother Godric challenged him.

"Their coin will be well used, and in their service," Robin said, "as the church should do." He gestured grandly to the trees that surrounded them. "This is all the cellar I need, and my only castle, and you see here, good monk, my only pair of boots. Were I a thief, believe me you, I'd be better clad, for all my winnings. But here"—Robin's voice dropped—"we follow the old ways, the ways of the Greenwood. We open our hands to those who suffer and those whose hearts are true. But to liars and to hoarders and to thieves"—he clenched his hand—"we close our fists."

"And I suppose I'm free to go," the monk said dryly, "now that you've stripped me of my coin? Or are you murderers as well as thieves?"

"You mean Mary's coin," Robin corrected him. "Now that our secrets are laid bare, monk, and you have relinquished all your lies, we are equals again—your pockets as thin and empty as ours. So you might ask me for a drink, or for a favor, or you might take your horse again and leave."

Godric's emotions played across his face, Jane could see. He was wondering whether there was another game, a way to take back some of his coin. But sense got the better of him. Looking around warily, he drew himself to his feet. "That's it, then?"

"Of course." Robin bowed. "Unless you'll join us for more drinking?"

The monk snorted. "Nay, by God, I might have dined cheaper at the finest inn in Blythe." He smoothed his habit and picked up his empty saddlebags with a baleful look at Jane.

"But we can't send you off alone," Robin said, and the monk

froze. "My men will shield your eyes and guide you back to town. Can't have you sending the shire reeve here to raid my castle."

Wyll fetched the monk's horse, and he and Tuk tied the bags on for him, putting only the underclothes back in, keeping the gold chalice.

"Little John," Robin said to Jane, "bind the monk's eyes and wrists. Tightly, please. Then you and Wyll must lead him through the forest."

Jane obeyed, and Wyll took the reins once they had stuffed Brother Godric awkwardly upon his horse.

"Greet your abbot for me," Robin called as they led the horse away. "Tell him I'd be happy to have a monk buy my dinner every day!"

It was only Nones by the sun, but the woods seemed to darken faster than the sky, shadows crawling around them. Wyll's face was unusually blank, blank as Robin's could be when he had a game up his sleeve.

"Robin Hood," Godric said, his voice trembling. "Never thought I'd see his face. They tell stories of him at the abbey, they do, like he's a demon in the night."

Jane frowned. Surely the monks and their stories had it wrong. They were just angry for being robbed, weren't they, and hoping to make Robin look like the one in the wrong. But a little worm of doubt gnawed at her navel. She thought of her own anger, the way she had felt when she found Brother Godric's hidden coin. Some part of her worried that if she'd been the real Little John, large and powerful and hidden in the forest, she might have put her own hands around the monk's throat and . . .

"I s'pose you said the right prayers, then," Wyll quipped. "For this time, the demon spared you."

"I suppose I did," Godric said. "Or is it that you two villains have brought me out into the woods to kill me off quietly, where your master doesn't have to stain his hands?"

Jane stilled, her own hands suddenly sweating.

"Robin ordered you safely home, monk. And so, you'll be safe," Wyll said.

"And if he'd ordered otherwise?" Godric asked.

"Change your ways"—Wyll grinned—"and you'll never need to find out." They reached a clear path, and Wyll pulled the horse to a halt. He looped the reins around a tree trunk. "Stay here," he ordered Brother Godric. "I need a word with Little John."

"As if I could go anywhere." Godric raised his bound hands.

Wyll led Jane far enough away that the monk wouldn't hear them. "Can you find your way back?"

Jane nodded. "Yes, but . . ."

Wyll cut her off. "Go back to camp, then. It'll be faster if I ride with him, get him farther off track."

Jane looked at him uncertainly. "Wyll, you wouldn't . . ."

"Wouldn't what?" A slow smile crawled across Wyll's face. "Worried about the monk, now, are you?"

"I just mean . . ." Jane's voice shook. "He'll get home safely, won't he?"

He studied her. "My mother always told me, *Little John*, not to ask questions I didn't want answered."

"But Robin wouldn't . . ."

"Robin told me to send the monk home. But if he'd told me otherwise, I would do what he said. And if he'd told me nothing at all, but it was what would keep him safe, I would do that too. That's loyalty." Wyll's eyes darkened, thick brows pressing to-gether. "You'll have to choose who you're true to—the broken old church, or the Greenwood's lord. We've got no room for cowards here."

He stepped toward her as he spoke, menace in his eyes, and she stepped back, her heart thumping in fear. "Of course," she said softly. "Robin knows best."

"That he does, and you'd best not forget it. Now, go on back, before it gets dark," he warned her with a smirk. "All manner of bandits and brigands in these woods. Anything could happen."

Jane watched Wyll stalk back to Brother Godric and mount up behind him on the horse, and she kept her eyes on them until they disappeared into the trees. Robin had played his own trick that day, a game he played with honor, and with justice. But she was sure that if John and Wyll Scathlock had their way, Brother Godric would have lost far more than just his coin and his cup to the Greenwood.

Chapter Fourteen

Jane wiped her face with her scarf, sweating despite the clouds that had tumbled in, spoiling the warm day. The best thing to do, she told herself as she walked back to camp, was to make her excuses and get back to King's Houses before the sun went down. She and Emmie could have a laugh about the scraps her mother had left her at the old place and the airs she was putting on in town, or she might curl up against Bran in the stables like she used to, watching firelight dance across his chest through the whorls of burnished hair. She might even hear word of Godric's safe return; surely he wouldn't ride all the way to Saint Mary's now, not with his empty saddlebags and bruised body. He would return to King's Houses, and he would heal, Jane would play the servant girl again, and no one would be the wiser.

When she returned to camp, Robin grinned and raised his cup to her, and it flashed gold in the dim forest light: it was the chalice she had taken from the monk. "You were brilliant, Jane!" he called to her. "A sharp arrow among dullards."

Jane blushed at his praise, even more so when Tuk raised his own cup and Mooch gave her a small, guilty smile. John wouldn't even look at her, though, and everyone was strangely quiet after Robin's words. She knew that sort of silence, like a still pool waiting to be shattered by a rock. They had been talking about her while she was gone.

"Wyll sent me back," she said awkwardly, her voice tiny as a mouse's squeak.

"Then he's the first one out here to show any sense," John snapped, and he looked at her then, finally, with a question in his eyes that she didn't know how to answer.

"Come now"—Robin thrust the monk's chalice into Jane's hands—"let's have a drink to the new Little John! She's far less of a piss pot than the old one!"

"Aye!" Mooch said, relief in his eyes, glad to be back to joking. "She's slimmer, and smarter, and lighter on her feet."

"And a much better dinner guest," Tuk added.

"I've half a mind to keep her," Robin said with a bold smile at Jane, one that made her skin turn to sparks and fire.

"And what would our Bran say about that?" The heat was high in John's face now, his great fists clenching. "You picking at his table while he's off doing favors for you?"

"John!" Jane's words burst out in a flash of shame, and she spoke as if she were scolding one of her brothers. "That's not what Robin meant!"

John stood up, brushing off his clothes. "He'll play you for a fool, girl, just you wait. The Lord of the Greenwood is a thief of coin, and of hearts. He only wants what another man has. Once he knows you're his, he'll be as cruel to you as he is to me, and you'll be ruined for anything else."

Robin rose to his feet, sleek and quick as a weasel, and Tuk straightened, making his shoulders broader, his cloak drifting over

Jane's knees as if to shield her. "Come now, old boy," Tuk said, his voice smooth but cold as a blade. "Are you so sore that she's stolen your name? Never known you to get your blood up over a jest."

"He's right, John." Robin eyed him. "'Tis only a jest. Leave the girl be, or I really will replace you with someone more agreeable."

John whirled on Robin, alarmingly fast for his size. "Someone who's still fooled by you, you mean. Someone too struck to see your games?"

"John, it's just a joke," Mooch said. "She doesn't want your place, or your name, or . . ."

"You witless ass!" John shouted. "Do you *really* think I'm mad about the name? She can paint my name all over her face for all I bloody care! Don't you see what he's done today? Don't any of you see? He has us drag a bloody monk into the woods—a *high* cellarer, a rich man's kin—and gives him his name, and *my* name, and *your* name"—he pointed to Mooch—"and Wyll's! And then bloody lets him go running back to the abbot, and the reeve!" John was steaming now, a towering blaze, his face pink with it. "And you're all out here drinking like children playing battles with wooden sticks while he starts a bloody war!"

"That's enough, John." Robin's voice was chill as winter.

"No," John shouted, pointing in his face, and Jane suddenly realized how much bigger he was than Robin. "I'm not finished. Do you have a *plan*, O Lord of the Greenwood, or are you just stroking your own cock and making us watch?"

Jane went cold: What would happen if John raised his fist to Robin now? What would happen to *her*?

But everything shifted as quickly as a March windstorm when

Robin hauled back and hit John in the face instead, spinning the great man's head to the side.

Robin drew his blade and held it to John's throat. "Speak to me like that again," he hissed, "and you won't live to see another bloody war."

A chill settled over the camp as Tuk, Jane, and Mooch all but turned to stone.

Somewhere, deep in the ocean of shock that had stunned Jane to stillness, she noticed the sun sinking, the daylight slipping away. She was out here alone, in the woods, with all these men. And their tempers were high, and they were deep in their cups, and Bran wasn't here to act as her guardian.

Bran. Guilt hit Jane, sharp and jagged, like a blade to her stomach. Would John tell him what he thought of her? She remembered her longing to see Robin, the almost uncontrollable force that had pulled her into the woods. God's bones, she was such a fool. What was she doing out here? This was a place where men fought with knives, and monks were robbed, and men like Wyll threatened murder. It was no place for her.

John backed away from Robin, his hands held high, blood trickling down his face. Jane had been sure he would hit Robin in turn—why wouldn't he?—but something in Robin's manner made that impossible, despite the difference in their sizes.

"That's it, then." John's voice, colder and steadier than Jane had ever heard it. "I ought to cut that pretty face of yours right off. But the reeve'll do it for me, and the blood will be on his hands, and mine own will be clean for once." John picked up a satchel and swung it onto his shoulder. "And you, you fucking whoreson, will get no more blood from me."

"John," Tuk called after him as he stomped away into the trees, "at least take your share of the coin!"

"Shove it up your fucking arse!" John called back, and then he was gone.

They all looked at Robin. "What?" he snapped at them. And he too stormed off, the opposite way.

Jane let out a long, shuddering breath. "I should go," she said, even as her legs shook almost too violently to stand.

"Come now," Tuk said. "Mooch and I will see you home."

Mooch looked uneasily in the direction that Robin had gone.

"I've my horse," Jane said. "I know the way." Some part of her didn't want to tell them that she had a house nearby, that she'd be home in moments. Or what used to be home.

"Well, *I'll* ride back with you." Tuk glared at Mooch.

"Really, I don't need . . ."

"No arguments," Tuk said. "I won't have you thrown to the wolves, not after all you've done today." He helped her to her feet and followed as she trod off toward Moll, and Jane wished she could run back to King's Houses on her own, far from all of them, where no one would think the things of her that John thought. Although surely, *surely*, all of them were thinking of it now.

Tuk misinterpreted the nervous look on her face. "Look, girl, your virtue is safe with me. Robin and I go back a long way, and I'm old enough to be your father."

Jane had to laugh. "You're much nicer than my father."

"Ah, he was a fiery one, then?" Tuk said. "So you've a type."

"What do you mean? Bran's sweet as cream."

Tuk gave her a long, knowing look. "I don't mean Bran."

Jane's cheeks burned. "Don't be silly," she said, and started walking again, faster, to cover her shame. "John was talking nonsense."

"I'll say it once because I like you, Jane, and because I think you're good and kind. Heed John's words about our master." Tuk spoke softly, but with no heat in his voice at all, almost as if he were resigned. He seemed to see through Jane, right through to the ache and the yearning that she could hardly admit to herself. But she couldn't let it show on her face, couldn't let him suspect he was right, for fear it would get back to Bran, or to Robin.

"You're a grown girl," he added, "but you should have a warning. Not everything is what it seems out here in the Greenwood, if you get my meaning. Especially not . . ."

They both drew to a halt when they reached the clearing where she'd left Moll. For there stood Robin, looking bored, but also guilty, the hand he'd hit his man John with wrapped in cloth as though he were hiding something shameful.

"Speak of the devil," Tuk breathed, too quietly for Robin to hear. Then, loudly, he said, "I'll get the girl home."

Robin straightened, his eyes bright. "No need. I'll see her back," he said to Tuk, but he was looking at Jane.

Tuk's jaw twitched. "We can both go. It's safer with two than with one."

They stared at each other in a silent standoff until Jane finally burst out, "There's no need for anyone to take me. There's still enough light to ride by."

"What kind of chivalry would that be," Robin asked smoothly, "to let a damsel ride alone through the woods after dark? I'll see you home, and no more words about it. Back to camp, Tuk. Mooch needs help cleaning up."

Tuk hesitated, looking between them.

"I'll be all right," Jane said, wishing that Tuk and his knowing stare would leave her be.

"As you say." Tuk nodded, grudging, but Jane could see his face clouded as he walked away, swallowing the words he wanted to shout.

Robin smiled at Jane as if satisfied, and it made her unsure what to do or say next. So she nodded at his wrapped hand. "Does it hurt?"

He pressed it to his chest with a mocking smile. "Not so much as my heart hurts, being abandoned by my man."

"You didn't have to hit him," Jane said, more sharply than she intended.

Robin feigned surprise. "But I did! I can't have the man besmirch your honor, Jane, right there in front of my entire court. I did it for you!"

He was lying, and she knew it, and John's words, and Tuk's, came back to her in a torrent that made her fingertips go numb with anger. She took off his cloak and handed it to him, coolly. "You did not," she said. "You did it for your pride and for nothing else, and for no one else."

Surprise opened Robin's green eyes wide as windows. A light breeze whistled through the forest leaves, fresh and teasing, and Jane suddenly worried at what she had said. It was bolder than she'd ever been with him. Would he be angry? She felt acutely aware of the silence around them.

To Jane's relief, Robin smiled coyly, taking his cloak back from her. "You'll always see through me, won't you, little crow? Well, you may fill your heart with watching, and one day you'll understand what it takes to lead." He took her own cloak from her saddlebag and held it up for her to step into, as though she were a fine lady and he were her maid. "Come now. 'Tis a long ride out to King's Houses."

"I can go alone," she said, her voice cracking, for she was imagining what would happen if Robin followed her home, imagining his touch, his slim body against hers, even though she could almost burn to ashes with the shame of it.

"And if the monk should come back with an army of men? If he should find you?" He lowered his voice to an intimate whisper. "Would you know how to hide?"

Jane fought the urge to lean against his chest as he set the cloak gently, ever so gently, upon her shoulders. "You must let me go alone. If you take me, everyone will think . . ." She found she couldn't finish her words. They caught in her throat as Robin reached around to fasten her cloak, his fingers brushing across her neck, lingering where her collarbone met her shoulder.

Jane stayed there, frozen, and his hands still sat on her shoulders, his lips near her ear.

"So let them think it," he whispered, his breath hot. "Would that be so bad?"

Jane was flooded, once again, with the image of Robin as a cat who loved cornering his prey. He enjoyed her putting him off, she realized. It was a game to him. It angered her, and she silently gave thanks to Mary, who must have loaned her the strength to step out of Robin's grip and face him, for she knew she didn't have that strength within herself.

"Is that what you want from all this?" she demanded. "To have your way with me and cast me aside, just as John said?"

"Don't flatter yourself." Anger flashed across Robin's face before he turned from her, reaching for his own cloak and shrugging it on. "And *don't* listen to John."

Jane's heart sank. She had gotten what she'd wanted, hadn't she? He was letting her go. But now, bereft of Robin's warmth, she felt as if she were in a frozen river, sinking beneath the ice, and she was desperate for the heat of him. What a fool she was. He didn't *want* her. She didn't matter at all, or, if she did, she mattered only because she was Bran's. Her Bran. Steady and sure and safe.

"I'm not even going back to King's Houses." Jane tried to make her voice softer, as though she were explaining, as though she hadn't meant to challenge him. "I'm going to my mother's old house. I can get there myself, it's near."

Robin turned to her again, his eyes bright but distant. "That *is* close. I know it."

"You do?" Jane took a step back.

"Did you think we'd take you on without knowing where you came from, Jane?"

Jane flushed with shame. "I'm sorry, Robin," she found herself saying. "I was a fool to let John's words and the drink get to me." She laughed to try to make amends. "Surely you have better prospects than a peasant girl who slices onions for her bread."

Robin warmed immediately to her modesty, his green eyes intense again, his stare deep enough to swallow her. He strode forward, coming right up to her, his face inches from hers. She stepped back again, but he seized her hand, pressing it against his chest. "None quite so wise, nor quite so intriguing." His other hand took the nape of her neck, gently, weaving under her hair, and she gasped as his lips grazed her cheek. "Let me come to you, then," he whispered, his voice hoarse. "After dark, when no one will see. There will be no shame in it for you."

She trembled as longing surged inside her. Still, she murmured, "I can't do that to Bran."

"Bran's a good man, but a dullard. He'll never know."

"How can you say that?" she whispered, but she didn't move away. She couldn't.

"Admit it, Jane. Does Bran fill your heart and your mind, or does he only fill your bed? Can he give you what you need?"

"Stop." Jane pushed futilely against his chest. "I can't. It would break his heart."

"And what of your heart?" Robin studied her. "Do you love him, Jane? If you truly love him, I'll walk away right now. I'll never trouble you again."

Jane began to panic. What she and Bran had was kind and fond and she had seen far worse between women and men. Their story wasn't a romance, though, a tale for knights and ladies. Whatever they felt for each other, it was a thing that shifted with the seasons and with circumstances.

But something settled in her at the thought of things shifting. It calmed her. Right now, here, with Robin, was just one moment, one small choice where she had to be strong. Life was made up of those small choices. Her brother Adam had always said so. There was comfort in that, after this day, in which she had pretended to be someone she wasn't.

One small choice. One small word, really, and Jane could save herself from being taken for a fool.

"Yes," she said, though her voice shook. "Yes," she managed the second time with more confidence, "I love him."

"Liar." Robin stared at her, hard, still gripping her hand.

"I'm sorry." Jane pulled her hand away, quickly, while she still had strength left in her to do the right thing. "But I do."

Jane's heart was pounding in her ears, and she could no longer tell her fear from her longing. Half of her wanted to jump on her horse and ride home as fast as she could, the other half to take

Robin into her bed, to feel him against her in the dark and quiet, in the old, abandoned house, where no one would ever know.

But Robin had tired of the game. His hard stare only held her for a moment before he released her and bowed, as if he were a fine suitor she had rejected. "As you say, Jane." And then he held out his hand. "May I have my knife back?"

"I . . . of course." Emptiness yawned inside her like a snake's widening jaws as she returned his knife, her hands trembling. But that was foolishness, and drink, and high emotions after such a day. She had to get her head right. She was on the verge of cracking her whole life open like a walnut, leaving the meat of it for birds to plunder. Or for men to plunder. Just as her mother had.

Jane shuddered at the thought of Sibyl, and how she must make sure to be different from her, steadying herself as Robin helped her onto Moll. As her longing began to diminish, she felt relief. She deserved to be proud, proud of herself, and of her strength. She had sworn she wouldn't be like her mother, and she would *not* be. She had proven that to herself today, and she would take heart in her own courage. It would light her ride home through the darkening trees.

Then Robin let his hand fall to her thigh, light as a bird's touch, and the tower Jane had built inside herself crumbled into dust.

"I am a patient man," he said, softly, his voice intimate, his hand pressing, burning her leg as if his fingers were made of fire. "Especially when a thing is worth the wait."

And then he lifted his hand, smacked Moll on her flank, and Jane rode off alone into the dusk.

Chapter Fifteen

Jane had tossed and turned all night in her childhood bed, sweating out sour wine and jumping at every rustle outside her window, every light wind rattling the door, but Robin never came to her. She did not know which she regretted more: letting things get so far with Robin, or telling him no.

Because what if he had come?

It would have been the worst thing, and the best thing, that Jane could have imagined happening. It could have opened up her world forever, or it could have ruined the small, uncertain new life she was building for herself. The one that relied on her relationship with Bran.

And it was Bran Jane had to worry about, not Robin, as she quietly led Moll back to the stables well before Bran was normally awake in the morning.

So she was startled to see him come out of the shadows.

"There you are," he said, in a voice that was detached and dull—and knowing. Or was it Jane's guilt making her think so?

"You're up this early?" she asked, as lightly as she could.

"I couldn't sleep. I was waiting for you." He was uncomfortably still, leaning up against the stable wall with his arms crossed, a bigger, thicker version of Robin, but with a frown on his face instead of a smile. "Where were you?"

"I . . . Robin had a trick."

"On Brother Godric?"

Jane gaped. "You knew?"

"I knew," he said crossly. "And I know you weren't meant to be a part of it."

Worry rang through Jane, like an axe against a tree. "Have you talked to John? Or . . . anyone?"

"I haven't. Not yet."

"I . . . I went out to the woods because I finished early and . . ."

"You went to the woods?" Bran's face darkened with something Jane had never seen before. A cloud promising a storm. "Why?"

"I went there looking for *you*," Jane said, though she hadn't been able to convince Robin of the same lie. But what else could she say? How could she explain what she had felt—the loneliness, the longing, the hole carved into her soul that she'd been certain, in that one brief moment, only Robin could fill? She could barely admit it to herself. She could *never* admit it to Bran.

And besides, it had all gone wrong anyway. So why did it matter? She had gone out there for a chance to feel good about herself, to feel a part of something, and she had sunk far out of her depth in sin and crime instead. Jane felt she had learned her lesson well enough. So what was the point of making things worse, of risking the one safe place she still had to go?

Bran shook his head. "What the hell were you thinking, going out there alone?"

"It was a mistake. For John was angry as a whole hive of bees, he was. Stormed off in a rage," Jane said, hurrying the story at him as Emmie would have, quick and fluttering, to distract him from his worries. "Robin even hit him! Had you been there like I thought you would be, everything would have gone better, I'm sure of it."

Bran's shoulders eased, just a little. He moved toward her, and Jane felt the pressure in her chest begin to lighten. "Tell me," he said.

So Jane told him of the fight between Robin and John, but not the true reason for it. She only said it was about the monk and both their fiery tempers, and Bran nodded like he understood, although he thought her playing the role of Little John was a great joke. As they talked, he warmed toward her, leading her up the ladder to his little bed above the stables, where the blanket and straw were mussed. The whole place smelled like him—earthy and close and safe.

"I wish I could have seen it." Bran laughed, and he was beside her on the bed now, close enough to touch, but not touching her, not yet. "It doesn't sound like John to get his blood up over a game, though."

"I suppose it wasn't about that. Not really. I think it was about the monk." Jane leaned her head against his chest and almost sighed in relief as he took her in his arms, circling her like a great, woolen cloak against the cold. "I think they really wanted to hurt him, Bran. John did, and Wyll too. They couldn't see it was just a game Robin was playing, that he only meant to take his coin and shame him."

Bran was quiet.

Jane looked up at him, met his eyes. "It *was* just a game, wasn't it? Robin would never . . ."

Bran's look was grim. "Not unless he had to."

"But he wouldn't kill a man just for a trick, would he?" Jane asked, feeling her stomach grow hard and cold at the thought of it.

"Not just for that, Janie. We've a code, after all."

Jane looked away, nestled her head against him again. "So for what, then?"

Bran began stroking her hair, soft and soothing, even as something in him drew back a little, pulling his thoughts and his heart away. "Did I ever tell you that Wyll and I came up together?"

"Did you?" she murmured.

"When we were little, he was . . . he was hurt by a priest. I wanted to help him, to do something. But we were small, skinny. Just kids. Especially Wyll. You should have seen him, Janie. He was like a little colt. All legs and elbows." He laughed fondly. "He wasn't so angry then. Not before Father Thomas. He had no brothers, so I was like a brother to him. That's why he came to me." Jane held her breath, listening.

"I said we should go to the law," Bran continued, speaking into her hair. "But Wyll wouldn't have it. He knew they wouldn't take our side. And now that I'm older, I know he was right. The reeve back then was a nobleman, a lord's son. He wouldn't have helped people like us. Not against a priest. But we'd been hearing whispers of a hero in the woods, one who would right your wrongs, and Wyll, he wanted to go find him. Thought he might do what the law wouldn't."

"Did you know him then? Robin, I mean?"

"I didn't even think he was real. But I went with Wyll anyway, searching the forest, and we sent word around that we were looking. I thought it would take Wyll's mind off things, help him move on." He finally looked at Jane then, and his eyes had grown soft around the edges. "But Robin *was* real. And when we found him . . . when he found *us*, because of the word we'd put out, I couldn't believe it. I thought I must have been dreaming."

"And did he help Wyll?"

"That priest got what he deserved," Bran said, but the warmth in his voice was gone.

Jane let Bran's story wash over her, heartsick. She knew of men like that priest, and sometimes they were driven out of town when they were caught. But if they were too powerful to tell on, what recourse did anyone have? Especially a child?

"Wyll was right," she said finally. "The law wouldn't have helped." She wondered at the sour, hard feel inside of herself, wondered what she would do, had anyone hurt Adam like that, or Ralf. If she'd had the power to stop them, she would have done it—she knew she would. She could even imagine Robin's knife in her own hand, feel the serpents swirling across its hilt. The familiarity of her anger frightened her, for it was the same hot surge she had felt at seeing heaps of silver in Brother Godric's saddlebags.

But she hadn't known this about Bran—his bravery, his compassion. Robin had called him a dullard, but that was cruel, she saw it now. Bran was here for people: he was here for her, and he had been there for Wyll, and that was what she had always liked about him.

She buried her head in Bran's chest, breathing in his soft smell, earth and horses and malt. "You're right, you know. I shouldn't have gone out there alone. I don't know what I was thinking. I was just upset."

"About Sibyl?"

"About Sibyl, the empty house, things falling to rot . . ." Bran had told her a truth, and she offered him this one, almost as an apology. "There's no place for me there, not anymore." Jane felt the tears gather, exhaustion settling on her like a great weight. "I thought, maybe, that if Robin could find me useful . . ."

Bran took her face in his strong hands, tangled his fingers in her hair. "I find you useful," he said. "You'll always have a place with me."

"Oh, really," she teased him. "Going to make me a bed here in the stables, are you?"

"Oh, aye." His pupils grew great and dark as they did when his fire was up. He eased her onto her back, coaxing her hips beneath his until she could feel him pressing hard against her. "You can stay right here all day and night. Eudo can send us our supper."

Jane laughed, her heart thudding in her chest. "And what about Robin? Won't he be angry when he needs me for another trick?"

"You're mine," Bran said, "not Robin's," and he kissed her roughly—almost too roughly—his tongue flooding her mouth.

PART III

A False Owtlaw

Chapter Sixteen

Weeks passed without word from the woods. Brother Godric was convalescing in a dark, lonely chamber at King's Houses, and Jane avoided him as much as she could, even though reason told her that he would never connect a lowly servant girl to the menacing, voiceless bandit in the woods.

Godric had passed word to the shire reeve that Robin Hood lurked in the woods with a pack of bandits, and the rumor was that all of them had been hired by Sir Richard to take vengeance on the clergy. That last part was a falsehood, of course, but there was no story so persistent as a tale that people wanted to believe despite its falseness. Walter de Stircheley sent hunting parties to raid the woods, but Jane knew they wouldn't find Robin. The men had made sure to confuse the monk when they'd stolen him away, and Wyll had set him loose far south, near the trysting tree where Robin had lured the reeve—which meant he was still searching the wrong forest. No one knew where Robin was really hiding.

Robin and John were still at odds. Wyll thought John had gone back to Holderness, where he was from, but Bran had seen him drinking in Mansfield. "Why does he hang around here?" Bran wondered. "What's there to do without Robin?" But Jane was beginning to understand: even in the absence of Robin, even when he had forsaken you, you still had the hope of him. The promise of adventure, of pleasure, and the joy of having his eyes and his attention turn to you.

Jane had been so distracted with worry—and with Robin's silence—that she had burned two pies and even dropped a clay pot, shattering it all over the floor. Eudo had scolded her harshly and had been cold to her ever since, so when Emmie offered to take on extra kitchen duties so that Jane could go to Mansfield for Whitsunday, she leapt at the chance.

Whitsunday was a fine spring day, the sun bright and high and the air crisp and flower-scented. The townspeople had donned their very best for church—bright, cheerful tunics in red and green and yellow. A line of women holding infants wrapped in white, waiting to be baptized, slithered through the crowd like a great worm. The Mansfield priest, Father Paul, greeted folks at the door—and her brother Adam stood beside him, his face as sunny as the sky. Jane had suspected he would be there, but her heart still sped up when she saw him, and despite how things stood between them she couldn't help but smile at how wise and grown he looked.

At that moment, Adam found her face in the crowd. Nervously, cautiously, he smiled back.

Jane smoothed her kirtle. She had been careful not to look too extravagant, which would have given Adam reason to suspect her yet again. She pulled at Bran's hand, moving toward the line of people Adam was greeting.

"Oy, the saintly brother, is it?" Bran grumbled. "Thought you two were having a spat."

Jane clucked her tongue. "Come now," she said, softer than she'd have liked. She found herself eager for the chance to forget her feud with Adam, because the sight of his face made her remember the hollow feeling she'd been burying, the one gnawing at her insides, that came from losing her greatest friend. She had tried to put him out of her mind all this time, to fill it up with her work at King's Houses and with Bran and Robin, but seeing his face put the lie to all of it. She had missed Adam, and from the look in his eyes, he had missed her just the same.

"At least Robin's not here to see me making friends with the enemy," Bran said as Jane dragged him into Adam's greeting line.

"Adam's not the enemy. He's draped in wool, not gold. See for yourself. He only wants to help people."

"That's what they all say, even as they take their tithe from your earnings," Bran groused, but good-naturedly, with a glimmer in his eyes, which was the way he said everything, even the hardest things.

Jane and her brother exchanged a long look as she approached him. "Hallo," she said brightly, but then the tears came into her eyes like little traitors, and she was soothed only by seeing her brother's eyes flood with water too.

"Are you well?" Adam asked, his voice strangled. He could not embrace her, not here, but she could see he wanted to, that he leaned toward her as if he could. Instead, he took Jane's hands in his own, as if he were giving her a proper blessing, and pressed them tightly, like she was a rope and he was drowning in the river.

"Well as I can be," she said around her tears. "This is Bran."

Adam sniffed, blinking rapidly, his face schooling itself into manly neutrality for Bran's sake. "Of course. You're taking good care of Jane, I hope."

"Well as one can care for a colt who runs her own path." He laughed, and Adam looked distraught, for the joke about Jane's free spirit had not landed as Bran thought it would. Adam was far too serious, and he read extra syllables into every word. "Your sister is practically running the king's kitchens on her own already," Bran added, seeing his mistake.

"Bran." Jane smiled shyly, embarrassed but also proud, for here was Bran at his best: when he was on her side. "I am not!"

"Are too!" He leaned close to Adam, as though he were sharing a secret. "Has the cook wrapped around her finger, she does. Her sauces are even better, though she has the good sense not to let him know."

"Jane always has good sense," Adam said humbly. "Even when the rest of us behave like fools."

Jane knew his apology for what it was, and she squeezed his hands to let him know she had heard it. "Have you been lonely out there?"

But Father Paul had joined them, and there was no more time for sharing. "No one is ever lonely when God is with them," he declared.

Adam dropped her hands. "May He watch over you in all your endeavors, Jane."

"And who is Jane?" the priest asked suspiciously, and Jane saw what he was seeing, what with Adam holding her hands for so long, and his feelings flooding to the surface at the sight of her.

"I'm his sister," she said. "And I miss him terribly."

Adam gave her a grateful smile, for he was always slow to see what others were thinking. He spent so much time wandering around in his own mind.

"Oh! Then welcome, Jane!" the priest said, and Bran stifled a smirk.

"Have you seen Mother?" Jane asked.

Adam's face closed, firmly as a door, and he shook his head. "She has her own life now. Best to let her be."

Jane had known Sibyl would want to forget them, but it still hurt to hear it.

Father Paul sensed her awkwardness, though he couldn't know the reason. If he did, Adam would be shamed right out of church. "Well," he said, "we had best get the townsfolk inside or we'll be listening to the high lords' stomachs grumble instead of the liturgy." Adam nodded, a mask of wise contentment crossing his face, and Jane saw that her little brother—once so vulnerable and soft—had truly become a man, and she was proud of him, no matter what Bran and Wyll and the others thought of priests.

Then Jane heard a familiar, high voice behind her, and she spun to see Walter and Betrice whisking past her. She stumbled out of the way with a nod to Adam as Father Paul welcomed the reeve.

"Why, good Shire Reeve! You honor us with your presence today. And my lady"—the priest greeted Betrice with a hungry smile—"we've so appreciated your alms, and your generous heart."

Betrice looked like an enormous, walking flower. She wore a violet dress embroidered with gold thread and swimming with flounces, and a matching caul woven with tiny white buds. She gave Jane an apologetic smile, for she saw how she'd taken her place, but to Betrice's mind, that was just the way of things. So

Jane smiled back, until she saw Walter's glower. The man looked as though he'd broken his fast with fire and planned smoke and ashes for dinner.

"You can honor me by getting these people inside," the reeve said. "The vermin that used to slither through the woods have grown bold, and I've reason to believe they'll show their faces today, since that fool monk decided a trip to church was more important than his life."

"Walter, please!" Betrice was thoroughly embarrassed, but the priest was forgiving enough.

"Good Lady Betrice, there are men of the cloth and men of the world, and neither may serve without the other. Mansfield is grateful for your husband's stout heart, and his sword, for it allows us all to pray in peace."

"Come now," Bran whispered in Jane's ear, sultry and teasing, "can't have you out here where the bandits might get you." Jane stifled a laugh, following him into the church with a small wave goodbye for Adam.

"What was he on about?" she asked Bran as they stood together behind a stinking mass of townspeople doused in perfumed oils and musty spring linens. "Nothing's planned for today, is it? Not with John and Robin at odds?"

Bran shook his head. "All's quiet," he said, and scooted closer to her as more people filed in beside them, his thick body pressing against hers, his horsey scent filling her nose. He had been passionate, even doting, since that day she had come back from the woods. And the more he was around, and so kind to her, the more she felt like a fool for being so drawn to Robin. It was pleasant, she realized, being here with Bran in front of everyone, rather than sneaking around the kitchens and the stables.

Perhaps that's how my mother felt, having to hide her men, Jane thought with a shock. But they were different, completely different. Weren't they?

Jane shook her head to clear it, searching the stifling room, for Emmie had made her promise to say what everyone was wearing. There was Betrice, of course, in all her springtime glory, her back tall and straight as she took her place of honor near the front. Jane found Ibota in the back, her head buried in her wimple, beside her knight, Sir Roger. They stood with the peasants, despite being welcome at the front. The impression Jane got from the prioress, regardless of what everyone said about her, was that she only wanted to be left alone. *And to torment greedy abbots,* she thought, and almost laughed aloud. Perhaps if the prioress knew what Jane was really up to at King's Houses, she would even take her side.

Then, suddenly, Jane spied a man two rows ahead of her—a man who was also studying the crowd. He had a broad hat on, shadowing his face, but beneath it, green eyes glittered as they watched her, and fox-colored hair caught the light.

Robin winked.

Jane froze, ice shooting from her toes all the way to her jaw. "Bran," she whispered, her voice suddenly hoarse. "Did you see . . . ?"

It was clear just from how stiff he'd gone at her side that Robin had surprised Bran as well. "What's he *doing* here?" Bran whispered back.

"You didn't know?"

Bran shook his head, his jaw clenched tight.

"So *is* there a plan for today?" Robin couldn't be foolish enough to try a trick in front of all these people, could he?

"Robin always has a plan," Bran whispered back, but he didn't sound sure. And as they were whispering, Robin slowly, casually took off his hat, baring his face to the entire church.

"He wants to be seen," Jane gasped. "Why would he possibly want that?"

"Damn it. John swore Robin would do something like this now that he wasn't around to yank his reins."

Jane frowned, for it seemed to her that John had been the one wanting to take risks. He'd been the one willing to murder a holy man for a stack of coins. Still, here was Robin, showing his face to all of Mansfield town just when the reeve was hunting him. "Does he mean to get his head cut off?" she muttered.

So far, no one else had noticed the rogue in the middle of the church. Everyone was chatty and bright, with no sense of what was coming. Jane tried to stay calm. Maybe no one would notice. The reeve was still outside, which meant Robin had slipped past him and his guards. Perhaps he wasn't looking to be caught after all. Perhaps he had a way out. Jane wanted very badly to clutch Bran's arm, but that would be improper in church and cause people to stare, so she just pressed closer to him. He danced his fingers across the tops of hers, between their hips where no one else could see. "It'll be all right," he whispered.

Finally, the doors closed, and the fierce buzz of the great town church dulled to a quiet hum, like a circle of flies. The procession of clergy began, a thundering of men's footsteps across the clean-swept wooden floorboards, the creaking of those boards under their girth, the wave of sweat and incense that rolled from their bodies as they passed.

It was grand, Jane thought, to see them march in their parade of white and red silk, even with the Benedictines trailing past, all tonsured heads and black robes, looking like a dull funeral procession behind the rest. Brother Godric was among them. His bruises had healed, but he looked thinner, gaunter, and sallow with fasting. She hung her head as he passed and tried not to stare at Robin. Surely he knew how these ceremonies went, and that the monk, if he was here, would be walking by. Surely he would take extra care not to be seen.

But as Brother Godric approached Robin's row, the Lord of the Greenwood let out a high, sharp whistle.

Everything dropped out from under Jane then, like she was tumbling into a vast, fiery pit—like hell had risen up to swallow her for her sins. Godric turned to the source of the noise, slowly, crawlingly, until he saw Robin Hood's bare, foolish face.

The monk raised his arm, hand shaking, black robe falling from his wrist like a shroud. His mouth opened and closed as he tried to find words, but he couldn't, so instead he gaped like a fish, pointing, his eyes wild with fear.

Jane gripped Bran's hand, not caring anymore what anyone thought.

The monk finally found his tongue. "It's . . . it's him!" he shouted. "The thief who robbed me! Get the bloody reeve!"

In an instant, everything was chaos.

Robin offered the monk a low, sweeping bow, his green cloak swirling around him. "Robin Hood, at your service." He grinned, looking around to see everyone in the church staring at him, pointing, some in shock, and some in admiration. He loved it, Jane realized. *That* was what he had come for.

From the front of the church, Betrice caught Jane's eye. Her own eyes were as enormous as a trapped hare's. She was clearly hoping for commiseration from Jane, who was supposed to be surprised too. *I can't believe Walter never told her who the potter was,*

Jane thought. The reeve was more worried about his pride than he was about his wife's safety.

"I did take the monk's coin," Robin shouted over the noise, commanding silence even in the rattling din, "but only to give it back to you!" And he pulled from his cloak the monk's stolen saddlebag, opening it to show that it was full of silver.

The crowd erupted, hooting and cheering in disbelief. Jane hadn't counted the monk's coins—she had only taken her small share—but she could see that Robin had held back the lot of it specifically for this moment.

"You are the ones who earned it," Robin continued, "through the hard work of your hands, through the labor on this monk's fields, through your service at his table. Why should he hoard it all himself, like some great dragon? It's you all who have a right to this coin, not the church!"

A few brave voices cheered, and Father Paul shouted, his voice shrill, "Would you blaspheme against the church, here in the house of God?"

"I am not the one who blasphemes," Robin said smoothly. "You are. You who would glut yourself on another man's hard-won bread and call yourself holy."

The crowd had been murmuring, their whispers escalating. But now, more of them began to cheer. At that moment, the reeve burst through the doors, his sword raised, his men at his side. "Bar the doors behind me!" he ordered the guards. "No one is getting out until I have my hands on Robin Hood!"

Robin's eyes glanced off Jane, his smile lifted at the corner, like it did when he thought he had mastered someone. He did have a plan, Jane thought. He must. And she thought she knew what it was, for the saddlebag was still open, its treasures gobbling up the light that came through the stained glass windows.

"Good Shire Reeve," Robin declared in greeting, even as a thick wooden bolt slid in place across the doors, "would you violate the law of sanctuary, here in this church, in front of all these people?"

"Sanctuary, my arse," the reeve growled. "I'm here on King Edward's orders. He can work out whether thieves are allowed in his church after they've attacked a holy man." He strode forward, his sword glinting, the lines in his sun-weathered skin carved deep, his eyes focused on his prey. "I should cleave your head from your shoulders right where you stand, after what you've done." His sword lowered, just an inch, and his shoulders squared. "But you'll be tried and hanged, as the law says. And I'll have my justice when all of Mansfield sees your corpse."

"Such a shame," Robin said, "that a sinner cannot even pray for Mary's grace when man's law takes the place of God's."

"You'll need more than Mary's grace to save you now, boy." The reeve ground his teeth, looking hungry, as if a great feast were before him and he'd been starving for days.

Robin and the reeve locked eyes for several breaths, and for those brief moments, it seemed as if there was no one in that church except for the two of them. And then Robin's smile grew broader.

"Well then, if that's the way you want it. The hunt is on, Shire Reeve. Catch me—if you can!" And then he hurled the saddlebag high into the air, sending coins flying everywhere in a snowfall of silver.

With a bloody battle cry, the reeve surged forward, a bull with a man in his sights. The crowd began to scream and shout, some hitting the floor to pick up coins, others scrambling out of the way, as Robin drew his sword and darted backward, letting the townsfolk form a human shield between the reeve's blade and his own. "Come and get me!" Robin taunted him, waving the sword, shrinking ever farther into the press of bodies.

Bran gripped Jane's hand, tugging her to the back of the church. "You have to get out of here!" His voice was frantic, high, and all the color had drained from his face.

Jane reluctantly tore her eyes from Robin. "But . . ."

"Now!" Bran said again, pulling harder, nearly yanking her off her feet. "You have to go for help. Go find John."

"The doors are barred." Her words came slowly, so slowly, as if she were speaking in a dream.

"They'll break them open soon. These people won't be penned in here, not with blood coming." And Bran was right, for those wise enough not to scramble after Robin's bait were already shoving toward the reeve's men, careless of their swords, and the two guards at the door were backed against the wall with their blades high. Jane heard an ear-piercing infant's wail—the children, she remembered with a sick feeling in her stomach. They had all come to be blessed, and now . . .

Bran shielded her with his body as people jostled past them, wrapping his thick arms around her like a barrier. And even though she knew he was getting banged and bruised on her account, she felt a fierce flame of resentment whip through her, for she could no longer see Robin, or the reeve, and she needed to know what was happening between them. She needed to know Robin would make it out alive.

From beneath Bran's arm, she saw Robin weaving through the

church, leading the reeve on a merry chase, but the crowd between them was thinning and, soon, they would be blade to blade.

"Find John," Bran insisted. "Do you hear me, Jane? Try Mooch's place. It's a little house, out past the mill pond, where the path ends. Take my horse."

"They'll never make it here in time!"

Bran shook his head, his face grim. "No. But if he's captured . . . if he falls . . ."

"Then they'll kill him, Bran," she rasped, the words catching in her throat.

"Maybe he'll make it out." Bran's voice was heavy with dread, and when their eyes met, she realized neither of them believed it.

Jane felt another hand on her shoulder, and she looked up to see her brother Adam, his cheeks red and drowning in sweat, his eyes urgent. He'd come to find her, she realized, awash with guilt. He'd pressed through the crowd for her, risked himself, and she hadn't thought of him at all. She'd only had eyes for Robin.

"There's a side door," Adam shouted, his eyes wide as platters. "Come, Jane! Let's get you out before you're crushed!"

"What about you . . . ?" she started, but Bran spoke over her.

"Good man!" he said. "Lead on." And he trundled her off after her brother, who led them toward a small door near the front of the church, the one the priest used when he wanted privacy. As they pushed through the mad, scrambling crowd, Jane realized that all the clergy had gone. They'd rushed out through their secret door and left the townspeople in there to die. All but her brother. Children huddled in a corner, a few women—their mothers, most likely—linking arms in front of them, trying to hush them.

The reeve and his men had finally cornered Robin at the front of the church, behind the altar. Their swords crashed together and Jane gasped. Robin's face was fierce, determined, still smiling. He feinted, dancing back, and the reeve charged forward with a growl.

"Now, Jane!" Bran shoved her through the door, ripping her eyes away from the scene. They followed Adam down the stone steps, through a cellar musty with the sweat of hurrying men, and then heard a sharp crack, and a triumphant cry—Walter's, she realized. Not Robin's.

She stopped. "What was that?"

Bran swallowed, looking pale. "A sword. Shattered, sounds like."

"Bran . . ." she whispered.

"Not now." He pushed her, gently, but it was enough, for Adam had turned to gawk at them.

"Come on!" her brother urged them.

Finally, they burst through the cellar door into the sunlight, right beside the stables. Jane swallowed air as though she had been drowning.

"Go on," Bran said, meeting her eyes, his own full of meaning. "Get to safety."

"You need to go with her," Adam said. "Those guards won't be easy with their swords, not if anyone gets in their way."

"No!" Jane said, too quickly. "You need to watch over him! In case he . . ."

"I'll be fine, Jane," Adam said, confounded. "They won't hurt me! I'm a priest!"

"I'll watch him," Bran said, his hand on Adam's shoulder, even as his eyes stayed locked to Jane's, making sure she knew that he understood her, that his watch would be for Robin. "Come on, good man. We've a safe way out, so let's get the children through that door."

"The villain must be caught now, I think," Adam said. "If his sword is rent, he's finished."

"Never bet against the Lord of the Greenwood." Bran smiled. "At least, that's what the townsfolk say. You watch yourself out there, Janie," he said before he led her brother back through the cellar, and Jane understood the meaning of that too, without him having to say another word.

Chapter Seventeen

Jane found the pond and the house easily, tucked away off the northern road to York. She was sweaty and parched, and even though the air was warm, thick with the dense, powdery smell of trees and flowers spraying themselves into springtime, Jane still felt the cold fear that had swallowed her in the church—along with her own guilt, her shame. What Bran had done—protecting her, saving the children, looking out for everyone who mattered—well, that was why she'd taken to him in the first place. His warmth, humor, and strength.

But Jane's own fears had been for Robin—and only Robin. Not for her brother, and not for Bran. How could she be so faithless?

She was tying her horse to a dilapidated post, her fingers shaking, her breath short, when the door to the house burst open. Wyll Scathlock stood there, leaning casually, a cup in his hand and an amused smile slanting his face sideways.

"Why, Jane," he said, "did you miss me so much that you rode all the way out here?"

"Jane?" Little John called from inside. "How'd she find this place?" Past Wyll's slim form, John and Mooch sat at a small table before a jug of ale.

"Well, come in, then." Wyll swung his body aside and gestured to the table. "Have a drink if you want one. But your man's not here, nor is Robin."

"I know. I need . . ." And her voice caught in her throat.

Mooch rose to his feet, sensing her urgency. "What is it? What's wrong?"

"It's Robin." She forced the words out, still disbelieving, though she'd seen it with her own eyes. "He's been caught."

Everyone jumped as John's fist slammed down on the table, causing the cups to spill. "That fucking arse-wisp! He went to the town church, didn't he?"

"What happened, Janie?" Wyll's face turned fierce, cruel. "Did the priests turn him in?"

"The monk saw his face," she said, "and called for the shire reeve. They trapped him in the church and . . ."

Wyll scowled. "Surprised they didn't take his head right there, those cowards."

"The reeve wants to put him on trial," she said. "You have to get him out."

Jane's plea was met with silence. All she could hear was a bird outside, shrieking alone, too late for sunrise and too early for the night call. "John, did you hear me?" she asked again, her voice softer. "We have to . . ."

"Do we, now?" John finally said, his face hard.

"We can't just leave him there!" Wyll gaped. "You know what they'll do to him."

"I know bloody well what they'll do, all right. And so did he when he got it in his fool head to go to church in town at Whit-sunday."

Wyll and Mooch exchanged a look, but neither of them said a word. John pushed an empty chair away from the table with his boot and said, "Sit down, Jane. Take a rest. 'Tis not right to have you run so ragged for our master's own mistakes."

"It's not like that," Jane tried to explain. "He fought hard, and his sword broke, and . . ."

John rolled his eyes. "Yes, I'm sure it was a grand show."

"But . . ." Wyll began.

"But what?" John's anger rose. "You'd have us all run off to break him out of the reeve's clutches? For fuck's sake, we don't even know where he's being kept, do we? Unless you saw where they hauled him?" he asked Jane.

She shook her head. "I don't even know if—" Her voice broke again. Robin couldn't have fallen in the fight, could he? Robin couldn't be dead. "The reeve wants to bring him to Nottingham," she said, as if convincing herself.

"So we have to get him out before they ride south." Wyll leaned toward the door as if he wanted to bolt out and steal her horse and ride off to save Robin all on his own.

John gave Wyll a sharp look, then his voice was soft, almost embarrassed, as he said, "He's done this to test me, you know. To see if I'll rescue him."

Jane scoffed. "Why would he do such a thing?"

"Because Robin hates to lose things once they're his." The big man shook his head. "He won't have it. You'll see, when the time comes that you think you want to leave all this behind. He'll find a way of having you back. He's playing games, and I'm full as a stuffed pig of his games."

"It's not a game, John!" But even as she spoke, she remembered Robin throwing his coins up in the air, remembered the satisfied smirk on his face as all the townsfolk looked at him in awe.

"It's a bloody game, and you know it," John said in a tone that brooked no argument. When she didn't respond, he sighed, leaning back in his chair. "Let me tell you something. I grew up in Holderness, out by the sea. 'Twas a hard place, all frost and fishing and wet winds. Me da died when I was but a boy—fell off a boat, he did, trying to get the catch—and me mum had to raise us all on her own, I and my two brothers. It wasn't pretty, but she did what she must to feed us, you understand?"

Jane nodded, understanding immediately. "My mum raised me and my brothers herself too. Well, with my help," she couldn't stop herself from adding. She felt ashamed of saying so, though she didn't know why.

John raised a bushy blond brow at her, a flash of respect. "Your da die too?"

Jane shook her head. "He left."

John turned and spat right on the dirt floor of Mooch's house. "Good as dead, then. So we had this priest in town. Richer than he should have been, since they sent him carts of money out from York. Rumor said he was a nobleman's son gone wrong, serving God for punishment. But he took the alms around to poor families, as he was supposed to, and he gave great speeches, and he was fine to look at, so the villagers loved him, they did."

John had a way of storytelling that made Jane feel as if she and he were the only two people in the room. He sounded wiser, a great deal more clever and sure of himself, when Robin wasn't around. The thought troubled her. It put her in mind of Betrice shrinking herself to please the reeve.

"But when the alms came to our house, he wanted something in return, if you catch my meaning."

Jane winced, for she caught his meaning indeed. "Is that why you left?"

John looked away, flushing. "Naw, he died when I was still small." Then his mouth hardened. "I wanted to kill him. 'Course I did. I thought about it all the time. But he went and died on his own. His heart it was, they said—black as burnt wood. The spots took me mum, not long after, and there was nothing for me there, so I left and went to war. But this story isn't about that, Janie. The thing is, that priest. It's about him. Had you not seen him in your own house—with his bare arse pumping yer mum like she was nothing to him but a cow or a sheep, and him a bull or a ram— oh, you'd have thought he was saintly indeed. The folk of Holderness hung on his every word. Who he told you to love, you loved. And who he told you to hate, you'd hate. And you'd give him the shirt off your back and the crops off your land and more, if he asked for it.

"He'd say it was all about God, what he said and what he did and what he took. But 'twasn't about God at all. It was about *him*."

Jane flushed. This didn't sound right to her. It couldn't be right. "And you think that's how Robin is too? Even though he's fighting to make things better?"

John leaned back, chewing on a cracked lip, his pale eyes meeting hers directly. "Is he?"

A thousand protests died on Jane's lips. Robin had helped Sir Richard, to be sure, but Sir Richard had been a knight, and had become an ally, someone who Robin could use. Robin had helped *her* too, but it was hardly an act of charity, for she was useful to him as well, wasn't she?

Jane knew Wyll's story, and that seemed like charity, though it was not a story Wyll would want her to mention now, she felt sure of it.

Wyll broke the silence, glaring at John. "And who are you to judge him? Robin wouldn't sit around and tell tales when a friend was in danger. I know that as well as I know my own arse!"

John spread his hands wide, daring him. "Then go be a hero, Scathlock. No one here is going to stop you."

"So you won't help?" John met Jane's plea with stony silence. "Where's Tuk, then?"

"On a job," Mooch said finally. "Outside town. Had the good sense to hire on as a guard after these two fell out."

"Or maybe he finally caught the scent of Robin's horseshit," John grumbled.

"He'll be back," Wyll insisted, still angry.

"Might be," Mooch said. "But not in time."

Desperation grew in Jane, and the sound of Robin's sword cracking in two rang over and over in her ears like a bell. He had saved Wyll—had saved John more than once, to hear Bran tell it. How could John just abandon him now? She had to get past his grudge somehow, had to make them all see what was at stake.

"He knows your names," she blurted finally. "That monk. Knows your names, and your faces."

"Oy, he does that." John laughed scornfully. "Robin made sure of it."

"Do you think the shire reeve will stop at Robin? I've met Walter de Stircheley. He's a hard man, and a cold one, and he's set on this hunt. He'll come for you no matter what."

Mooch grimaced. "Most like he'll torture Robin, he will, and find a way to track us all down like runaway dogs."

"Might be we all ought to get out of town, then," John said, watching Jane as if he knew just what she was doing, as if he were amused. As if he were playing a game with her himself—testing her, just as Robin would have.

"And go where?" Wyll demanded. "You're both a couple of cowards!"

"There's nowhere the reeve won't go to find you." Jane pressed on. "You know he'll come for you, John. He'll come for all of you."

John's mouth worked for a minute as he drummed his thick fingers on the table. Then, finally, he let out a foul curse. "Do you know what it is you're asking, Jane? Do you *really* know?"

Jane's shoulders eased, for she saw that she had won him, saw the resignation in his eyes. "I just want Robin to be safe."

"If you want him safe," John said, "we have to get him before the reeve takes him back to Nottingham. And that means we need a distraction."

"What kind of distraction?" Jane asked.

"One you're going to help us with." John's eyes narrowed.

"But I have to get back to King's Houses!" Jane said, her heart feeling trapped in her chest. What did John expect from her? Hadn't she already ridden all the way out here to warn them? Shouldn't *they* be the ones to go up against the reeve?

"Do you think you're some fair maiden out of legend, meant to give us a quest and then flutter off to a tower full of silks? That's not the way the real world works, Janie. Either you're in, or we're all out."

Wyll started to sputter an objection, but John silenced him with a glare.

"What do you want me to do?" Jane asked, the fear clenched around her heart squeezing harder still.

"We'll see, won't we? Tell a lie, hold a sword—whatever we need."

"But I can't . . ."

"Do you want Robin free, or not?"

Jane tried to steel herself. "I do."

"Right, then," John said. "First, we go find us a monk. Then, we teach that shire reeve a lesson."

"What kind of lesson?"

John rose, his whole girth towering over her, his shoulders square and broad, and he looked a warrior then, rather than the soft, drunken storyteller he had seemed a moment ago. "That Robin Hood isn't the only lord of these woods. And he's not the only outlaw to be feared."

Chapter Eighteen

It had been easy enough for Wyll to track Brother Godric down. When he returned, ripe with the smell of sweat and horses, he conferred with John quietly, as though Jane and Mooch couldn't be trusted. As though they weren't the ones who'd had to drag John into action. Mooch gave Jane an uneasy glance. Whatever Wyll was plotting, Jane was sure she wasn't going to like it.

John leaned against the door, his arms crossed, a grim smile on his face. "Seems we're in luck. Brother Godric has had enough of Mansfield. He's riding back to York this very afternoon."

Wyll smirked, copying John's stance, but doing it poorly, looking more like a leering gargoyle than a watchman. "Fleeing in the shadows, he is," Wyll said. "Fast as he can, scared as a rabbit, with no time to hire a proper guard. Says he's not safe at King's Houses anymore. And soon, he'll see he's not safe anywhere." His eyes were too eager. Jane thought of Bran's story again and felt as if she had plunged her hands into icy water.

"The road to York runs right by us," Mooch said, sober now, but looking tired, older than his years, creases deep around his eyes.

"Exactly." John nodded. "So, are we ready?"

Jane felt that sinking feeling in her stomach again. "Ready for what?"

John kicked himself off the door, making it rattle, looming over her again like a great giant. She wished she could crawl under the table and hide forever.

"Ready to play our parts." He handed her a knife. "Put this somewhere hidden."

Jane remembered the knife Robin had given her on the day she played as Little John, intricate and cared-for, worn from his own grip, redolent with him. John's knife was a bare, sparse thing, rust climbing its edges, like he never gave a thought to it. "Shall I cover my face?" she asked.

"Not this time," John said, his voice grim, his eyes keeping a hold on hers.

"But he'll know me, won't he? And if he comes back to King's Houses . . ."

"He won't come back." John's eyes, steady, willing her to see the truth despite her awful stubbornness. She knew what he meant. She knew *exactly* what he meant. But neither of them would say it. The truth crackled around them like the bristling charge before a storm of light and rain.

"What do you want me to do?" Her throat was dry as dust.

"You'll run out there, right in front of his horse, and tell the monk you've been robbed." He walked over to her and mussed her hair, pulling half of it out of her braid. Jane felt the hairs move against the back of her neck, smelled the ale on John's breath. She stood very, very still, even though she was desperate to look away, even though her face and spine were burning with the effort. "Describe us"—John's hands pushed hair into her face, delicate, but firm—"with as much detail as you can. Leave nothing out. Make sure he knows us." Finally, he reached down and yanked her sleeve, hard, and she gasped as it split in half, flailing uselessly over her arm.

"John!" she cried, thinking that it was her best tunic, and then thinking what a shallow, foolish thought that was, given all that had happened, and all that was about to happen.

"You do your skirts," he said, and gestured to where she had hidden the knife, then turned his back as if he were some sort of gentleman. Jane closed her eyes, then tore and cut. She couldn't bear to look. That kirtle was a week's wages, at least, and it was better not to see it. Better not to think about the consequences of any of this.

"We don't hurt women, though." Wyll looked affronted, though he did not turn away as John had.

"Right, but *he* doesn't know that, you dullard," Mooch said. "The church men think we're all demons anyway."

John turned back around with a grin. "So, let's go be demons, then. Are you ready, Jane?"

No, Jane wanted to say. *No, I'm not ready at all.* She gathered her courage, though, and forced herself to meet John's stare, despite his towering height. "I'll do it for Robin," she said.

"Brave girl," Wyll said.

"Fool girl," John corrected him. "He's made fools of all of us, and me, the worst fool yet. But let's get out to the road. That monk will ride by soon enough."

-«««•»»»-

It all happened so quickly. Like one of the nightmares that would shake her awake just before dawn. The moment they heard horses

coming, John led Jane onto the dirt road. He and Wyll and Mooch
ran back to hide in the trees near the house. They left her alone
on the path, waiting either to be run down by a scared monk's
horse or to lead him to his doom. John and the others had put
a lot of trust in her, she tried to tell herself, leaving her out
here alone, where she could warn Godric off or run away if she
wanted to.

But not really. Not really at all, because they were close enough
to come for her if she failed them. And they knew where to find
her, and where she worked, and how to take it all from her in an
instant if they wanted to. She wished fervently, selfishly, that Bran
had come with her instead of helping at the church, that he could
be at her side right now. He would have known what to do—how
to talk to them, how to keep her safe, how to stop all this from
happening.

But Bran wasn't there. There was no one there but Jane, Jane
with a thick, hard rock in her stomach as she watched horses
come toward her at a dreamlike speed.

And then, suddenly, time sped up again. A blur of black and
brown flashed onto the path, hurtling toward her, and almost as if
it were instinct, Jane waved her arms and shouted, "Stop!" The
monk and another rider, a young man on a smaller horse, slowed
their horses to a halt. Both looked wary, cautious, and Jane realized she had shouted a command, which was wrong, wrong for
the game John wanted her to play, so she tried to sound and look
more desperate. "Please!" She tore at her hair as she had seen
other women do when they were scared or grieving. "Please stop,
for the love of God!"

"What is it, woman?" The monk's face twisted with irritation.

Jane saw that the second rider was barely a man at all—just a boy, really. Her heart seized in her chest. The boy's face—a noble one, with soft skin and a slim little nose like a girl's—was concerned, compassionate. He was one of the monk's pages, she realized. She had seen him at King's Houses with the others. Jane stuffed down the urge to scream at him, to warn him, to beg him to run away. She thought of Wyll's knife flashing, the violence it promised, the vengeance. Would he spare the boy? Or would he see every churchman in the same way and punish the boy along with the monk?

"She's been hurt, Brother," the page said, and Jane fought a surge of tears at the kindness on his face. Then, she thought fleetingly that the tears might help her after all, so she let them spill.

"I've . . ." She could barely get the words out. She was choking on them, they were filling up her throat, for she did not want to say them. But she remembered John's face, thought of what he would do if she betrayed him, and she forced herself to speak. "I've been robbed," she cried finally. "By outlaws, villains, cruel and false!"

"Who were they?" the monk asked warily.

Jane fought to get ahold of her words, letting her hair fall into her face so he couldn't see her clearly. "'Twas a big man, bearded, and a small man"—she thought of her own disguise—"a small man who didn't speak. And . . ."

"It's all right," the page said. "We can help you." He looked at the monk, his innocent young brow creased with worry. "We *can* help her, can't we, Brother Godric?"

"Like hell we can!" The monk had turned white with fear beneath his hood. "That's the same men who robbed me! We have to get out of here!"

"But we caught their leader!" the page argued. "You said so yourself, you said . . ."

"And now they'll bloody well want vengeance!"

"Please!" Jane shouted, trying to pitch her voice high, over theirs. "Please, m'lord, if you'll just see me home."

"We must," the page declared. "Are we men of God, or are we cowards?" Birds cried out somewhere in the distance, and insects hummed around the pond, and the noise began to ring in Jane's ears, as if all of nature were angry with her for what she was about to do.

"Cowards live. Fools and heroes are the ones who die."

"Well, *I'm* going to help her," the page said, determination on his young, small face.

"This isn't a knight's tale, boy." The monk softened. "These men are true villains. You saw what they did to me."

"I see what they did to *her*," the page answered. "Plain as day. What kind of men are we if we let them do something worse?"

Jane stared at them, disbelieving, as they argued over her fate. She had known Brother Godric had no honor, that he thought nothing of stealing from people like her to fill his purse, but she hadn't thought him so craven. She flushed with rage. She had poured this man's ale and his wine. She had fed him meals she made with her own hands. And the whole time, he hadn't even seen her, no more than he saw the boy who rode by his side. The monk was a coward and a thief. Perhaps he deserved whatever John and Wyll might do to him.

But not the boy. The boy was innocent, though Jane knew John wouldn't care. She had been a fool to follow his plan, knowing what he was capable of. Robin would not want the page to come to harm, not in his name. Robin would want her to be clever—to trick them, not to kill them.

After all, Jane realized, Brother Godric and the page could summon the reeve into the forest, and away from Robin, just by running back to town in fear. And pay for it with their dignity alone, rather than with their lives.

"He's right," Jane said, her voice shaking, and she did not have to use any wiles or falseness to put the tremor there. "Your master is right." She reached up and grabbed the page's hand in her own, speaking as quietly as she could, so that only he could hear her, and not whichever of Robin's men lurked behind her in the woods.

"What's she saying?" Godric demanded.

"These men are cruel, and dangerous"—Jane kept up her whispering, fervid, frantic, the tremor leaving her voice as her heart swelled—"and you should run. Run and find help. Find the reeve and bring him here. Tell him . . ."

But before Jane could say another word, two figures flew out of the trees and onto the horses' backs, their bodies blurred with movement, their faces so vicious and cold that they would be burned into Jane's memory forever. John and Wyll grabbed the reins of each horse and slammed the monk and his page to the ground as if they were sacks of grain. As Wyll leapt on top of the little page with his knife raised high, his teeth bared like an animal, Jane opened her mouth to scream and found herself yanked into Mooch's arms.

He pressed her head into his chest, forcing her eyes away as the page cried out, bleating like a lamb at slaughter. Jane's screams died against Mooch's heart, though she struggled to pull her head back, to shout a warning that was far too late. Her breath choked on the smell of his sweat, ripe and old and crusted into his tunic, like beer and onions and unwashed linen.

"Shhh," he whispered to her, breath acrid with fear. "Don't look, Janie. Don't listen. Just keep your head right here."

Jane sobbed against him, soundless, saliva running out of her mouth and all over his filthy shirt.

"It's okay." Mooch stroked her hair, but she could feel him shaking too, though he tried to pretend, tried to hold her firm like he was strong for her. "The worst is done."

She finally pushed him away, not caring for the mess of her face or the stains she had left on his tunic. "It's not," she said, garbled through her own tears and snot. "It's not. He's just a boy. They can't . . ."

"*Where the fuck is he?*" Little John bellowed, and Mooch lost his grip on her, and they both turned around.

John crouched behind Brother Godric, holding the monk still with one great arm around his chest, his legs wrapped around the monk's hips, crushing them. His other arm held a sword to Brother Godric's neck. Wyll stood over the monk's bared legs, standing in the puddle of piss that had seeped into the mud, his blade stained red. And the little page's body lay crumpled on the ground, curled up as if he were a sleeping child, a thin stream of blood running from his throat.

Jane gasped, her hand flying over her mouth, and she almost lost her feet until Mooch took her in his arms again.

"No," she murmured, "no, no, no. He was good. He was kind. He . . ." She felt a scream and a sob rising in her throat at once, and she tried to force them down, making a strangled, keening noise around her own fist.

"Nothing you can do for him now," Mooch whispered in her

ear, fiercely. "You hear me, Jane? Wyll has blood in his eyes, and so does John. Stand clear of them, you understand? Stay out of their way." He paused as she sank her teeth into her hand, tears still streaming. "Show me you understand."

She nodded, and he loosened his grip, just a little.

"Why should I tell you?" the monk sputtered, his voice choked with tears and terror. "You'll kill me anyway, you sack of shite!"

"Right." Wyll had a gleam in his eye as he tossed his knife back and forth in his hands. "But if you talk, you'll go as swift as he did." He jerked his head to the side, to the innocent boy's body. "And if you don't talk . . ."

"Did I tell you how much my friend here hates church men?" John said, his voice sounding cold, so cold, like a frozen lake with a great creature lurking beneath it. "He'd love to give you a taste of hell before he sends you there."

The monk found his courage in his final moments. "Do it, then! God will take me at His side, and He'll roast your corpses on a pyre!" He hocked up a huge ball of snot and spat, hard, right in Wyll's face. "Do it, you cowards!" Godric shouted, and before Wyll could move in, John had dropped the monk's head to the ground, cracking his skull against the earth. Then he leapt over him, raised his sword, and stabbed Brother Godric between his ribs, thrusting the blade up into his heart.

Jane stood stock-still, frozen, as she watched the monk die. The thrust was fast—too fast for anyone to have stopped it—but his death was slow. The life bled from his eyes like a candle's flame guttering as the tallow buried the wick.

And then, Jane's stomach heaved up and she vomited all over Mooch's feet.

"What did you do, you arse?" she heard Wyll cry even as

Mooch stroked her hair, pulling it back from her face. She thought Wyll might be shouting at her, but she didn't care, and she couldn't stop. She heaved and heaved again, until nothing was left in her stomach.

"I cleaned up Robin's fucking mess!" John yelled back. "And yours! Once you killed the boy . . ."

"What are we supposed to trade for Robin now?" Wyll whined, as if he were a hurt dog, not a brutal killer of boys, a torturer, a man who would give monks a taste of hell. "We've got nothing! You've spoiled our barter!"

"Don't be an ass, Wyll," John growled, but the chill in his voice was wearing off, and he sounded tired. "The reeve doesn't know he's dead. We can still draw him here, and keep him hunting."

Jane's head swirled, her mouth full of stinging bile. She started to slip once again, and then felt arms under hers, Mooch's arms, lifting her and trying to drag her away despite the mess she had made of his shoes. Filled with sudden fear and disgust, she pushed away from him and found her feet. "I have to go," she said, the words slow and heavy, her tongue sticking to her mouth.

"You're in no shape to . . ." Mooch began.

"I *have* to go. Now." Her words still thick, still clumsy, as if she were drunk.

"You can't let her go," Wyll said, eyes hungry for blood, knife still gripped in his hand. "Not now. Look at her."

"Fuck you, Wyll Scathlock," Mooch said, raising his voice for the first time Jane had ever heard. "She did what you wanted, and this is your mess, not hers. Leave her be."

"Left a mess of her own, she did." Wyll nodded at Mooch's soiled shoes.

John was still steady, still cruelly calm, staring at Jane as he wiped the blood off his sword. "Jane's right. She has to go. Someone has to tell the shire reeve that Brother Godric was caught in the forest."

Jane looked back at him, hollow, what was left of her guts sinking deep into her bowels like stones. She wished John would look anywhere else with that grim, canny stare, the one that said he knew what she had done, what she had tried to do, and failed. That he was watching her now, that he didn't think she had what it took to serve Robin, to be one of them. But she stared back, feeling like a corpse herself, dead and empty and dry. She held his eyes. She didn't shrink from him, didn't run. She would be proud of that, later.

"And if she turns on us instead?" Wyll demanded. "If she tells him what we've done?"

John put his sword back in its sheath. "She knows what kind of game this is now. So go on, Jane." He held her gaze still, but he didn't soften to her, not this time. "Get the reeve out here before he rides away with his prize."

"What should I tell him?" Jane asked, her voice so soft that even she could hardly hear it.

"Tell him there's thieves and bandits in the forest," John said, as simply as if he'd been talking about the sun rising or the rain falling. "Tell him that they took Brother Godric. And tell him you're scared they'll come for you next."

Jane saw things clearly now—John and Wyll and even Mooch, turning their heads from the killing as though that could wash away the sin, the memory. But Robin would be furious at this. Furious with John, with Wyll. Maybe even furious with her. She remembered the way he had struck John in the woods, struck Wyll when he mocked her. Robin had a code. He had a code, and they had all broken it.

Robin had to be freed. He was the only one who could fix this. And once he was back, Jane could explain everything. She could tell him what John and Wyll had done. She could tell him she had tried to stop it. If she helped to free him, she could make sure he knew what had really happened. And if she didn't . . .

Jane's breath caught in her chest. For if she didn't free Robin, he would pay for their crimes—for *her* crime—with his life.

And the page would have died for nothing at all.

Jane finally broke away from John's stare. She let Mooch help her onto Bran's horse, torn clothes and bile stains and mussed hair and all, and she rode back to the King's Houses, into the darkening dusk, the echo of the little page's screams following her all the way home.

Chapter Nineteen

Jane rode back to King's Houses as if she were riding through a nightmare, the path hot and dark and twisted. She returned Bran's horse to the stables and took a spare cloak from the hook, wrapping it around herself despite the warm weather so she could steal away to the servants' chamber unnoticed. She knew what she had to do. She had to go to the reeve and tell him what she had seen, to lure him away long enough to get Robin free. And a dark, fluttering hope in Jane's heart whispered that the reeve might even defeat John and Wyll in battle, might punish them for what they had done.

But what they had done, Jane had done too. What if the reeve took *her* prisoner instead? He was not a stupid man. He had seen her with Robin. He would not believe that Jane had been involved with any of this by accident, not a second time, and there would be no mercy in Walter de Stircheley if he knew the truth of what Jane had witnessed. What she had watched John and Wyll do while she stood by and did nothing, her words too feeble, and far too late, to save anyone.

By the time Jane reached the room she shared with the other girls—which was quiet and desolate, for all the staff were either madly scrubbing up the evening feast or gone for Whitsunday festivals in town—the thought of facing the reeve, her hair caked with mud and vomit, her breath reeking of fear, made something inside her shatter. She sagged against the wash basin, her head in her hands, and let her tears fall, water running from everywhere on her face as though she held a rainstorm behind her eyes.

And that was how Emmie found her.

"Jane! Jane, what's happened?" Jane felt Emmie's hands on her shoulders, her hair, and she turned her head away, frantically wiping at the tears, as though Emmie hadn't already seen her sobbing.

"Jane, please, tell me what's wrong!" But Jane couldn't respond. She had run out of words, but not out of tears, for they kept coming, like she was a river that would never run out of water.

"All right, it's all right." Emmie took her in her arms, let her sob against her chest. She smelled of ash soap and butter and cream, and Jane could have swooned into her. Emmie's hands were small and birdlike as they wove through Jane's tangled hair. "Whatever it is, we'll fix it, Jane, I swear. Where's Bran? Should I fetch Bran?"

"H . . . he . . ." Bran. Bran hadn't been at the stables. He should have been back by now, and she hadn't even looked for him. Had he been captured along with Robin? What would happen to him if he was? What would happen to *her*? Fresh sobs swallowed her words, and Jane heaved into tears again, retching.

"Jane . . ." Emmie's voice lowered, soft but resolved, as she asked against Jane's hair, "Jane, did Bran do something to you? Did he hurt you?"

The shock was enough to stir words from Jane's mouth. She wiped her eyes, her running nose. "Not him," she managed. Her voice was hoarse from crying, the words, spare as they were, burning her throat like fire.

Emmie let out a sigh, relieved, and wiped at Jane's face. "Sweet Mother Mary, you're filthy! Are you hurt? Tell me the truth now. I can fetch the witch for you." She smiled, making the joke gentle, trying to bring Jane back to herself. Jane could see it, but it was as though Emmie, and safety and goodness, drifted away toward the end of a long, dark corridor, leaving Jane with nothing but shadows and echoes. "Your prioress will know if you need a draught or a poultice."

A flame sparked, suddenly, in Jane's desolate heart. Ibota *could* help, if not in the way Emmie meant. She wouldn't help if Jane told the truth, but if Jane lied—told her that the monk and page had been taken for ransom—Ibota would go to the reeve on her own. It was a risk, but maybe, just maybe, it was a way out without Jane being seized by the reeve herself. She just had to say that Brother Godric was still alive.

The thought made Jane's nausea rise, and she covered her mouth with her hand.

"Shall I fetch her, Jane?" Emmie asked urgently.

Jane nodded, then turned her head away so that Emmie could not see her face, could not see the fear on it, or the relief.

A rustle of skirts, Emmie's powdery, milky smell, a whispered, "I'll be back," and Jane was alone again. She sank onto the bed. Emmie had lit a candle for her, and Jane watched shadows flicker across the floor, growing and shrinking, until the door cracked open and she heard Emmie's voice again, small and desperate.

"I don't know, m'um. She won't tell me what happened. But I thought if anyone could help . . ."

She trailed off, and Jane heard the chill wind of Ibota's voice. "Is she hurt?"

There was a torch now, and the smell of chamomile and mint.

The torch filled the room with so much light that Jane had to close her burning eyes. "I don't think so, m'um," she heard Emmie say. "But I'm not sure."

"Shut the door." Ibota's voice was cold, and so were her gloved hands as they turned Jane around for examination. "Gentle, not there, clean her face." A soft, damp cloth, warm as a mother's touch, smelling of clary sage. It pressed against Jane's neck, wiping around her mouth, cleaning away the stains on her face, the stains that marked her crime. Her sin.

"Jane," Ibota demanded, her hawk's eyes penetrating the fog in Jane's mind. "Are you ill?"

"Look at her tunic, m'um," Emmie hissed sharply. "She isn't ill."

Ibota's eyes snapped down only for a moment before they returned to Jane's face, but it was enough. Her eyes glistened, but her jaw was firm and set. "Go to my chambers," she ordered Emmie. "There's a draught in a violet jar. Bring it here, with wine from the kitchen."

Emmie hesitated. "But, m'um, I . . ."

"Leave us!" Ibota snapped, and Emmie scurried out, abandoning Jane to the prioress's unflinching gaze. She sat down beside Jane on the bed. "I know you have your secrets, Jane," she said softly. "And I know you're scared, and you're upset, but you must tell me if you've been hurt. I can't help you if you don't tell me, and if there's a wound or a cut, something may fester."

Jane shook her head. "No, m'um."

"Are you sure? Because sometimes, sometimes even in privy places, you might feel pain but you might not . . ."

Jane shook her head again, as hard as she could, but the concern on Ibota's face made tears spring to her eyes anew. She knew what the prioress thought, and some small part of her treacherous mind wondered if it was something she could use, which only made her feel guiltier, more ashamed. Words—even the words she knew she had to say to save herself, to save Robin—still wouldn't come. Nothing was coming to her now. Only tears.

Ibota removed her glove and pressed a cool, soft palm to Jane's forehead. "No fever, though you've been sick, it's clear. A drink and a bath will help with that." Her hand dropped to Jane's, and she pressed it, strong and firm. "When you're ready, Jane," Ibota said, her voice like a swift, cool current beneath the heat of Jane's tears, "you must tell me who did this to you."

Jane shook her head fiercely, tears leaking out, the prioress's kindness pressing the breath out of her. "It's my fault. There's no one else to blame. I should have known . . ."

"No, Jane." Ibota took her hands in her own again and said fiercely, "I know you think it's your fault. But it's not. They'll make you think it was, but it isn't. You remember that. It *never* is."

Jane sniffled like a child. "This is different."

"Women always think they're different. But not a one of us is. Not a one of us deserves to suffer, no matter who we think we are. No matter what we think we've done."

Her kindness made Jane suddenly want to confess everything, and see what Ibota could do with the mess Jane had made. Perhaps she would forgive her, perhaps she would send her off to Kirklees, hide Jane away there, where John and Wyll would never find her.

But Jane knew she would not. Not even Mary would have mercy for a wretch like her, someone who stood and did nothing when innocent lives were cut short like weaver's thread. And Ibota was the king's cousin. She would tell King Edward the whole of it. She might even hand Jane over to the reeve herself. Ibota was one of them, no matter how kind she seemed—bound to them by her noble blood. And in the face of that bond, Jane was no one.

Before Jane could speak again, Emmie returned. "I've brought what you asked, m'um."

Ibota handed Jane the potion, which smelled sharply of vinegar and bitter herbs. "Drink this. It will taste ill, but the wine will wash it down."

Jane drank and it seared her throat. She doubled over coughing, a sickly floral taste coating her tongue, tearing through her nostrils.

"Easy," Ibota said. "You must keep it down."

"Take this!" Emmie thrust a cup of wine into Jane's hand, and she swallowed it all at once. Anything to chase that foul taste out of her mouth. Still, the bitter herbs lingered like knives upon her tongue.

"Now, Jane," Ibota said again. "You must tell us what happened. Tell us who put you in this state."

Jane began to speak, a cough raking her throat like a claw. She thought of John's stare, his warning—*She knows what kind of game this is now*—and it forced the words out of her. "It was bandits, m'um. And . . . and it wasn't just me," she said, her heart pounding against her ribs so fast that Jane thought it might burst. "They took a holy man," she said, the words breaking in her throat, "a monk, and a boy."

"Brother Godric. Brother Godric and his page." Ibota turned gray as ashes. "Jane, you must tell me where. *Where* do they have him?"

Jane sucked in air, a shuddering breath, which made the lie sound more real, making her heart hurt all the more. "In the south woods, near the trysting tree. I think they're the ones the shire reeve's hunting. He caught one bandit . . . at the church." Jane's head was starting to cloud from the prioress's draught, its cloying taste coating her tongue like an ice slick, making it numb and slippery. She remembered what the monk had said, right before she led him to his death. "I think the others want their vengeance," she whispered.

The prioress pressed her lips against her teeth, and the lines around her mouth quivered with the effort of holding in words that weren't proper to be uttered. "And they don't care who they hurt. Typical." She rose. "She'll sleep soon," Ibota said to Emmie. "Make sure her face is clean, and make sure she's comfortable. I need to get a message to the shire reeve. He'll want answers from you, Jane, when you're ready."

"No!" Jane found that she and Emmie cried out together, almost as if they shared a voice.

"*No?*"

Jane thought desperately for an excuse, but Emmie saved her from having to speak. "M'um, forgive me, but you mustn't!"

"I mustn't? Whyever . . ." Her sharp, angled eyebrows crouched over her eyes, suddenly suspicious. "Do you understand how serious this is, either of you? You must stop them before they hurt Brother Godric and the boy! Men like that live by no rules. They'll spare no one if revenge is what they want."

Fear swelled in Jane, for Ibota was right, and here Jane was, a coward for not telling her that there was no sense in rushing, no urgency, for John and Wyll had indeed not spared anyone at all.

"No, m'um." Emmie's voice was meek—falsely so, Jane thought, for Jane knew Emmie didn't have a meek bone in her body. "'Tisn't that, I swear, it . . ." She sprang up from Jane's side, little hands pressed into each other, eyes pleading. "It's just . . . they'll question her, m'um. Ask her things. They might force her."

"Force her?" The arched brows pressed together. "Of course." Ibota's face went white. "They torture witnesses to crimes."

Emmie looked sorrowful, contrite. "You don't know what they'll do to girls like us, m'um. They hardly need any excuse, any reason at all."

The prioress let out a long, resigned sigh. "Fine. I'll tell the reeve about the bandits, and where they are, but I won't say it was you who told me. Is that fair?"

Emmie nodded. "More than fair, m'um."

"Thank you," Jane whispered, her lids closing of their own accord now, desperate to drag her into sleep.

"But Jane," Ibota said, her voice heavy with dreadful warning, "I have questions of my own. And I expect you to answer them when you wake."

Jane tried to nod, but her eyes were rolling back in her head, such a heavy head, like it was full of wool and lead, like the bed was sucking her down. The last thing she remembered was Emmie leaning over her and whispering, "You didn't want to tell. And so I made sure of it." She kissed her on the forehead, light as a butterfly, lips thin as air. "I'll keep your secrets, Jane. So get some sleep," she said, as if Jane could help it. Ibota's potion had taken her now, and she fell into darkness, and into nightmares, as if she had lost her footing somewhere out in the wild and tumbled directly into hell.

‑‑«‹‹‹*›››»‑

Jane awoke in Ibota's bed, sprawled out shamelessly on her soft, clean linens and silks. The smell of herbs was cloying. Her mouth was sour and her belly empty, gnawing, and growling obscenely, as if it hadn't witnessed all those horrible events right along with Jane. Moonlight poured through the prioress's little window, and Jane's mind reeled in panic. Had she been too late to pull the reeve away? Had the prioress's message missed him? Her heart filled with dread. She should have gone to the reeve herself, no matter the risk. She never should have trusted Robin's freedom to anyone else.

Then, she heard raised voices in the hallway.

"How the hell am I supposed to find them then?" Walter de Stircheley bellowed outside the wooden door.

Jane tried to pull herself up to sitting, her heart hammering, but her head felt heavy as a pail of milk, and all she could do was prop herself up against the bed. What if the reeve came in here? He would know it was Jane, then. He already remembered her face. But he couldn't come into a lady's chambers, could he? Not even the shire reeve was allowed to do that.

Still, he had come, which meant he had not yet ridden off to Nottingham with Robin Hood in tow. Robin could still be freed.

But at what cost? Jane's mind whispered to her, and it was in the prioress's voice, or Emmie's or some other good and pure woman, the kind who Jane would never be again.

"A servant told me, but I can't remember which one." Ibota's voice, full of false haughtiness, false lightness.

"Damn it, woman! This is important!"

"I *know* it's important." The prioress couldn't keep up her innocent act for long. It hung on her foolishly, like an ill-fitting girdle. "Why do you think I summoned you?"

Walter heaved a heavy sigh. "Was it a male servant, or a female servant, or . . ."

"A boy, I think. But were I you, Shire Reeve, I would leave the servants be. Let them do their jobs, and you do yours. Hunt your prey where it's been herded for you."

"That's why you're *not* shire reeve," Walter snapped. "If you were, you'd know not to walk into a trap!"

Jane heard the heavy tread of Walter's boots, and then Ibota's muttering as she came back through her door. "*That's* not why I'm not shire reeve, you giant foolish . . . oh, good!" she said when she saw Jane. "You're awake." She frowned. "I hope I've done enough, Jane. I hope protecting you hasn't cost us innocent lives."

"Thank you," Jane tried to say, though her voice came out a rasp, and all the other things she wanted to say—like, *I'm sorry* and *It's already too late*—were lost. She swam in guilt as if it were a wild river, and she could barely keep her head above its rushing waters. She could have told the prioress exactly where they were, could have traced the path to Mooch's house with her eyes closed. But that would have led the reeve right to them, quickly. Far too quickly for any of them to get Robin free. And then they would send the reeve after her.

The prioress shook her head, mistaking Jane's sorrow for illness, then stirred together something in a cup on her side table. "I'd give you water, but it will cool your bile, so this is hyssop and honey and warming cloves, to help your throat. *Sip* it," she warned as Jane took it between her hands. "Small sips, like a bird. Count five Ave Marys in your head before you drink again."

Jane took an obedient sip. It was so soothing to her dry, flaming mouth that she was desperate to swallow the whole thing, but she didn't dare, not under the prioress's watchful eye. She counted slowly, silently. When it was finally time, she let the minty hyssop soothe her again. "I told Eudo you were ill," the prioress continued. "And Emmie sent word to that boy of yours, the one at the stables . . ."

"Bran," Jane croaked. "Is he . . ." She swallowed hard, her throat feeling full of needles. "He's all right?"

The prioress focused on her like a hawk. "Was he with you, Jane? Does he know who hurt you?"

Jane shook her head fiercely, not trusting her voice.

"Jane, please. I can't help if you won't talk to me. Are you beholden to them somehow? You said you had brothers. Are they involved?"

"No!" The absurdity of it eased her tears a little. "My brother is a priest!"

"Your lover, then. Was that the man I saw you with? Not the stable boy, but the other one?" She looked at Jane knowingly, and Jane remembered with a shock that the prioress had seen Robin near the stables. And she had been there, at the church, to see him stand up and challenge the reeve. Had she been close enough to know it was the same man?

As Jane struggled between silence and words, the prioress snapped, "Drink. It's been more than five Marys."

Jane drank, and she found her throat clearing a little more. "I'm not . . ." she started, but Ibota's eyebrows raised sharply, as if daring her to lie. "It isn't . . ."

Sympathy warred with disappointment on the prioress's face. "All right, Jane. I won't press you, for now. You've done the right thing. You're saving a man's life. But it's clear to me that you're in over your head," she said, her stare so intense that Jane wanted to run, to hide away and never meet that stare again. "You'll see, soon enough, that a silver-tongued man is nothing but shining paint on a low coin. He'll promise you your freedom, he'll promise to change the world for you, to shift the moon and stars. But the only way to be *truly* free is to be your own woman. Not his."

Jane felt anger rise up in her. Ibota didn't know her. And she didn't know anything about what was between her and Robin. But Jane could not fight back, could not defend Robin the way she wanted to, for her own fate hung on a knife's edge now, and she was smart enough to know it. She needed to play the game, for Robin's sake and her own. And for that, she needed to keep Ibota on her side. "I don't deserve your kindness, m'um," she said, the words not reaching her heart. "Not after what I've done."

Jane's false words brought a flush to the prioress's cheeks. "Nonsense. I'm a healer, and this is what I do. Everyone deserves a chance to be whole."

"M'um, you're very generous, but I can't . . ."

"Quiet, now." A frown appeared on the prioress's face, candle-light twinkling in her eyes. "I didn't say I was doing this out of charity. I have questions for you, Jane Crowe, like I said. And I expect you to answer everything I ask you once you're back."

"Back from where?"

Ibota stared heavenward and sighed. "You're wanted by Be-trice de Stircheley. The reeve has set up his fool wife here, of all places. He says it's not safe for his lady in the house. He's got an outlaw locked up in the cellar."

Jane almost dropped her cup. The reeve's house. His *cellar*. Of course that's where Robin was. Where else would the reeve keep him before dragging him off to Nottingham? "Why did she send for *me*?" she asked, gripping the cup harder.

"I suppose she trusts you," Ibota said wryly.

"Eudo will be furious. I've already missed a day."

"I'm certain he'll understand," the prioress said, and Jane

nodded agreeably, even though she was certain that he wouldn't. "Betrice de Stircheley will be safe in your care, and you'll be safe with her. Well guarded," she added, and it was both a promise and a warning. Ibota stood, straightening her robes, staring out the window. "I'm taking a chance on you, Jane. I can see that your heart is good. And I can see that you're trapped, even if you can't. I want to open a window for you, give you a way to save yourself." She seemed to summon her courage for something, taking in a deep breath. "And when it's done, and when they're caught, we're going to have a long talk, you and I." She met Jane's stare with eyes full of fire and pain. "And we're going to make sure no one else gets hurt by those men in the woods."

Chapter Twenty

The sky was dark gray at dawn, heavy with clouds. At least Jane would be indoors today, waiting on Betrice. The prioress was already gone, but Eudo had sent Jane a bowl of stewed grains and a caudle from the kitchens. She picked at the porridge, for caudle disgusted her, particularly when it had begun to cool and set. She ate slowly, just as the prioress had told her, and her stomach took the food surprisingly well, as if she had purged everything out of her, all the horror and the fear, and her belly had become a stone pit, incapable of feeling.

She changed into the fresh kirtle and stockings Emmie had left for her, then wandered into the corridor, trying to decide what to do with the caudle. Perhaps she could find a place to bury it in the dirt outside so she wouldn't seem ungrateful. As she crept out of the prioress's chambers with her burden, Jane almost walked into Milla, who had bowls of her own in her hands.

"I'll take that," Milla sang, and then she looked at the full caudle with disdain. "She never does finish things, does she? Spoiled as old fish, she is."

Jane nodded, agreeing with Milla to spare herself embarrassment. Her lies were beginning to feel like a thicket full of clinging vines and thorns, like she might stumble with any step and be swallowed by them.

"Has her claws in you now, does she?" The older servant seemed almost sympathetic, which she had never seemed before. Jane prayed fervently that Emmie hadn't told her anything. The last thing she needed was for everyone at King's Houses to think her a victim. She couldn't bear it. It was bad enough with Emmie and the prioress.

"I'm to wait on the shire reeve's wife today," Jane said. "Do you know where they're keeping her?"

Milla rolled her eyes. "You've gone from bad to worse, then, haven't you? She's in the far chamber, out by the chapel. Thick as an oak tree, that one, but acts as if a light breeze will knock her off her feet."

Jane found Betrice pacing the floor in emerald-green slippers, her chestnut hair loose and frizzled by wear and wind, streaked with thin silver strands that Jane hadn't noticed before.

"Oh, thank God, Jane! You're here!" Betrice cried in the high, false voice she used with her husband. She rushed toward Jane, then stopped herself, backing away a little, her pale face folding into a worried frown. "They said you were ill last night. I hope it's not catching."

Jane smiled weakly. "Just my courses, m'um." It was a ridiculous lie, but it was the only one she had come up with over her porridge.

"Oh," Betrice breathed. "A good, stout ale for that." She smiled shyly, as if they were friends. "They say it gets better with children, but don't believe a word of it. Did you know we have two boys and a girl, Walter and I? Sent them to London when they were young. He said it was better for them to come up with my cousins. They'd have a better lot in life, he said. I was sorry for it then, but now, after all that's happened . . ." Betrice drifted off, her hands catching at her fur collar.

"Of course," Jane said, and something inside her found the role she was playing soothing, like a mask she could slip on to hide her inner turmoil, her private thoughts. "What do you need of me, m'um?"

"Well . . ." Betrice flailed a little. "My hair, I suppose, and my clothes and things." Jane hadn't seen a true lady's maid at Betrice's house. The older woman who served the table and cleaned and shopped likely also had to dress her mistress's hair. It made Jane feel sick. Robin had placed her so well, she thought, sparing her the endless labor of serving in a private home.

"Are you still feeling weak, Jane?" Betrice's brow creased. "I can have the cook bring something to make you sturdy."

"I'm fine," Jane said, her voice thin. "Shall we comb your hair?" She felt like she was talking to a child, but Betrice responded by beaming at her.

"I know it's not your role." Betrice settled into a chair and handed Jane a comb. "But you're the only person I can bear to see right now. That's what I told them. I told them you were the only one I trusted!"

Jane started combing Betrice's hair, thick as a horse's tail, smoothing the little silver hairs back into the brown. She didn't know what to say, so she murmured, "I'm honored, m'um."

Betrice shook her head, her hair snagging the comb, and Jane lifted it away carefully until she finished moving. "You know about the potter, of course. Robin Hood." She turned to look at

Jane with wide, stricken eyes. "Oh, Jane, isn't it awful? Had you any idea?"

Jane shook her head. "He had us all fooled, m'um." Gently, she turned Betrice's head around again so she could continue her combing, and Betrice whimpered a little with her strokes, whether in pleasure or distress, Jane couldn't tell.

"I just can't be there in that house with *him* downstairs any longer. I thought he had eyes for me, and it was flattering, even though I've grown so old and Walter can be so . . ." She looked up, blinking, waving a hand across her eyes as though she could will the tears away with magic, and Jane had to lift the comb again. "Well, I was a fool, is all I was. He was so kind, so familiar. But I suppose it was just to get at Walter. None of it was real."

Jane felt a little stabbing pain within her heart at this confession, a low jealousy that she did not deserve to feel, but also sympathy for Betrice, for Robin had made Jane feel adored too, and John had called her a fool for it. She repeated the warning that John had given her: "They say the Lord of the Greenwood is a thief of coin, and of hearts. He only wants what another man has."

"Yes." Betrice sniffed. "I suppose that's all it was, wasn't it?" She looked out the window, a shadow falling over her face as the clouds thickened outside. "I wish I had thought to take my things," she said sadly. "Just a few. But I can't bear to go back to that house. Not now." Her hand fell idly to the cluster of keys at her belt. "Not when I know he's lurking down there, with only the floor between us."

A spark lit in Jane, and her mind began a slow march back into formation, like soldiers waking from sleep. Betrice would keep her wine, her ale, and her onions in her cellar. She was the lady of the house. She would have the key to Robin's prison. It must be on that belt.

Jane could scarcely breathe. She struggled to keep her voice measured, calm. "Of course," she said, the words catching a little, and she cleared her throat. "I can fetch a few things from the house, m'um."

"Really? Would you?" Betrice seemed relieved, even knowing that she had agreed to send Jane into danger. "I understand if you don't want to," she added quickly. "The wind is high today, and it's a long walk, and I can always send someone who . . ."

"I'll do it," Jane said, far too fast, the words rushing out of her like a gust of air. "I don't mind."

"Please, Jane, if you're unwell, I shan't press you." Betrice's eyes were stricken, her mouth tight, nervous, and Jane could see that she did, indeed, want to press, but she knew it wouldn't be proper.

Jane wove her face into a mask of sympathy. "But, m'um, if it's your privy things, it must be someone you trust, especially after all that's happened. All that's come out, I mean." She was alarmed at how smooth, how confident she sounded. It wasn't a lie, not exactly. She was merely using Betrice's own words, shifting them a little to suit herself. It wasn't nearly as hard as it should have been.

"Exactly. You understand me so well, Jane, and you're so kind to do it."

You understand me so well. It was the same sort of thing Robin had said to her.

Betrice seemed lighter now, like a great weight had been lifted. She handed Jane a satchel. "I'd send you with a cart," she said, "but Walter would never let me hear the end of it. Just the necessities: a few privy things from the chest—ladies' things, you know, for

Walter didn't think to tell me how long I'd be away." Her fingers ran through the keys, stopping at an iron one with a square head. "He has him in the cellar. In my very own house. Don't go near it, Jane. I know he was . . . kind to both of us when he played at being a potter"—Betrice flushed a little with the memory of Robin's "kindness"—"but he's not a good man."

"I wouldn't want to see him again, m'um," Jane lied, wishing she could simply grab the keys out of Betrice's hands and be done with it, for, surely, *that* was the key to the cellar—the key on which the reeve's wife had lingered. "Not now that I know who he really is."

"No." Betrice's eyes creased with sadness and memory. She looked haunted as she thrust the keys into Jane's hands. "Maybe he's not even a man at all. Maybe he's a devil sent to test us. Walter doesn't believe in such things, but I'm not so sure."

And Jane wondered, as she clutched the keys, her hands sweating, if Robin was the devil, just who and what *she* was becoming.

-≪≪◆≫≫-

Bran was waiting for Jane when she came for a horse to ride to the reeve's house, his face drawn and tense. "There you are!" he said, his voice a rushed whisper. "Have you found anything?"

He reached for her, trying to pull her close, but Jane backed away from him, fury rising in her chest. He must have had word from John, must have known she was meant to search for Robin. Did he also know about the bodies they had left behind? "Did John tell you what he and Wyll *did*?" she demanded.

Bran paled. "He sent word, is all. They're waiting on you to . . ."

"Did he tell you they did it right in front of me?"

Bran reached for her again, but she stumbled out of his grasp. "Did they hurt you?" he asked softly, disbelieving.

"No, but they hurt . . ." Jane thought of the page, his child's body, crumpled up, the soul fled out of it, that thin stream of blood. "They killed an innocent. A boy." The page had barely been older than her brother Ralf. He'd been cut down like a stunted crop before he could even reach his full height.

"We only do what's needed," Bran said, though he was still pale as the morning sky. "If they had to do it, if they had to find Robin . . ."

"*I'm* the one who found Robin!" Jane shouted, the outburst startling them both.

"You found him? Where is he?"

"The shire reeve's cellar. He's guarded. He . . ."

"John will find a way."

"I have the keys. You need to fetch John and tell him where to meet me." But her words were thin and quiet. The thought of having to face John again had doused her fire.

Bran's eyes grew wary, softer, as if she were a horse he needed to tame. "Look, Janie, sometimes, when you try to help people, bad people get hurt. You remember my story about Wyll's priest . . ."

"But it isn't only bad people getting hurt!"

"No one's hands are clean in the church. They lie and rape and steal and . . ."

"No one?" She bit back her anger, trying not to shout, not to draw attention from anyone else. "What about my brother?"

"Adam's different. He's not one of them in his heart. Not yet. But if he chooses the wrong side, when it comes to it . . ."

"Then when it comes to it, you'd cut him down too? Knowing

how hard we had it, knowing how hard he worked to get where he is now? Would you . . ." Jane's words ran out, and her hand flew over her mouth, stifling a sob. She squeezed her eyes shut to stop the tears.

Bran tried to put his hand on her shoulder, but she shoved it away. "I said *don't*! I can't believe you're taking John's side. Robin would never kill innocents. But what does it matter? They'll blame him, and you know it, and they'll hunt him to the ends of England!"

Bran leaned back, his face darkening. "You talk of Robin like he's a delicate urn, not an outlaw." He looked at her as if there were something he wanted to say, but he thought better of it. "Maybe it was a mistake to get you involved," he said instead. "You can't pull off a trick if your feelings get the better of you."

"Anger is a feeling too," she said, her voice as cold and hollow as she felt inside, "even if men like to tell themselves it isn't. Wyll's anger killed that boy yesterday. It wasn't justice. And even if we get Robin free, he'll never forgive us for it." She swallowed the sob that threatened to rise in her throat. "Maybe he shouldn't."

"Jane"—Bran's voice dropped—"you should just let me handle this. Give me the keys, and you can go back to the kitchens . . ."

"They'll never let you into that house!" she snapped. "But they won't even blink at me. I'm just a servant girl. I'm no threat to anyone." Jane couldn't keep the bitterness from her voice. "Besides, I think we both know what John will do to me if I disappear."

"John wouldn't hurt you, Janie!"

"Don't tell me what he would or wouldn't do! You weren't there!"

"Jane"—Bran raised his hands, still trying to soothe and calm her, as if she weren't thinking clearly—"you don't have to do this. I can fix it for you. I can find you a way out."

"You can't." She shook her head, backing away from him. *Robin is the only one who can fix this*, Jane thought, but she knew enough not to say so. "I have to do it myself."

A shadow crossed Bran's face, like he was haunted by a spirit only he could see. "Promise you'll come back to me, Janie."

"I promise," she told him. But it tasted like a lie.

Chapter Twenty-One

J ane sheltered from the wind beneath a great tree, clutching at the empty satchel the reeve's wife had given her and trying to control her pounding heart. The shire reeve's house was just up the hill, but she couldn't go up until she saw John or Wyll or Mooch, until she was sure Bran had found them and told them where Robin was being held.

Even still, she jumped when she finally saw John's bulky form round the corner toward her, another man at his side, their cloaks flapping in the wind. She worried it would be John and Wyll both, and that their anger would have come with them—their heads weren't cool when they were together, no matter what Bran thought. But she saw with relief that it was only Tuk. Tuk who had always been kind to her.

Jane sucked in a deep breath. She couldn't look at John, though she could feel his eyes on her. "You came back," she said to Tuk, and it was a weak thing to say, after all that had passed.

His face was stony, grim. "John sent word."

"What do you have for us?" John's tone was curt.

Jane lifted the belt of keys from her waist. "A key," she said, looking at the keys instead of John. "This one's for the cellar, but I don't know how to unfasten . . ."

John took the belt in his own hands, examined the clasp, and squeezed. "There." He held up the key. "Simple as that."

"I'll need it back," Jane said. "If she sees that it's missing, and Robin's gone missing too, she'll . . ."

"We're not dullards, Jane," John snapped. "You'll get your key back."

"Easy, old man," Tuk said. "She's here to help."

"That's right." Jane felt indignant enough to meet John's eyes, her nostrils flaring. "I'm helping you in spite of what you did."

John shook his head. "You're soft, Jane. You've got no idea what this takes. I told Robin you would be soft. Told him early, I did."

"I just don't want innocent blood on my hands. Not again."

"Then you had better run far from us." John tried to sound gruff, but his voice had a hint of sadness, and so did his eyes.

"Let's get on with it," Tuk urged them. "We'll need to see where he's held."

In the fall, the reeve's house had been lively with the warm smell of food and the stink of men and ale. Now, it looked as if Walter had set it up for a battle. The house teemed with lean, hungry mercenaries, dirt and weeds caking their boots. None of them were the same men who had been there before—perhaps Walter had cut those men loose after they got him stuck in Robin's trap. Tables were stacked in the corners, chairs overturned, the floors cleared of rugs, tapestries stripped from the walls. Betrice would have fainted clear away to see it. She had abandoned her old servants there, along with her privy things, and they skittered between the men like mice, their faces drawn. The whole house stank of fear—fear and boasting, like a pen of trapped animals.

Jane left Tuk and John in the trees near the house and approached with her jaw clenched tight, but the guards just waved her through when she showed them the keys and murmured something about fetching the lady's necessaries. Their eyes were on the door, the way in and out, and they paid no attention to servants, or women, or anything they felt was beneath their notice. After all, what danger could there be in a peasant girl with her head low and her arms full of ladies' underclothes?

"The cellar is down the steps," she said when she returned. "At the back of the house. It's not near any windows."

"Bloody hell," John groaned. "We'll never get through the guards."

Jane's heart sank. There was no way in to Robin. No way in at all. She should have known. Walter was an arrogant man, but a canny one. She stared hard at the ground. Robin was down there, beneath the dirt, stored up with the flour and Betrice's precious spices. Would the reeve's men have beaten him? Would he be hungry? Would he know that Jane and John and Tuk were coming for him, or would he have surrendered to his fate? She imagined him, bruised and bound, his head hung, his fox-colored hair smeared with blood, and her heart surged back toward the house. She felt suddenly that if she had the strength, she would have burst through the guards herself, killed them with her bare hands just to get to him.

"We'll need a distraction." John chewed his lip. "To get the guards outside, so we can slip inside and use your key."

"What kind of distraction?" Jane demanded, worried—the last time John had used that word, a monk and a boy lay dead.

"Let me think, girl." John waved her off, as if she were an insect buzzing at his ear. "I need to make some noise, get them all outside."

"Promise no one will get hurt," Jane said weakly, feeling the sweat from her palms slick across Betrice's oiled satchel. "I want to make sure that . . ." She swallowed, fighting tears. "I want to make sure you get him free, but . . ."

"Are you forgetting whose idea this is?" John said, his fire growing. "You were the one who came to me and begged me to rescue Robin! You were the one who said she would do anything!"

Jane flushed deep, her face boiling like winter pottage. Is that what John told himself—that this was *her* idea? That she should have known what he was capable of? Is that what he would tell Robin? And she was about to shout right back at him when Tuk snapped, "Enough! You're acting like children, both of you. Robin is a dead man if we don't get him out of there before the reeve finds the bodies. He won't wait for trial in Nottingham: he'll take his head right here and now, and all of ours too, if he catches us. So stop sniping at each other and *think*!"

Jane swallowed her accusations. Tuk was right. She couldn't stand here arguing with John with all the guards close enough to hear: there was more at stake now than her pride. "There's a garden, and stables," she said, "'round the other side of the yard. But I don't know what you can do there."

"Cut the horses loose, burn the flowers." John flashed a wicked smile. "Raise hell."

Tuk laughed, but Jane could only think of the crops burning

along with the flowers, the way the servants would have to dig deep into the scorched land to rebuild it.

Maybe not, though. Maybe Walter and Betrice would leave town for good this time, taking Jane's shame and humiliation along with them. Suddenly, she was filled with an intense longing to be back in the kitchens, hands sticky with dough, listening to Emmie and Eudo's banter. Cooking was hard work, but it was a happy, warm place, and Jane always felt satisfied as the bread rose and the smell of meat and herbs fought the wet winter wind outside. Kitchen work had never left her scared, or ill. It had never made her heart pound so hard that she feared it wouldn't stop. She could be content with life in the kitchens; it could be enough for her. What kind of a person was she to keep casting herself into danger and fear?

And John's words haunted her. For he *had* warned her, hadn't he? *Do you know what it is you're asking, Jane?* Perhaps she had been a fool to think that Robin's code would still mean something when Robin himself was gone. And when he was back, would he see it John's way—that blood was on Jane's hands as much as John's and Wyll's? It was a selfish thought, in the face of everything— Jane knew it was—but it made her heart ache with loss. What place would she have in Robin's life, or even at the King's Houses, if he lost his faith in her? What would any of this mean, all that she had done for Robin, if Robin didn't want her anymore?

Chapter Twenty-Two

The sky was growing dark by the time Jane returned to King's Houses with Betrice's satchel. All the way home, she kept smelling fire—burning harvest and wood and weed— but that was foolish. She was a long way from the shire reeve's house. It was merely guilt haunting her, like a nightmare she could barely remember, one that left nothing behind it but the fear.

When she returned to Betrice's chamber, the reeve's wife nearly toppled her with an embrace, and it was so shockingly improper that Jane staggered backward. "Oh, Jane!" she cried out. "I'm so glad you're back! Was the house all right?"

Jane remembered the bare hall, the furniture pushed against walls, the men's boots tracking mud. And the fire she knew was coming but hadn't seen. "It's fine, m'um," she said, dizzy with the scent of Betrice's perfume hanging like a cloud in her hair. "All's well. I have your things."

"Thank you so much, Jane. I don't know what I'd do without you," Betrice gushed, and it sounded so false, for she had been without Jane for most of her life and would be again, as soon as someone could arrange it.

"The prioress wanted to see you," Betrice said offhandedly, sorting through her things, "but I asked if she could wait. Oh, do you have my keys?"

Jane nodded and unbound the key belt from her own waist. The cellar key wasn't on it. Not yet. She could only pray that John would keep his promise and get it back to her, that he wouldn't get her in trouble with the reeve out of bitterness or spite. And she had to pray that Betrice didn't notice. But why would she look for the cellar key, unless she was thinking about Robin?

"Just set them over there, Jane." Betrice gestured to a little table beneath the window, and Jane nearly swooned in relief. "Thank you for staying," she continued, although Jane hadn't agreed to do any such thing. "I just can't bear to be alone. Not now. Not until Walter is back."

Betrice sat nervously as the sun disappeared into gray sky, and Jane bustled around, arranging the reeve's wife's few possessions and lighting candles. The evening grew darker still, and rain finally broke from the clouds, and all Jane could hope was that whatever fire John and Tuk had started would soon be washed away. But there was still no sign of either of them, or the key. How would they even get it back to her, under guard as she was? Why had she thought to do something so reckless, so foolish, after all she had already done?

"Shall I send for food, m'um?" Jane finally asked. Her own stomach was surging, despite her fear and nervousness waiting on the key, waiting on word of Robin, waiting on the reeve—waiting on *everything*. She could barely breathe from the pressure in her chest. But she knew the kitchens would be cleaning up soon, and

it was the last chance to get whatever Eudo had in mind for supper. She'd had nothing but the morning's porridge, and she'd lost
most of what she'd had the day before. Perhaps she should have
forced the caudle down after all. *When did you get so used to food and
drink*, she asked herself, *like a fatted calf?*

"Thank you, Jane, but I couldn't stomach a thing," Betrice
said from her chair, her tall form dwarfing it, rocking it back and
forth on its weak legs as she busied her hands toying with her
rings. "Well," she said, "perhaps a clarrey. And some sop. Would
you fetch a clarrey?"

"Of course, m'um." Jane tried not to let her disappointment
show. If Betrice weren't eating, then *she* couldn't eat, unless she
snuck something. And that would require a conversation with
Eudo, who would already have plenty of questions, and Emmie
too. Jane flushed at the memory of the night before, of what Emmie had seen and thought. She was a fool to have offered to go to
the kitchens for Betrice. What if Bran came looking for her with
the key? For it would be Bran, wouldn't it? John wouldn't be fool
enough to come himself? Or would he, thinking himself brave?

A drop of cold sweat trickled down her back. She hadn't
thought any of this through. What was to stop John from taking
the key with him, forgetting her, or leaving it on the ground like a
brand upon her forehead, pointing to her guilt?

But when Jane opened the chamber door, the old laundress
stood there, her hand raised to knock.

"What is it?" Jane burst out, churlish, her mind a tangled web
of fear.

The laundress pressed something into Jane's hands, wrapped
in a filthy cloth. "All's well at home," she said, her voice a harsh
whisper.

"At home?" Jane looked at her, confused. It was as if she had slipped back in time a moment, back to when she had a real home.

"Aye," she said. "At the old house."

"Is everything all right, Jane?" Betrice called out. "Tell her I have no washing. I shan't be staying long."

Disgust flickered across the old woman's face, a pale mole on the end of her nose quivering. "Your reeve's back, m'um," she croaked to Betrice, with no pretense of courtesy, for she didn't have to have it, did she, this old woman who slipped in and out of the shadows, her head and body bent? "Tying up his horse right now, he is."

"Hide that," the laundress breathed to Jane, but Jane had already searched the bundle with her fingers, already felt the thin rod of iron with the square head. It was the key. It was the key to the cellar, and Robin was free! The realization came to her like the sun clearing the clouds at dawn, like a ray from the heavens. *At the old house*, the laundress had said. Robin knew where her house was. He had said so. And it was the perfect place for him to hide, safe from the reeve and anyone else who went hunting for him. Her heart lifted up, light as breezes, as though it could drift right out of her chest.

"Thank you," Jane whispered, but the laundress was already shuffling away.

Now she just had to get the key back on that belt. She turned to Betrice, who looked stricken, her face ashen as fine-milled flour, her hands clutching at the pendant hanging from her throat. The reeve's safe return was what Betrice had been waiting for, wasn't it? Why did she look so terrified?

"Shall I set your hair, m'um?" Jane offered. She could get close to the keys if she did, if she had Betrice's head turned away from the table.

"Oh, yes." Betrice tugged absently at the loose chestnut strands, staring at the door, over Jane's shoulder. "Perhaps. Perhaps before the clarrey. And Walter . . ." She looked around as though she hoped that her drink would magically appear beside her, as though fairies served the nobles at King's Houses instead of real people. "Perhaps Walter might want something. Better to wait?" Her eyes finally met Jane's, haunted. "You will wait with me, won't you, Jane?"

"Of course!" Jane said, and relief brought a flush back to Betrice's cheeks.

Jane had barely gathered all of Betrice's hair into her hands, eyes turned back to the table and the keys, when Walter de Stircheley burst through the door, sending it slamming into the wall beside it.

Betrice gasped and leapt to her feet, tearing her hair out of Jane's grasp, and Jane felt her own shoulders fly up around her ears. He was here. And Jane had to face him, knowing what she'd done.

Walter was a stone gargoyle of rage, his lips pressed white against each other, his eyes full of smoke and steam. His boots were white with ash, trailing burnt weeds, and Jane's stomach flipped over. They had done it. She could see the evidence of John's crime—of *her* crime—all over the chamber floor.

But Jane couldn't think about that now. She couldn't let it freeze her, or stop her. She *had* to get the key back on that belt. Betrice might be as careless as a butterfly, but Walter was a stinging wasp. He'd know just what to look for. And if his wife told him that she had loaned the keys to Jane, had sent her to the house, and the cellar key was missing . . .

Jane backed toward the table, eyes on Walter, who looked as if he was so angry that he couldn't see clearly no matter what she did. Better to look meek, though, and afraid.

"Walter," Betrice cried. "What is it? What's happened?"

"What's happened?" Walter thundered, striding toward her. "What did you *think* would happen?"

"Walter!" Betrice clutched her throat. "The door! Please!"

The reeve looked over his shoulder with a hiss, realizing the door was still open, that all the servants who came through the corridor could hear his every word, could see his rage. As he turned his head, Jane snatched the belt off the table and buried it within her skirts, her fingers feeling for the twisted piece of metal, the empty one, the one that had held the cellar key. The one John had told her would be easy to twist into place.

Walter slammed the door shut and spun back to his wife, his face a wild flame. "You want to know what *happened*? Do you mean the slaughtered monk I found in the woods, head stuck on a pike like a fucking battle standard?" Betrice gasped again, a strangled sob. "Or do you mean our garden, burned to ashes by the fires of hell?"

"Our . . . our gardens?" Betrice stumbled forward, still clutching at her throat. Her eyes pinned to the reeve and his wife, Jane's fingers flew through the keys until she finally felt the twisted metal, the loop without a key. *There.* It was pinched shut, and she cursed John silently, as if he had shut it again to vex her. She twisted hard with both fingers, trying to pry it open, praying that neither Walter nor his wife would look her way. "Walter, what do you mean? It's raining, Walter! How could our gardens . . ."

"It's raining. Oh, it's raining, she says." His eyes rolled in his head. "Well, it wasn't *fucking raining* when Robin Hood broke out of our cellar and torched our land for spite!" And with a great shout, the reeve suddenly turned and slammed his fist into the wall, leaving a thin line of cracks radiating through it, like a great rock had struck it.

Jane and Betrice both jumped, Jane nearly dropping the keys. Suddenly Jane was five years old again, her head ducked low, and she could feel her feet moving of their own volition, skittering backward across the wood, just as her own small feet had done as a child to avoid her father's fists. For her da had hit a wall like that, and more than once, and he had done worse too. She clutched hard at the keys, which had slipped low, and she lifted her skirts up a little too high to catch them. *Breathe, Jane,* she told herself. *Just breathe. Mend the keys and focus.*

"But . . . but how?" Betrice's voice was weak, timid. "How did he get out?"

"You tell me, woman!" The reeve stormed toward her, his shoulders hunched as if he were about to charge at her like a mean, angry boar, all red face and slavering jaws.

Betrice stumbled backward, and Jane found the little piece of metal again. She twisted, hard, desperately, as if her life depended on it, and finally felt a tiny gap open up, and she worked the key back on with small, quick movements, hoping it looked as if she were scared enough to be wringing her skirts.

"Walter, calm down! I . . ."

"I found Brother Godric *desecrated,*" the reeve spat, his shoulders shaking. Jane fought the tears welling in her eyes, pinching the key twist closed as hard as she could. "I went back to the house. *Our* house. I meant to torture that bastard. Wring everything out of him. Bleed him dry."

"You think he . . ." Betrice's hands scrabbled at her face. "You think Robin Hood did that? To the monk?"

"Who else?" Walter bellowed, and Jane's heart sank. She had known, hadn't she, exactly what the reeve would think. He had aimed his arrow at Robin Hood's heart and he couldn't see the other outlaws in the forest, didn't need to see them. He would never believe that Robin was different from the rest. "He was free, wasn't he? Smuggled out of the house without a trace!" The reeve started toward Betrice again, and she backed away until she met the wall. "No locks broken, no doors off their hinges, easy as you please." He snarled, his face close to hers now. "But you wouldn't know anything about that, would you, my *love*."

"Walter," Betrice stammered. "Walter, I don't know what you mean."

The reeve stopped moving, cold washing over him like black ice on a winter path. "Show me your keys."

"My keys? Why do you need my . . ."

"Your keys, Betrice," he demanded. "Now!"

Jane pretended to turn around and take the key belt from the table, slipping it out of her skirts while Walter's eyes were focused on his wife, then she strode forward and placed the belt, gently, into Betrice's hands. "Here, m'um," she said, keeping her eyes on Walter, as if her presence might stop him from doing anything violent. Though that was foolish, for Jane's presence had never stopped anything before, and Walter would surely remember . . .

"*You.*" A snarl formed on the reeve's lips, his eyes widening. "*You* were there when he was."

Jane nearly fell over when Betrice stepped in front of her,

shielding her with her tall, stately figure. "Jane has been a great help to me today. Sent by the angels, Walter. You leave her be."

"Fine." Walter snatched the key belt out of his wife's hands, and Betrice jerked as the metal scraped her skin.

Behind Betrice's strong back, Jane felt tears gathering in the corners of her eyes, guilt gnawing at her stomach. She wouldn't let Walter hurt his wife, she decided. No matter what. Even if she had to confess. She couldn't stand by and watch it happen. Not as she had before, with Sibyl. She stepped out from behind the taller woman's shadow.

But Betrice had drawn herself up, indignant, righteousness swallowing her fear. And *she* strode forward, toward Walter, and Jane noted again the difference in their height, surprised to find that Betrice was so much taller when she stood up straight, squaring her shoulders as she was now. "I can't believe you think I let him out! Why would I do such a thing?"

"Oh, you *know* why," Walter growled, his face twisting like an ogre's. He hunched over the keys, thumbing through them. And when he found the cellar key, he held it up, studying it in the candlelight, and closed his eyes.

He heaved a great sigh then. He dropped the keys to the ground. And then, he sank into a chair, put his head into his strong, brown, corded hands, and began to sob.

"Oh, Walter!" Betrice rushed to him, bending over him, stroking his back while his shoulders shook. "Walter, it's all right. It will be all right."

"What will the king think of me now?" Walter shook his head, moaning a little. "He'll hang me, is what he'll do."

"He won't!" Betrice stroked his hair, damp from rain and

sweat, black wire sprinkled with smoke. "Edward won't hang you just for losing a man."

"He will," the reeve sobbed, pitiful. "I've failed him. After he gave me such a grand chance."

"Your chances aren't through," his wife said. "Perhaps you'll find Robin Hood yet. Perhaps he's run from town, and you've scared him off."

"It won't matter to Edward. He'll shame me, he'll strip me of my title, and they'll all say they were right about me. That they never should have sent a lesser man to do a noble's job."

Betrice looked down at her husband again, her fingers still moving through his hair. "Edward sent you out here with nothing but churls for hire. Robin is a soldier. He could have an army in these woods, for all you know. What are you supposed to do against that?"

"Well, you know who he'll send to do my job now," Walter said bitterly. "One of his turned barons. A rotten coin. You should have taken a man like that as your husband, not a low-born man like me."

Betrice sighed wearily, as though this were a complaint she had heard from him before. "I'll forgive you that, Walter. But only if you stop with this foolishness. I'll have words with my father and he'll make things right."

"And what sort of man am I, who needs his wife to plead excuses for his failures?" But he relaxed a little, cracking his well-muscled neck, breathing deeply.

Betrice took his hands, lifting him to his feet, and she smiled. "That's a lord's life, my dear," she said dryly. "They make excuses all the time. If you mean to be one, you had best get used to it."

And then, Walter actually laughed.

Jane's head whirled as if she were caught in a storm. Betrice had calmed him. Or perhaps he had never meant to hurt her at all. She had thought them at war, as all married couples seemed to be. But that wasn't quite right, was it? There was something more between them. A partnership, a deal, warm and weathered, even if it wasn't the romantic love of chivalry and stories.

"Let's go." Walter grasped his wife's hands in his own, as if he'd forgotten they weren't alone, as if Jane weren't there at all. "Let's ride back home tonight."

"Back to Nottingham?" Betrice asked, but her voice was light and lifted as a child's. "Are you finally giving up this silly quest, so we can leave this dreary hovel and get back to our lives?"

"I'll see you home safely tonight, but I'll be back on the morrow." Walter's smile was sharp and hungry. "Let them all laugh and call me common. Let Edward send any other hunter he pleases. I'll show him I'm better than any one of them, no matter how fat their purses or how bloody their swords. *I'll* be the one to bring him the outlaw's head. I'll flush these woods out with fire, if I have to. And this time, there will be nowhere for Robin Hood to hide."

Chapter Twenty-Three

Jane rode out to her old house even though it was dark, even though she had to sneak out of the servants' chambers with a hood pulled over her head and take Moll right from under Bran's nose. She left her little token for him, an aged scrap of linen with a flower embroidered on it, so he would know who had taken her, but she couldn't face him, for there was no excuse she could have given for taking the horse in the night, no way he wouldn't read the truth in her eyes. She had to talk to Robin. She couldn't let him hear John's tales of her without the truth of what had happened and how she had tried to stop it—tried and failed. What if John decided to tell Robin it was all her fault, her plan?

Yet even as Jane's thoughts kept getting tangled in doubt, her heart sang to her like a little trilling, fearless bird. For Robin was at her house—*her* house—which had seen her change and love and suffer, held all of her secret hopes and shames. Robin was free, by her hands.

She would go to him, and she would confess. He would see the truth of it, Jane hoped, even if he was angry at first. Either way, she couldn't lie to him. Not to him, and not about something like this. Rain was still spitting from the dim sky, the dark clusters of clouds, and the wind blew her hood back and sent raindrops thumping against her face, as if the air itself were trying to steer her back to King's Houses. But nothing short of lightning striking could have stopped Jane from seeing Robin now that he was finally free.

When she reached her old, abandoned house, she stood by the front door, dithering. There were boot prints in the mud before the door, more than one set, and a foul smell in the trees beside the house, where someone must have tossed a basin. The door was shut, though, and the curtains drawn, no sounds of laughter or revelry. She should have realized Robin might not be alone. But she was here, now, standing in the rain like a fool. Should she knock? It was *her* house. But if he was in there . . .

Jane tapped weakly. She listened, feeling as if she would burst. She heard nothing but the soft howl of wind, the sound of rain smacking the roof, the one that Hugh had criticized. She remembered the leak she had seen the last time she was there, the pool of mold where the water had dripped, and she flushed with embarrassment. It would be far worse now, after all the rain. Would Robin think she had lived her whole life like that, in filth and squalor?

Finally, drawing up all her courage, Jane pushed the door open. It creaked loudly, horribly, and she only had time to swallow her despair at the mud tracked through the straw on the floor before she heard someone stirring in the back of the house, behind the partition that kept her mother's room private.

"Hallo?" she called, and it came out strangled, as if she were underwater.

"Hallo?" It was Robin's voice, Robin's call back to her, filling

Jane with so much relief that she rushed to the back of the house, where her mother used to braid her hair while her father was away, before Sibyl started taking lovers and Jane became afraid of what she would find behind the partition.

Jane skidded to a halt when she saw Robin, his head propped up and his long legs spread across her mother's bed, shadows crawling across the walls in the candlelight. "Jane," he said, and it was more like a breath than a word, like he was breathing out her name. His cheeks were shrouded with fine, russet hair, slick with sweat, and his green eyes glistened, the right one swollen red, purpling around its edges. He struggled to focus on her, bleary with fever—or with drink, she realized, as she saw the jug by the foot of the bed, the cup clutched in his hand.

He lifted his cup, his face sliding into a soft smirk. "For the pain," he said, and Jane's eyes fell to the wrappings around his torso, the tearing and stains on his tunic, the bruises on his arms. The thought of Walter beating those marks into Robin's lean, strong body made her swell with fury.

"How did you know I was here?"

"The laundress at King's Houses told me," she answered, hearing her voice tremble. "I thought you meant for me to know."

"You mean Tillot?" He took another drink. "That withered old trout! Ha! She's been mine for ages."

Jane frowned. "She must be very loyal, to work for you so long."

Robin snorted. "Right, very loyal. Very loyal to the wine we steal for her, that's for sure."

"Really? That's all it takes?" Jane's confession beat hard against her chest, but, somehow, the words wouldn't come.

"Don't judge her too harshly." Robin wiped his mouth on his

sleeve. "Life is hard for so many, and a little sweetness in a sour pot is the only way they can make it through." He frowned, looked to his side as though staring out a window, but of course there was no window in her mother's room. "They're not like us, Jane. Few people are. Most people don't need a greater purpose, a reason. They just need a bit of honey to wake up for. Tell me"—he looked back to her with that old, familiar twinkle in his eye, that half smile on his face, and Jane nearly tumbled in relief to see the old Robin who she knew and cared for—"how did you get the key to my prison?"

"I was waiting on the reeve's wife," Jane said. "He had her hidden at King's Houses."

"Well, well." He raised his vessel. "Suppose he knows what a wild mare he has now. Maybe he'll ride her better."

Jane bristled. He had a foul name for the laundress, he did, and fouler words for Betrice, and she wondered suddenly how Robin referred to *her* when she wasn't in the room. "They're gone now," she said, a little snappish. "The reeve has taken her home to Nottingham."

"He's gone?" Robin's eyes widened. "We drove him off?" He thrust the drink at her. "We've *won*, Jane! *You've* won it for us!"

"We haven't won," she said, but she took the cup anyway. Maybe it would calm her wild nerves, her fluttering heart. "He'll be back, and . . ." She took a sip and nearly spit it out, the taste of rotting flowers was so strong. "God's bones, Robin!"

"You like it? John's own recipe. A mother hen, that one is." He grinned. "Come now. Don't worry so much, Jane. The reeve is a coward. The man can only face me with an army at his back."

"You're wrong about him. He's no coward. And the king will send someone worse now, he said. Someone outside the law."

"Well, we're all outside the law here in Sherwood." He laughed. "Why are you so set on spoiling our victory? You've freed me, Jane! You were a hero yesterday, just like the old tales, the ones of Lancelot and Ywain trapped in towers, where the ladies come to save them!"

"I'm no hero." It came out like a whisper, from the bottom of her throat.

"Oh, John and Tuk told tall tales of their rescue, they did." He leaned forward, then winced, his hand falling to his ribs. "But *you're* the one who really saved me, aren't you?"

"Don't get up!" Jane said urgently. "You're hurt!" She set the cup down and rushed toward him, straightening the rough blanket that was tangled about his feet, trying to pull it over him. She winced at the tang of blood and sweat that wafted up from his body. John might have fed him, but he hadn't bothered to bathe him. Robin still smelled of sickness, and bruises, and old blood, and the dust of his makeshift prison.

"Stop. Jane, stop it. Don't mother me." Robin took her wrist, his grip loose and gentle, and patted both of their hands on the bed together. "I've John for that." He dropped his voice until it was a soft, sensual purr. "Sit with me instead."

Jane shook her head, tears coming to her again as she remembered the page and his emptied eyes. She had to tell Robin now. But what would he think of her when she did? What would he say when he knew the truth of her cowardice?

"Jane, what is it? What's wrong?" Robin's hand moved to hers, and she let him pull her down to sit beside him. "Come now, you can tell me anything."

"It's John. He . . ." She nearly choked on the confession. She didn't want to lose Robin's regard, not for turning on John, and not for standing there and watching and doing nothing but running away. "He murdered them," she whispered. "He and Wyll both. The page was just a boy, Robin. He was innocent."

Robin frowned, something crossing his face that she couldn't read. "Aye. He was."

Jane pulled back in horror. "You *knew*?"

"We've had words, John and I."

"Words? That's it?" she demanded, suddenly feeling indignant in the absence of Robin's anger. "Only words?"

Robin sighed, and Jane felt like she had lost all the breath from her chest. "Do you want me to do more, Jane? Shall I beat him for you? Take a limb? What do you think is fair?"

"I . . ." She flushed, even as she tried to stop the tears, thinking what a mess she would look, hair matted from her nighttime ride, face blotchy and water-stained. "No! That isn't what I want at all!"

She moved to stand, but Robin gripped her hand, firmer now, to hold her still. "What *do* you want, Jane?" His voice, his eyes, were heavy with meaning, but Jane's own heart had frozen, her thoughts gone blank. Suddenly Jane wanted to be anywhere but there, in her mother's room, sitting on her mother's bed. It was too full of emotions and memories and terrible choices. Both her mother's and her own.

"You've a code," she finally managed, "and now it's gone. It's ruined. And *I* had a part in it!"

"Oh, Jane." Robin pulled her back to him, brushing her hair away from her eyes, even as she tried to turn her head, to look away, for she didn't want him to see her as she was now, soft and weak with guilt and shame. "You mustn't blame yourself. Please don't blame yourself."

She was helpless against the tears that flooded her eyes, helpless against him. "But I helped them trap the boy! I couldn't stop it!"

Robin watched her, his face serious, as he brushed away her tears. "This is a terrible fight we're in, Jane. A war. There are times—awful times—when we face grave choices. Sometimes, that choice is between the people we love and care for, and the people who would throw us to the wolves." His fingers lingered on her jaw now, his palm against her chin. "John knew I would be cross with him, but he placed my anger and my life upon a scale, just as Lady Justice would, and he weighed it as he must. That's family, Jane. That's *loyalty*."

Jane felt as if she were drowning in a churning sea. She swallowed against the sickness that threatened to rise in her throat. *That page*, she wanted to protest, *that page wouldn't have thrown me to the wolves. And he died anyway.* But Robin hadn't been there. He couldn't know.

And if he had been there? The question froze Jane's heart.

"Would you have done it yourself?" she asked softly. "Out of loyalty?"

"If I had to choose, you mean?" he murmured, leaning closer to her still, studying every part of her face as if she might disappear and he would be left with only his memories. "An innocent life for yours?"

"No, not mine!" Jane's breath caught. "That's not what I meant! I . . ."

"I would do anything to free you, Jane. Whatever it took." Robin's eyes, green lit with amber, were so penetrating, so focused. Bran had never looked at her like that, as though he were dying of thirst and wanted to drink her down, all in one swallow. Bran had never made her feel so vital, so alive, so *wanted*. "No matter what the nobles tell you about how low you are, about how little you're worth, you mustn't believe them. Your life, your strong heart, are worth all the treasure in the world."

"I . . ." She tried to turn her face away, her head spinning, but he pulled her back, her chin in his hand, his touch so firm and warm.

"You came for me," Robin said. "Just as I knew you would. You're like me, Jane. Loyal. We'll always come for each other."

And then he wove his hand into her hair and pulled her close, bringing her mouth to his.

Jane jerked a little at the heavy smell of his breath, and then his tongue darted past her lips, quick as a hummingbird, and she opened to him and sighed as his whole scent, the warmth of his tongue, filled her. She found herself kissing back, suddenly urgent, as though she could devour him. But he toyed with her, pulling as she pushed, nipping at her lower lip, holding her back even as her whole body yearned toward him, tight with hunger.

Just then, a shadow fell over them both. A giant, looming shadow in the candlelight. And Little John cleared his throat.

-«««◆»»»-

Jane leapt to her feet, but she was tangled in the blanket, and she yanked it off of Robin in her distress. He groaned, pulling the blanket back, sending her tunic all askew.

John merely watched her struggle, silently, his face contorted in disgust. He was sopping wet from the rain, his pale eyes blue-gray stone.

"John," Robin cried in greeting. "Did you hear? The reeve has fled the coop! Jane came to tell me!"

"Is *that* what she came to do?"

Robin laughed shamelessly into the tense silence, meeting Jane's eyes with a look that was intimate, teasing—and far too fond in front of someone like John.

"Nothing happened," Jane breathed, trying to keep quiet. She still tasted Robin's mouth in her own, knew his smell was all over her. "I just wanted . . ." But she stopped. She couldn't make the rest of the excuses come out of her mouth. Not to John, who looked as if he were a great demon made of rock.

"Come on, you dour old goat!" Robin gave John his most charming smile, though she knew his face must ache for it. "Pour a drink. I had a dream I need you to read for me."

John ignored him. "You should go," he said to Jane, his voice a chill wind. "The others are coming."

"But we didn't . . ."

"I don't care if you did. I'm not your lover. Not your priest."

"'Twas a dream about a bird," Robin said loudly. "A sign, I think."

John finally turned to look at him with a tired groan. "What kind of bird?"

Jane let out a breath, relieved to be free of John's judgment and his stare. She needed to get out of there, get somewhere quiet and safe, put a little bread in her stomach to settle it. But she felt trapped by Robin's presence. She and John both were, no matter how they churned inside.

"A black bird. I'd hit it with an arrow. I nursed it back to health," Robin said, "kept it by me. But then it lunged for me, pecking at my eye." He rubbed his face as if he could feel the bird there and he hoped to drive it away. "This one. The right one."

He finally moved his hands away, leaning back and looking be-tween John and Jane. "What do you think it means?"

John snorted. "I think it means that arsehole reeve punched you in your eye."

"Not a deep thinker, is he, our John?" Robin laughed ruefully but he shook himself, as though he could shake off the dream and its portents.

"Never did put much stock in dreams," John grumbled, then reached for the jug, which had dripped onto the floor. "But in sleep, and in drink, I'm a great believer. I'll refill your cup and see Jane out."

"He needs food, John," Jane urged him.

"*Don't,*" John snapped, then caught himself and said more softly, "tell me what he needs. We've been through this more times than you can count."

"That's right, Jane." Robin pulled the blanket over himself again. "I told you not to mother me. That big rooster there will chase you right out of the henhouse."

Jane followed John out from behind the wall, shuffling her feet, her face burning with humiliation, but also fury. Who was John, of all people, to look askance at her for what she did—or didn't do—with Robin? "I know you dislike me, John," she said through gritted teeth, "but you can't just chase me out of my own house!"

John slammed the jug onto the wooden table, just as her father had, and her older brother, so many times, taking out their end-less rage on tables and cups and walls. "It's not your house any-more. Your place is at King's Houses, doing the job Bran bought for you. Or have you forgotten?"

The words were like a fist in Jane's stomach. "I . . . I haven't forgotten."

John settled into a chair, weary, rubbing at his bristling yellow beard, and Jane noticed for the first time the shadows beneath his eyes, the creases in his skin, the pallor of his cheeks. He had been caring for Robin this whole time and hadn't had a moment of rest himself. She would have felt sympathy for him, if she hadn't known him to be a monster.

"I don't dislike you, Jane." John's gaze was steady, though his eyes were red-rimmed and bloodshot. "I just thought you were different."

"Different from what?" Jane asked, the floor shifting beneath her like sand on the river's bank. "Have there been other . . ."

"You're smarter than to ask that. Though not as smart as I thought."

She looked up, defiant, suddenly wanting to fight for herself. "Because I got angry about murder? Because I wouldn't . . ."

"It's not that," John said, weary, and Jane didn't know why she was pushing him. It wasn't like her at all, and she worried it was her own guilt sending her sideways. "I don't give a damn about your qualms about the monk."

"Qualms? Is that what you call it?" She felt her chest swell. "The reeve's not gone," she said. "Not for good. And the king will send more men after Robin because of what you did!"

John's eyes widened. "You think *I'm* the reason the king is after Robin's head? You think he hasn't done worse?" He shook his head. "Unbelievable. Got you hooked like a fish, he does."

"He doesn't . . ."

"Just like all of us, Jane. He's got us all hooked on his line, waiting for the final cut. And there's nothing we can do about it.

Not even you." John groaned, pulling himself to his feet. "Now, get out. I have work to do, and your man won't be glad to know you've been here."

Jane couldn't gather her thoughts at all. "You won't tell him?" she asked weakly, for she couldn't think of another thing to say.

"Robin needs you at King's Houses, Jane," John said, grim. "And he needs me here. So let's both get back to work."

Chapter Twenty-Four

The sun had risen when Jane finally got back to King's Houses, soaking wet and starving and racked with shame. Bran was hovering around the stables like a thundercloud, and when Jane climbed down from Moll, he grabbed her wrist and yanked her toward him a little too roughly. "Where have you been?"

Jane snatched her wrist out of his grasp, feeling like she'd been slapped. "Where we've all been! Saving Robin!"

"Robin was *saved* last night," he said, his dark eyes hard as stones. "It's the morning. Did you go riding off into the forest after dark? To see *him*?"

"He's not . . ." Jane rubbed at her forehead. Why hadn't they told Bran where they were keeping Robin? There must be a reason. Or was it just because they knew that Jane's house, that intimacy with Jane, would set him off? "It's not as if he's alone. He's with John," she said, suddenly angry, even though she knew she had no right to it. "He's at John's mercy. They're alone together, and I don't trust John. Neither should you."

"Don't put this onto John, Jane. Why did you go riding off to see Robin in the night? Why didn't you come to *me* when your task was done?"

"I wanted . . ." She stumbled over the words, for Bran was as wrapped up in his rage as she was in her guilt, and she had earned them both, she knew. "I wanted Robin to know the truth. I wanted him to know what happened. I thought he would be angry, that he would feel . . ."

"You wanted *Robin*. All your thoughts are for *him*," he said, his eyes hot with some emotion Jane had never seen before. "What he thinks of you, and what he feels. You think I didn't notice the way you looked at him in church? The look on your face when he was caught?"

"He'd been *captured*, Bran! How did you expect me to look?"

"I expected you to think of me!" he bellowed. "*I* saved you that day! You and your brother! And what thanks do I get? You running off to see our master in the night!" He pointed at her, finger hard and stiff and inches from her chest, his face so fierce that she backed away even more.

Bran's voice softened as he read the fear in her eyes, saw what he had done to feed it, and he stepped back, running a hand across his jaw. "I should never have got you into all this. They warned me, they did, from the moment I brought you out to the Greenwood." The morning mist gathered on his cheek, glittering in his soft hair the way she used to like. "But I thought you had a level head. You weren't the type to get lost in stories. You had your feet planted so firmly on the ground." He shook his head, eyes to the sky, as if he were too disgusted even to look at her. "I thought you were different. I thought *we* were different."

He spoke as though he had already lost her, so much so that it pierced Jane's heart. But he was right, wasn't he? She *had* only been thinking of Robin. And she had gone to him in the night, even when he hadn't called, pulled to him like he was a lodestone and her heart was full of nails.

But it wasn't just Robin's words that pulled to her. It was more than that. Robin could see Jane right through to her core. He knew who she really was, what she really felt, in a way that Bran never could.

"What did you think we were?" Jane asked softly. She hadn't wanted much from Bran, and she had thought he felt the same. He had asked nothing from her, let her run free, and she had loved it. And until Robin looked at her—like he wanted her more than anything, like there was no one else in the world who mattered—Jane hadn't known how much she wanted more.

"Does it matter now? You pranced around for Robin as soon as he turned your way. He's spun you up in all his lies. And here I thought you would see through him. You, of all people."

"Robin's not a liar, Bran. He isn't that. You act as if he hasn't saved you more than once! As if he isn't doing this to save all of us!"

Bran's face closed like a locked door. Then he let out a wry laugh, dark and cold. "You believe him. You believe him over me, even though he'll say anything to get what he wants. I thought you *knew* that, Jane."

"Why do you follow him if you think he's so false?"

"Because"—Bran looked at her as though she were a dullard, a fool—"that's what makes him good at the trick."

The trick. Is that all this was—all she was to Robin? To Bran? Part of a game to turn nobles on their heads and empty out their purses? She refused to believe it. She *knew* Robin cared about more than that. He had said so. Either Bran couldn't see it, or he was lying to her out of spite.

"You're talking out of anger, Bran," she said, as much to herself as to him. "Out of envy. You're jealous of Robin and trying to win me back! God's bones, I feel like a bag of coins you're fighting for!"

"Win you back." Bran stiffened like a corpse. "So I'm right. He did take you to bed."

"It didn't happen," Jane said, swallowing the truth, knowing that she would have, if it hadn't been for John. "I didn't do it." She didn't know what the point was now, of honesty. Their courtship already had one foot in the grave.

"Well, maybe you should have," Bran said bitterly, "because clearly this means nothing to you, this thing between us."

"You act as if it means something to *you*," Jane said, her throat raw with tears.

Bran shrugged, his eyes blank, cold, and she could see, then, the truth of him. He did care for her—but it was the same way he cared for his horses. She was a thing of his—a charge for him to keep, a job he had stumbled into, and one he found pleasant, when it wasn't too much work. But he didn't care enough to fight for her. Not like Robin would.

"Maybe you're right, Jane," he said, and she could see the hurt in his eyes, and she could see how he fought to shut it out, to keep it out of his voice, his mouth twisting around the ice in his words. "Maybe it never meant anything at all. Maybe Robin was the only thing that ever mattered."

Jane wanted to do so many things, at that moment—to say she was sorry, to reach for him one more time, to soothe the hurt out of him like she would have done before. But there was no point to it anymore. He wasn't hers to comfort. Not now.

So she let silence fall between them instead, like a path that had been swallowed by snow.

-≪≪◆≫≫-

Jane tried to dry her tears as she rushed to the kitchens so she could help with cleaning up. She had been gone for two days now, and Eudo would be cross with her for how late she was today, and for all that had fallen behind in her absence. But Emmie stopped her before she could even walk inside. "The witch wants to see you," she said, but she seemed distant, cross.

"What's wrong?" Jane asked, her eyes searching.

"How should I know?" Emmie snapped.

"No, I mean"—Jane reached for her hand, but Emmie pulled it away—"what's wrong with you?"

"Me?" Emmie's eyes widened in anger. "What's wrong with *me*? What about *you*, Jane? Bran was asking me where you went this morning, and I had no answer, and none for the prioress either. Why would a girl who claims to be sick and hurt go out riding in the rain, before the sun's even up, without telling her lover or her healer?"

"I . . ."

"I don't have time right now." Emmie's open face was raw with hurt. "Just find the witch before she turns us all into frogs and minnows." And then she turned away, leaving Jane gaping in the downpour.

Jane leaned against the wall and ran a hand through her hair, smoothing water into the hasty braid she'd made. She felt as if she

had lived a hundred years in a matter of hours. And now the prioress had summoned her. And she and Emmie were both angry,
when they had doted on her before.

Do they know? Her thoughts whirled. *Do they know how I lied to
them, let them care for me, when they should have had me thrown in a
dungeon?*

Jane trudged to Ibota's door, as if her feet had moved on their
own when her mind couldn't make them work. Sir Roger stood
guard, as always, and he met Jane with a stern look. She should
have been afraid of that look, afraid of what awaited her inside,
but she was too beaten, gutted like a fish torn open by a cat. What
could the prioress take from her that she hadn't already lost?

"She's here," Roger called, and the door flew open.

A sea of emotions washed across the prioress's face before she
finally fixed it into sternness. "Get in here. Now," she ordered,
then spun away in a cloud of rosemary and sage, leaving Jane to
follow and shut the door behind her.

"Well?" Ibota stood by her herbs, as if she were working, but
her hands didn't touch them. They were shaking, pale and veined
and scarred. She had either forgotten her gloves, or she was too
upset to care.

"I . . . Emelyn said that you wanted to see me."

"I wanted to see you *last night*." Ibota bit off the ends of her
words, as though she could barely control her anger. "Last night.
When they found Brother Godric's corpse." She held Jane's eyes
like a challenge. "When they found his severed head."

"I've heard," Jane stammered. "It's awful. I . . ."

"And the boy who was with him? His page?"

Jane opened her mouth to speak, but words wouldn't come
out. Tears filled her eyes and throat.

"You knew. You knew they were already dead." Ibota's eyes pinned Jane's feet to the floor. "You knew that night, when I found you. And you let me think . . ."

Jane's whole chest shuddered, and she turned her head, looking out the window. She had to look away from that stare, for fear it would pry the whole truth out of her. "I tried to tell you," she said weakly, so weakly that her voice was barely audible. "Tried to tell you it wasn't what you thought."

"Did you try to stop it? Is that why you were so upset? You tried, and they took it out on you?" Ibota's voice was thin, as if she didn't believe her own story, no matter how much she wanted to.

"You know who killed them? Did . . . did the reeve catch them?" Jane trembled. The tears were pouring out now, and she could not stop them. She had led two people to their deaths as surely as if she had held the sword herself. And then, even after that, she'd led John and Tuk to the reeve's house, to burn his farm. Did Ibota know about her role in that too?

Curse her tears. They told her tale for her, without Jane even opening her mouth.

"Of course I know who killed them!" Ibota turned cold as ice then, when she said, "The man from the stables. The man at church. And they're the same man, aren't they?" The fog in the prioress's ice-blue eyes cleared, the crease between her brows straightening, almost in relief. "You're in love with Robin Hood."

Jane's mind spun, flailing around for something to grab on to, anything, to tell her what the right thing to say might be. Her stomach clenched, her bowels kicking at her, even though everything inside her was empty and dry. *Ibota knew.*

But of course she knew. Ibota of Kirklees was no fool.

All of Jane's denials died on her lips.

The prioress sighed, finally, pushing air out of her thin nose. "De Stircheley failed to catch him. Robin must think he's untouchable now that he's outwitted that dullard of a reeve, murdered a monk and a boy with no consequences. What do you think comes next, Jane? How much longer will you protect him?"

"Robin didn't kill anyone!" Jane protested. "The reeve had him then. He was locked away!"

"So his men did it for him! They beat two of the reeve's men, set fire to a field, and murdered two people in cold blood! What's the difference, Jane, if Robin Hood did those things, or if his people did them in his name?"

"It isn't like that," Jane said weakly.

"Sit down, Jane."

"I can't stay! Master Eudo will . . ."

"You can, and you will," Ibota snapped. "Unless you want me to call the reeve back from Nottingham and hand you over to him in chains."

Jane sank onto a little stool, feeling as heavy as a stone. She had thought she had nothing left to lose, but it seemed God meant for her to reckon with her sins today. All of them. And Mary's mercy was nowhere to be found. Jane would have prayed for it, silently, but she knew in her heart that it was mercy she didn't deserve.

Ibota heaved a great sigh. "I've borrowed you from the kitchens for a time," she said. "So you needn't worry about Eudo or Ancel or anyone else."

"For how long?" Jane asked softly.

"Until I'm finished with you," the prioress declared, ice crawling back in her voice. She pinched the flesh between her eyes as though Jane's mere presence made her head ache. "What do you know about the Barons' War, Jane?"

Jane's throat went dry. Why bring that up now? What did Ibota know? "I was but a child, m'um." Jane knew Robin had fought on the barons' side against King Henry. Perchance John and Tuk too, though Bran and Mooch and Wyll were far too young, closer to her own age.

"The barons said the king had too much power. That was what they *said*, mind you. They said they were going to be heroes, to take that power from him so they could share it."

"But Robin isn't . . ."

"Do you remember Sir Richard's visit?" She didn't give Jane time to answer. "Of course you do. You were the one who let him in, weren't you? No"—Ibota raised a scarred hand—"don't deny it. That's when I knew to watch you. His little performance for the abbot should give you some sense of the lengths a nobleman will go to cancel his own debts."

"But it was unfair debt, wasn't it?" Shame seared Jane's throat at the prioress's sharp look. "That's why Robin helped him."

"Any man thinks his debt is unfair when he owes his coin to someone else. No matter how he got himself into it. And no matter how much gold was showered on him beforehand by virtue of his birth." She looked away from Jane, her voice thinning.

"I was in Winchester when Simon de Montfort's son came through with his army of barons, with his fire and his swords. My closest friend there was a formidable woman. She was also a Jew." Jane's eyes widened. There were few Jews in Mansfield, but more in the cities, she had heard. "When the king wants to put a man in debt," Ibota said, "he goes through the city's Jews to loan his money, to avoid staining his hands with usury. And to use them as his shield when things go wrong." A tear appeared in Ibota's eye and hung there, as glacial and disciplined as the prioress herself.

"My friend had three children. Twin girls—they were seven years old, eight maybe. And a boy, just a babe, with a lick of red-gold hair like a little flame."

When she looked at Jane again, her eyes were fathomless with grief, like glass about to shatter. "The barons' soldiers killed them, Jane. Killed them all. Burned alive in their house. My friend, the girls, even the boy." Her voice caught and she blinked rapidly. "Their army killed hundreds like my friend. And when it was over"—her mouth twitched as she shifted, like a windstorm, from grief to rage—"when their corpses were piled high in England's cities, and the rest were thrown in prison—everything they had built their whole lives lost, stolen from them, by men who wanted their gold—*then* the rebel barons announced that their own debts were canceled, as though it were a great victory. They meant for us all to celebrate.

"Edward, my cousin, took the barons' side, at first." Jane nodded blankly, her mind reeling with the horror the prioress had painted. "I fought him. Not with a sword, of course. But with words. He sent me all the way to Kirklees for my troubles. He saw reason, in the end, but it was a close thing, Jane. Far too close."

Jane found herself without anything to say, her mind swimming with the images of children, hundreds of them, slumped and bleeding just like the little page. Robin had been one of the barons' soldiers. But would he have done that? Burned innocent people in their homes? Slaughtered children?

She shook herself. It couldn't be. Robin protected the weak. But John's words rang in her mind, mocking her. *You think he hasn't done worse?*

"When I heard about your forest rebels," Ibota said, as if she were following Jane's thoughts, "I suspected they were fugitives. So many went north once the barons lost. But they were just soldiers for coin, most of them barely grown themselves, so no one bothered to give chase. Not until Robin Hood started drawing attention to himself."

"And now?" Jane asked. "What threat could he be to King Edward, all the way up here?"

"The rebel soldiers know all the barons' dirty secrets. They know all the traitors to the crown. And they know about Edward, and all he did before he changed sides and rode beside his father as England's hero. So when my cousin heard tell of the rebels in the woods, he sent Walter. A blunt weapon for a subtle battle." She leaned back, sighing. "Now that this tool has inevitably failed, more blood will spill. He'll send someone harder than Walter, someone who won't care how many deer he has to cut down to get to his stag."

"And you?" Jane asked, her bones turning to ice. "Are you also hunting Robin on the king's orders?" If Jane hadn't seen it, had trusted her, well then, Jane really was the fool John said she was.

Ibota laughed, bitterly. "I'm afraid not. Rumors of my sorcery are greatly overstated. Besides, my pompous ass of a cousin would never trust a woman to do his bidding. I came here in *spite* of him. Because I'm afraid, Jane. I'm afraid these rebels will run free with their swords and their fires, just as they did when I was younger." She stiffened. "I will not see another Winchester slaughter. Not in my lifetime.

"And so," Ibota said, "I'm hunting Robin for myself, not for the king. And now"—she raised one eyebrow, measuring, testing—"you're hunting him for me too."

Jane nearly fell off her stool. "What?"

"You heard me."

"And if I refuse?" Jane asked, even though she knew it was a foolish question.

"How do you think Walter de Stircheley will feel when he finds out that the same servant girl who 'fetched his wife things,' the same one who dined at his own table, is sharing Robin Hood's bed?"

"It's not like that! I'm not . . ."

"I don't care what it's like. And neither will the reeve."

Ice seemed to fill the prioress's room as they stared at each other, Jane's heartbeat loud as a horse's thundering hooves. "What do you want from me?" Jane finally asked. "What do you think I can do?"

"You can do exactly what you did for *him*. Watch. Listen. And do everything I tell you."

"And if they catch me, if they grow suspicious? How am I supposed to explain it?"

"You're well practiced at falsehood, Jane. You'll find a way." Ibota leaned forward. "But if you lie to me again, then yours will be the head Walter de Stircheley brings to Edward as his prize."

Jane's anger rose before she could stop it. "You're forcing me to betray my friends!" She felt, all at once, like a petulant child. The prioress had caught her falsehoods, knew her lies, knew *more* than that, probably, stored behind that sharp, watchful stare. What was she thinking, talking back to a woman who could end her life with a snap of her fingers?

Ibota's face softened. "You'll understand, Jane. Once you know more, see more. Once you listen for me, and you watch them for me, you'll see what I see."

If she thinks that, Jane thought, *then maybe she knows nothing after all. She certainly doesn't know Robin.* But she lowered her eyes and murmured, "Yes, m'um." For she remembered her place, now. The prioress had made sure of it. And the only way a servant could fight back was to agree, to be appeasing, and to tell people whatever they wanted to hear.

And do whatever they pleased when their mistress's eyes were turned.

PART IV

An Arrow Broade

Chapter Twenty-Five

What do you know about hell?" Jane slowed her horse to a walk beside Ibota, who rode a gray palfrey, a lady's horse, elegant and graceful. Jane felt short and mulish beside her.

"What a thing to ask," Ibota murmured. She had been keeping Jane close all week, giving her small, insignificant tasks in her chambers, without any consideration for Jane's real responsibilities in the kitchens. Jane knew Eudo must be grumbling about it, and Emmie would be mocking her for it to the rest of them, but the prioress behaved as they all expected her to behave—flighty and cold, as if she couldn't be bothered with rules or social graces—and so everyone bent to her whims. The other servants probably saw Ibota's attention as an incredible spin of Fortune's wheel for Jane. They didn't know her new, enviable friendship was nothing but a prison.

But the worst prison was the one around Jane's heart, for there had been no word from Robin for days—no orders, no missives, no whispers from Tillot or anyone else at King's Houses. Was

Jane to be shut out now that she had almost tumbled into his bed? And was that Bran's doing, or Robin's?

Still, even without messages from the Greenwood, Jane had to give Ibota something to keep her from calling in the reeve, so she told the prioress stories, each one as though it was a truth she had just learned instead of a tale she had been carrying for months. She told her of the men in Robin's gang, like John and Wyll, and of their characters. She sheltered Mooch and Tuk, who had both been kind, and she sheltered Bran, in spite of the way he was avoiding her. She told the prioress about the spot by the trysting tree that the reeve already knew, but didn't say a word about her own house, the way her feet had tread Robin's paths so well that she could walk them from memory. She knew better now than to defend Robin to her anymore, to say he was different from his men. She had tried it once, and Ibota had berated her for it in her cold way, making her feel a fool. "The longer you wait to open your eyes, Jane," she had said, "the more the truth will sting you when it comes."

"Hell is . . . useful," Ibota answered Jane now. "It's soothing to believe that people who do evil will suffer when they die, as they have caused others to suffer." Sweat trickled down Jane's back despite the cool day, for the prioress was a fast rider, and the spring sun was bright and high. The scent of dry leaves and kitchen fires tangled with the warm, earthy smell of horses as they neared the stables, and Jane missed Bran's scent, his easy laugh—the way he always used to wait for her—with a sudden, sharp pang. "Some believe we are all destined to suffer for man's first sin. And there are others who feel that our soiled bodies, with their earthly needs and slow decay, are punishment enough."

"You mean, you don't think hell is real? You don't think anyone is punished?" Jane shouldn't have been surprised. Her brother Adam had said that the further he went into holy teachings, the less he felt he knew. Jane found it vexing. Among all the questions priests contemplated, how and why a person might be punished for the evil they had done should have been the first thing they figured out.

Ibota looked pointedly at Jane. "I sometimes wonder if a sinner's own mind traps them in hell during their earthly lives. It's easy to be haunted by guilt, and to suffer because of it."

Jane looked away. That was no help at all, even though Ibota meant it to be.

"But redemption is available to all of God's children," Ibota added, much more decisively. "If that weren't so, there would be no reason to keep trying."

Jane nodded, but she knew it was a false answer, for Ibota had seen through her question. Jane felt as if she had been suffering in her own private hell for days. Her guilt for the deaths of the monk and the page was so mingled with her shame over Bran and her longing for Robin that it felt like a pit of sand was swallowing her whole.

Jane and Ibota drew up the main path to King's Houses and found a commotion in the courtyard, servants and stableboys hurrying about, though Bran was still nowhere to be found, keeping clear of her even now. One lone figure stood in the center of the chaos, tall and broad and clad ostentatiously in black. His hair was almost the color of Robin's in the sunlight, but worn long, pulled into a horse's tail at the nape of his neck. The stranger moved with arrogance. She could see it in his walk, in the way he pushed through the servants as if they were a cloud of gnats.

The shire reeve was there too, and Jane tried to steady herself at the sight of him.

"Do you know who he is?" The prioress nodded at the black-clad stranger with a warning in her voice.

Jane shook her head, feeling frustrated. Were she still with Bran, she would have known all the guests days ahead of time. But he wasn't going to whisper that kind of thing to her anymore.

Ibota frowned. "I fear he's Edward's hunter. They have a look about them. And he's someone important enough that you and I are left to stable our own horses."

"I'll take care of the horses, m'um," Jane said, instead of what she wanted to say, which was that if Ibota had allowed her to keep her place as a scullion, she could answer any question she wanted. When she finally returned from stabling the horses, her arms heavy with baskets of dried herbs and soaps and wax to seal their potions, Ibota was pressing Walter for answers.

"He even hunts in a *mask*," the reeve was grumbling. "Like a real arsehole." Walter's shoulders slumped more than before, and the sun's touch had faded from his skin, turning it waxy and pale. He watched the stranger with his jaw working, as though he were chewing on something. Jane felt a twinge of pity for the reeve. The nobles had delighted in his failure to capture Robin Hood, just as he had predicted; she had heard them whispering that had Walter de Stircheley been a true knight, born with better blood, the outlaws would already be caught.

"You said he was a baron?" Ibota looked perplexed, like she should have heard of him.

"Was." Walter spat to the side, as if to ward off a curse. "Family cast him out, so he changed sides in the war and hunted his own people."

Ibota's face froze, growing even paler. "It's Guy de Gisborne, then?"

"Do you know him, m'um?" Jane asked.

"I know enough, Jane," Ibota started. "I . . ."

"Jane?" The reeve's head snapped in her direction, his eyes dark with suspicion. "Why do you pop up everywhere I turn, like a garden weasel?"

"I decided to put her to good use," the prioress said smoothly, "after I saw the care she gave your Betrice." Ibota had a way of telling the truth in a secret way, twisting it so that no one else could hear it.

Walter squinted at Jane from beneath those wild brows. "Come a long way from selling conserves, girl."

"Has de Gisborne come to hunt your outlaw?" Ibota asked abruptly, with a warning look to Jane. "Isn't that your job?"

"It was." The reeve said the words like he was chewing on rocks. "But Robin has crossed a line now, and Edward has lost his patience. He's making a trial of it. If Guy catches him first, he'll claim my title."

Most people would have expressed sympathy, but not Ibota, who got right to the meat of things. "And if *you* catch him first?"

"Then I get to keep my head," the reeve said.

"The switch instead of the golden ring. That was always Edward's way."

Walter shook his head. "I want to take Robin clean. Show what he truly is, a coward and a snake. But if Edward's man gets there first, well"—Walter frowned—"nothing he does is clean."

"And the town will have its hero still, and a martyr besides." Ibota scowled. "The people will turn on Edward for it. He isn't thinking."

Walter whistled, and his eyes danced, amused. "Might be you can say that about your cousin, Lady Prioress, but those words are too sharp for my tongue." He drew himself up a little, as if commiserating with Ibota had lightened his spirit. "Well, I'd best go greet the competition. Oh, and Prioress . . ." Walter looked between her and Jane. "I'd keep clear of that one. Nasty piece of work, he is." Jane allowed herself a little sigh of relief that he hadn't been referring to her. "Keep your girl away from him too. He's left a trail of unhappy women in his wake."

Annoyance flashed across Ibota's face before she smoothed her features. "I can assure you that I won't be tempted, nor will Jane."

The reeve looked grim, his eyes sad for the briefest moment. "That isn't what I meant."

The prioress paled, then hurried Jane off to the safety of her chambers.

True to the reeve's warning, Jane found Emmie quietly sobbing in the middle of the day, her shoulders shaking. When she looked up at Jane, her lips were wet, eyes swollen and rimmed red.

"Emmie!" Jane rushed to her, though things had been strained between them. Jane had tried to confide in her about ending things with Bran, though she left out the cause of it, but Emmie had seemed ill-soothed by the explanation and still kept her distance. "Are you all right?"

Emmie laughed, a tiny snort. "Do I look all right?"

"What is it? Is there anything I can do?"

Emmie wiped her nose on her sleeve. "Can you get Guy de Gisborne to ride away on his stupid black horse?"

Jane tried to make her voice light, though she was not feeling light at all. This was the most Emmie had said to her in days. "Maybe," Jane said, knowing how Emmie liked to keep everything fun and easy. "Shall I challenge him to a duel?"

Emmie snorted again, but the mist in her eyes cleared. "Was that a joke, Jane? From *you*?"

Jane smiled sheepishly. "Can you believe it?"

"Maybe your time with that witch is actually good for you."

Jane touched Emmie's shoulder very, very gently. "Did he hurt you?"

Emmie shook her head, blinking at the tears. "Just my pride. But it was a near thing. I'd not be alone with him if I was you. Although I s'pose you don't have to worry about such things anymore, do you?" Those last words had a tinge of bitterness, and Jane realized with surprise that Emmie was actually envious of her time with the prioress, for all her mocking. If only she knew the truth.

"He's here for Robin Hood," Jane said cautiously. "That's what the reeve says, anyway."

"Talking to reeves now, are you?" Emmie smiled through her tears. "Well, I hope Robin gives him what for."

"Me too," Jane said.

"Thought you didn't even think he was real, Jane." Emmie smirked. "*Only tales*, you said. Isn't that what you told me?"

Jane hung her head. "All right, all right, you can say you told me so later." Her contrition was real. She had kept secrets from Emmie all along, lied to her since the day they met. Her heart stung at what Emmie must think of her. No wonder she didn't see Jane as a true friend. "If you need to go to Guy's chambers, or need to fetch anything for him, come and find me first," Jane said. "I'll ask the prioress to keep her man's eyes on him too."

Emmie rubbed her nose, still sniffling. "So she can know my shame?"

"It isn't *your* shame," Jane said back instinctively. She realized she spoke with Ibota's voice and thoughts, and not her own. Perhaps Emmie was right. Perhaps the prioress was good for Jane after all.

But for all Jane's worry about Emmie, she had her own encounter with Guy de Gisborne later that day, as she was fetching water, her mind full of dark clouds. She should be warning Robin that Guy had come, that the king had finally sent another hunter. But how was she meant to escape the prioress to do it? And worse, what if they had all turned on her for what she had done to Bran? Why hadn't Robin sent word, after everything that had happened between them? Didn't he want to see her again, or did he feel she had hoped for too much from him, that she was too much trouble? Or what if he *had* sent word, and Bran or John or one of the others had swallowed the message out of spite?

Jane's flying thoughts, her fear and hope and her scattered mind, sent her stumbling right into the hunter with her basin. She darted out of the way and muttered an apology, but not quickly enough, for Guy grabbed her arm and yanked her back, causing water to slosh all over the floor.

"S'wounds!" Jane gasped.

"Shite! Stupid girl," Guy said at the same time. "You wet my boots!"

"*I* wet your boots?" Jane said, uncharacteristically bold. But anger had overtaken her. Anger at Bran, at John, at whoever else was keeping Robin from her, keeping him hidden.

Suddenly, Guy struck her across the face, hard.

The basin fell to the ground. Jane gasped and staggered backward.

"Don't you talk to me like that, girl! Who the hell do you think you are?" He grabbed Jane's arm as if to rip it from her shoulder, but at that moment, Ibota rushed into the corridor.

"What's going on out here? Jane, what's happened?"

"He hit me. M'um." Jane glared at Guy, feeling her lip split open with the words, but she held his eyes just as she had held John's that day at Mooch's house. She would have been afraid of Guy once, but she had seen far worse now than a nobleman who bullied servants.

"He did *what*?" Ibota whirled on him.

"What's it to you, Prioress?" Guy de Gisborne glared at her.

Ibota drew herself up to her full height, broadened her shoulders. "That's Mother Ibota to you, hunter. And keep your hands off the servants. I've half a mind to call the shire reeve back and have him haul you out of here."

"The reeve? That chicken-hearted coward?" Guy rubbed his bulbous nose, and Jane kept glaring at him, wondering how she could have thought he had Robin's color of hair at all, for his was dull as rust, pulled back to hide its sparseness. "You can tell him to try. Get this farce of a contest over with." He leered at Jane. "Well, scat, you. Your mistress saved you from a beating."

Ibota stepped in front of Jane. "Don't you know who I am?"

"Don't know. Don't care. 'Tis not my job to care about church-women or their servants. I'm a hunter, here on the king's call."

"*I* am the king's cousin." Ibota's voice was frost, but her shoulders shook as she spoke.

"Well, pansies and flower crowns for you, then," Guy said.

"You could be the king's whore for all I care. He sent me to get Robin Hood's head, and the heads of all those helping him." He peeked around Ibota, as if he were playing a game with Jane. "Every last rat. Even the ones hiding their heads behind king's cousins."

Jane's heart went cold, her lip still stinging. This had been no accident, no sour turn of Fortune, like what had happened to Emmie. Guy was a hunter, and he had come to the prioress's corridor hunting *her*.

Ibota shoved him away, firmly. Jane was surprised by it, but the prioress was almost his height. "You're out of your place, hunter. Come near this girl again, and it will be your head sent back to Edward." Guy moved as if to lay hands on Ibota, but she stepped swiftly out of the way. "Sir Roger!" she called, and the knight came 'round the corner as though he had been waiting on her word.

"Yes, Mother Ibota?" Roger said stiffly, formally, his lean body pulled straight, his armor clean and bright and woven with metal. He stared down Guy de Gisborne, reminding Jane of childhood stories about weathered old kings protecting their castles from usurpers with demons for hearts.

Roger's hand was on his sword.

Guy looked between them, eyes narrow, as if wondering whether to test his blade against the older knight, and against the two women, who did not have blades at all.

"Sir Roger is one of my cousin's handpicked guards," Ibota said. "He is completely loyal to me, and to the royal family. As are many of the guards at the King's Houses. Sir Roger, please show Guy de Gisborne back to his chambers. Remind him of his place."

Guy's mouth twisted, his rough shadow of a beard, russet woven with iron, bristling. "Right." He took a deep, mocking bow. "Ladies, I take my leave. No need to show me back," he added to Roger. "I know exactly where I'm meant to be."

Ibota hurried Jane back into her chambers. "Guard the door," she ordered Roger. "Shout if he comes back." He nodded, though he was no fool and she needn't have given him such an order at all.

Ibota bolted her door and sagged against it with a sigh.

"Thank you," Jane said around her aching lip.

"For what? Using my cousin as a shield?" Ibota took Jane's chin in her hand, examining her cut lip. "We need to tend to that." She shuffled through her pots to find a poultice.

"Has Edward really sent men to protect you?" Jane's hurt lip made the words come out garbled.

"No," Ibota muttered. "Roger is loyal to me, and only Roger. But Guy doesn't need to know that." She turned, a small pot reeking of violets in her hand. "Come now, Jane. Remember your herbs. What will keep you from bruising?"

"It's violets. I can smell them," Jane admitted.

"And do we put it on the wound, or around it?"

"'Round it," Jane murmured, but the prioress was already smearing the violets and oil onto her mouth. "No, on it," she corrected herself, making a mess of Ibota's work.

The prioress shook her head. "On it when it's bleeding, 'round it when it starts to heal, for swelling." She sighed, a puff of lavender and rose, and Jane felt as if she were breathing in a dusty old garden. Ibota had been trying to hone Jane's herbcraft in their days together. To Jane's surprise, Ibota worked with poisons as well as poultices—plants and funguses and berries that Jane had learned to avoid in the forest, but that the prioress said also had their uses, making Jane wonder if some of the rumors about her witchery might be true.

"So you lied to him? Guy, I mean?" Jane's lips still felt swollen, but the stinging had been soothed.

"I lied to protect us. He'll leave you be from now on."

Jane laughed, the smile turning to a grimace with her cut. "He will not. He'll try to find me alone, he will."

"Then don't be alone," Ibota said sharply. "Take Roger, or take one of the other girls, until we can get Guy sent away. Don't forget, the reeve wants him gone as badly as we do. We'll think of something."

But Jane had already thought of something. "Let me bring word to Robin," she said. He was in danger, and so was Jane. He would want to protect her, she knew he would. And she would be protecting him too. "It's as you say, m'um," Jane said. "If Robin is killed for vengeance and not for justice, they'll turn him into a saint, they will. And more will follow his path."

"Of course, you have your own reasons for wanting Robin spared," Ibota said with a sharp look at Jane.

Jane shrugged and tried to seem embarrassed. She waited, for she was learning that Ibota needed time to think things through, to get to where her mind was going, and to believe she had thought of things herself rather than having the ideas put there by Jane, or by anyone else.

"But if Robin knows Guy is hunting him, if he humiliates him . . ." the prioress mused.

"Then Guy will be gone, m'um, with his head hanging. He won't trouble us. Or anyone else." She weighted the last few words with meaning.

"Have you heard things among the servants? Has he . . . ?"

Jane nodded, and let real anger flash across her face, for that part was not a lie, after all.

"I'll admit, it would be a delight to see him crawl back to my cousin like a whipped dog." Ibota considered her. "All right, Jane. Meet with Robin and warn him. But he can't fly free forever. In exchange, I want to know Robin Hood's plans, whatever they are."

Jane's heart leapt, a flame bursting to life inside her. It was sad, she thought fleetingly, that she should be so thrilled by her own danger. But her caged heart beat loudly enough to drown out all her doubts. She would have to keep Bran from finding out, for surely he would foil it if he could, but that would be a small thing. Just one more secret, one more lie, that Jane buried deep in her belly as she nodded obediently, bowed her head, and held her tongue.

She sent her message through Tillot, the old laundress, whispering of a new threat to Robin and all his loyal servants at King's Houses. Then, she spent a torrid, sleepless night in her chambers, blanket twisted around her as she jerked awake over and over, soothing herself with the memory of Robin's touch, his kiss, his mouth on hers, only to awaken with fear throbbing in her heart, for what if he didn't answer her? She found herself praying to Mary, although it was a selfish thing, a heartless thing to pray for, that her lover should come back to her and want her again, knowing the blood she had on her hands, and knowing who she had hurt to get to him.

-<<<◆>>>-

Jane's prayers, selfish as they were, were answered. Robin summoned her to the trysting tree the very next day, and he sent the message back through Tillot too, not through Bran. Did he know that Bran and Jane were through, that she could be his now? And did it please him? Her heart leaping, her feet light as air, Jane nearly ran to the prioress for permission.

"You'll need to bring protection," Ibota said, her parchment brow creased, making Jane's stomach ache with guilt. The prioress was worried for her, and Jane didn't deserve it. "I'll give you hemlock, and monkshood, and something more. You mustn't touch it, but . . ."

"You want me to bring *poisons* to the Greenwood?"

"You do remember your lessons, then," Ibota quipped as she pressed a cold lump of metal into Jane's hand. "Bring it in this."

It was a ring, an ugly thing, mannish and stern, silver with a thick yellow jewel that concealed a wax-sealed hole in its side.

Jane shook her head. "I could never wear that. No one would believe I had come by it."

"Can you keep it hidden, then? Only take it out if you need it?" Jane looked at her skeptically. "If anyone asks, pretend you stole it from me."

"I wouldn't . . ."

"You must take it with you, Jane." Ibota's face was grim. "In case you can't get back. You may have forgotten the state you were in the last time you saw Robin Hood, but I have not."

"But it wasn't . . ." Jane swallowed her objections. Perhaps, one day, she would be free to speak her mind, but for now, her silences kept building like snow on a straw roof, threatening to break a hole in her. She closed her hand around the ring. "How do you give it to someone?"

"Well, normally I would tip it into a drink, discreetly. But if your need is great, I know you'll think of something."

Normally? Jane thought. *How often do you poison people?* She didn't say it aloud, and she kept her eyes down to study the ring as if awed by it, in case the prioress could read her face.

"Jane"—Ibota pressed her hands around Jane's, the ring cupped inside—"if you see Guy in the Greenwood, if he catches up to Robin before you do, don't try to use this. Just run."

Jane nodded. "Yes, m'um."

"I mean it. He's not to be trifled with. Promise me you'll run the moment you see him."

Heat washed across Jane's face from the guilt, the shame, as the prioress thought only for her life and her safety, and all Jane could think about was how she wanted to tear her hands away, leap onto a horse, and throw herself into Robin's arms.

"I'll run," she whispered. "I promise." But she had already abandoned Robin to danger once, that day in the church. She knew, in her heart, that she couldn't bear to abandon him again.

Chapter Twenty-Six

Jane's lies, her guilt, followed her like shadows as she rode through the forest. She jumped at every little sound, every breath of wind. She could have sworn there were hoofbeats behind her, just on the edge of hearing.

But her guilt lifted when she saw Robin. He was shooting arrows into a makeshift target molded to look like a man, tied to the trysting tree. The seashell ropes on the tree shook and clattered with the impact of his arrows, new leaves that had burst out green for springtime tumbling from the great oak's limbs.

Robin wore his secret, private smile, the one that was just for her. "Jane." He bowed, and Jane thought she noticed new creases near his eyes when he rose, though his bruises were fading, and though he stood as gracefully as he used to stand, lean and tall. "There you are! It's been so long since I've heard from you, I thought you had forgotten me."

"Bran hasn't been sending your messages . . . I mean, if you've sent them. I . . . ." Jane gushed, then felt foolish, girlish. "Well, Bran and I are through, is all."

Robin laughed, a pleasant flush blooming on his cheeks. "So you're a free woman now, are you?"

Not free, Jane thought stubbornly, her jaw clenching. *Not free. Yours.*

He reached for her hand, helping her down off the horse, and she stumbled a little, letting him steady her in his arms. He was clean-shaven, his cheekbones sharp, setting off his green eyes. The beard that shrouded those cheeks when the reeve held him captive, the sourness of his skin, had made him seem like something lesser, a mere man, subject to nature just like everyone else. Now he smelled of woodsmoke again, and herbs.

Jane tried not to let her longing show. Instead, she blurted out, "Is it safe for you to be here?"

"The shire reeve has been tricked here twice. He won't think to come again, at least not for a while." Robin looked around him, drawing in a deep breath.

"I suppose you know he's back, your shire reeve. And there's another man after you now, a worse one. Guy de Gisborne has come."

"Aye," Robin said. "Tillot passed that along. Did you come all the way out here just to tell me about him? Or"—he smiled coyly, knowing—"for something more."

Jane scrambled for more information, something the other servants might not have told Robin, feeling bewildered at his distance, as though all the kind things he'd said—his touch, his kiss, just days ago—had meant nothing at all. Was it true what John had told her, then: that Robin only wanted what another man had? Was Jane really such a fool, as much of a fool as Betrice had been? "King Edward has them in competition now," she stammered, "the reeve and him. They're both here for your head, and the man who wins will be shire reeve from then on."

"Did that hunter hurt you?" Robin's glance flew to her swollen lip. She nodded, suddenly unable to speak. She had thought Guy's blow hadn't really moved her, but Robin's concern seemed to stir emotions she had buried, and tears stung her eyes, sudden and surprising.

Robin reached out and stroked her injured lip, his fingertips gentle as feathers. "And no Bran to protect you," he said softly. "Am I the cause of that, Jane?" His eyes took her in, bright, devouring, and Jane breathed a sigh. She had his regard again. It didn't matter that his question was a game, meant to force a confession out of her, when he knew—he had to know—that she couldn't ask for him first, not with him being who he was, and Jane being who she was. For she was nothing, no one, and Robin Hood—well, he was everything. That he would toy with her now, after all she had given up for him, troubled her in a way she could not bear to think about, so she swatted the thought away as if it were a fly circling summer fruit.

"Guy de Gisborne . . ." Robin turned his head to study the woods, and Jane hurriedly wiped at her eyes. "A traitor he was, in the Barons' War, even more than Edward. What false courage men must feel in their bones, to mark themselves hunters before they catch their prey. So, Jane"—Robin turned back, his eyes dancing with light—"what are you hoping I'll do about him?"

"Well," she said, "I was hoping you would protect them. The servants, I mean. Especially the girls."

"And you? Do you want me to protect you too?" His smile was playful, his eyes still glittering.

"I . . . well . . ." Jane felt like vines were crawling up her heart, choking her breath. "I understand if it's too much of a risk, with so many men on the hunt for you. Perhaps it's best if you don't. Perhaps it's best if you stay hidden."

"Are you calling me a coward, Jane?"

Jane found herself at a loss, like she was drowning in an unexpected sea. "No! Of course not! I . . ." He grinned at her then, mocking her, and she burst out, confounded, "What do you want from me?"

"Little Jane." Robin's smile softened. "Of course I'll help. But it *is* nice to be asked."

"I'm so sorry. I should have asked properly, but I . . ."

"You're worried, and you've been hurt. I should not have teased you. It wasn't right. But I do like to see you stumble, like a baby deer over forest tangles. It brings a pretty color to your face." And then, finally, *finally*, he came to her and kissed her cheek. Warmth spread throughout her body as his mouth traced a line down her jaw, then to her lips, kissing her gently, his tongue flickering over her bruise.

He pulled her to him then, hands circling the base of her back, and Jane was swept away on the wave of him, full of his taste. She pressed closer, but she was afraid to reach up, to touch his face, to show her longing, as though their kiss was so delicate that she could break it with a breath.

"You taste of violets." He sighed. And he stepped away.

Jane could only blink at him. It had been so many days since she had been under Robin's spell that she had forgotten what it was like not to know her own mind. She had begun to think she was mastering people, that she had skill at it—that she was above being mastered herself. But no one mastered the Lord of the Greenwood. She should not have forgotten.

"So for all that time you spent together," Robin asked with a coy smile, "Bran never taught you how to protect yourself?"

Jane felt welcome again, comfortable enough to joke. "I can hardly go attacking all the nasty lords at King's Houses, can I? Not if I want to keep working there."

"There are ways of fighting back, of making people know not to trouble you because you're trouble yourself."

"Everyone already thinks I'm trouble. That's how I earned this mark upon my face. The hunter and the reeve both suspect me."

Robin took her by the shoulders, breath hot and close to her ear. "And what if the hunter had you cornered? What if he decided to take you by force." His nose tickled her neck. Jane trembled, feeling heat climb up her face and chest.

"Robin," she murmured, secretly pleased, even though she knew she should not be.

"If you mean to keep working for me, you must be able to defend yourself." He released her, then fished out his knife, the one with the strange knots and creatures on it. "I loaned you this once, and you didn't have call to use it, but I hadn't realized you wouldn't know how." Robin tossed it up in the air, then caught it cleverly by the hilt again. The blade, kept just as clean as it had been the last time Jane had held it, glimmered in the shrouded sunlight, warm gold against silver. "Did I ever tell you this knife's story?"

Jane shook her head as if to clear a fog. "You didn't."

"It belonged to an Irishman who fought alongside me in the war. We were all hired men, you see, and the Irishman, well." Robin paused, his eyes clouding. "Like many of us, he was running from something. He used to talk to me about his homeland, the great green hills across the sea. When he spoke of Ireland, it sounded like a free place, a wild place. It sounded like a dream."

Wind whipped through the trysting tree, rattling the shells again. "And you never went?" Jane asked when the shells had finished their song. "To visit, I mean?"

"He always said he would take me. But instead, the war took him, and all I have left of him is this knife." He smiled at it, sadly. "What I realized, Jane, is if you're not willing to protect your own land, your own people, then there's nowhere you can run that will be safe. No land on this earth can be free without spilling the blood of those who mean to take it from you. I found my paradise right here in these woods, my freedom right here in these woods, and I will always fight for it." He took her hands in his, pressing them so hard that the knife's hilt bit into her skin. "And you, Jane, you must learn to fight for it too, and not rely on others to win your freedom for you."

And at that, a slow, loud clapping sound came from the western edge of the clearing. The noise of the wind and the shells had covered someone's approach.

"Pretty words. Very pretty words. You're an ass and a fool if you believe them, but they are pretty." Jane's shoulders shot up to her ears when she heard the voice, for she knew exactly whose it was, even though she had only heard it once before. Even though, when she turned around to face him, she saw that Guy de Gisborne was on the hunt, for his face was hidden behind a leather mask.

-◄◄◄◆►►►-

Guy stood before them, arms crossed. His mask was fitted to the top of his skull, a poorly stitched seam running across it like a scar. His red-gold tail hung out of it at the back, whipped across his shoulder. He looked bigger and more menacing here in the forest, with a wicked pair of swords at his belt, a bow strapped to his back.

All Jane could think when she saw him was the prioress's warning. Had she *known* Guy was coming? Had she sent him after Jane, planning to trap Robin? He had arrived here too quickly, as if he'd known exactly where to go. Or worse, had Guy chased *her* into the forest, and she had just been too foolishly smitten, too eager to see Robin, to realize she was being followed?

Guy pointed at her with a gloved hand. "Knew there was something off about you. That reeve thought me a fool for nosing around a plain servant girl." Guy straightened and tapped his nose beneath the mask. "Hunters should have a nose for that kind of thing. Seems he's a rusty blade indeed." Jane tried to keep her face neutral. The reeve suspected her—she knew he did. Apparently he hadn't wanted to share that information with his rival.

Robin stepped in front of her, just as Betrice had, as if he'd noticed her trembling. "And what, good sir, are you hunting on this day?"

Guy chuckled and spat on the ground beside him. "Birds. Robins, specifically."

"'Tis a poor time for such a hunt," Robin said. "I haven't seen a robin in these woods for days."

"Aye," Guy said, with a grin that said he thought himself clever. "But wolves hunt best when robins hide."

"So if you're a wolf looking for a robin, why are you following a girl?"

"Is she your girl, then? Bit beneath you, isn't it, Lord of the Greenwood? But between you and that prioress, seems she's got some value to her." Guy's hands dropped to his swords. "Perhaps I'll find out what it is myself."

"Lord of the Greenwood?" Robin said innocently. "Why, I'm just a humble archer romancing my fair maiden. It is a cruel wolf indeed who interrupts a man's courting. What could you hope to gain by stealing the sunlight from a peasant and his maid?"

"Drop the foolery, Robin Hood. I know exactly who you are, and I'd like to have this girl back before dinner. Or, perhaps, *for* dinner." His grin showed a missing tooth in the upper left corner. "The wolf is hungry, after all."

"I can't have you stealing my maiden, hunter. Not without a fair fight." He took up his bow casually, even as Guy's hands twitched at his swords. Robin grinned, feigning surprise, and opened his arms wide, brandishing the bow. "A *contest*, I mean. I'm not so good a shot as the bird you're hunting, but I *am* the best shot in these woods. Or are you all wolf and no man, here merely to plunder another man's hard-won harvest?"

"You're a bigger fool than I thought if you believe such contests are fair."

"Perhaps not in the king's court, where men's sight is fogged by the glitter of gold. But this is the Greenwood. If you're the better shot, you can have the girl."

Sickness rose up in Jane. She was sure Robin could win. She had seen him shoot before. But Guy didn't seem like the sort of man to follow the rules of an archery contest if he lost. Was Robin really willing to risk her life for another one of his games?

"And what's to stop you," Guy asked, "or me, from drawing swords and having it done if we don't like the way the wind blows our arrows?"

"Jane will guard our baser weapons while we settle this like gentlemen. Here, Jane." Robin held out his sword. "I'll even offer mine first, as a show of goodwill, before our hunter offers you his. That is, unless he is afraid of losing."

Guy snorted, then spat into the dirt again. "All right, archer. I'm bored and it's a pleasant day, so we'll play your game until I tire of it." He threw both of his swords on the ground before Jane, and she staggered backward a little, for they came quite close to her feet. Scowling, she knelt and picked them up. "But I have my own rule to add, my own stakes."

"And what is your rule?" Robin asked.

"For every shot I make," Guy said, "I'll tell your girl a secret about the rebel she's been bedding."

"And for every shot I make?"

"Every shot you make, boy, is another moment added to your life."

"One can't expect a fair trade from a wolf, I suppose." Robin winked at Jane, who sat on the ground to watch with the swords beside her. She chewed her lip, opening the cut and tasting blood. What would happen if Guy mastered Robin? *Could* Guy master Robin? Robin seemed confident as ever, but without his men around, Jane felt less sure. She thought of Ibota's poisoned ring, heavy but useless in her belt, and cursed herself for not heeding the prioress's warning. *Promise me you'll run the moment you see him*, she had said. And Jane should have. But how could she have left Robin behind?

"I don't accept, hunter," Robin said, as though he had actually considered Guy's offer. "You mean to take something precious from me, so I must ask the same of you: each shot I make, I'll choose a thing of yours to claim as mine."

"Like *what*?" Guy snapped.

"Oh, I don't know." Robin pretended to think. "That horn at your side, or your horse. Or that silly mask you wear."

"You watch your tongue, or I'll . . ."

"Are you so afraid of being bested that you'd bring us to blows before we shoot?"

"Oh, I'll show you fear," Guy boasted, pretending to be bold, but Jane could see that Guy was caught, that he was no wolf at all. Merely another hare who had stumbled into Robin's trap.

"You know," Robin said as Guy removed the bow from his back, "'tis a lucky thing you met with me today instead of Robin Hood. I hear the Lord of the Greenwood is a dangerous man and can't be trusted."

"Oh, I'll tell you a thing or two about . . ."

Robin clucked. "Not yet, hunter. You must beat my shot first. Then, and only then, can you loosen your tongue." He shrugged at Guy's irritated look. "It's your rule. Not mine."

"How many are we shooting for?"

"We'll play until you feel you've lost too much."

"Or," Guy said with a hungry grin, "until your girl here knows too much."

"I've nothing to hide," Robin said, "and nothing to be ashamed of. Unless you intend to lie, hunter. A wolf will pretend to be a dog, or a sheep, just to fill his belly—or so the fables say."

"I've no need to lie to fill my belly. My bow is good enough."

"Let's see it, then." Robin bowed. "The first shot is yours, since you're a guest in my home. Gentlemen's rules, though you prefer to play the churl."

Guy hit the target directly where the heart would be, if the target were a man made of flesh instead of straw. "Heart shot," he said. "Beat that, archer."

Robin's arrow flew light and graceful, as if it were the very bird de Gisborne hunted. And it split Guy's arrow in twain.

"And here I thought you meant to give me a challenge," Robin said. "So, hunter, which will it be first? Your mask, your horse, or your horn?"

Guy snarled, took the horn from his belt, and tossed it at Robin's feet. "We'll see about next time."

Robin lifted the horn up, frowning at it. "This isn't nearly as nice as the shire reeve's horn. Or"—he grinned—"so I've heard. Let's keep this in our treasure hoard, shall we?" He lobbed it gently to Jane, and she caught it and put it in her pile, feeling sick, for surely she was meant to be part of the hoard as well. She found herself gripping Robin's sword with her other hand. She didn't know when the gentlemen's rules, or the facade of gentlemen's rules, would collapse around her, when things would turn to blood and chaos the way they had at Mooch's house. She didn't want to believe they could turn that way with Robin, but she couldn't chase the fear away, couldn't shake the smell of blood, the sound of screams, that haunted her still.

"Next shot," Robin said. "You call the target. I'm sure I won't be as lucky this time." He turned to Jane and winked, and she knew at that moment that he meant to draw the game out, to toy with Guy de Gisborne the way he had toyed with his other victims. She felt tired, all of a sudden. She just wanted to go back to King's Houses and crawl into bed until the sun set and she could sleep. When had King's Houses begun to feel like a safe place to her? She supposed since she got there. She supposed King's Houses was the first safe place she had ever known, because her own home was never that safe. Someone was always threatening to tear it out from under her. And now, she had lost even that. She had been thrown on the prioress's mercy, and there was no safe place for her at all. Jane's throat started to choke with tears, and she wiped her eyes as swiftly as she could, when the men weren't looking.

The game moved along without her. Guy shot and hit where the target's eye would have been. Robin shot next and landed wide of the mark, but not so wide that he could be called a poor shot. He still had his pride, even when he was playing games. Jane remembered that from the contest at the reeve's house.

"Ha!" Guy barked. "I knew my luck would turn. Now I'll spill a secret of yours, I will. So, little girl"—and Jane's skin crawled when he said it—"did you know your man here is a deserter? That he scampered away from war like a scared rabbit, leaving other men to pay for his crimes?" He smirked. "And pay they did. With their heads, and worse."

Defiantly, Jane met Guy de Gisborne's masked gaze and shrugged. She had known about the war. She had known that Robin deserted, but not for the reasons Guy said. Was this something the hunter really thought would turn her heart? She was no nobleman, no knight, fool enough to believe that wars were fought with honor.

Guy laughed, surprised. "Oh, so she knows, then. She's fallen for a traitor with wide-open eyes. Doesn't speak well for you, girl. Seems to me you ought to be punished for your associations. And I'm just the man to do it."

"Let us leave justice to the shire reeve, shall we?" Robin said. "And not to wolves. Unless we have stopped pretending to be men of honor?"

"Boy, I lost my honor long ago."

"But that's the *game*, hunter," Robin said with false earnestness. "Or have you already forgotten the rules? Call a target."

"We'll soon run out of targets," Guy said, "and your little game will end. I call the other eye."

"But I'm so bad with eyes." Robin grinned.

"You shoot first, then," Guy said. "I insist. If we are to play at having honor."

"As poor a player as you are, I accept." Robin shot at the target's left eye and hit the mark.

"A good shot," Guy grunted, "but we'll see." His shot nicked Robin's arrow so it wobbled free from the target and fell to the ground.

Robin actually looked surprised. "Very good. A wolf with a mind for a bow."

"Another secret, then," Guy proclaimed. "Today, your lover has targets made of straw and plays at courtesy. But once he held his blade to any throat he was sent to cut, no matter how delicate, no matter how young and fragile. And he did it all for coin."

Anger flashed across Robin's face like a little storm, a swift black cloud, before he regained his composure. "I thought you weren't going to tell lies, wolf. Nothing in the Barons' War was done for coin, not by Robin Hood or his men. Everything in that war was done for freedom."

"Freedom from being poor, you mean?" Guy laughed, and Robin tried to smile, but it was strained. "This wolf has followed you for some time. He knows the scent of your tracks."

"Shoot, then," Robin said. "You first this time. And since you insist on telling secrets, if I win this one, I'll see your face. We shoot for the mask."

Guy was feeling cocksure now, but Jane could see violence rising in Robin, just as it had before he hit John. A coolness came over him, not like an ordinary man's rage that burned hot and showed on his face. Robin's anger was as silent and chill as the death that came in a man's sleep. Jane gripped the sword harder, though she still didn't know what she might do with it.

"All right," Guy said. "Let's shoot for the liver, where a man's courage lives and dies."

"A fine choice," Robin answered, "for a man's true face is revealed with courage. Only cowards hide behind a mask."

"I'll let that go," Guy said, though his shoulders tightened. "Only because you're about to lose." But he shot just wide of the mark. "Argh!" he said. "A foul wind caught me!"

Robin laughed. "And here I thought that was the wolf's foul breath." He shot easily, directly into the mark, and then he shot another arrow into Guy's for good measure. He turned around with a deceptively kind smile. "Unmask, hunter, and we shall see the truth of you."

Guy took his mask off, grumbling. "Too warm a day for this thing anyway. They said the north was cold, they did, but they . . ."

And suddenly, just as the mask was off and the hunter's sweaty, bulbous nose and pockmarked cheeks met the springtime sun, Robin whipped out his Irish knife—the one he had meant to give Jane—and hurled it right into Guy de Gisborne's eye.

Chapter Twenty-Seven

Guy screamed. He fell to his knees, clutching his face. "My eye! You fucking bastard!"

Jane leapt to her feet, sword in her hand, fear a river of frost pouring down her spine. "Robin!" she gasped—but her words, and the sword in her hand—none of it meant anything at all. For what could she do, really, now that Robin had changed the game, had turned it into a battle with a flick of his wrist?

Although, Robin had changed too, now that he had drawn blood. He had an empty stare, and he smiled without a hint of humor. "Seems I am good with eyes, after all." Wind blew through the seashells on the trysting tree again, another dance of bone, and Jane felt every clatter ring deep within her spine.

"You fucking coward!" Guy bellowed, his hands around the knife. He tore it out and hurled it into the dirt, his eye spurting blood. His face twisted and gory like a demon's, he spotted Jane with his good eye, the sword in her hand.

He lunged for her. But he wasn't fast enough.

Even as Jane skittered backward, clutching the sword as though her life depended on it, Robin grabbed Guy by the collar and flung him away. Guy recovered, struggled to his knees, but Robin stalked over and kicked him in the stomach. "Knew it was you," Robin said, his teeth gritted, but his voice so impossibly light. "Knew you were the one who took my men from me in the war. The ones you could catch. I just had to see your face to be certain."

"You . . . bloody . . . snake!" Guy managed, gasping, clutching at his face. He started crawling toward Jane, but it was a doomed thing, his body, his quest, for Robin kicked him again, rolling him against the tree.

"I'm the snake? *You* fought by our side until you saw which way the wind was blowing, then you slithered through our ranks and took coin for all your brothers' heads!"

"No one has brothers in war," Guy spat.

Robin picked up his knife and stood over Guy's writhing body, mindless of the blood and filth and gore that marred his hands. "That's where you're wrong. War is all *about* brotherhood. And when a brother is wronged"—he gripped the knife with purpose now—"a loyal man gets revenge."

And then, Robin turned to Jane. She had thought John's anger had been an awful thing to behold. But this was worse. Robin was worse. His face, his demeanor, hardly changed at all. You wouldn't even notice it, if you hadn't spent all your time—too much time— watching him. Watching him, but somehow, stupidly, not seeing what lurked behind his smile.

"Be a good girl, Jane," Robin said, his voice all cloying honey, "and fetch water from the stream."

"But I . . ."

Guy had pulled himself upright, pressing a torn piece of cloth to his wounded eye. Blood ran from it, thick and blackened with dirt. "Wouldn't argue with him, girl. Mayhap you didn't know what you were bedding, but you know it now."

His warning freed Jane from her stupor, and she ran, stumbling over her feet, scrambling over twigs and brambles and tree stumps. Guy's screams shattered the woods behind her, raw and animal. Only when the sword fell from Jane's hand did she realize she had still been clutching it. Robin's sword. She dropped to her knees beside it.

Another scream, and a gurgle at the end, like a beast being slaughtered. Those weren't fighting sounds. There was only one voice screaming, and it wasn't Robin's.

Jane tried to force herself to move. She had to get water. She did not want to go back there empty-handed. Robin had never hurt her, but she had to admit to herself, finally, that she did not know this man, not fully. Not this man with all the warmth behind his eyes snuffed out like a candle flame in a storm.

Somehow, Jane made it to Robin's makeshift camp by the stream, the same place they had ambushed the reeve, back when Robin's games had seemed so innocent. She found a water skin there, alongside dried food and blankets. Where were his other men? Had he brought no one with him? Or had they known—suspected—why she was coming to meet Robin and let him come alone? Shame flooded her, though it was such a silly thing to worry about when she was fetching water to wash Robin clean of blood.

Jane forced herself to fill the skin, cold water running over her hands, numbing her fingers. Her mouth was dry as grave dirt. She thought of drinking some of the water herself, but she knew she could not keep it down. Even now her bile threatened to rise, but a part of Jane refused to lose control again. Not in front of Robin.

And why not? another part of her mind asked her, for it felt as though her thoughts had cracked into fragments like a broken jug, and all the different pieces were screaming at each other.

Another piece tried to calm her as she knelt in the stream, her stockings soaking through at the knees. It whispered that perhaps Robin had sent her away to protect her, to keep her from seeing what had to be done. That he was killing Guy to save her. And so it would be a hard thing to see Guy's corpse, but not so hard as what John and Wyll had done, murdering a man right in front of her eyes. Murdering a boy.

But why was it taking so long? Jane thought she heard another scream, but the wind was whipping through the trees now, and Guy's voice had become so faint, so light, as if it were a part of the wind itself.

Jane let out a deep, shaking breath. This was what it meant to be one of Robin's people, to be close to him, to be loyal. She had to steel herself. She could do this. But as Jane gathered enough courage to make her way back to the trysting tree, she found herself still haunted by the specter of Robin's face, the ice in his smile. What if she had run, or been in his way, or failed him? She had seen him hit John and Wyll both, and they were his friends and allies. Would he stay his hand just because she was a woman?

And when Jane came back to the trysting tree, when she saw what Robin had done, she dropped the skin and the sword, and water spilled into the dirt, turning the earth beneath her boots to mud.

Robin stood beside Guy, playing with his knife, but the knife was black with gore now, and Guy's face . . .

Once, Jane had found a little dog mauled by a forest creature— a wolf, or a boar, she'd had no way of telling. It was dead, and there was nothing to be done, and all she could do was mourn and turn away, but her heart still pressed against her chest as though it would burst with sadness whenever she thought of it, whenever the image slipped into her thoughts like an intruder, unannounced and unwelcome.

Guy's face was like that now. But there was no question about what had done it. No question that it was a man, not a beast. That it was Robin—*her* Robin—if a man who could do such a thing could be called a man at all.

Jane couldn't even scream. She just stared, mouth open, boots sinking into mud, limbs as stiff as though she had been locked in a tomb.

Robin had bound Guy to the tree with his horse's reins. Guy was dead—surely he was dead, for Robin couldn't do this while he lived—his head slumped, his face a thicket of wounds, a cobweb of cuts and pouring blood.

And yet, Robin kept staring at Guy's body as though it would speak.

"What do you think, Jane?" Robin asked calmly. "Might he pass for me, now that he has no face?"

Fear froze Jane's feet to the ground like blocks of ice. Her mouth was too dry even to swallow.

At her silence, Robin spun to look at her. The evil, knowing face he had worn before was gone, replaced by a wide, innocent stare, a wounded one. "You've dropped the water," he said as though he were scolding a child, but one he was fond of. "Now I'll have to go get more."

"Robin," Jane whispered, her lips sticking together, pasty with fear.

"Oh, Jane," he said, still speaking as though she were a partic-

ularly stupid girl and he was trying to explain why the sky went
dark at night. "What I've done to him, he would have done to me.
And that's nothing to what he would do to you. He said as much.
Or don't you remember? Did you think it was only threats instead
of promises?"

"I just—" Jane's voice cracked, and she cleared her throat. "I
thought you'd do it quickly. Show him mercy."

"And would he have shown *you* mercy?" Robin's lip curled,
and Jane shrank back a little, but he sighed instead of moving toward her. "I should have known this was the thanks I'd get. It's
just as John said. He said I should let you be, that you were too
delicate, like a flower pretending to be a tree. But I didn't want to
believe him."

Words fled Jane like rats fled the light.

"We'll deal with this when I get back," Robin said, his voice
still hollow. "But I'm disappointed in you, Jane. I really am. I
thought you were a stronger woman. I thought you knew what we
were up against."

Robin disappeared into the trees. Once no one could hear her,
Jane whispered to herself, "I should have listened to her. I should
have run."

Or she thought no one could hear her, until a gurgling sound
came from Guy's slumped body. "Mercy," he mumbled.

Jane gasped, her mind blank as fresh snow. He was alive.
Robin had left him alive, alive and suffering. Suffering on the edge
of death, but alive enough to feel pain, alive enough to beg. *Mercy*.
Was he just repeating the word she had said, or did he want . . .

"Mercy," Guy rasped again from his wreck of a face, blood
and froth spilling from his mouth. Jane could see cuts on his neck
too, patches of skin carved away, like a deer cut up for roasting.

Jane shut her eyes. This was a nightmare. It had to be a nightmare. Like all the times she was lost in the woods and the trees took the shape of wild beasts, and the air howled at her, and she woke up foggy and stifling and praying thanks to Mary that it was a dream after all. She tried to conjure the portrait of Mary she had seen at Robin's camp—bronze and gold and blue. The seashells on the trysting tree spun and chattered in the breeze.

If she took a blade to Guy's throat, made it fast, perhaps she could do it. She had taken chickens before, and hares, and if she was very, very quick, perhaps this would be no different. Perhaps.

But Robin would know. He'd see the killing cut, for she could not make it hidden. He had made all the marks on Guy's face, and on his neck, and he had meant them, and he would know. She couldn't do anything but watch. And would she have to keep watching, when Robin came back? Horror slid up her fingers like a wet pair of gloves.

Jane did not want to look at Guy. She did not want to see or smell him, or taste his fear, or have his mangled face burned into her mind like a brand. But she summoned her courage. She went to him. Perhaps, if he was still alive, she could cut his bonds, set him free. She crept up slowly. Guy didn't talk, didn't move, as she went to him. The forest was so still, the sun hot on the back of her neck, like the moment was frozen in time.

Jane drew close enough to smell him—the blood, the stench of his innards, the way he had soiled himself. But Guy still didn't move. His single eye was staring, but not at her, for she had moved past it, and that was when she realized, with a turmoil of horror, of relief, threatening to burst from her chest in a sob, that his last words had been a prayer, and Mary had shown him mercy after all.

She placed a hand, tentative, beneath the wreck of his nose, and felt nothing—no wind, no breath, no spark of life or spirit. Trembling—with rage, with horror and fear—Jane closed his remaining eye for him.

⟶⟨⟨⟨•⟩⟩⟩⟵

Robin returned with a full water skin and an axe. Jane wondered what the water was for, after all, and whether the axe was for her, but she wondered it idly, as if some part of her were floating up above the forest, like the crow he had once called her, watching in a detached, disinterested way.

She tried not to flinch at the sight of him.

She forced herself to study Robin's face the way she had watched Guy's. She forced herself to read it, openly this time, with no illusions. *I know you see me, Jane*, Robin had said once, *more than anyone ever has.* He had called her wise. But some part of her knew that she had merely seen what Robin needed and given it, just as she had soothed her father's lightning rages, her mother's thunderstorms of sadness. Just as she had known what Eudo wanted to hear when he sounded cross, what Bran wanted when he warmed her with his smile.

Robin wanted her devotion. Her gratitude. He thought himself a hero even now, even with Guy's mutilated corpse proving the lie right beside him, even with his tunic and stockings painted scarlet with blood and gore. He had cleaned his face and hands, but not his clothes, as though he knew they would be bloodied again and there was no point to it.

There are no lies so powerful, so pleasing, as the lies a man will tell about himself, Jane thought, feeling like a carrion bird in truth, picking at his insides.

348 THE TRAITOR OF SHERWOOD FOREST

All she wanted to do was to get away from him, to run. But she couldn't run. Robin would never let her go. Not until she showed him that she was loyal. He had told her he would kill for her, would do anything to free her. But what he had done to Guy had only been for himself—his pleasure, his vengeance. And she saw it now, clear as winter ice, that this was what Robin's tricks had been for all along.

Jane took a deep breath. She knew how to beg forgiveness. She had learned it as a child, over and over. "Robin, I'm so sorry. You were right," she said.

Robin looked at her skeptically, but his face softened, just a little bit.

"You were only protecting me, and I was . . . I was just . . ." Jane's lip trembled, and her fear was a real thing.

His shoulders eased, the hint of a smile lighting his face. "You were scared, Jane. Of course you were. War is not an easy thing. It never is. But I knew you'd see it. I knew you'd understand."

"You had to kill him for me. You had to kill him for *us*." That part, at least, was the truth.

Robin's brows knitted together. "Kill him? Oh, no, he's not . . ." He turned to Guy, axe and water still in his hands, and probed Guy's stomach with his boot, sending the corpse slumping sideways. "Well, look at that! He left us! Slunk away like a coward!"

Jane braced herself for Robin's rage, in case it came, in case he blamed her. But Robin only shrugged. "Wanted to seem strong, he did, but no man is strong when he hides behind a mask." Robin turned, brow still creased, worried. "But you do understand, don't you, Jane? Why I couldn't just kill him. Why I had to . . ."

"Of course," Jane said. "What he did to your friends in the war, what he would have done to me." She looked away as if she were sickened by the thought of it, and not at the sight of Guy's mutilated face. "He betrayed you."

"Yes," Robin said eagerly. "Yes, you see! I knew you would. It's about loyalty, Jane. He had the nerve to call me traitor. But I stayed loyal to my men in the war. And I'll stay loyal now, to you."

Jane looked back at him beneath her lashes, halting, like the stumbling fawn he hoped she would be. "You forgive me for my fear?"

"Please. There's nothing to forgive." Robin set down his axe, his water, and took Jane's hands, pressing them to his soiled chest. If she kept from looking at his stained tunic, kept her eyes latched on to his, she could pretend he was still the same Robin, courteous and gentle and kind. "You're part of my band, and that's forever, Jane."

"What happens now?" she asked, trying to sound light, curious, but her throat had gone dry with the question.

"Now we lay a trap for the shire reeve."

"And after that?" Jane cursed herself for asking. Was she looking for some greater good, some plan, when all Robin had ever wanted was vengeance?

"Sir Richard promised me a title for my favors. You were right, Jane." Robin grew excited, his eyes green as river mold. "He's raising an army. He means to have me lead it."

"And what will you do once you have your title? Once you have real power?" The question came like a whisper, for she glanced at Guy's ruined face when she asked it, and she was flooded with fear that she knew the answer.

"I'll be a guardian, a steward. I only want freedom, Jane, for us. Freedom from kings and churches, which toss men to and fro like our lives and our bonds mean nothing." Robin finally dropped her hands. "I thought Edward would be different. I defended him, at first. He's not his father, I said, and I was right. But not in the way that I thought. He's something worse. He has no principles. Do you know, he tried to turn me to his side when he turned on the barons? He wanted me to be his shadow, his blade in the dark. He wanted to be my master." His jaw clenched. "But the Lord of the Greenwood *has* no master."

Then he grasped Jane's shoulders, pulling her almost off her feet. "Nor should you, Jane," he said earnestly, and she cursed herself, for her heart still fluttered when he said her name, in spite of everything. "You must join me freely. Your loyalty must come from your heart."

And if it doesn't? Jane wondered to herself. *If it comes from fear instead? How will that make Robin any different from the people who rule me now?*

"You'll see, Jane." Robin's smile was back, and it was real, and warm, and lit his eyes with fire again, and Jane could almost ignore the corpse beside them, the blood all over his clothes, he shone so brightly. "We'll drive the rich from their thrones, rob the church clean of gold, and whip the priests and monks and abbots until they flee our land for good, dropping coins behind them as they go."

"All of them?" Jane thought of her brother Adam, kind to animals and children, donating his pittance of a salary to help families who hadn't made it through the winter. Adam, who, if Bran had been true to his word, Robin didn't know about. *Couldn't* know about. "I . . . just . . . there are poor ones who love the Virgin just as you do. Do they not deserve our mercy, our . . . ?"

"*All* of them"—Robin's voice cut through her own like a blade—"serve the devil and his gold. They kiss his ring and call it holy. We are at war, Jane. Make no mistake," he warned, and Jane felt as if she couldn't breathe. "In war, you choose a side. So choose, Jane. The time is now. Choose which side you're on."

Jane sensed the danger. She pressed her lips together, running her tongue over them, dry as they were. Sweat broke across her brow. "With you," she whispered, staring into his eyes with all the devotion she could muster. "I'm with you, m'lord."

He pouted, looking ridiculous with all that gore, with Guy's blood all over his tunic. "I told you not to call me that."

He pulled her even closer, and she winced as he pressed her body against the bloody cloth. He kissed her, hard, his tongue rough, probing now, as if he could find forgiveness, absolution, in her mouth. Then he stopped, sighing into her skin. "I know you think me cruel, Jane. But it's best to learn now. Loyalty is the law of the Greenwood. It's the *only* law that matters. I've proved my loyalty to you this day. And now, you must prove your loyalty to me."

Jane turned her head away so that she did not have to smell him. "What would you have me do?"

At that question, Robin finally released her. He walked over to Guy's corpse and lifted the mask and horn, dangling them from his hands proudly, like he had caught a pair of fat fish. "You're to help me with my trap. Tell the reeve that Guy de Gisborne has caught and killed his bird. That he waits for a final contest at the trysting tree, a battle for Robin's head."

Jane swallowed back bile. That's what the axe was for.

Robin tied Guy's mask around his own head. "What do you think, Jane? Do I look like our wolf here, before he lost his face? Or do I look like myself?"

"You don't look like Robin Hood at all," she said. "You look just like a wolf."

Chapter Twenty-Eight

Jane sucked in huge gulps of air as she raced back to King's Houses, riding as fast as she could go. The air had turned chill as the sun began to drop, and her eyes and nose ran with water in the bracing wind. She could not push the memory of Guy's carved face out of her mind—it kept appearing in front of her as though he were riding the wind, a demon guiding her into hell. Would Robin do to the reeve what he had done to Guy? Walter de Stircheley was not a bad man, though he was not a good one either. But if she warned him away, she might face the noose herself. Or worse, she would face Robin's anger. Not to mention the others who would suffer for her treachery, like Bran.

Bran. Suddenly, he filled her thoughts, coating her heart like a warm clarrey. How could she have betrayed him? How could she have given him up? She had been such a fool for Robin when Bran was right there the whole time, his arms open for her, his bed warm. Robin wanted war, wanted bloodshed, but Jane and Bran, they were simple people. They weren't made for war. Jane had tried to soar too high, she saw that now. Robins—red-breasted, proud—took what they wanted in the sunlight. Crows lurked in the shadows, guarding their nests, watching and waiting for what was left.

Perhaps Bran would forgive her, she thought wildly. If she went to him, if she told him she was wrong, what a fool she'd been. They could run away together, someplace far away, where Robin and John and the reeve couldn't catch them. For they couldn't stay at King's Houses, or in Sherwood Forest, that was certain. Whoever the victor was in Robin's war, there would be blood spilled, and it would be the blood of people who didn't have power, spilled by those who did. It always was. Powerless people—like Bran, like herself, like the little page who rode alongside the monk, innocent and chivalrous—would suffer. People who had no real idea of what was coming, or what beasts warfare made of men.

Jane stabled her horse, resolved. She would go to Bran, and she would tell him everything, and he would see sense. She knew he would. She didn't hear him upstairs, but she would wait there for him, safe and warm, and he would comfort her. He would forgive her, for she would be sorry enough to soothe him. Sorry enough for a thousand years of mistakes. She knew just how to crack the ice around his heart. She longed to feel his thick chest pressed against hers, his safe, strong arms around her, his horsey smell filling her senses until there was nothing there but him, no fears or memories or longings she shouldn't have. Her heart was pound-ing and her face hot when she reached the top of the ladder, though her hands were slippery and cold.

And that was when she realized Bran was gone.

The blanket lay neatly folded on the bed, which Bran had never done, not once. He always left it in a sweaty tangle, half on the floor, covered with straw, and she used to complain about it, but he would just wink at her and say, "Shouldn't keep the bed so busy, then." The saddles and gear he sometimes kept beside his bed to clean in the candlelight, gone. The clothes he left hanging over the loft to dry, disappeared. The bag he kept of his privy things, packed and ready to go anywhere at any time, so close at hand that he and Jane had sometimes joked about it, nowhere to be found.

Jane gasped and stumbled, falling three steps down the ladder.

If Bran had run away, run away and left her, run away because he knew it wasn't safe, that meant . . .

"There you are," Emmie called out as Jane staggered down the ladder, out into the open air of King's Houses. "Eudo's been running me ragged while you . . ." She stopped as her eyes searched Jane's. "Ah. You didn't know."

"He . . ." Jane found her mouth tight, full of dirt. "He's gone?"

"Said he found a new post, he did, somewhere better. Nottingham, I think." Emmie raised one eyebrow. "Surprised your prioress didn't tell you."

"*Nottingham*," Jane murmured, and she dizzied, like the world had tilted around her with her still on it, struggling to stay upright.

Watching her, Emmie sighed, and something in her face softened. "Come on, Jane. Let's go sit. Eudo's got a cooking wine he won't miss." She held out a hand in truce.

"The prioress," Jane said, and her voice was more like a whisper, a croak. "I'm meant to meet her."

"Of course you are." Emmie rolled her eyes, crossing her arms over her chest, and just like that the door that had opened closed. The flour caked on her sleeves, crusted on her hands, sent a pang of longing through Jane for a soft, warm life that was lost to her now. Lost because she had ruined it. "She's in the gardens. Don't worry about us," she added wryly, already turning her back to Jane. "The kitchens will go on without you, as we always have."

The king's gardens were sprawling, bright with spring herbs and early flowers. The prioress knelt in the dirt to fill her basket, mindless of her clothes and hands.

Jane approached her with her heart pounding. Ibota seemed to want to help her, but people seemed to be many things, both at King's Houses and in the Greenwood. Jane should have learned that lesson long ago. She had seen it in her own parents. Her mother, who had seemed to be strong, had turned out to be a willful child who wanted nothing but a man to tend to her. Her father, who had seemed jolly and warm to the outside world, was a devil in his own home. Adam, who had seemed to be a loving brother, had turned on her the moment she stopped helping him and started helping herself. Now even Bran had turned and run. Run away, and worse, if his fleeing to Nottingham meant what she thought it did.

"Jane," Ibota said, her back still bent over the ground, "I'm glad you're back safely. Come down here and help me."

She turned to see Jane standing rigidly behind her, words trailing off. The prioress drew herself up, and for the first time, Jane noticed the weakness in her knees, the time it took her to stand, the curve of her long back and the stoop of her shoulders. "Jane, what is it? What's happened?"

"Did you send him after me?" Jane asked, her voice trembling. "Did you send him to catch us in the woods?"

"Him who?" Ibota asked sharply. "Did the shire reeve find you?"

"Guy de Gisborne," Jane said. "You warned me to run if I saw him. And he followed me. Just like you said he would. Did you send him to kill Robin?"

"Don't be ridiculous!" Ibota snapped, anger and confusion warring on her face. "Do you really think I'd put you in that kind of danger?"

All the air went out of Jane then, and she stood like a straw figure, stiff and hollow. "I don't know," she whispered, her voice breaking, and she turned her head to look away. "I don't know anymore."

Ibota softened. "Jane, what's happened? Did Guy . . ."

But Jane could only shake her head, speechless.

"You must tell me. We agreed." The sun was slipping away, the wind rising. It seemed the whole earth longed for darkness so it could shut its eyes and rest.

"I can't tell you." Jane's eyes filled with tears. She did not know what to do. She did not know who to trust anymore. She didn't know if she had any way out, or if she even deserved one. "I can't tell you"—she finally forced herself to meet Ibota's eyes—"for what you will think of me if you knew what I've done, what I've seen."

The prioress seemed to sense that Jane was on the edge of breaking. "All right," she said cautiously, as if Jane were an angry cat who needed soothing. "Well, is it over, whatever it is?"

Jane shook her head again.

"I see," Ibota said, her face pale with worry. "What about de Gisborne? Is he . . . ?"

"Robin tortured him." And the words rushed out of her, suddenly, like a river in a storm. "He's dead." And Jane's head dropped. She couldn't face Ibota's knowing, penetrating stare. Not after all she had seen and done.

"And is that something a hero would do, Jane?" Ibota asked softly.

Jane broke then, under her cool gaze. "Robin Hood is no hero," she said, choking out the words through a rush of tears, finally telling the truth, to Ibota, and to herself.

"So," Ibota breathed, but her back stayed rigid, "now you see."

"I don't know what to do," Jane sobbed. "I thought he was helping people. So many people have stories of him helping. I thought . . ."

"The truth is"—Ibota softened her voice—"men who call themselves heroes are often the greatest disappointments. And it may be he did help people, or that he meant to. That he flowered for a time." She gestured toward a few pale yellow primrose buds, only just beginning to open, as if testing the air to see if it was time for them to blossom. "Nature," she said, "knows when it is time to rise, and when it's time to stop struggling against winter. But man never does. Man would drink the world dry if he could, and never give himself back to the land to heal it."

Jane closed her eyes, for the thirst she had seen in Robin, for blood and slaughter and vengeance, was just as the prioress said. And Jane was supposed to lure the reeve into his trap. She didn't even need to lay a hand on the reeve herself—like the monk, and like the little page, he would die because of her anyway. She bit her lips, pressing them together, as she remembered Walter's bent head, his wife standing over him, stroking his hair, the love they had for one another, the children they had sent away. He would not be killed in front of her, not like Guy and Brother Godric and the little page, but his death would stain her soul all the same.

Bran had abandoned her. Her mother and her brothers had their own lives. Emmie and Eudo wouldn't want her back—she had lost their trust. There was nothing left now but Robin and his war, and Jane was no warrior. Perhaps it was *her* time to stop struggling against the winter. Perhaps her time in the sun had come and gone.

"Can you . . ." Jane's voice broke, and she had to clear the fog from her throat. "Can you send the reeve a message for me?"

Ibota looked at her steadily. "What message shall I send him?"

"Tell him," Jane said, "not to go to the Greenwood when Guy de Gisborne summons him today. Tell him it's a trap."

-««•»»-

"You can't stay here, you know." Ibota sipped her drink, looking pointedly at Jane. She had sent Roger with Jane's message, then sent for clarrey and sop and some cheese from the kitchens. Milla had delivered it with a cold, hard stare for Jane, and Jane didn't know whether it was for Bran's leaving, or for her being in the prioress's care instead of in the kitchens where she belonged. There were so many secrets and lies swirling in the air at King's Houses, and most of them were Jane's own fault.

"Even if de Stircheley catches him," Ibota continued, "it's far too dangerous for you now."

Jane hung her head. "You're right," she said, but she did not say that she had nowhere to go. All because she had chased her heart into the forest like a stupid deer, running right toward the hunter's horn.

"You'll come with me to Kirklees," the prioress said firmly, as if she could hear her. "There's a place for you there."

Tears rose in Jane's throat. It seemed all she tasted was tears on this day, like she would never be rid of them. "I'm no nun," she whispered, imagined herself cloistered, surrounded by women, her collar pinned at her throat, her hair covered, sweeping the floors for her betters—women who would disdain her, who would turn up their noses at her, and not a single man around to warm her bed.

"Not yet, but you can be," Ibota said. "I'll tell everyone you're my apprentice. You can take your vows, and no one need know where you came from, or why."

"I'm not you," Jane croaked through her tears. "I don't want a life without . . ." She trailed off, for she knew it was foolish.

"I know the church seems stifling, but you'll see, Jane. It's one of the few places women can find their voices in our world, and live our lives the way we choose. You can have a full life at Kirklees, if you're careful." A sly smile crossed her face, her cheeks frosting pink. "Surely you know Roger is not simply my guard."

"But you must hide it from everyone," Jane said, although everyone knew. Everyone at King's Houses, anyway.

"It's not so hard."

But I'm so tired of hiding, Jane thought. She could not say it, not out loud, for she would sound like a whining child if she did. Hadn't she seen enough to know that everyone's true nature was hidden, that no one could live as they pleased? Who was she to think she might choose her path in life? What kind of person had that freedom? Only outlaws. And John had been right about her all along. She didn't have the stomach to be an outlaw.

"I don't deserve your help," Jane said.

Ibota looked somewhere past Jane's head, toward the darkened window. "There was a time I felt the same about myself, you know. Edward sent me to Kirklees to silence me, to punish me. I had failed him, and I had failed to protect my friend and her children. But the prioress before me made sure I could grow strong in her care. She made sure I would bloom. And I see something in you, Jane, the way she did in me. You're special."

"You keep saying that," Jane said, "but I'm not special. I'm no different from anybody else—Eudo or Milla or Emmie." She frowned bitterly. "The only different thing is that I've caused trouble."

"You don't think you're special? You don't think you're worth protecting?" The prioress leaned forward. "But you thought Robin Hood was?"

Jane was silent. She had no answer for her.

"Perhaps no one is special," Ibota conceded. "Perhaps it is all Fortune's wheel. But Fortune placed me here, and you, for me to offer you a chance, for me to hold out a hand. Unless you're determined to spit in it."

At that moment, there was a quick, urgent knock on the door, and then Roger rushed into the room without even waiting for permission.

Ibota looked up with concern. "Did you deliver my message?"

Roger had always looked pale to Jane, losing his color with age as some men did, but now he looked as white as snow. He glanced around the hallway for eavesdroppers, then shut the door behind him. "I went to find the shire reeve, to warn him. But he's already gone to the Greenwood." He stopped for a moment, swallowed air, cleared his throat. "Someone told him Guy was waiting for him out there. Someone lied to him and said he'd taken Robin's head."

Chapter Twenty-Nine

It had been too dark to ride when Roger brought his news. There was nothing left to do but wait for morning. The prioress dozed in her chair while Jane paced the room. Sleep was impossible. Ibota had offered her one of the draughts that sat on her messy table, among the dried and scattered herbs, but Jane did not want to be outside of her own mind if the worst happened. Though after what she had seen Robin do to Guy, she wasn't sure what *could* be worse.

It was dark and still and even the night birds had grown quiet when someone finally pounded on the door.

"Open up!" Walter de Stircheley shouted. "Open up *right now!*"

Jane waited until Ibota wrapped a long crimson mantle around herself, which drained what little color she had left. Then, at her nod, Jane flung the door open. The reeve stood there, soaked in mud and blood, with three of his mercenaries. They seemed impassable shadows in the door, like a row of giant stones. One of them held Roger still in his massive arms. Ibota's knight had been stripped of his sword.

"That's her." Walter pointed at Jane, his jaw firm, his eyes rimmed with red. One arm hung limply at his side, bandaged with bloody cloth. "Take her."

"Wait!" Ibota said, sleep still in her voice as she shuffled forward.

"Oh, no," the reeve said. "I've waited long enough."

"You were ambushed, weren't you? Jane tried to warn you."

Jane flushed with fear. Ibota wasn't supposed to tell him it was her. But if it could protect her now . . .

"And why would she want to warn me," the reeve demanded through gritted teeth, "when she knows I'm after her very own lover? Afraid I'll take his pretty head, are you?"

"No, it's not like that . . ." Jane stammered. "I wanted to . . ."

"Don't bother lying." Walter scowled, and she noticed the dried blood in his beard, coloring it redder. "Your stable boy told me everything."

Jane almost lost her feet. So it was true. Bran had turned on her.

Ibota gave Jane a warning look before she could speak. "The stable boy?" the prioress said haughtily. "He's nothing but a jilted lover. He's the one who works for Robin Hood. Tell him, Jane."

Jane was still stunned, still reeling. Of course, she knew Bran was angry. He had every right to be angry. But somehow, she hadn't imagined that he could turn on her. She didn't think he had the cruelty, or the boldness. There were so many things she should have seen, so much that Robin's glow had blinded her to, like she had spent all her days squinting at the sun.

"She's upset, Reeve," Ibota said when Jane lost her words. "The stable boy was jealous. She left him because of what he was wrapped up in, and this is his revenge."

"Oh, *she's* upset?" the reeve snapped. "I went into the wood with six men and came out with three corpses and a useless sword arm! And *she's* upset?"

"Jane, you must tell him the truth. It's time." Jane knew the prioress didn't mean the real truth from the way she chewed out the words, lingered over them. Jane was meant to lie in a way that left her clean. And what did another lie matter now? Her lies to herself and other people had buried the truth so far into the earth that there was no recovering it.

"Yes, m'um." Jane hung her head to hide her flush. "I found out what he'd done, m'lord, and told him we were through."

The reeve's stare blackened. "And when you ate my food and drank my wine at Robin Hood's side?" he demanded. "Where was your stable boy then?" He caught the surprise on Ibota's face and laughed. "Didn't know about that little trick she pulled, did you, Prioress? I wouldn't lie to me again if I were you. Not when I have a sword to your man's throat."

"Let him go," Ibota said, and Jane could sense real fear in the prioress for the first time, despite her cutting words. "Do your job and stop bothering holy women and frightened girls." The torch-light in the hall made a shadow of Ibota's long nose, made her eyes seem to glow with ice, and Jane wondered which version of the prioress the reeve saw—the mask she wore to make herself powerful, or the frightened woman whose lover balanced on the edge of death.

"He stays with me," Walter said. "And the girl is coming with me too."

"You *will* obey me, Reeve. I'm the king's own cousin."

"I don't care who your cousin is, and I don't care who you are. I don't even care what Edward wants of me. I'll not be made a fool of by a pair of lying women. Not again."

"We're not the ones making you a fool," Ibota muttered under her breath.

"What did you say to me?" The reeve growled.

"I said"—her smile was all clenched teeth—"be reasonable. Hear us out. We could help you, if only you would listen." Ibota softened, made herself more womanly, which looked a farce to Jane. "You didn't catch Robin today, did you? If you had caught him, you wouldn't be here. Won't you take what we know willingly instead of forcing it?"

Walter squinted. "Why are you, king's cousin, protecting Robin Hood's girl?" he demanded. "She's hardly a cowering child."

"She's not his," Ibota said. "She's mine."

Walter's wild brows drew together. "And what in the hell is that supposed to mean?"

"What I mean"—Ibota let the words draw out, as if the reeve were forcing the confession—"is that she's been watching Robin Hood for *me*."

"Explain yourself, woman. I'm too tired for games."

"If you'll release my man, and come sit down so we can talk like courteous people, I'll explain it to you. But not like this. Not with your men and all of King's Houses listening to my privy business."

Jane's heart felt frozen in her chest. She did not know what would happen, and she could not speak for herself. Not here, where both the prioress and the reeve had a claim to her.

"My man is unarmed now," Ibota said. "And Jane and I wield nothing deadlier than silk and herbs. You're in no danger from us, and we can save you further suffering, if only you would cast aside your pride."

The reeve studied the two of them as if they were walnuts he could crack open with his eyes. After a long, slow, endless silence, he finally assented. "Fine." He nodded at the three men behind him, who still held Roger. "Take him outside. Better make it quick, Prioress. My men are hungry for vengeance."

"Sir Roger will wait inside with us," Ibota said coldly, "unless you intend to invade a lady's chambers without providing her a guardian."

The reeve rolled his eyes. "All right," he conceded. "But we'll keep his sword."

"That's very reasonable," Ibota said, pleased now that she had gotten her way. She ushered Walter inside and offered him a chair, though not her best one, not the one she reserved for herself. Jane sat rigidly on a small stool as the reeve and prioress took their seats and Roger stood at the prioress's back like a guardian angel. Jane tried not to stare at the bruises and cuts on Walter's collarbone, the swelling of his wounded arm. Had Robin done that to him? Had John? How had he gotten away? Jane couldn't ask any of this. She could barely open her mouth to speak. It seemed as though anything she said, anything she admitted to knowing, would only prove her guilt.

"So is the stable boy your man now?" Ibota asked the reeve. "Will you let him feed you more lies?"

"I let him go," Walter said warily. "He didn't seem a dangerous one, and he didn't want to be found." He shrugged, but he looked at Jane with a question in his eyes.

"He's not dangerous," Jane agreed, her voice a whisper.

"So you needn't fear him, girl. It's time to tell me what you know."

Ibota nodded her encouragement, although Jane did not quite know what she wanted her to say. "Jane, tell him of the . . ."

"Let her speak," Walter demanded. "I won't have you guiding her. I want the truth this time. And all of it."

Ibota tried to hide the worry in her eyes. "Very well. Go ahead, Jane."

"Well"—Jane cleared her throat—"I'd heard that Guy was dead, m'lord, and that Robin would pretend to be him to trap you."

"Heard it from the stableboy," Ibota interjected. "He's loose with his talk after . . . you know." She waved her hand and turned up her nose, as if her own lie had embarrassed her. "She came to me and let me know, but we were too late."

"I *said*, let the girl speak for herself." Jane knew from the bend of Walter's brows that he did not believe Ibota's story. He had caught the scent of his prey now. He knew the truth was just on the edge of his vision. And Jane would have to twist it better than Ibota had to avoid his blade.

"I . . ." Jane looked out the window, mustering the stomach to say the words, to confess. If it would help, if it would finally finish things, she would do it. "When I heard Robin's plan, I'd hoped you would catch him then, and so I sent word with Roger. But he . . ." She stammered, took a breath. "He couldn't reach you in time."

"And why would you want to see your lover dragged off in chains, when you've helped him so many times before? Oh, don't you start again," he warned as Ibota opened her mouth to interrupt. "How long have you known about her and Robin? I ought to haul you off right alongside her!"

"No!" Jane was surprised to find she was shouting, surprised at the strength of her own voice. But she was tired, suddenly, of all her lies, of all her shields. For what had it gotten her? Nothing but pain, and loss—for her, and for Bran, and for Ibota and Betrice.

For brave pages and braver women willing to put themselves on the line for Jane. Who saw something in Jane even more than Robin did, something she had never seen in herself. And who meant it, when all Robin had meant from it was to work his way into her heart like a worm into an apple. "No," she said again, softened by the shock on both their faces. "You mustn't. She's only trying to protect me. And this is my fault. I was fooled by Robin. I thought he was a hero, and not . . ." She swallowed. "Not a killer. You know the stories, m'lord. You know what they say about him."

The reeve grimaced. "Aye. I know what they say about him. And I know what they'll say about me." Walter leaned forward, rubbing his head and neck with his good hand, staring at the floor instead of them. "I didn't catch Robin Hood," he admitted, "but I took one of his men, and wounded another, left him close to death. Hard fought, it was, and I came home with corpses for it. But Robin is near alone now, so far as I can tell."

"Does that sound right to you, Jane?" the prioress asked gently. "How many men does Robin count on his side?"

"Who do you have?" Jane asked, the question sticking in her throat. "And who did you hurt?"

"I took the big one. A yellow-bearded, silent type. And we hurt a skinny one who loves to talk."

Jane was surprised to feel a flash of sympathy for Wyll, led into more suffering by Robin's trap. She wondered if Robin would care for him now, the way John had cared for him, or whether he'd seek vengeance instead, cutting through anything and everything else in Wyll's name. "That's Wyll, then," Jane said. "The one you hurt. And the bearded one is Little John."

"How many more does he have?" the reeve asked.

"Two, m'lord," Jane said softly. "Without Bran, there's only two."

"Now, that's a number I can work with." The reeve seemed satisfied. "You're sure he can't get more?"

Jane shook her head, and Ibota studied her.

"Not if you're fast enough to catch him," the prioress said.

"I wasn't fast enough to catch you, was I?" The reeve scowled at Jane. "But rats are always hard to catch."

"Will Robin come for his man John?" Ibota asked her. "Or will he leave him to his fate?"

"It doesn't matter." The reeve looked at Jane as though she were a hare in his trap. "Your stable boy said Robin would come for *you*."

"No," Ibota said before Jane could respond. "Why would you believe him? I told you . . ."

"Because they're lovers. Because Robin thinks himself a gentleman and she a lady, like the fool he is. Or maybe . . ." Walter leaned forward, narrowing his eyes with threat. "Maybe he knows she's a traitor and wants to take her head for it. Either way"—the reeve stood, straightening his shoulders despite the wound to his arm, and despite how tired he must be after a night of making war with Robin Hood and failing—"I'm not taking any chances. You're coming with me, girl. You're going to help me draw him out."

Ibota leapt to her feet. "Hold on, Reeve! I'm not putting Jane in danger just because you . . ."

"And what do you think you're going to do about it?" The reeve's hand dropped to his sword. It was only a moment, but it was enough for the prioress to freeze, enough for Roger to move forward, meaning to step in front of her, until Ibota put a calming hand upon his shoulder.

"Do you *really* think Edward will reward you if he finds you've gone against his cousin?"

"His cousin who's been hiding a traitor?" the reeve demanded.

"Edward is a cautious man, Shire Reeve, and a thorough one. He doesn't trust anyone. Not me and not you. You ought to have realized that by now. The most important thing to Edward is that he *does not lose.* The method of his victory, and his loyalty to those involved, will weigh very lightly on him, compared to that."

Walter's lips twitched. "I see you know your cousin as well as I do."

"If you want to make sure you win," Ibota said diplomatically, "then you should take my help, and Jane's, instead of forcing it."

"I don't need your help. Not when I have her," he said.

"You can't just *take* her," the prioress demanded. "Jane is under my protection."

"And how do you plan to stop me?"

Jane could smell violence brewing in the room. It would not go their way, she knew, no matter how brave Sir Roger might be. The reeve knew his sword, and his men were right outside. Jane remembered the way that Betrice had stepped in front of her to protect her from her husband's ire, and the way that Ibota had protected her from Guy, and she could see that the prioress meant to do the same again. How much longer was she going to let other women, better and stronger women, risk themselves to cover up her sins?

Jane took a deep breath, summoning her courage. "I'll go."

"You really don't have a say in it," Walter snapped, and Ibota flushed with indignation.

"Will you slap a helping hand away, then, Reeve?"

"Don't you dare . . ." he started, then growled as Ibota raised a hand to silence him.

"If she's willing to go with you," the prioress said, resigned, for she could see Jane's resolve, must see the way she suffered for her sins and meant to make herself clean, "I'll allow it. But under certain conditions."

"You're in no position to . . ."

"Conditions, Reeve." Ibota drew herself up tall and straight. "And you will hear them now. First, Robin's men must think you've caught her. They can't know she's been disloyal."

The reeve nodded, clenching his jaw. "Fair enough."

"Second, you'll return Jane to me, *unharmed*, when this is over, and you must consider this little test of yours her punishment and trial. She will not be tormented any further for what she's done, or"—she curled her lip—"what you think she's done."

"And if she turns on me? If she helps her outlaw lover?"

"She won't do that." Ibota was steady. "But I can give you one more surety: Sir Roger will go with you. He can pose as one of your guards."

Walter smirked. "Is he there to watch my men, or to keep your girl from bolting?"

"What does it matter to you?" Ibota asked, and she was cold again, for although she had not won, she had taken back some fragment of her power.

"I want the girl at my house before dawn. And you"—Walter pointed at the prioress—"you'll help me make it known just who I have. I want Robin to come for his girl and his man, hot and hungry and careless as a fox after a hen." He smiled, a cruel smile.

"And tell him that if he doesn't come by Terce, I'll have them both dragged by a horse and hanged."

"Reeve, there's really no need for . . ."

"That's what we do to traitors," he said, his mouth firm. "And God help you, girl, if my trap fails. Because before Robin kills me, I'll tell him exactly what you are, and how you turned."

Chapter Thirty

The shire reeve dragged Jane into his house with her arms bound, her eyes covered with cloth just as they had been when Bran first led her to Robin Hood's camp in the Greenwood, where the air had smelled clean and fresh, full of hope and promise. The reeve's house smelled like nothing but fear and men's sweat.

She was forced onto a stool and bound with rope to another body, and Jane knew from his scent, from the bulk of him, that it was Little John she was being tied to, his warm, broad back pressed to hers, his breath steady, more so than it should have been. Roger removed her blindfold, and as gentle as he was, Jane was not sure it was a mercy.

The house was still set up for battle: the chairs and tables still pressed against the walls, though they were gray with dust and ash from Little John's fire. Walter's three remaining men guarded the outside, pacing past the windows on their watch. The sun was rising lazily, but surely, and it would be hard for anyone to sneak up to the house once it did. It was an obvious trap for Robin, unless he was a fool. The reeve's plan relied on Robin's emotions getting the better of him. But he hadn't seen what Jane had seen in Robin's face—the blank stare, the hunter's focus, the way he could become one with whatever weapon he held.

Ibota's noble lineage, even in the face of Jane's lies and sins, had bought her some measure of dignity: Jane had been allowed to keep her clothes instead of being stripped to her shift. But it couldn't save her. She felt the weight of Ibota's ring hidden in her belt—another attempt to help her that had come to nothing. What was a ring, a potion, no matter how deadly, in the face of all the brutal violence Jane had seen? Perhaps the prioress was a force to be reckoned with in churches and in abbeys, but this was Robin's world, a world of torture, and murder, and bodies lying in the woods like trophies. The prioress and her kind had no power here.

Jane and John stayed quiet for a time, breathing into each other's backs while the reeve watched them. Sir Roger tried his best to blend in with the guards outside, but it was clear—to Jane, at least—that he was not one of them. He was a gentleman, quiet and thoughtful, and he held himself above these mercenary men with their mismatched armor and their crass jokes. Jane worried for the prioress's lover, even though sense told her she should be far more worried about herself.

John spoke first. He took a long time, though, to test his words. The day was warm—one of those days when clouds threatened rain, but the rain hadn't come yet, so the sky was gray and the air was trapped, with no wind to relieve the stillness. Jane felt the sweat of her back against John's, sticking their tunics together. Normally, she would have been mortified for him to feel it, but there was no point being embarrassed about anything given the state they were in.

The reeve paced away to look out the west window yet again, his sword in his good arm, the injured one bound and cradled against his chest, and that was when John finally spoke.

"Who did you in, then?" His voice was soft, almost apologetic. "I didn't talk."

"It was Bran." The words stuck in Jane's throat.

John snorted. "Guess he found out about you two. Can hardly blame him. Though Robin won't feel the same if he catches him." She could hear the sideways smile in his voice, as though he were joking, though it clearly wasn't a joke.

"He's gone," she said. "Run away." Jane was surprised to hear real bitterness in her voice, even though it was her own fault Bran had betrayed her.

"Hope he ran far." John took in a breath against her spine. "Wyll went down in the fight. Might not keep his leg, and that's if he's lucky." He cleared the emotion from his throat. "Robin won't forgive that. He'll hunt Bran to the sea and back."

Jane felt her nausea rise. It was hard to imagine Bran's face under Robin's knife, in spite of what he had done.

John's voice deepened. "You know," he said, "I thought we were rid of you."

Jane laughed sadly. "You mean you hoped."

"Hoped you had come to your senses. Found something better," John said, sorrow drifting through his voice like a thin cloud before he became gruff again. "Should have got out while you could. Should have seen how this was ending. I tried to give you a thousand warnings and a thousand ways out and you didn't take a single one."

"Finally found your tongue, did you?" Walter stalked back over to them to taunt John.

"Wanted you to know my voice," John said, calm as a breeze, "so you'd know just who was mocking you when you die."

The reeve laughed. "You think Robin's coming for your sorry arse, then? Didn't think you were his type."

"Mayhap," John said. "Though it's more likely to be her arse he's after, and don't I know it. But I'm smart enough to take my fortune when it comes."

Jane flushed, though she was surprised she had any shame left in her at all, with these men who knew so many of her secrets. The reeve could have shamed Jane further, show he had been proved right about her, but he looked away instead, and Jane had to be grateful.

"I wouldn't thank Fortune yet, if I were you. Your master has but two men left, by my count. And we've five of us here waiting for him."

"Robin don't need more men than he has. Not for the likes of you. Though you've hardly made it a fair fight, have you?" John twitched within their shared binds, his muscles pulsing against the rope. "What kind of shire reeve hides from outlaws?"

Walter snorted. "If Robin were an honorable man, like you all pretend he is, he'd have fought me fairly instead of setting up bloody ambushes and tricks. Only a fool doesn't see treachery coming twice."

"Thrice, if we're honest, Reeve." John's laugh strained their bonds, and the rope scraped Jane's flesh raw. "And our Robin doesn't fight like a man. He fights like a demon. That's why you people wanted him for your war."

The reeve's predatory smile turned to a grimace. "Wasn't my war."

"It's your war now," John replied.

The reeve paced over to the window again. The sun was brightening the clouds now and there was still no sign of Robin. What if he didn't come? What if the reeve thought Jane had warned him away? What if he really did tie her and John to horses and have them dragged through town, just to draw out his enemy?

The dust drifted past her in the silence, as the sun grew too warm and sweat poured down her back. She was beginning to panic, her heart beating faster and faster, as if her mind were a crazed horse being chased by wolves. Why hadn't she eaten before she left? What if she never ate again? What if she had to make water here, in front of all these men? Would the reeve untie her, give her privacy? Or would he force her to shame herself in front of everyone, tied to Little John?

"Easy, girl," John whispered, feeling her heart pound against his back. "Won't be long now."

Jane tried to calm herself, still her breath, agonized that Little John, of all people, could feel her fear. That he knew what a coward she was.

The reeve, growing agitated, walked by the window again. "Is that bloody dog ever going to . . ." And then something flew through that window, reeking and flaming and pouring smoke, smacking the dusty furniture with a thud.

"What the hell?" The reeve leapt out of the way as the rank odor of burning horse shit flooded the room.

John laughed against Jane's back, pulling the rope into her chest. "Here we go," he said.

Just as Walter regained his balance, another flaming sack flew through the far window, landing in the center of the straw-covered floor, catching it alight.

"Shit!" Walter cried. "He's here! Where are my lookouts?" He brandished his sword with his good arm and raced back and forth between the windows, trying to see what was happening outside.

Jane's whole body went tense in her bindings, she and John coughing as the smoke hit them, crushing the ropes into her chest. The stench was awful and the smoke was rising, but over the choking smell of the flames and shit and the mercenaries' shouts, she heard a scream outside and a sound, wet and thunking, that might have been an arrow to a man's flesh.

"Get outside!" the reeve shouted. "Now!" He shoved Roger, who was trying to kick out one of the flaming bags. "I said get the fuck outside!"

"What's happening?" Jane coughed out to John.

"That'd be Mooch," he said, laughing even as he gagged at the smell. "Flaming shit is his specialty." He seemed incredibly calm, despite the prospect of them both burning to death. "Sit tight, Jane. We're just getting started."

Just then, arrows flew through the window, and they were also wearing flames, like a storm of shooting stars. The house was not on fire yet, but it would be, with all the dry wood about the place, with all the old straw on the ground, covered with grease and dirt and men's filth.

"Shire Reeve!" Jane heard Robin shout over the din, the chaos. "What have you done with my loyal charges?"

"I'll hang them like the traitors they are," Walter shouted back, "once I'm through with you! Come out and fight me like a man!"

"We can't fucking see him for the smoke!" one of the reeve's men shouted. "We have to . . ." His words shortened to a strangled cry.

"Silent as a cat, Tuk is," John said proudly. "Never see him coming."

More blazing arrows flew into the house, and Jane cursed. "Does he mean to burn us out, then?"

"Aye," John said, still calm as a windless day. "Don't fear, Jane. Robin knows what he's doing."

Robin was taunting the reeve through the windows. "Did you think they taught us to fight like men, your barons, those gentlemen astride their horses with their shining swords?"

More arrows shot inside, and another man screamed outside. "Fuck!" someone shouted. "Around the back! He . . ." And then, a muffled shriek.

"But what if he . . . what if we . . . ?" Jane looked around, but she could barely see a thing anymore, the smoke was so thick, her eyes stung so badly from the stench.

Robin's voice came back through the window over the sound of the flames, clear as a bell. "That's not what they taught us, Reeve. We were the beasts they sent to cull their fields. They claimed the glory. They claimed the prizes and the gold. But for all their talk of honor, for all *your* talk of honor, not a one of you wants an honorable fight when your life is at stake." Another flight of arrows shot through the window, searing fabric, lighting sparks, filling the room with more smoke.

"Look at you, cowering inside like a child!" Robin mocked him. "Would you rather burn to death than face me?"

"You fucker!" the reeve shouted, and barreled toward the door, egged on like a fool. He stumbled outside, sword raised high, leaving Jane and John alone.

"Hold on, now," John coughed at her. "We're going down."

"What do you mean we're . . ."

Jane's whole world tilted sideways as John thrust his weight to the left, sending them crashing to the ground. His body softened most of the blow, though Jane's jaw smacked against the floor, rattling her teeth together.

"We've got to get undone!" John shouted. "Press your wrists to mine." She obeyed and felt John working at the ropes until he finally freed Jane's hands. "Help me with the binds around us! Quick!"

As they struggled together on the floor, wriggling in ash and smoke and straw to get loose, a pair of muddy boots rushed up to them. "John! Look out!" Jane cried, but then, blessedly, Sir Roger's face emerged from the smoke. He knelt beside her, his skin streaked with mud.

"I'll get you loose!" the prioress's man said, his voice hoarse. He began sawing at the bindings on her chest with a knife.

"No," Jane warned him, but her mouth and throat were so full of smoke that the words weren't loud enough, even though she sighed in relief as her chest and arms were freed. "Run!" she tried to shout, but then Little John was free, standing tall, standing over Roger.

"Got a heart, then, this one. Fucking idiot." John kicked Roger in the face, then ripped the sword from his hand. "Thanks for this," he said, raising the sword high.

Jane tried to roll over Roger. "Don't!" she shouted, but Roger was fast, and strong, and he leapt to his feet and pulled her up with him, dragging her away from John, shoving her through the door.

"Come on!" he cried. "We've got to go!"

Jane took Roger's hand as they raced into the open air, praying that John couldn't see what she was doing in the smoke, how she was following the prioress's man. "He'll kill you!" she warned Roger, gasping for breath. "You have to run! Leave me!"

"I'm not leaving . . ." But John had caught them just past the threshold, and he grabbed Roger by the shoulders, hauling him away from Jane, hurling him aside.

"Oh, no, you don't!" John said. "You're not making off with her!" He thrust his sword toward Roger, and the knight danced away, but not in time. He took a cut to his hand.

John grunted and lunged again, and Roger, swordless, dodged, parrying his blow with a leather-clad arm, then went to hit him in the stomach. But John moved out of the way, faster than Jane thought he could move, flipped his sword around, and slammed Roger in the face with its hilt.

Roger staggered back with a moan, clutching his bleeding nose.

"John, let him go!" Jane gasped, still coughing, still trying to clear the smoke from her chest. "He tried to help me!"

"Fuck you if you think . . ." And then, a dark figure flew out from the trees.

"You bloody bastard!" the reeve screamed, and flung himself at Little John.

John threw him off like a horse bucking off a fly. "Oho, you want to fight, now, Reeve? My hands are free, and ready!"

As John and the reeve crashed together like a pair of bulls, Jane grabbed Roger's bloody hand. "Now! Let's go!"

Roger staggered forward with her, stumbling. The blow to his face had cost him both his balance and his breath, but she dragged him on, merciless. If they could only get to the road. If they could only get out into the open, into town, they would be safe there. They could hide. "Jane," Roger wheezed. "They'll know you turned!"

"I don't care!" Jane cried, heedless of who could hear. "I don't care anymore! He would have killed us all for his own pride and I don't . . ."

Jane stumbled over a body, lying right there beside the reeve's burning house. This one was in plain clothes, not armor. This one had no helmet to cover his face.

It was Mooch's body. And he had a knife stuck in his chest.

Jane swallowed her scream, her horror. Screaming wouldn't save Mooch. He had already died for her crimes, died for her lies.

But she could do one more thing that mattered. She could get Roger to safety. No more kind, gentle men would have to die. If she could only get him to run faster.

"Come on!" she shouted, and she and the prioress's knight ran around the corner of the burning house, scrambling for breath, their eyes stinging from smoke, blood running down his face.

And then a cloaked, hooded figure stepped out in front of them, silent as nightfall, a bow drawn taut, an arrow poised to fly.

"Where do you think *you're* going?" Robin asked softly, and then he shot, and there was a horrible, sickening noise as Robin's arrow pierced Roger's throat and sent him sprawling to the ground.

Jane fell to her knees beside Roger, her whole body shaking. It was over. She was caught now. She was at Robin's mercy. And no one was coming to save her.

"I told you, Jane," Robin said as he lifted her to her feet. "I told you. We're loyal, Jane. We're the same, you and I. And we'll always come for each other."

Chapter Thirty-One

Someone had tied the reeve up in the burned-out garden, bound him to a withered tree, his arms spread wide, bleeding from sword cuts. His armor had been torn away, his tunic ripped open, exposing his chest, his skin solid but sagging around his breast, the hair across it a nest of faded steel. His head lolled to the side, mouth slack, his face a tapestry of cuts and bruises.

The fire had calmed. Embers smoldered inside the house, leaving the air thick with smoke and ash. There was enough stone in the house, Jane supposed, to keep it whole. Though who or what it would be kept whole for, she didn't know anymore.

Tears stirred in her burning eyes at the sight of the reeve's body. He had given Jane a chance, and he had lost his life for it. Ibota had given her a chance, and she had lost her love for it. Why would anyone ever give Jane a chance again? She should just give herself to Robin and stop fighting. He would tire of her, she knew, and then she could escape him. But where would she go?

Robin crossed his arms over his chest and frowned. "He's not dead, is he? That would spoil the game."

"What game?" Jane asked, her voice so small she could barely hear it herself.

"Why, a shooting game," Robin said, his smile playful, but cold. "We mean to use him as a target, just as he meant to target us."

"What's this *we*?" John grunted. "*I* said we should get our fool arses out of here while we still can."

Robin paced to the middle of the courtyard, spreading his arms wide, inhaling deeply even though the air was full of smoke. "And who do you think is coming for us, Little John? Who is *left* to come for us? Mansfield is ours now, and the whole forest. We're finally free, old man. Enjoy it a little, will you?"

Tuk stood stock-still in the smoky air. Jane couldn't read his face, but she saw the caution in his eyes. Not fear, exactly, but readiness.

"And you mean for us to play games right now? You really do?" John demanded. "With Wyll bleeding out all over *her* old bed . . ." Jane shuddered at the thought of it, but of course that was where they had hidden him. "And with Mooch . . ." John trailed off. His voice would have caught on tears and grief had he been anyone else, but he was John, and there was nothing left in him but anger. "Do you mean to mourn him? To care for his body? Or have you already forgotten about his corpse?"

"There will be time for mourning, and pouring out good ale, and for tending to our Wyll and seeing him whole again. But for now, I've a mind to finish this battle, right here, against my enemy. And I've a mind to be the winner. So line up and shoot. Don't spoil my fun. I've earned it with your rescue."

John just glared at him. The wind picked up, scattering ash across Jane's boot. She stood as still as she could. She didn't know what else to do but watch.

"Fine." Robin sighed. "I'll shoot first." He drew his bow. "Wake up, Shire Reeve." He sang the words, a taunting call, and then, almost casually, barely looking, Robin shot his arrow right into the reeve's wounded arm.

Walter stirred enough to scream. His eyes opened, red and raw, his skin bled of color, and he looked old, then, so much older than Jane remembered. He breathed hard, trying to gather his courage, trying to pull himself free. But what was the point of courage? What was the point of trying to act like a man when you were nothing but an animal, at the core of it? Nothing but a beast caught in a trap.

"You see me, Reeve? I remember the feel of your fists, old man." Another arrow flew, the reeve's good arm now, jerking his whole body with the impact, and he howled. "And I remember the taste of your wife's cunt," Robin added with a laugh.

Jane choked back vomit.

"How long do you mean to make him suffer, Robin?" Tuk asked, his voice deadly soft.

"Oh, don't whine at me," Robin said. "I just want to give everyone a turn." He looked between his men, and found their faces closed to him, cold. And then, his eyes alighted on Jane, still trying to hold down her stomach, and his smile sharpened like a knife's edge.

"How about you, Jane? Surely you want your vengeance for what the reeve did to you? Ruined your little job at King's Houses, drove off your lover?"

Jane's throat closed with horror, her insides a pool of black bile, of fear. "No . . ." She stepped backward, small steps, as if he wouldn't notice. As if he wouldn't see. "No, I . . ."

"Don't refuse your rescuer his boon. It's not courteous." Robin walked closer to her, fast, fast like he was hunting, and grabbed her wrist. He pulled her into his arms, even as she whimpered, his rough touch stinging all the places the rope had rubbed raw. "Come now, Jane," he said, arranging her hands on the bow, his body at her back, his arms around her, and it would have been intimate, it would have been so close, and she would have felt so stirred by it before. But now, all she felt was terror. "Show me your courage. Show me your heart."

"Jane," the reeve murmured, and when his eyes found her, they were deep, fathomless pools of rage. "Jane," he said again, and blood fell from his lips.

Jane's heart seized, even as Robin pulled her arms back, pulled her arrow back. He would reveal her, the reeve would. She knew it. For what did he have to lose? He would name her traitor right here, while she stood in Robin's arms, his grip tight enough to crush her. Robin would know her heart and he would kill her for it, and she shivered with terror, even as he whispered in her ear, his breath against her neck, "Easy now, one swift shot, not too close to the heart, for I want to . . ."

An arrow flew past them, right into the reeve's heart. He lurched forward in his bindings, and died, right in front of them, his eyes still staring at her.

Robin dropped his grip on Jane and whirled around, the bow in her hands clattering to the ground.

John stood there, bow raised, eyes still focused on the reeve's heart. When he saw Robin looking at him, mouth open in shock, he said, "Game's over."

Jane ran. It was foolish, and useless, but she did not know what else to do. She heard someone following her, but she was too distraught to turn around. Her eyes and nose still stung from the smoke, and she stopped to wipe them on her sleeve, but it was filthy too. She felt as though she would never get clean.

"John ended it quickly," Tuk said beside her. "He did right."

She looked at him, his face streaked with ash, his hair whitened from it. "Why? Why couldn't he just kill him and be done with it?"

"Don't know the answer to that. Or I do, but it would take explaining, and that's time I don't have." He looked out past the smoking house as if searching for something. As if he could see anything at all. "The time has come, girl, for staying or for leaving, if you've no appetite for blood. For there's death on the wind. Anyone can taste it."

"Are you staying?" she whispered, her voice raw with the words, with the smoke, with the horror of this day.

He handed her a wine skin, and she drank from it deeply. It was fine stuff, she could tell, but that didn't stop it from burning her parched throat, didn't stop her from feeling sickened by the sharp tang of its fruit. She coughed, sputtering, struggling to keep it in.

"I'm an old man, Jane. I've no taste for blood anymore."

His words, stark as they were, filled Jane with dread. They were a warning, after all—and a promise, the same promise Robin had made when he forced her hands around the bow, when he claimed the torture of a beaten man as his boon, his reward. There would be always blood on Robin's path. Blood and vengeance drove him—more than loyalty, more than honor, more even than the Virgin he knelt to and claimed to serve.

Claimed falsely, Jane knew it now. For Mary demanded mercy of Her knights, and Robin Hood had never known its taste.

Robin emerged through the smoke, along with John, whose face was grim. John had made the kill clean as he could, Jane thought, just as Tuk said. And then was surprised at herself for thinking such a thing so coldly. But it was true. John had killed Walter de Stircheley cleanly because there was no other way. Same with the monk. And if he had been there for Guy's death, he would have killed him cleanly too. Jane saw him clearly now, and she wished she had seen it before. She had thought Little John was a monster, but he was an angel of mercy, he was. An angel who served a vengeful god of death.

"Well," Robin said, though not unkindly, his voice still rough with smoke. "Now that John has spoiled my game, where shall we go?"

"We bury Mooch's body," John said. "You owe him that, to save his family from his shame. They never knew he was an outlaw, and they shouldn't need to. After that, we tend to Wyll."

"I can see you mean to ruin all my fun today. Is this how you thank me for my rescue? What about my reward?" Robin pouted, playfully, and Jane knew he didn't mean it, but John was in no mood for his playing.

John looked at Jane, his lip curling. "Ask *her* for your reward."

"Now, John, that's hardly a chivalrous thing to say." But Robin's voice was light, mocking. Jane flushed, her chest growing hot as she caught their meaning.

Robin mistook her silence, her flush. "Never mind him, Jane. He's just jealous of us, for he has no prize of his own."

John wiped the sweat from his face. "Fuck you, Robin," he said, and he turned toward the front of the house, where Mooch's body lay, abandoned in the dirt and ash.

"I'll help him," Tuk said. He had been standing silently, watching, measuring, and Jane could see that he had made a choice now. And so could Robin.

"Perhaps I should follow too," Robin suggested, his eyes narrowing.

"The two of us can handle Mooch," Tuk said.

The Lord of the Greenwood cocked his head. "You mean to leave for good, don't you?"

Tuk's smile was sad, steady, but Jane could see a hint of fear behind it, dimming it like a shadow. "The wind has changed. It blows me south again."

"Is it as ill a wind as the one that blew you here?"

"Perhaps," Tuk said. "But follow it I must. I presume our debt is settled now?"

"Tenfold, my friend."

"Then I'll be off," Tuk said.

"Wait." Jane held out the skin to return it, for it was still mostly full. "Your wine." She pleaded with him with her eyes, hoping he would stay. Hoping she would not be left alone with Robin. But it was pointless, wasn't it? This was her fate. She could no more fight against it than she could free herself from the ravages of winter or of age.

"Keep it, girl." Tuk bowed to Jane. "There's plenty more and better where I'm going." And then he turned away and disappeared into the smoke.

Jane tried to keep her breath steady and calm, her voice light. She couldn't reveal her fear, not now. "What kind of debt did he owe you?"

"A debt between men, Jane. You wouldn't understand." Robin's gaze followed after Tuk, wistful. "Well, little crow." He sighed. "John will be back, he will. Once his anger is worn off. Shall we go to our place in the forest, finish that wine, and play a few games of our own?"

He turned, then, his green eyes gleaming, but tired, as if he were resigned to her now that the hunt was finished, now that he had caught his prize.

She knew his mind. And he knew that she did. He mocked her now, with his frankness, with his teasing smile. There was nothing she could do but play the game with him, smile back. He held out his hand, and she took it, and when he led her over to his horse, and said, "My lady," and helped her up, she climbed on, keeping her smile frozen to her face.

But Jane could not be with Robin. She knew she could not—not now. Not knowing what he was. Who he was. But there was no other way out.

And then Jane stilled. For there was one way, wasn't there?

When Robin turned to mount the horse, Jane slipped the prioress's ring from her belt. She opened the wine skin. By the time Robin settled in behind her and squeezed her leg fondly, too fondly, Jane had made her choice.

She handed him the wine. "A drink, m'lord? We've a long ride out to the forest."

"Now, Jane. I've told you over and over not to call me that. Will you ever stop?" Robin took the wine, draining it deep, wiping his lips before he handed it back to her. "Although"—he smirked—"if you'd like to call me that abed, perhaps I shall allow it."

"As a game, you mean?" Jane asked, her smile biting into her skin.

"Everything's a game, Jane," Robin said. "I only hope you're as good at playing games as I am."

Chapter Thirty-Two

The poison began its work on Robin's mind first. Jane had been riding with him, clinging to his back, long enough for the sun to fall. The sky was dim and the moon in hiding, and night was coming down like a scythe's blade, when Robin started to sway a little. He stopped, and they climbed off the horse, breathing in the cool, loamy air of the forest.

"I feel unwell." Robin rolled his head, cracking his neck. "I think . . . do you think it's fever, Jane?"

Jane looked at him cautiously. "Were you wounded in the fight?"

"Was I? I don't think so. I didn't let anyone catch me." He looked himself up and down, poking his chest with a shaking finger. "I don't think they did, but I don't remember."

"You hit your head, perhaps," Jane suggested softly, her stomach churning.

Robin rubbed his head. "Perhaps. Would you lead the horse for us?"

"Of course," Jane said. As they mounted the horse again, a plan formed in Jane's mind, which was as cool and calm as settled snow, now that there was no changing what she had done. She could not take Robin to the woods. The poison would take too long. She would be trapped there with him until John came to find him, and he would see her with his dying master, and he would know what she had done. She needed to bring Robin somewhere else. Somewhere John didn't know about.

She had been riding east through the forest for what seemed like an hour as Robin dozed against her back when, finally, he stirred and spoke. "Haven't we reached the camp yet?"

"I'm not bringing you there," Jane said.

"Hiding from old John, are we? Worried he'll barge in on us? Or want to watch like the lecher he is?" Robin laughed and groped at her thigh, reaching around the front of her before she pushed his hand away. "Oh, stop it, Jane." He shoved his hand back to her crotch, crudely, and she shifted her hips to move him. "What's the point of playing modest? It's inevitable, you and me."

"I thought you liked games," she said, cringing at his touch, breathing in the cool wind. Robin only laughed.

Darkness had swallowed the sky by the time Jane reached their destination. Robin didn't seem aware of where they were at all. "What of your Bran?" he asked as she helped him down from the horse. "What would he say if he saw us together?"

"Bran turned on you," Jane reminded him, "after I left him." Robin looked at her, confused. He had forgotten that too, then.

"Did he? Well . . ." He tried to straighten his body but wound up slumping against Jane. She caught him in her arms, leaned him up against the horse. "We'll kill him together, okay?" His smile was so sweet, so vulnerable, and she could see the fire in his eyes, even by starlight. But she steeled herself against that smile.

"Wait here," she said.

Robin looked past her and his mouth dropped open. "Did you bring me to a *church* for our tryst, Jane? Naughty, naughty girl."

"You aren't angry, are you?"

"Ha!" He laughed. "I love it."

"I'll get rid of the priest."

"Shall I kill him?" Robin swayed, hand falling to his sword.

"No need," Jane said quickly. "I'll persuade him."

"Well," Robin slurred, "you are very persuasive." His eyes fluttered, open and shut, and Jane hurried inside.

Adam was there, just as she knew he would be, down in the cellar having his spare bread and sop. He shot to his feet at the sight of her, crumbs falling from his lips.

"I thought I heard a rider! Jane! What are you . . . oh, God in heaven!" He gaped at the ash, the soot, the torn clothing and flesh where the rope had cut into her. "What happened to you? Are you all right?"

"There's no time. I need your help."

"What do you mean? Are you hurt? Are you in danger?" His face was white in the candlelight.

"No." Jane looked worriedly over her shoulder. "Not yet. But you're in danger if you stay here. Is there a back way out?"

"What have you gotten yourself into? Tell me the truth, this time!"

But Adam hadn't earned the truth. Not the whole truth. Not from her.

"If there's a back door, Adam," she repeated calmly, "I need you to take it. Ride to King's Houses, fast as you can, with a message. And stay there, or stay in town with Father Paul. Just don't come back here. And don't go home, to our old house. It isn't safe."

"I'm not leaving you to . . ."

"Ask for the prioress," Jane said, as if he hadn't spoken at all. "The one from Kirklees. Tell her there's a man here who needs her healing." She swallowed. "A wounded bird, tell her."

"What have you to do with the Prioress of Kirklees?"

"I work for her." The words were true for the time being, Jane supposed, though surely they would not be true when Ibota found out what she had lost. What Jane had taken from her.

Adam looked indignant. "So that's where your money has come from? That's what you've been doing all this time? And you let me think . . ."

"That's right," Jane said, letting the lie stand, hoping it would be her last, but knowing it wouldn't. Not if she wanted to live through the night. "I couldn't tell a soul. She had me swear it. Now, will you finally listen to me and go?"

"I just," Adam sputtered, "I wish you would have told me."

I wish I didn't have to, Jane thought, *to make you care for me again.* But she held her tongue, hurried him out the back door, and went outside to face her sins.

–‹‹‹•›››–

Jane put Robin in her brother's straw bed. He was sweating now, hair stuck to his fevered head, and she sat beside him, stroking his brow.

"Will you lie beside me"—he grabbed at her, but limply now—"like you did before?" She stared at him, her thoughts and stomach swirling, the memory of his touch, his kiss, the trail of fire his mouth had burned into her skin. His touch used to pull at her like she had the devil in her loins, but now her heart recoiled.

There was still a game to play, though, until Robin was gone, until Jane and everyone else could be safe. And so she lay down beside him, trying to still her own squirming skin. She felt she was being eaten alive by ants everywhere his body touched her own.

"I think I need a healer, Jane." Robin took her hand in his, his touch hot and limp.

She pressed that hand, not looking at him. She couldn't. "I've sent for one. It may take time for her to get here, though. You should rest."

"I don't think I can . . . claim my reward." Robin coughed, and she could hear the sheepish smile on his face, even though she couldn't see it. "Not right now."

"Like you said," Jane stared at the low, cracked ceiling dully, her heart slick with ice, "we have all the time in the world."

"We do." Robin stopped straining to look at her, and he rested his head on her breast instead, closed his eyes.

"What will you do," Jane asked him, "now that the reeve is gone?"

"Burn the churches, starting with this foul place." Robin's laugh was wet with phlegm. "It stinks of rot and mold."

"And then?"

"Stick all the monks' heads on poles. Kill the abbots and the king." He coughed, his chest shaking. "Kill *all* the kings."

"And what about the Virgin?" Jane asked softly. "You said you honored Her, Robin. You said She guided you. Wouldn't She want you to show mercy?"

But Robin didn't answer her. He had finally, blessedly, fallen asleep.

The prioress arrived when the sky was still black and the stars were high. She wore a plain, homespun cloak, the hood pulled up over her head, making her look like a long, tall drawing of Death from a monk's book, her shadow wavering in the flickering candles Jane had lit while Robin slept.

"Jane," Ibota whispered into the dark.

Jane ran to her, took her hands, and found herself weeping, water cracking through her frozen heart. "I'm so sorry, m'um. It's Roger. It was a mistake. He . . ."

"I know," Ibota said, and her voice was dry as ashes. "I knew when he didn't come back, but I . . ." Her words broke off a little, and she shuddered.

Then her tone turned dark and menacing. "Where is Robin Hood," she asked through gritted teeth.

"Downstairs," Jane said, and the word came out with all that was left of her breath.

The prioress stalked down the stairs, leaving Jane to hurry after her. Ibota sat on the edge of Robin's bed, wordless, and pulled back her hood. Her face was drawn and tight, and fully drained of color. Jane could see the grief etched across it, even in the candlelight, the lines around her eyes, her lips pulled taut. She looked at Robin with a fixed expression and began pulling things out of her bag.

Robin stirred, his eyes wet and green and unfocused. "Jane? Who's there?"

"The healer's here, Robin," Jane said, her voice a whisper.

"Good." He closed his eyes again.

When Jane turned back, the prioress had set her lances and her bowl upon the bed. Her leechcraft tools. Jane blanched.

"Must you . . . must we . . . ?"

Ibota's eyes were steel. "Perhaps it's better if you go."

Jane turned back to Robin, feeling suddenly desperate, grief rising in her chest. She studied his face as though she could etch it into her mind forever. Soft cheeks, though with little lines she hadn't seen before. The fall of his lashes, the color of old flame, against those cheeks. His lips curved up on the right side, thinner there so that he always seemed to be smiling a little.

Those lips had kissed her, and she remembered that with a rush of warmth. Perhaps she should have let him take her to bed. Just once, while she still could. Just once, so she could have the memory, like she had the memory of his face, his touch. But it was too late for that. It was too late for anything, now.

"I'll stay," Jane said, tears choking her throat, still watching Robin, still gripping his hand. "I can't just leave him."

Ibota softened. "It will be faster this way. The other way, the herbs. It could be days, Jane. He would be very ill."

"And this way," Jane whispered back. "Will he suffer?"

"Not as much," Ibota said, and Jane thought she heard regret in the prioress's voice.

Jane held Robin's hand as the prioress cut him open, slicing his flesh in one clean stroke. Ibota tied his arm to the bed's base with a rope, placing the bowl on the ground beneath it.

Robin's eyes opened, and he looked at his bleeding arm. "What's happening?" he asked, dazed. "Why am I bound?"

"She's got to bleed you." Jane turned his head back to face her, so she could hold his eyes steady, though her voice shook with sorrow.

"There's poison in your blood." That part was true, or was truth wrapped in a lie, or a lie in truth. It was so hard to tell now.

Robin gripped her hand tight.

Jane watched him. She watched him through the whole thing. Watched the color drain from his face. Watched him wither as his spirit fled him. At one point, Robin's eyes fluttered, and he cried out, "It's too much! It's too much! Stop it!" And Jane only stared at him and held his hand, and the tears flew out of her eyes like a flock of crows.

Robin met her eyes then, and he knew. Just before he died, he knew.

"Why?" he asked her, his voice so light, as though his soul were flying away, drifting out of his body.

"You asked me to choose," Jane said through her tears. "You asked me to choose . . ." She stroked his fox-colored hair. "And I did."

-◄◄◄◄•►►►-

They stood outside the church together, watching the sun rise in silence, the sky thin and gray, creased by a purple line. "They say the pagans used to sacrifice a wild god each year to bring in summer." Ibota's voice was flat, distant. "He ran through these forests as a stag. But this looks a winter sky to me, not a spring one. The blood spilled here has brought us nothing."

"Betrice will want to be told." The words clawed at Jane's throat. "About Walter."

"We have all lost something today. Women always do, in war."

"I'm so sorry," Jane said, and it felt so hollow. She knew it would never be enough.

Ibota still wouldn't look at her. "It's not your fault, what happened to Roger."

Jane bit her lip, grimaced. "You mustn't lie to soothe me."

"No. I wanted to blame you. I blamed you all the way here. But I'm the one who ordered you to spy for me. I'm the one who sent you off with the reeve. Who sent . . ." Her voice broke. "Who sent him, knowing he would do anything I asked."

The air hung still and cold between them, as if even the wind were mourning. "What will you do now?" Jane's voice was hoarse, and the question hurt her throat, for she knew she was asking for herself, as well, and she did not know if there would be an answer. Not one she could stand to hear.

"I'll go back to Kirklees," Ibota said, still looking away from her, into the rising sun, as though she could not bear to see Jane's face. "And you should come. As the cook. I'll stop trying to make you my apprentice. I was wrong to try to change you." She smiled sadly, and the tears she had held back finally fell down her pale, thin cheeks. "Our cook is dreadful. Roger always thought it was on purpose. He thought he . . ."

And then the tears came too fast, and Ibota's hands flew to her mouth, as though that would stop them.

"I'm so sorry," Jane said again, "I tried to . . ." But her own tears swallowed up her voice.

Ibota sniffed, wiping at her eyes. "There's a cottage for you there, and a life."

And Jane tried to imagine it. A quiet abbey, a kitchen of her own, a life that would be smooth and unbothered, except for petty things, the fickle whims of those above her station, the ones that had gnawed at her so at King's Houses. Ibota was offering Jane safety that she didn't deserve, a peaceful life she thought anyone would want. But she didn't see Jane, not really, though Jane once thought she had. Just as Bran hadn't seen her, or Adam. *Robin* was the only one who had seen her, in spite of everything he had done, in spite of who he was, and who she was. He had seen that Jane was meant to soar free, to fly in the night and in the shadows, and to roost where she pleased, without a tether at her wrist.

"We'll see," Jane answered the prioress, for grief had struck her in the chest again, hard as a sword thrust, and she could not say more.

"Whatever you do, Jane," Ibota said, "don't stay here and die. Not for him. He isn't worth it." She blinked hard to stop the flow of her tears. Her back straightened, and when she finally looked at Jane, her ice-blue eyes glittered with rage. "They'll sing songs of Robin Hood, of course. They'll say he lived and died a hero. But you and I will know the truth."

"And what will they sing of me," Jane whispered, "the woman who betrayed him? Who led him to his death?"

"If you're very lucky, Jane," Ibota said, "they'll never sing of you at all."

ACKNOWLEDGMENTS

This book belongs as much to me as it does to two brilliant women: Sam Farkas, my agent, who convinced me that the world actually *would* want to meet the medieval version of Robin Hood, and without whose deep intelligence, encouragement, and clear-eyed guidance, I would be completely lost; and Nidhi Pugalia, my editor at Viking Penguin, who *understood* this book—and what I wanted it to be—in the fullest possible way, and whose alchemical gifts for story, character, and prose pulled the gold out of *The Traitor of Sherwood Forest* and made it shine. Both Nidhi and Sam loved Robin Hood in the same way I did, their hearts raced and dipped and swayed and fretted along with Jane's, and this book would not be the same without their hard work, their advice, their insight, and their passion.

The whole team at Viking Penguin is an absolute joy to work with, and they also deserve credit for the book you have in your hands: Andrea Schulz, who helped to sell me on Viking from the very beginning, and whose advice was a vital part of the book's progress. Thank you also to Yuleza Negron, Alex Cruz-Jimenez, and Molly Fessenden, who all introduced Jane and

Robin to the world for me—and brought me into the modern era. My deepest thanks to my production editor, Jennifer Tait; my copyeditor; and my proofreader, Chelsea Cohen, all of whom have eyes as sharp as Robin's arrows. Any remaining errors are my own. I also want to thank the entire team at the Jill Grinberg Literary Management. Everyone at the agency got behind this book, and I'm so incredibly lucky to have found an agency that makes me feel like a valuable part of the family. And I have undying gratitude for the divinely talented Micaela Alcaino, who captured the heart and soul of this book with her cover illustration.

Thank you to my earliest readers, who were also my friends, who listened to me gripe and reassured me and rode with me through all the hopes and fears of bringing a book into the world: Dawn Addonizio, Megan Leitch, Jenna Mann, Derek Nylen, Usha Vishnuvajjala, Rick Waugh, and Vsevolod Zaikov. Thanks also to Kella Campbell, Jessica Li, and Mackenzie Reide, who read portions of the book and cheered me on. And special thanks to Mark Feenstra for welcoming me into Vancouver Genre Writers and for his friendship and support. Every one of you gave me the confidence and community I sorely needed, and you made the writing process fun and encouraging instead of lonely and agonizing.

Finally, thank you forever and always to Mike James, the love of my life, my partner in doing brave and impossible things. Here is another one for our list!

HISTORICAL NOTE

The Traitor of Sherwood Forest is a Robin Hood retelling, but in many ways, this book is a return to the past rather than a revision of it. Most people today know Robin Hood as "Robin of Locksley," the exiled noble, paramour of Maid Marian, champion of the poor and oppressed, and the mortal enemy of a corrupt King John. But that Robin Hood is nowhere to be found in the medieval ballads. Their Robin Hood is brash and childish, alternately charming and bullying—dashing and heroic in one stanza, brutal and ruthless in the next. He devotes himself to the Virgin Mary rather than a mortal woman. And his king, when the king is named at all, is King Edward. So how did this complicated, morally gray medieval trickster become such a squeaky-clean hero in the present day?

Medieval people didn't need their heroes to be perfect. They didn't even need their heroes to be good! Robin Hood was popular in the Middle Ages precisely *because* he was a violent, irreverent rogue who stuck it to everyone in authority. But he underwent a "reboot" during the English Renaissance, thanks in part to Henry VIII, who had a penchant for comparing himself to legendary medieval men. (He loved to dress up as Robin Hood, and he had his own image painted in King Arthur's place on the Winchester Round Table.) Robin Hood's rebellion against the clergy would have been delicious to Henry, who had himself broken with the Roman Catholic Church. But the outlaw's vendetta against the aristocracy and his devotion to the Virgin were different matters entirely—*that* version of Robin Hood could not survive the relentless pens of the nobility or the Protestant Reformation.

Thus, the post-medieval Robin Hood transformed from a rough, chaotic criminal who pitted himself against both church and king into an exiled noble fighting an evil King John in the name of King Richard. He also acquired a girlfriend. Like many medieval heroes, the early Robin Hood devoted himself to the Virgin Mary, but "Mariolatry" grew dangerously unfashionable during the rise of Protestantism. As for Maid Marian, she may have originated as part of a medieval May Day tradition. In early (and sometimes bawdy) versions of her story, she had a lover named Robin, but they were both shepherds, not outlaws. When their stories eventually merged, both Robin and Marian were promoted to nobility, their former Catholic and pagan leanings all but forgotten.

Robin's legend continued in England, growing increasingly didactic with the rise of Puritanical (and anti-Catholic) fervor. Then nineteenth-century writers, who were infamous for bowdlerizing medieval legends and cleaning up medieval heroes, got hold of Robin Hood. They polished off the grime and made him innocent and righteous. Sometimes Robin returned to his yeoman roots—in Sir Walter Scott's *Ivanhoe*, for instance—but he was still made to serve the royal cause. Children's literature starring Robin Hood also emerged in the nineteenth century, featuring Robin as a boyish, romantic gentleman, playful rather than subversive, loyal to England and the crown. This is the Robin Hood that Disney eventually brought to life as the clever, lovable cartoon fox that most of us grew up with: a childlike figure that the medieval Robin Hood probably would have knocked off his horse with a well-aimed shot from his bow, just for the fun of it.

The question of whether or not Robin Hood was a real man still rages among enthusiasts and scholars—and I'm happy to leave the debate to them. The main question I wanted to explore with this retelling was: What did *medieval* people think of Robin Hood? What did he mean to them, and what did he inspire? I wanted to write Robin as the Middle Ages imagined him— tempestuous and contradictory, both chivalrous and cruel. He steals from the rich, and he sometimes protects the poor, but he is also violent, erratic, and deeply flawed. This medieval Robin Hood has a story too—not because he was a disinherited noble, like the later Robin Hoods, or because he was someone privileged who had his power taken away, but because he was *no one*—and he wanted to make the world see him anyway.

I'm indebted to Stephen Knight and Thomas Ohlgren for their collection and curation of the ballads in *Robin Hood and Other Outlaw Tales* (TEAMS Middle English Texts Series, 2000). TEAMS and the University of Rochester have done incredible work putting medieval texts and sources online, and a whole history of Robin Hood legends along with rich introductions and explanatory notes can be found at: https://d.lib.rochester.edu/robin-hood/authors. Of course, I didn't practice absolute fidelity to my source texts. Robin wouldn't have either. Once you start writing characters, they take on lives of their own.

Mooch, for instance, is the one who kills the little page in the ballad "Robin Hood and the Monk." (He's better known as

"Much," but I spelled it in this book the way it might have been pronounced in Middle English.) My Mooch grew so soft over the course of my writing him, so kind and gentle, that I wound up reversing his role with Wyll, who became darker and more haunted in the telling of this tale. Friar Tuck was a late addition to the Robin Hood canon, so I borrowed his name for "Tuk," a Muslim mercenary, to make him part of a modern tradition of more diverse Merry Men who are grounded in history, a tradition that includes Morgan Freeman's character, Azeem, in the 1991 *Robin Hood: Prince of Thieves* and David Harewood's Brother Tuck in the BBC's *Robin Hood* (2006–2009).

As with Mooch's name, I modernized some words to convey the right image or meaning: "stockings" take the place of "hose," for instance, and "fireflies" replace "glow worms." "Lavender" has become "laundress," and "cleft the prick" (an archery term) is "cleft the peg"— for obvious reasons. Sometimes I do the opposite, using an archaic or translated term as a creative choice, as with "shire reeve." Variations close to the modern word (*screffe, shyref*, etc.) are used in the late medieval ballads, but in the time of Edward I, the spelling (typically *syrreue*) would be closer to the literal meaning of the word. Likewise, I use "Nottingham Shire" to distinguish it from Nottingham town, even though it is sometimes a compound word in medieval texts the way it is today.

Although I used plenty of creative license in this book, many of the tricks Robin plays, and even some of the dialogue lines, come directly from the medieval ballads. Most of the dates indicated below are estimates, since extant manuscripts often transcribe earlier ballads whose sources are lost texts, analogues, or part of an oral tradition.

Part I is from the ballad "Robin Hood and the Potter" (c. 1500 or earlier), including Robin's disguise, his attempt to sell pots at the market, the archery contest, the flirtation with the reeve's wife, and leading the reeve into an ambush the next day. Part II, the Sir Richard episodes, is from *A Gest of Robyn Hode* (c. 1400–1450), a long compilation of earlier ballads. Sir Richard shows up at the abbey instead of the dinner table in the poem, and the prioress's role is my own addition. I translated several of the original lines for these scenes, including "Thou arte ever in my berde," which was just too good to cut. Parts II and III, the episodes with Brother Godric, are from a combination of *A Gest of Robyn Hode* and "Robin Hood and the Monk," which scholars believe is one of the earliest Robin Hood ballads (pre-1370s, though it was recorded later). Both poems tell the story of Robin and his men besting a greedy monk, after which Robin and Little John come to blows—they are often getting into fights in the medieval stories, though they always prove loyal to each other in the end.

Part IV is from "Robin Hood and Guy of Gisborne," a later ballad that showcases Robin's brutality. The ballad puts an inexplicable emphasis on Robin's "Irish knife," so I decided that knife deserved a story of its own. The final chapters are based on both the *Gest* and a later ballad, "The Death of Robin Hood" (c. 1600s). The *Gest* recounts the reeve's capture of Little John, and both poems tell of Robin's tragic death at the hands of the prioress of Kirklees (and her lover, Sir Roger). Unlike the authors of the original stories, who blame the wicked nature of women for Robin's demise, I tend to think the prioress had her reasons.

Finally, Jane Crowe is my own invention. There are very few named women in the medieval Robin Hood stories (although there *is* an anonymous girl in "Robin Hood and the Potter" who carries the pots for Robin and the sheriff's wife, helping him pull off his trick). Medieval literature is full of such unnamed women and servants, and to me, those untold stories are just as important as Robin's—maybe even more so, since real social change often happens through the hard work of ordinary people whose names are lost to history, rather than through celebrities and heroes.

Jane is not a noblewoman born to greatness. And she's no hero either. But she still matters. She is the kind of woman who has been there throughout history—unnoticed and unsung—changing her world from the shadows. And even when the ballads and stories leave her silent, anonymous, and invisible, she can still press the world with her finger and force it to tip.